B+
3.97

AN HOUR
OF LAST THINGS
and Other Stories

Books by George P. Elliott

GEORGE P. ELLIOTT

AN HOUR
OF LAST THINGS

☙❧ ☙❧   and Other Stories

HARPER & ROW, PUBLISHERS
NEW YORK, EVANSTON,
AND LONDON

1817

The author gives grateful acknowledgment to the following magazines in which these stories originally appeared: *Epoch, Esquire, Harper's Magazine, The Hudson Review,* the *Magazine of Fantasy and Science Fiction, Northwest Review,* the *Pacific Spectator, Quarterly Review of Literature, Stand, Tri-Quarterly,* and the *University Review* of Kansas City, Missouri.

FIRST EDITION

LIBRARY OF CONGRESS CATALOG CARD NUMBER: 68-16310

D-S

To Sara

Contents

AN HOUR

OF LAST THINGS

and Other Stories

Into the Cone of Cold

1

"Brother Carl?" said Stuart. "Why, I saw him in the coffee shop just a couple of weeks ago—yes, the day before Christmas vacation."

"But you haven't seen him since," said Brother Joseph. "Did you speak to him?"

"No."

"Did he look at you?"

"I guess not," said Stuart, scratching his chin with his thumb. "I've never really talked with him, just a word or two the time we were introduced. There was a pile of bluebooks on the table beside him, and also one styrofoam cup of the sort in which coffee is served in the coffee shop and I presume it had coffee in it. He was reading what appeared to be a bluebook."

Brother Joseph, his elbows on the leather arms of the chair, leaned forward, his substantial belly pressing against his clasped hands. "Do you know why he was there?"

"My God!" Stuart clutched his hair with both hands, then flung his arms up. "What are you, in training to be an inquisitor?"

Stuart, in some ways a shy man, but also open-faced, good-looking, with an ingratiating smile, was given to bursts of self-mocking buffoonery. Brother Joseph might have smiled at the extravagance; but he did not smile.

"He was there under my orders."

"What kind of a deal is this," said Stuart, "that a distinguished professor of mathematics can be ordered to go grade papers in a student coffee shop?"

"I realize this is your first semester with us." Brother Joseph searched Stuart's eyes, which did not waver. "You may not realize it, but St. Anselm's is also a priory and I am both president and prior. Brother Carl was under the vow of obedience." Brother Joseph noticed a little smile on Stuart's lips, and paused to see what would happen.

Stuart, in whose mind a prior had more in common with a unicorn than with a college president, was smiling because he had restrained an impulse to say something imprudent. The two previous colleges where he had taught had "not kept him on." Now, instead of saying anything, he made up the last line of a limerick: "And the prior was a buyer of fryers." He became conscious of the heaviness of Brother Joseph's gaze, and quit smiling.

"Why are you telling me all this?"

"To impress upon you the severity of the crisis we of St. Anselm's find ourselves in. In order to understand that, you must understand its history." He paused. "I had already noticed that Brother Carl was withdrawing from community life. He left us on New Year's Eve in order to become a hermit."

Stuart had seen photographs of bearded, naked hermits in India, and he had even toyed with the notion of hermitage himself a time or two. "Great! Where's he going to live? How will he get food?"

Brother Joseph adjusted his black, apple-sized penholder so that it stood exactly midway between the left edge of the blotter and the left edge of the desk. There was nothing else on the desk except a black telephone exactly midway between the right edge of the blotter and the right edge of the desk.

"I had thought a man in his mid-thirties," he said, "a man of some learning, a poet, even if you are not a Catholic . . . No matter." He swiveled his chair sharply so that it was at a right angle to its former position. "I did everything in my power to dissuade him. This is a teaching order. You must take my word for it: St. Anselm's is in a state of crisis."

"Brother," said Stuart quietly, "I've got a wife and two children, I haven't worked here very long. St. Anselm's doesn't mean too awfully much to me."

"I suppose not."

"I got my own crisis."

It was saying things like this, and in this same voice, that had made Stuart a good many of his enemies in the colleges where he had taught, though he did not admit it to himself. Because the voice in which he uttered such words was bland and slick instead of abrasive, he sort of thought no one would notice what the words implied; and he did not believe—though it had been suggested to him one way or another by a friend or two—that the smoothness of his voice made the implications of his words penetrate the deeper. He often complained that he had been laid off his jobs because of the mediocrity of administrators, who cannot stand to have excellence near them. But he did nothing to placate them. Instead, the more convinced of this he became, the oftener he spoke to them as he had spoken just now.

Brother Joseph was staring at the carved oak door in front of him. He shook himself and stepped toward the door. "Would you care for a drink?" There was a certain intensity in his voice but no forced cheer.

"Well," said Stuart, deciding not to leave right away after all, "that sounds like a good idea."

The closet behind the door was a compact bar. Stuart was so astonished at the array it offered that he did not say what he wanted.

"Bourbon all right?" said Brother Joseph, pouring copiously into a tall glass. "Say when."

"When," said Stuart. "Back when. Sorry, I like it weak."

Brother Joseph shrugged and put it aside for himself. He was a man of forty-five, blond with thin hair, pop-eyed, his face smooth and well-fleshed, a network of fine blue and red lines visible under his fair skin.

Eggface, thought Stuart. Maybe if he drinks enough I'll get an idea what's inside that egg. Not that I really want to know.

Brother Joseph poured a third glass. "Brother Nicholas will be here shortly. You know him?"

"We were introduced. Funny rimless glasses?"

"Yes, a round face. He's in cryogenics."

"That a fact?" said Stuart, settling back in his chair. "Cryogenics."

"Extreme cold? Absolute zero?"

"Oh, yes, sure."

"I don't understand it any better than you do." Brother Joseph sighed. "He explains how it works, but I . . ." He waved. "He'll tell you whatever you want to hear about the physics of it."

"Why?" said Stuart, meaning *Why should I get involved in all this?*

"Why not?" said Brother Joseph with a contemptuous snort.

This time Stuart restrained himself from speaking only because he did not want to lose this job right then in mid-year. He chewed his tongue, blinked, and took a deep swallow of the highball.

"Pardon me," said Brother Joseph, "I have been under a considerable strain. We are turning to you for help because we are at our wits' end."

"Thanks a lot," said Stuart, indulging himself to a quick swipe at least.

"We have a Brother Frederick at Sansom, but he's too lop-sided. Besides"—Brother Joseph shrugged—"you're much the better poet."

"And less lopsided?"

"Quite symmetrical, as a matter of fact, and you've got a brush cut. Moreover, your poems are a record of yourself. You have done half the job already."

"Aha," said Stuart and asked for another drink. "Now that we're in the middle of things, why don't we double back to the beginning for a minute. What are you talking about?"

"A scientific experiment. We hope you will be able to give an account of what happens."

"What's the matter, the meters break down?"

"Precisely. In that region there are no meters."

"Hey," said Stuart, beaming, "I'm needed. What's a poet got other people haven't got? Built-in meters. John Stuart the meter man. Take me to your zero. I'll come back and tell you all."

"Precisely," said Brother Joseph. "If only you weren't mar-ried."

"I've had the same thought myself on occasion."

"You aren't contemplating divorce, are you?"

"I'm human," said Stuart.

"I mean, seriously."

"Well, now, Brother, I'll tell you. Since our daughter was born, my wife and I've given up the idea of separating. Susie's such a pretty little thing we neither of us could bear to be with-out her. The first one, the boy, he was so rambunctious and the like that we weren't sure there for a few years. But Susie made up our minds for us. She's just three, you know. She's not as smart as Charley, but she likes nursery rhymes better. Besides, the income tax people give us such a rebate for the kids we just couldn't afford to get divorced, the way we live now. If I had a Ph.D. I might. I could get a better salary than you're giving me. But being that all I've got is a B.A. and a couple of books of poems, I guess not. Anyway, Charley's fun to play catch with of an afternoon after school."

The door flung open and Brother Nicholas came in saying Hi in a hearty voice.

He was a medium-sized, fleshy, black-haired man with heavy jowls and large pores. His oblong, rimless glasses with wire shafts gave his coarse features an air of sly, peasant stupidity. What was known about extreme cold, he knew.

"You got him briefed?" he said.

Brother Joseph half-shrugged. "He's ready for you."

Brother Nicholas took his drink, then leaned back against the presidential desk and studied Stuart. "You know how a cone is generated?"

"Yes," said Stuart, feeling balky and ready to kick. "Why don't you sit down so I won't have to be craning my neck up at you all the time?"

Brother Joseph chuckled, and Brother Nicholas sat down.

"The reason I ask," said Brother Nicholas, "is that a lot of laymen think a cone is one thing, a nappe, like an ice cream cone."

"No, it's twins. You revolve a line around a fixed point."

"Tha—at's right," said Brother Nicholas in the inflection of teacher approval. Stuart wanted so much to kick him that he crossed his legs vigorously instead. "Now think of a double cone generated from the point of absolute zero. The cone we live in is the cone of heat. Got it?"

"No," said Stuart. "I thought there wasn't any heat down near absolute zero."

"Labels," said Brother Nicholas scornfully and snorted through his big lips like a horse. "Heat, cold, all they are is customary labels. You can take them off to suit your convenience and stick them on anywhere they work better."

"Not me," said Stuart. "I'm a poet."

"I'm a physicist," said Brother Nicholas, "and physicists do it all the time. You understand, this whole thing of getting a poet in on it was not my idea."

"Whose idea was it?" said Stuart to Brother Joseph.

"Brother David's," said Brother Nicholas.

"Who is he?" said Stuart to Brother Nicholas.

"The provincial," said Brother Joseph.

"Oh, sure," said Stuart, speaking to the air between them, "the provincial." He had never heard the word used that way before. "Well, how would I refer to him—His Grace the Provincial?"

"Just Brother David," said Brother Joseph coldly. "It is an administrative position. Come on, Nicholas, we have a job to do. Let's get it done."

"That's right," said Brother Nicholas, staring straight at Brother Joseph, who turned to the window and gazed at the sprinkler on the lawn.

"We've got a friend coming in for dinner," said Stuart, preparing to bolt. "I told my wife . . ."

Brother Nicholas slapped a hand at him lazily and said, "We're about to get down to business. Let's go over to the lab. Joe, you coming?"

"Later," said Brother Joseph, turning around. "I really have nothing to contribute at this stage."

"What he means," said Brother Nicholas to Stuart, "is, he doesn't want to come along because he hates my lab. What he'd really like is to smash it up."

"If it were totally irreplaceable, I would do that," said Brother Joseph.

"Irreplaceable!" Brother Nicholas laughed heartily. "In science there's no such thing. Brains are as replaceable as laboratories. Buck up, Joe, you'll live. See you in a while."

As they were approaching the side entrance to the science building, Stuart slowed almost to a halt.

"There's a fellow I know in Berkeley," he said. "We waited

table in the same fraternity one year when we were in college, and I keep bumping into him the way a person does. He seems like a good enough guy, but I don't know him too well. All he does, all day and half the night, is work, a biophysicist, and he never got married. He's a monk of science."

Brother Nicholas' laughter got flatter as it got louder. "A monk of science."

"No," said Stuart, laughing a little with him, "I mean it. To a married layman like me, it's all pretty weirdo, you celibates in your cells."

"Come on," said Brother Nicholas, tugging at his sleeve.

"Wait a minute, I'm not positive I'm going in there with you. You see, a year or two ago this fellow took me up to his lab in that big parasitology building they've got on the hill. He has an electron microscope in it and I don't know what else, but the way he showed it off I could tell what it meant to him, the world and all. He told me the military paid for the whole shebang, including his salary, but they left him alone to do any research he wanted, by himself or in cooperation with other scientists. He also told me he didn't think there was anything he could do, scientifically, but what the military might use it. He says there's a team there that took one of the experiments he did just to find out, and they used it to perfect a nerve bug that'll cripple any adult it doesn't kill. They've got it down to where it'll leave a good many children alive. Of course it'll kill a lot of kids and most of the survivors will be invalids for life like the adults, but enough will get well to carry things on. The way the team put it to my friend was, Think how humane this nerve bug is compared to atom bombs. Anyway, Americans being goodhearted like they are, the army will add on a Child Care Corps with the best medical attention money can provide and a Teacher Corps to train those little gook survivors to love democracy and hate Communism. What this guy I know can't keep from brooding over is: how can you educate bugs to tell people apart? To them we all look alike, friend, foe, and neutral; black, brown, and beige."

"Don't worry," said Brother Nicholas. "The army doesn't even know my gadget exists."

"If they did know, what could they do with it?"

"Nothing."

"They're mighty clever."

"Look, all my dynocryne does is push one thing at a time into the cone of cold, which we're not even sure is there."

"Not there?" said Stuart.

"And even if it is there," said Brother Nicholas, "the army couldn't use it. All I've got's this hypothesis, really, and I can't figure out how to verify it. That's where the provincial thought a poet might get in on the act."

"Oh?" said Stuart. "And how does Brother Hermit fit in?"

"It was Carl's hunch in the first place, half a dozen equations on a piece of paper. I just worked out the engineering."

"The more I know, the more I don't know."

"Tha—at's right," said Brother Nicholas, grinning. "Come on."

"Well, all right," said Stuart. "Maybe my biophysicist friend's so bitter just because he's not big enough to get a Nobel or any of those nice soothing prizes they've got for scientists with inflamed consciences."

"Now you're getting there," said Brother Nicholas.

In the basement they took a large slow elevator down about thirty feet.

The laboratory was a medium-sized, concrete room furnished with pipes, pumps, dials, shelves, a sink, a cluttered desk, a coffee pot on an electric hot plate, and an oversized bathtub; just above floor level in the wall with lots of dials, there was a round door that looked like the entrance to a safe. Stuart said he wanted to understand everything, and Brother Nicholas told him to fire away. But Stuart asked directionless questions ("What's this for?") to which Brother Nicholas gave dead-end answers ("Oh, that's just a dehumidifier to keep the walls from sweating") generously sprinkled with jargon ("reversed Carnots"). One phrase, "a space of many dimensions," bemused Stuart into a long silence ("How do we know what it's like there? Maybe it's a Hilbert space of infinitely many dimensions"). It was not long before they reached the main thing, what lay behind the round door.

"The important stuff," said Brother Nicholas, "is buried in cement where you can't see it. I'll show you what I can."

He pressed a button, and the door gradually opened.

"Good Lord," said Stuart, "I never saw anything like it. It's honed."

Brother Nicholas snorted. "Microhoned. This door cost as much as everything else in the lab put together."

"How much?"

"Less than you'd expect for what it does. We had to seal against implosion. We get quite a vacuum going around the core. I'll fix it so you can go in and take a look." He lay on a dolly, then wriggled himself into the hole in the wall, head first up to his knees. Presently he emerged from this entrance tube, holding a round, thick, concave metal plug which he laid carefully on a rubber pad. "Your turn. Take this flashlight."

"Flashlight! Is it a coffin?"

"A sphere with nothing in it."

"Not even a seat or pad?"

"Nothing."

Stuart balked. "Why should I go in there?"

"Just get the feel. When you really go in for the experiment, you don't eat or drink for twenty-four hours beforehand, you take an enema, you strip off rings, wrist watch, things like that; take out any false teeth; you spend an hour washing from head to foot the way a surgeon washes his hands; and you go in in the buff and curl up."

"*If* I go in?"

Brother Nicholas roared. "All you have to take off now is your shoes."

"You know," said Stuart mock-ominously, taking them off, "somebody's wasting somebody's time around here."

He gave his head a little shake as though he had just won a skirmish, lay on the dolly, grabbed the bar above the entrance hole, and wriggled in on his back as neatly as Brother Nicholas had done.

He inched along the entrance tube, which was somewhat longer than he was tall, until he was head and shoulders into the hollow ball. It was bigger than he had expected. The flashlight revealed nothing to look at except two small holes about a foot apart in the top of the cavity. The dark metal lining looked smooth as glass and felt slick as though it had been greased. He turned off the light and held his breath. The only sound in his ears was the beat of his heart. So far from feeling trapped, he did not feel enclosed. He lost all sense of place and, but for gravity, would have been free even of a sense of direction. Anchored by gravity somewhere, he floated nowhere. He lost interest in time. A verse began to surface, "I swooned into total consciousness," but presently submerged again.

Feeling a tug on his foot, he wriggled out. Brother Nicholas was standing on one side of the opening and Brother Joseph on the other. They seemed ready to support him if need be.

"Wow," he said, "it's marvelous."

"I was afraid you might run low on oxygen," said Brother Nicholas, "somehow."

"Who knows," said Stuart, "what I was running low on?"

"You seem to find the experience exhilarating," said Brother Joseph.

Stuart, detecting a hint of eagerness behind Brother Joseph's judicious reserve, shuffled about the room for a minute, frowning, trying to decide how to bargain with him: he'd trade a trip into the cone of cold for a class of freshman English next semester; or no, he liked classroom teaching, so he'd settle for an assistant to correct his papers for him. But the thought of a half hour of negotiating with this smooth egg of a college president was altogether distasteful to him at that moment; besides, he was afraid he'd forget the line that had come to him in the ball.

He stopped in front of them and puckered up his eyes. "I'll do it," he said to Brother Joseph. Then he turned to Brother Nicholas, giving Brother Joseph his shoulder. "How long does it take?"

"Twelve hours, start to finish."

"Tomorrow?"

Brother Nicholas shook his head. "You've got to fast for a full day. Besides, day after is Saturday."

"Shouldn't you consult your wife?" said Brother Joseph.

"Is there much risk?" Stuart asked Brother Nicholas.

"No animal or person who's ever taken the trip," said Brother Nicholas, "has even gotten a runny nose out of it."

"Of course," said Brother Joseph, "we will take out twenty-five thousand dollars' worth of life insurance on you for a year, with your wife as beneficiary."

Stuart thanked him with distaste and turned back to Brother Nicholas.

"Blood doesn't freeze? Eyeballs?"

"The temperature drops too fast for that. The thermal acceleration is so great you zip right through the freezing zone into cryostasis."

"Unconscious the whole time?" Stuart detected an odd look in Brother Nicholas' eyes when he nodded to this question. "Who all have gone?"

"Brother Carl first—he insisted. Then me."

"Anybody else?" said Stuart.

"Three," said Brother Joseph, "who wish to remain unidentified."

"What's the symmetry bit?" said Stuart. "How come Brother Poet was too lopsided?"

"That—" Brother Joseph began.

"I'd just as soon hear it from Brother Nicholas," said Stuart. "The horse's mouth, as it were."

"One reason," said Brother Nicholas, "it occurred to us that the dynocryne may push things into the cone of cold and not just down near absolute zero is, when physical objects come out they're reversed, mirror images of themselves."

"Animals?" said Stuart. "People?"

"Some. Not always. Just a part of them at most."

"What if you put them through twice? Won't they come back right?"

"A warm-blooded animal's got to wait three or four weeks to go there the second time," said Brother Nicholas carefully, "and even so it doesn't always work."

"For example," said Brother Joseph, "Carl's right testicle stayed lower than the left. You think your wife would notice a thing like that?"

"My God," said Stuart, blushing and ducking.

"Any moles or birthmarks?" said Brother Nicholas.

"Maybe he'll want to tell her about it first," said Brother Joseph disdainfully.

Stuart glanced at him and noticed how symmetrical his face was. "You gone too?"

Brother Joseph half-shrugged and half-shook his head, went over to the sink and drew a cup of water, and stood there sipping it, looking at the floor. "We must mention that there may be some question of personality change."

"Oh?"

"One timid cat we put through," said Brother Nicholas, "came out scrappy as all get out. But nothing happened to me, so far as anybody has noticed. I haven't even gone through twice. The part in my hair went from the right side of my head to the left—that's why I had a butch there till it grew out wild like this. But I'm still the same old loudmouth."

"There's handedness," said Brother Joseph.

"Ah, yes," said Stuart, "there's always handedness."

"I suppose you are right-handed?"

"Left."

"Well, expect to come out right-handed," Brother Joseph said and chuckled. "Everybody else has switched."

"Except Carl," said Brother Nicholas. "He stayed left-handed."

"When left is right," Stuart said, "right is wrong."

Brother Nicholas gave a belch of laughter. Brother Joseph just gazed at Stuart.

"It is possible that some values get reversed sometimes," he said. "That is Brother Carl's hypothesis."

"But not re-reversed the second time?" said Stuart.

"Take Carl himself," said Brother Nicholas. "Six months ago he was charged up about math, the way he's been all his life. Now he's gone off somewhere to pray all the time. He says he's off math for good."

"And," said Brother Joseph, "he's left the college."

"To say nothing of the order," said Brother Nicholas.

"But he's still a Catholic?" Stuart asked.

Brother Nicholas averted his gaze, and Brother Joseph said "Of course" brusquely.

"I'll run the risk," said Stuart. "I've always wanted to trade the old psyche in on a new model. Well, back to the womb Saturday morning."

"Gah," said Brother Nicholas, flapping, "we've done the

Freudian bit. A man going in the tube is a penis in a vagina, and once he's locked in the ball he's a fetus in the womb. It's so obvious it's stupid."

"I was just joking," said Stuart, smiling weakly. "I'll come up with some idea better than that for a poem or else I won't write one. Don't worry. Well, I certainly do thank you for giving me this opportunity."

"You're sure," said Brother Joseph, "you don't want more time to think it over?"

Stuart looked inward. "Why am I in such a hurry?" Neither of the brothers moved. "I don't know. Maybe it's because I haven't written a decent poem in over two years. I pretty much used myself up and I have nothing else so good to write about, the way I write."

"My God," said Brother Nicholas.

Stuart could not tell whether Brother Nicholas spoke in wonder or disgust or disbelief, but he had no trouble interpreting the down-turning of Brother Joseph's tight lips. Unable to utter the rudeness he felt, he said, "Off with the old, on with the new," and chuckled inanely.

He drove home more slowly than usual, so he could get "I swooned into total consciousness" placed in the poem that was beginning to accrete about it. But a variation on the line began nagging at him, "A trance of total consciousness." He was not sure he liked the alliteration of this; but "swooned" was dangerously poetical, not to say flabby, and he could think of no suitable alternative for "total." There was no question of discarding or postponing this poem, as he had recently taken to doing with so many. He wanted a before-and-after pair, and he wanted them hot off the pulse. He foresaw a hard night, of the kind he liked.

Stuart wrote on a card table in the bedroom. Shortly after ten that evening Marguerite opened the door partway and stuck her head in like a child seeing if it is safe to enter a forbidden room. When he looked around at her she batted her eyes.

"Honey?" she wheedled.

"What?" he grunted.

"I'm sleepy and I want to take a bath. Everything's hunky-dory in the dining room, and I cleared the table for you."

He shuffled his papers together and laid them on the dresser. "If I just wasn't a poet," he growled as he was folding up the card table, "I'd earn enough money to have a room of my own to write in."

"Aw, honey, was it going well? I'm sorry I interrupted. You haven't written at night like this for ages." Her tan skin was smooth and her figure was good, but though she was only thirty her hair was nearly white. She hunched over and made what she called her granny face. "Forgive?"

Clearly if he did not scowl too hard she would try to seduce him away from his work. He had finished a first draft of the poem. He was willing.

"You are forgiven," he said severely.

In the dining room he tried to fiddle at his poem, but phrases from the afternoon kept cluttering up his thoughts—Hilsch tubes, vortex streams, Landau theories, and especially a phrase concerning superfluid helium, second sound, which according to Brother Nicholas had to do not with sound but with heat conduction; it kept bobbing up in Stuart's mind anyway, second sound. At a yodel from Marguerite to please come scrub her back, he leaped up and went to the bathroom. Usually she put in the bath water some foaming stuff, made from horse chestnuts, which she said made her skin feel young. But she knew he disliked the smell of it. He found her stretched full-length in the tub, no foam on the water, the moist air pleasantly scented from perfumed bath salts. Because there was no archness in the smile with which she replied to his grateful glance, he did not even pretend he did not desire her; he sat on the edge of the tub and began soaping her back.

"Sweetie," she said, "you know Saturday afternoon Charley's

going to Orrin Crowell's birthday party, and Mother just told me this afternoon that she's going to be in the city all day Saturday, and I thought I'd drop Charley off at the Crowells' and go shopping for a couple of hours and pick him up on the way home, so I just wanted to make sure you'd be home to look after Susie, you know, you can watch football on TV or anything, she doesn't mind just as long as she's got you to herself. Okay?"

"Aw," he said, "I'm sorry. I'm going to be over at St. Anselm's all day."

"All day Saturday? Since when?"

"Well, yes, it just came up this afternoon."

"I knew you were crazy about teaching but I didn't know you were that crazy."

"No, it's different, it's sort of an experimental deal."

"Is it."

"It takes twelve hours."

"Does it."

"Yes, you see, for me what it amounts to is a free physical. They want subjects of various ages and I fit in."

"What are you going to let them do to you?"

"Nothing. The whole thing doesn't amount to a hill of beans really."

"So. What's the experiment about?"

"Some scientific stuff, physiological and psychological, in that area."

"I suppose there's some Catholic angle to it."

"Oh, honey, there's nothing Catholic about it. I tell you, I get a free examination out of it, thorough, head to toe, lab tests, the works. Why not?"

"You sure can be slippery when you want to be. Poet."

"Not as slippery as you, my love," he said, running his hands under her arms.

"Quit slithering around over me," she said crossly. "So you won't even be home till all hours? What about dinner?"

"Half past seven."

"Okay, lambie pie," she said, squinting at him. "You go get yourself into bed right now. Stepping out on me, eh? A day with the monks, eh? You get in bed and in two minutes I'll come in and give you something to come home to."

He gave a playful little shake of the head and leaned forward to kiss her, but she drew back and flicked water in his face.

"Go on," she said. "I'm not just messing around. Monk."

As soon as they had made love, Marguerite turned over and went to sleep. Stuart, however, so far from relaxing, lay awake, his thoughts darting about patternlessly like waterbugs on a scummy pool. Every noise and motion she made irritated him, and he was especially irritated by having to restrain his own movements, hardly scratch an itch, for fear of disturbing her. After a long time, he felt himself sinking toward sleep; the very noticing jerked him wider awake than ever. She half-moaned, and he glanced at her anxiously, ready to propitiate her if she should awake. But her sigh had come from a dream; he saw her eyes move under the lids. His prepared resentment melted. He got himself to look at her as though he had never seen her before.

Her face on the pillow next to his was toward him, her neck extended. Like Nefertiti, he thought, even if she does have a button nose. Her mouth was slightly open. Why did I lie to her? She sighed again, and this time, because he expected no reproach of himself, it seemed like a mildly pathetic little whimper. She's not as bad as I make her out to be. I just don't want to upset her, that's why I lied, I want to protect her from worry. But if I am not afraid, why should she be? Maybe I ought to go make my will. That seemed a responsible thing to do. He got up.

By the time he had turned on the lights in the dining room and plugged in the electric heater and made himself a cup of decaffeinated coffee and settled down at the dining table, he had talked himself out of writing a will—California was a community property state and what did he have to bequeath anyway? He got to work on the poem instead. The best lines in the first draft could be counted as three-stress lines, so the whole poem was obviously meant to be in three-stress lines. This cleared up the problem of the line that had first come to him. It should be "in a trance of consciousness," and as such it was no longer very important; the poem had grown so far in another direction that this phrase had ceased to be at the center. It became clear to him that the last word was going to be "dead" and that the game of the poem was to spring "dead" on the reader to his shock and delight. In an hour Stuart had done this, and at the sound of the first birds of dawn he quit fiddling dopily with syllables and went back to bed.

Marguerite had turned over. When he tried to snuggle his cold feet against her warm legs, she whined and kicked them away. He sighed. Why am I going to do this stupid experiment? I don't want to. Here we are, a tender, loving family, and I end the best poem I've written for years with "dead." In fact, it's the best poem I ever wrote. Maybe I'm scared? "The cone of cold," what a lot of crap. Who cares what it's like? Here I am going to let them change me all around, maybe, and I'm not even getting anything out of it. Well, I've got something they haven't got and they need it. He shifted into a more comfortable position. I don't see why I shouldn't be afraid. It's dangerous, that's why I lied to her, it's a twenty-five-thousand-dollar danger. I won't tell her about it till afterward, so she won't worry. I really ought to make a will, to save her any possible complications. I could write it out and mail it to myself at school where it would be found next week, in case. But he made no move in that direction. I know damned well I'm not going to make a will, so why do I keep on telling myself to? Maybe I really am afraid? Good, that's it. I'm afraid and just don't know it. Again as he was about to fall asleep, his eyelids flew open. Why don't I let myself feel how afraid I am? This is too important a thing just to feel jittery about. What's the matter with me—I'm scared of being scared?

He was wide awake when the alarm went off, but he pre-

tended to be asleep while Marguerite got up with the children—
Charley was already banging around. It seemed to him she made
far more noise in the bathroom and then in the bedroom dressing
than she had any right to make. He lay there in a clench of
irritation, as though she had awakened him carelessly from a
deep sleep, and he let the noises of breakfast nag at him.

I didn't lie to her to shield her. At least I don't need to lie to
myself about that. I lied to her so she wouldn't nag at me. She'd
want to know all about it. She'd tell me what to do and not do.
She's a roadblock, with tentacles. How can I get out of the house
this morning without having to pretend to be nice to her?

After his two o'clock class that day, Stuart found the door to
his office open and a short, middle-aged brother pacing, hands
behind back, head thrust forward.

"Mr. Stuart?" he asked, closing the door, and when Stuart responded with a nod, he gave his hand a vigorous pump, saying,
"Brother David."

Whatever Stuart had expected in a provincial, this sharp-eyed
little man with bushy brown hair and delicate hands was not it.

"Well," said Stuart, "I was just going over to the president's
office as soon as I put these themes in my briefcase."

"I changed my mind," said Brother David. "I decided to see
you here alone before the conference with Brother Joseph."

"You're going to give me a pep talk so I'll be sure to write a
masterpiece?"

"Joseph warned me you had a sense of humor."

"Warned," said Stuart curtly.

"Warned," said Brother David and lifted an eyebrow. "Your
irony? In a community like this, it's apt to be taken for nothing
more than leg-pulling, when it isn't just taken straight."

"Oh, I don't know, Brother Nicholas seems to get my points.
At least he laughs in the right places."

"He's a laugher, yes. I was talking about people who think."

"Scientists don't think?"

"That's right, they tinker. I was a chemist who began to think. Therefore I ceased to be a chemist."

Stuart sat down at his desk and rubbed his eyes with his forefingers. Brother David was still pacing.

"Let me get this straight," said Stuart. "The way it came to me was, Brother Carl's idea is what caused all this furor in the first place, and he's a scientist."

"Are you being obtuse deliberately?" said Brother David. "Carl can barely screw in a light bulb. He's a mathematical philosopher."

"Brother David," said Stuart in his blandest voice, his voice of social judo, "is Brother Joseph gunning for your job?"

"That's the way the tinkers would phrase it," said Brother David, glancing at him scornfully, "personal rivalry." He did not even pause in his pacing. "Sure, Joseph would like to be in my shoes and have me under him where he could trample on me, and sure, if this whole thing blows up into a scandal that's what'll happen. But that's the least of it. There are really big things at stake. That's why I came here today, to fill you in."

"Just," said Stuart, "sooner or later, get around to mentioning why the hell I should be up to my tonsils in it."

Brother David took a melodramatic pose against the wall furthest from Stuart, hands at his sides flat against it.

"Joseph is a recidivist," he hissed. "He's sorry the Church no longer burns witches. He'd like nothing better than to have this dynocryne kill somebody so he could have it smashed up and forgotten. He's straight out of the Dark Ages." He began pacing again, and Stuart breathed.

Brother David went on and on about how the Church had to turn its face toward the future, to accept progress, because in this century to stand still was automatically to go out of date.

"Pardon me," said Stuart, "maybe they neglected to tell you. I'm not a Catholic."

"That's part of your strength. This thing has to mean something to everybody. We're going to put St. Anselm's on the map. We're too parochial. This could be our entree into the big time."

"The cone of cold, you're talking about?"

"Right. We believe this contraption gives man access to the antiworld, but there seems to be no way of verifying it." He grimaced. "The way Joseph thinks, if there is an antiworld it has to have an anti-God so we shouldn't have anything to do with it. You see what I mean about Dark Ages?— But the experience of going there, of having been there, maybe we can get a hold on that through you. We want to introduce this thing all shaped up."

"Well," said Stuart, "it sounds very interesting but it hasn't got much to do with me. I'm going to do this for my own reasons, and they have mighty little to do with your reasons. Anyway, I told my wife I'd be home early today and I have to get a haircut first, so if you'll excuse me . . ."

"Finals come week after next," said Brother David. "You have help grading papers?" Stuart shook his head. "Joseph didn't even give you that. What did he give you?"

"Nothing."

"The most precious thing for a poet is time, right?"

Stuart had uttered that sentiment a hundred times, but now, from Brother David's mouth, it sounded somehow off. "Well," he drawled, "other things being equal, yes, I suppose time's as important as anything else."

"How many hours do you teach a week?"

"Twelve."

"You shall have six next semester. Let's go."

"You're sure in a hurry for this poem of mine."

In the corridor approaching the door to the president's office, Stuart put his hand on Brother David's arm and stopped.

"This business of help with grading papers and free time next semester, I don't want you to think I anything but appreciate it, but how are you going to put it to him?"

"I'm going to tell him you need it," said Brother David frowning, "tell him you said you needed it for your writing."

"Fine, just so long as you make it clear I didn't initiate that but said it in response to your question."

Brother David glanced at him malevolently, nodded, and moved on.

"Because," said Stuart, "if you don't, I will."

That night as he was dozing off, he recalled Brother David's saying that Brother Joseph would like for the dynocryne to kill somebody, and he also recalled the inexpressive faces but unresting eyes of the two brothers as the three of them were chatting over highballs.

At five thirty the alarm wakened him unrefreshed.

When he came back out of the bathroom, Marguerite was no longer in bed. He thought nothing of it, but dressed.

He found her in robe and curlers at the dining-room table, sipping a cup of coffee.

"Here, honey." She gestured at a glass of frozen orange juice at his place.

"No, thanks. I told you yesterday."

"Not even a little juice?"

"Not even a sip of water."

"What kind of an experiment is this, anyway?" she said.

"I don't know. Pretty high-powered, I guess."

"Since when does a little old Catholic liberal-arts college get enough money for high-powered scientific experiments?"

"The government. The National Science Foundation is loaded"—he hoped there was an outfit in the government with that name—"and one of the biologists has a grant to do something in connection with cancer research."

"Cancer!"

"Research. Well, I've got to run. I'll be home by seven thirty at the latest." He kissed her on the forehead.

"There's something fishy about this," she said, and she was biting a thumbnail when he went out the door.

In the car on the way to St. Anselm's, he congratulated himself at having slipped by her with a minimum of trouble.

2

Curled in the hollow ball, naked, scrubbed, purged, bridge with three false teeth removed, hair cut as short as it had been in the army, Stuart could not tell whether his shivering was caused by cold or fear or general excitement. Only one sense was functioning properly: he heard the steady susurrus of oxygen coming in through one of the holes and also a muffled slow beat, perhaps of his heart, perhaps of the vacuum pump. He did not care. Brother Nicholas had told him he would be conscious for no more than ten or twelve minutes in the adiabatic stage before the abrupt chill-off. He could not think consecutively about anything, even the sounds. He had no idea how long he had been there nor any interest in the matter. Sentences occurred to him from time to time. "Nothing happened to me." "I was taken apart and put back together." But he took only enough interest in them to let them register. "What happened to me was nothing." He not only was without care or interest, he did not think about being without them; yet he was conscious. A huge spasm of shivering seized him, and he realized that the cold, which he had not noticed on his skin, had penetrated his vitals. He could not breathe, yet felt no panic of strangling. He quit trying to breathe.

Then he was breathing hard and the heavy thumps in his head were undoubtedly the poundings of his heart. Brother Nicholas had warned him this would happen when he regained consciousness. Only because of this warning did he think that he must have been there already, wherever *there* was, and returned. He tried to concentrate on his senses one after the other to see if he had changed. Except for the gentle hiss of the oxygen, his few sensations were still all internal. He remembered that as soon as he regained consciousness he was supposed to say something so that the vibrations of his voice would register on a dial. "One, two, three, four." His voice sounded odd, but no odder than the first time he was inside this lightless ball. "I was never nowhere, and nothing happened." The plug withdrew presently, and he slid out into the lab.

He was still left-handed, but otherwise checked out pretty much as expected. There were three signs of reversal: his heart was now on the right side, and his right testicle lower than the left; only the third change affected his appearance. He had removed his bridge filling the gap made by three missing molars on the upper left side; now the gap was on the upper right side. Apparently his smile had been more lopsided than he had appreciated, for now, with the gap shifted, he seemed to be trying simultaneously to smile and to not smile.

"It's just the teeth," said Brother Nicholas.

"Is it," said Stuart, staring in the mirror.

"You can get a new bridge Monday. Avoid complications. Go to a strange dentist."

"And give a bass-ackward name," he said, thinking, I'm reversed. "Stewart Johns, for instance. After all, I may not be myself any longer."

"Well, you still have the old sense of humor."

"Have I," thinking, I'm not even my own identical twin.

"Everything else okay?"

"No," thinking, I'll grow a beard.

The children in their pajamas met him at the door, and Marguerite waved from the kitchen and came up to him as he was letting them kiss him. Charley said he looked funny and Marguerite said, "Yes, what's the matter, honey, is anything wrong?" He told them it was just his teeth, he'd accidentally broken his bridge. They seemed satisfied with this, but Susie was not. When he stretched full-length in his chair in the living room to wait for Marguerite to serve dinner, Susie climbed onto him, laid her head on his chest, murmured, "Don't be sad, Daddy," and began sucking her thumb. He did not make a lap for her or hug her, and before long she ran into the kitchen. He heard her half-crying, "Daddy doesn't love me any more," and Marguerite's soothing answer, "Of course he does, lovely, he's just tired."

Why does she have to lie so much? he thought and spied a pun. They lie to become mothers that they may lie as mothers. He sneer-smiled a little, in scorn that the day before he would have been tickled by so flabby a joke. But then he thought, All the same *I* just made the goddamned abortion of a pun, and a dark stain of rage rose from his guts and blinded him. When he could, he went off to bed and lay rigid, jaws clamped. When Marguerite came, he was able to tell her, in a tight voice, but not rudely, that he had a ferocious headache and to let her feel his forehead and commiserate a little.

A couple of nights later when he heard her running a bath, he consulted his genitals and found them responsive to the occasion. He predicted to the minute the time when she called him to come wash her back, and to the note the coy inflection of her voice. He winced, and went to her.

The bath water was covered with foam and only her head showed, her fluffy gray-white hair framing her smiling face.

"See, honey." She raised an arm on which foam stood like powdery snow on a still branch.

"Eh, it stinks in here."

She batted her eyes and crooked a finger.

"Do you have to act like a starlet in a grade-Z movie?" he said, and not quite slammed the door behind him.

He stretched out spread-eagle in the middle of their bed and in a minute was dreaming cannibals and ransom. She spent the night on the couch in a sleeping bag.

Teaching became laborious and no longer gave him satisfaction. In class he uttered the same ideas in usual words, and had as well stayed home for all they meant to him or seemed to mean to the students.

The Friday following his trip he was summoned to the president's office.

He declined both the seat and the drink Brother Joseph offered him.

"I hope," said Brother Joseph, "you have found the experience a fruitful one."

"You mean," said Stuart, "have I got a poem out of it yet?"

"That too, of course," said Brother Joseph, "but there are many other facets of the experience which I am sure . . ."

"You mean, you hope to hell it's a bad poem. I've got one:

> I let them take me apart.
> What happened to me was nothing.
> They put me together, wrong.
> Nothing was still happening.
> I got them to return me never nowhere.
> I am back together again."

"That's no poem," said Brother Joseph, frowning.

"Would you know a poem if you heard one? Unrhymed?"

"Not always, but I can spot a non-poem. What you recited is just playing with words. You are not keeping your part of the bargain."

"Bargain, for Christ's sake. I lay my life on the line for what? An insurance policy?"

"We have already given you a full-time reader, and next semester we are going to give you a half-time load at full pay."

" 'We,' is it?" said Stuart. "Brother David and who else?"

"Brother David and myself, in consultation," said Brother Joseph firmly.

"Shit, Brother Joseph sir, shit."

He knew in his muscles that if Brother Joseph said anything rude, he would knock him down.

Brother Joseph swirled his glass, watched the ice drift, and said, "If that's the way you feel about it."

To this soap-opera line any response Stuart could think of would be just another soap-opera line. He left without speaking.

Afterward, he realized that he had been, and would again be, ready to translate his anger immediately into words and physical actions, as he had not been before. But this more natural, more spontaneous behavior seemed to him no more worthy of congratulation than being able to run when you needed to run, and thought of his earlier restraint (pusillanimity? he had not been in a fist fight since he was twelve years old) made him grind his teeth and pound his hips with both fists.

He told the children a story about a beautiful snowman in a park into whose chest gnomes cruelly put a light bulb so he would glow in the dark. He did glow one whole night, though nobody saw him except a dog who just barked a couple of times and trotted on. Next morning, from the heat of the bulb the snowman's face was gone and he was dripping and lumpy like a candle in a draft. So when the boys who had made him saw how ugly and melted he was, they kicked him to pieces and jumped on the pieces.

Charley and Susie loved him to make up stories for them and

they thanked him for this one. But they did not ask to hear it again.

After fifteen days he went back to Brother Nicholas and asked to be put through the second time.

"Too soon," said Brother Nicholas, looking at him warily.

"A couple more days of this and it'll be too late," said Stuart.

"Let's run another metabolism on you. If it's still significantly low, no soap."

"Shit," said Stuart.

"Shit to you," said Brother Nicholas. "Look, friend, I hear you've got it bad, and I'm sorry. . . ."

"What do you hear?"

"Like that brawl you got in, in the No Name Bar night before last."

"What have you got, your own CIA?"

"A couple of students were there on dates."

"What else?"

"Enough. Like I say, I'm sorry you're in trouble, but nothing, and I mean nothing, is going to make me risk killing you till your functions are back to normal. Got it?"

"Who else knows how to run this contraption?"

"Nobody. Carl, more or less."

"I'll go to him."

"Go ahead. All he really knows is a couple of formulas, and he's trying as hard as he can to forget them."

"You mean there's nothing whatever I can do but wait another week? Or even two weeks maybe?"

"Tha—at's right."

Stuart scratched his scraggly beard and bared his teeth in a smile.

Brother Nicholas shrugged.

The three new false teeth were not only on the wrong side;

they were rougher than the old ones. Stuart's tongue could not leave them alone. Several times he took the bridge out and stood in front of the mirror staring at his mouth. His lips skinned back, exposing his teeth, in full rictus; his eyes popped, and the tendons in his neck trembled; each breath rattled. He saw himself on his deathbed. He saw his skull.

He gathered all his poems, finished or unfinished, which had not already been published, and read them through. "Rot," he said to himself, "dry rot. Silent unspeakable solitary dry rot." So that Marguerite would not know what he was up to, he put all the papers in his briefcase one morning when he was leaving for campus, and dumped them in a public trashcan.

The blank in his memory tormented him.

I'm unconscious every night, he told himself. What difference does it make where or how? If you don't know, you don't know.

But it made a difference.

The void has spread into me. I went into it and it has come into me.

The only friend whom he could have talked with about this had, two years before, without apparent reason, killed himself.

I have no soul. The void in me is where my soul was.

With this thought, his rage and fear seeped down out of sight, and for the week till Brother Nicholas let him go back into the dynocryne, he walked through the routines of his life, absent-minded and absent-hearted.

"Honey," said Marguerite at dinner, "whatever came of that physical you took, that experiment?"

"Nothing. Why do you ask?"

"I just wondered whether you got any report on it yet."

"Do I act sick?"

"Well, not exactly, but you aren't eating too awfully much. How come you never told me what they said?"

"You never asked."

"Well, for Pete's sake. How am I supposed to know everything to ask?"

He restrained himself from saying, "If you cared, you'd find out." He said instead, "I'm going back for the follow-up day after tomorrow. No food for me tomorrow."

"Say," she said cheerily, "I'm glad they're doing a thorough job. Let me know what they tell you."

He drummed the table, not trusting himself to speak. It seemed to him that, if she should see him raise the loaded pistol to his temple, she would say in the same cheery voice, "Wait a minute, why don't you lie down and put it in your mouth so you won't get blood all over everything?" He pushed his plate away from him.

"Aren't you even going to finish your meal tonight?" she said. "You ought to stoke up."

"I've lost my zest for overcooked spaghetti," he said, staring at it. Susie began to whimper, and he turned on her. "If you're going to be a crybaby, go to your room." She leaned against her mother and half-sucked her thumb, half-cried. "Go to your room now."

Marguerite went with her.

Charley hunched over his plate and ate slowly, looking mostly at his father's hands.

When Stuart noticed this, he looked down and saw them clutching the edge of the table top so hard the ends were white. He played with the pressure on his fingertips, watching the color flow in and out under his fingernails. When he next looked up, Charley was gone too.

The first thing he did when he came to after the second trip was to run his tongue against his teeth: the three-molar gap was back on the left side where it belonged. He felt his testicles: the left was now lower as it should be. To the thump of his heart in his head a hymn tune began beating as it had beat when he was a child between his parents on a Presbyterian pew. He had not gone to church voluntarily since he was a sophomore in college. He and Marguerite had had a halfhearted quarrel a year ago about what to do if the children should ever ask to go to Sunday school; when she wanted to forbid it, he said that the whole religious bit was there, you couldn't get away from it, but Sunday school shouldn't be made to look tempting by being forbidden, just let the whole thing fade away of itself. But here he was rejoicing in a hymn tune whose words he was not even bothering to remember. He was lying on his back in the hollow ball, legs folded, head bent forward. He began wiggling his toes to the hymn beat, rolling his head back and forth, slapping his thighs. Then it occurred to him he was supposed to say something for the dial. "Let the lower light be burning," he sang, and his voice sounded so odd in his ears that he could hardly keep from laughing, but he went on singing. "Cast a gleam across the wave. Some poor fainting, struggling seaman you may rescue, you may save."

When he felt the plug begin to move, he fell silent, and when the first hairline arc of light showed, he burst out singing, "Some poor fainting . . ." but the whole disc of light at the end of the tube so delighted him that he had to roar laughing, and "struggling seaman" was choked out of sense. He managed to slither out of the tube, but as soon as he was standing and saw the worry on Brother Nicholas' face, he staggered about the lab helplessly.

Brother Nicholas poured a glass of something thick and white and followed him around, holding it out. "You've had too much oxygen."

"You look like you think," Stuart gasped, "I'm out of my

head. Well, Brother, you couldn't be wronger." He took the glass and managed to drink some of the liquid. "I'm back in my head, that's what. And my head's screwed back on my body the way it belongs. God, it's great to be a man again." He finished off the liquid.

"Now, into the tub," said Brother Nicholas. "You've got to warm up."

Stuart stood in the blood-warm water and gestured largely at the shelves of flasks and gauges and electrodes and hypodermics and pipettes. "Test me, Brother, I'll test clean, I'm here again; I'm back." He eased into the water and sighed. "Just bring me my old bridge first." He fitted it back onto his teeth. "What an improvement. Oh God, I am myself again. Oh Brother, I'm not nuts, really I'm not, just giddy. Oh, how intricate a wonder is man, most curious, most beautiful, worthy of the Lord's devices, and I am he. Oh Brother. Man, man."

Brother Nicholas stuck a thermometer in his mouth, and as he lay back into the water with only his face out, his eyes filled with tears.

3

Two months later he wrote a letter to the former Brother Carl and gave it to Brother Nicholas, who, promising nothing, undertook to send it to the one person he knew of that might know where to forward it. After ten anxious days, Stuart received an unsigned card, postmarked Oakland, instructing him to be at Al's Café, three miles above Stowe's Landing, at nine thirty the next Saturday morning.

He drove the two hundred miles up the coast the night before and got to the empty café a little after nine. The glum waitress did not look him in the eye but at whatever she could be fiddling with, the order pad, a spoon, a pencil. But when from time to time he caught her glancing at his bushy beard, he licked his lips so she would look quickly out the window. Just as she put a platter of bacon and eggs in front of him, a rusty old pickup parked by the highway and a squat man in work clothes and knee boots got out. Stuart, remembering him as quite an ugly man, would not have recognized this nondescript bearded workman. He walked straight to Stuart's table.

"Hello, Stuart."

"How do you do, Mr. Paulson."

"Call me Carl." He sat down across the little table from Stuart. "After twenty-five years nothing else suits."

"It is very good of you to see me. I need your advice badly."

"Why mine?"

"My letter explained."

"It explained that you need advice," said Carl. "Why mine?"

"If I didn't make that clear, why have you consented to see me?"

"Tell me again."

"You are the one who thought up the cone of cold."

"So you came to blame me."

"Not so!" cried Stuart, pushing the untouched platter to one side. "Blame has nothing to do with it, nor praise either."

"What do you suppose there was about your letter," Carl drawled, like a teacher playing guess-what's-on-my-mind with a confused, eager student, "that persuaded me to break the vow I made when I came up here three and a half months ago?"

"What vow?"

"Not to speak to anyone that has anything to do with St. Anselm's."

"Well," Stuart spoke slowly, "we've both had the same experience and it's affected us both quite a lot, and we've both severed connections with St. Anselm's because of it, you voluntarily, to be sure, and I because I've been fired as of the end of this semester, but still . . . We have a lot in common."

"It was a phrase in your letter," said Carl, " 'the total experience of otherness.' I want to know what that phrase means."

"If you don't know," said Stuart, laughing through stiff lips, "when you've been there yourself, it sure as hell won't mean anything to anybody else."

The waitress put a coin in the juke box, which presently began to emit loud, muddy heaves of seething sound.

"And you used the word 'nothing' a lot in your letter," said Carl. "I want to know what you meant special by that."

"I thought you mathematicians put big stock in zero."

"Zero is not the same as nothing."

"If I don't misunderstand," said Stuart, "zero made negative numbers and arithmetic possible, and without them the modern world would not be."

"The reason I went into mathematics," said Carl, gazing out the window across the highway up at the hills, "was that when I was a kid nobody could tell me what happened when you multiply zero by infinity."

"What does?"

"It depends on which kind of infinity you're talking about."

"Oh. How many kinds of zero are there?"

"One," said Carl with distaste, glancing sharply at Stuart and then looking up at the hills again, "so far as I know."

"And that," said Stuart, "is why you're a hermit today?"

Carl opened his mouth as though he were unsticking it. "I've seldom heard a short sentence with more wrong with it." His heavy brows descended, his eyelids half-covered his eyes, his upper lip twitched. "To begin with, I'm not a hermit. Obviously."

"Let's get the hell out of here," said Stuart. "I can't hear myself think."

"She'll turn it down," said Carl, and shouted for the waitress.

"I want to take a walk," said Stuart.

"I don't," said Carl. "It's cold and blowy." But at Stuart's expression he twitched, got up, and walked out.

The waitress came out of the kitchen and yelled, "What do you want?" from behind the counter.

"Check, please," Stuart called.

"Don't you want your food?"

Stuart walked to the cash register. "I'm not hungry after all. How much?"

"Some people," she said.

By the time he got outside, Carl was starting the pickup. Stuart ran over to the driver's side; the window was rolled up; he opened the door.

"Where you going? You can't go off and leave me."

"Get in," said Carl, with a jerk of the head. "If we're going to walk, let's go."

"What's wrong with right here?" Stuart gestured at the field stretching from the highway to the ocean.

"Private property."

Stuart went around and climbed in. "What do the farmers think we'll do, chase their sheep over a cliff?"

Carl did not respond, but pulled out onto the highway and headed north. He drove slowly, gripping the wheel and straining at the road.

"I see you have some tools," said Stuart, pointing with his thumb back at the truck bed. "The story I heard at St. Anselm's was that you weren't mechanical."

"Neither are tire irons and shovels," said Carl.

"Tire irons?" said Stuart.

"For prying abalone off rocks. That's one of the ways I make a living."

A mile up the road he pulled into a little state park in a valley of redwoods.

"Let's walk on the beach," said Stuart.

"Warmer up creek," said Carl, and strode off into the woods like a hiker.

He did not respond to Stuart's commonplace remarks.

He's furious, thought Stuart. He's as furious as I was before I went in the second time. Yet he's been there twice too. Maybe that's why he isn't able to stop himself from being rude. I mustn't let him go on. He mustn't get away with it. There's only one thing to do.

The path narrowed presently so that they had to go Indian file. After a couple of minutes of this, at a place where the path became a log across the stream, Stuart ran around Carl and jumped between him and the log, then stood staring him in the eye without speaking. Carl glared first at him, then over his shoulder into the little forest of redwoods, back and forth, back and forth. Stuart's head was thrust forward, Carl's was hunched down. Stuart's intention had been to confront Carl with a posed image of his own anger; but the moment Stuart assumed the posture the emotions became his own. His fists were clenched, as were Carl's.

Carl relaxed and his face cleared. "All right, I let you come up here; I'll take the consequences."

"That's more like," said Stuart and held out his hand, which Carl shook. Neither smiled.

"It opens up over there," said Carl and led the way over the log into a grove much like the one in which they had started out.

The breeze was soughing high up in the tall trees; they strolled in quiet, unencumbered by underbrush.

The sudden noise of two low-flying fighter jets whammed them.

"You see," said Stuart, "you can't get away, not really."

In the laughter with which Carl responded to this, they began to make friends.

"Tell me how you got fired," said Carl.

"At breakfast on April first," said Stuart, "I read in the paper an announcement that Brother David was appointed to a Presidential advisory committee on educational matters and was going to live in Washington."

"So."

"You expected this?"

"I used to be mildly curious whether David would get kicked up, down, or out. Up and out, it sounds like. Go on."

"The paper also said that Brother Joseph is taking over as provincial, beginning this summer."

"Naturally he is."

"When I got to my office that afternoon, I found a letter from him dated that same day, April first. It said my services would no longer be needed as of the end of this semester. I thought maybe it was an April Fool's joke."

"No."

"There's one sentence in it I'm keen on. He said he'd give me a good recommendation, my teaching was satisfactory. 'But it is felt that you are not happy as a member of the St. Anselm's family.' "

Carl gnashed his teeth. "Have you spoken to Joseph since?"

"Three or four times," said Stuart, "passing in the corridors. We're as cordial as ambassadors."

"He did write you the recommendation?"

"Oh, sure, and I've already lined up a job for next year. Same pay but lighter load."

"Good."

"I'm not sure how good it is."

"The lighter load?"

"Yes."

"It gives you more time to write, doesn't it?"

"That's the hitch," said Stuart.

"Hitch?"

"Well, anyway," Stuart said, "I don't have to worry about that goddamned cryostatic poem any more."

"You didn't write it?"

"I haven't written a verse since I went through the first time. I couldn't imagine what was going to happen beforehand, and now, afterward, I can't imagine what did happen."

"It's unimaginable."

"I hope so. But there's nothing else that seems worth thinking about, that way, imagining it."

"That poem scheme," said Carl, "has David stamped all over it—sounds brilliant but couldn't be stupider. Irresponsible. I wouldn't be surprised if it wasn't this poem he dreamed up for you that finally tipped the scales against him. You know, let's ship him off to Washington where idea men are a dime a dozen and nobody cares."

"It didn't seem *such* a bad notion," said Stuart. "After all."

"Poetry in the nineteen sixties?" said Carl contemptuously.

Ten minutes earlier, Stuart would have been infuriated by this. Now he was hurt. "As a matter of fact," he said, his chin drawn in, "I've given up writing poetry."

"I'm sorry to hear that."

"Sorry! After what you just said!"

"That was modern man I was talking about," said Carl. "And David's publicity schemes. Not myself. All I read, here, is philosophy and poetry."

"Well," said Stuart and kicked a fallen branch.

"My friend," said Carl, "what's the matter? Is it that you can't write?"

Stuart flailed the air with both arms, then burst out: "All I want to do is teach! Every class I teach as hard as I can. I can't keep from giving them everything I've got. At the end of every class I'm absolutely drained. It's just as though I'd been making love. They're boys, young men, maybe I'm a latent homosexual or something. I don't know. But the way I'm teaching these days is just like making love. You know what I mean?"

"No," said Carl harshly, but with an apologetic little duck of the head, "I don't know what you mean. I leave sex to my dreams."

"Tidy," said Stuart.

"I just put sex in my dreams and then don't think about the dreams. I assume they would analyze out to mean what everybody else's mean."

"Sigmund, thou hast not lived in vain." He meant to say this in his bland voice of insult, but it came out openly sarcastic and therefore unvenomous.

"It kept my head clear for thinking," said Carl softly, "and that turned out to be a mistake."

"Why did you bow out?" said Stuart in a clinging voice. "That's what I want to know, why you bowed out."

"Maybe something happened when I took my trip? I don't know."

"Did you have to think up those formulas?"

"Have to?" said Carl. "No."

"If you hadn't thought them up, would somebody else have? That's what we're always being told—scientific discoveries are in the air, it's just a question of who's lucky enough to get there first, simultaneous discoveries. Would somebody else have?"

"Of course."

"Then why haven't you ever published your findings?"

"You're pushing."

"I'm being pushed." Stuart suddenly felt hot behind the eyes.

"Maybe I'm wrong. Maybe no one will think of them independently. Maybe scientists and mathematicians aren't computers."

"Good," said Stuart, "but not good enough. Why didn't you publish them, really?"

"I don't like the practical consequences of those vile equations."

"Better," said Stuart, "much better." He thought about this for a while; something in Carl's silence drew him on. "Still not good enough. Were you ordered not to publish them?"

Carl snorted. "I was ordered *to*."

"Well, then," Stuart said. "Oh. Well, how can an equation be vile?"

"I'll tell you." Carl spoke in a strangled way, in short bursts. "I lied to you back there in the restaurant. There are two kinds of zero, plus and minus."

"That's nonsense," said Stuart. "Isn't it nonsense?"

"Sheer, trivial nonsense. All the same, these equations of mine, which Nicholas used to build the dynocryne, are based on minus zero."

Stuart held out his hands, palms up. "I thought the physical world was at least thinkable."

"Never," said Carl, "and especially not now."

"That should fill a religious man with joy."

"It does not fill me with joy. Does it fill you with joy?"

"It terrifies me," said Stuart.

"Are you religious?"

"I thought I wasn't. I didn't used to be. I want the world to mean now. Haven't you proved that the material world is just as unthinkable as the spiritual world?"

"Those equations of mine prove nothing," said Carl. "They stop argument, that's all. Because of them, you can't deny there is a part of the universe we can't think about. But the so-called proof for this is insane. Those aren't equations, they are anti-equations which work. It is the case that there is something in the world which you can't think about and which is *there,* but to understand this you have to think insanely. My particular insane thinking from nothing can be, has been, engineered in a way that fits the world. The world must be insane with nothing too."

Stuart cried almost in anguish, "That doesn't mean anything!"

"Yes, it does," said Carl and made a chopping little gesture with his hand. "It means that the world does not mean. Now tell me what you know about nothing."

"I told you I couldn't write my poem. I can't say something about nothing. I'm a poet. Words are things. Nothing is a thing."

"Phrases. So you're not going to tell me anything?"

"I can't."

Carl's eyebrows descended again. "That's that." He wheeled away.

Smiling impotently at the back of Carl's head, Stuart followed. "I'm glad I can't," he said. "If I could I probably would, and I'd sure hate to do that to people."

Carl's murderous scowl lightened only a little when they said good-bye back by the café. Stuart fiddled at starting his car, thinking to trail Carl. He had no particular reason for wanting to know where Carl lived; he just felt like finding out. But Carl outwitted him; when he drove away, Carl took off in the opposite direction.

"Well," Stuart said aloud, "what would you expect from a hermit anyway? All the same."

Past the first bend in the highway he turned around and raced back in the other direction. But after driving five miles he gave up; Carl must have ducked up one of the side roads. Stuart shook his head, and drove on north to Noyo, where he had fresh salmon for lunch in a restaurant by a fish dock.

There was still a cool breeze. The heart had gone out of his weekend. If he was to get home at a reasonable hour today, he should take off now. However, by the time he had driven south twenty miles, the sun was out and the wind had died down and he no longer cared whether he got home that evening but decided to walk by the ocean as long as the weather held.

An old station wagon was parked inside a gate which a man was closing. Stuart honked and turned off the highway. The man shook his head, waved him away, then got in the station wagon, in which there were several other people, and drove off across the pasture. The gate was locked, and there was a fresh NO TRES-PASSING sign on the hinge post. Stuart watched the station wagon drive a few hundred yards out, to about the place where a spit extended another quarter of a mile westward into the sea, and park. Then he climbed the gate and strode off down the middle of the spit.

Not far from the outermost point, there was a clump of dark green trees which, even though the air at the moment was still, leaned inland as though they were being swept by a stiff breeze. Against the far side of the trees there was a pickup, which he recognized as Carl's. He felt a surge of expectation that lifted him onto the balls of his feet and made his nostrils flare.

He went to the north edge; there was only empty sand below, stretching out to the lapping surf; the low tide was so sluggish that the waves often did not break but faded into ripples. Far inland, he caught sight of two or three of the station wagon party out among the exposed sea rocks.

On the south side of the spit, he saw many rocks and pools, gleaming with dark brown ribbons of seaweed. The sheer cliff was about thirty feet high at this point, and he spied no path nearby. Offshore a hundred yards or so, a tall rounded bald upcropping of dark granite with a high arch in it and a lop-sided boulder squat on top looked to him like a Henry Moore statue of matter becoming man. He lost interest in searching for Carl and stood watching the waves crashing and spuming against the little island.

He became aware of a movement a good way out, of something dark emerging from the other side of a large rock. At first he thought the large black lump was a seal, but then it reared up and he saw it was a cartoonlike man wearing a black rubber suit, gloves, and helmet, and some sort of face mask with goggles.

While the tide ebbed and turned, Stuart lay on the grass, in front of a bush so that his profile would not be visible from below, watching this solitary, edgeless figure which he knew to contain the man who of all men had had the most important effect on him, submerge, come up, move with his bucket from place to place, measure the shells of the great snails he pried off their rocks underwater, put some into the bucket, and toss more back into the deep water.

By the time the fog began to roll in, the tide was clearly rising, and Carl started back to shore. Stuart crawled to the other side of the bush so he might stand and walk away unseen. His last image was of the granite, oceanic sculpture.

For hours as he drove south toward home, he imagined he had participated in a ritual of revelation.

At one thirty, chilly, stiff from the long drive, glad to be home, he let himself into the flat on tiptoe, undressed in the dining room, felt his way through the dark bedroom to his side of the bed, and gently lifted the covers to slide in. But as he was easing down onto the mattress, Marguerite suddenly glurked, "Wha'? Wha'?" and began thrashing about. He said, "Sh, honey, it's me," and caught her arm. When her hands closed on his beard, she flinched as though she had been electrically shocked, and hollered *Help!* in a husky voice.

"Maggy! You'll wake up the children!"

"Stu? That beard? Oh, that beard! What are you, creeping up on a person—a rapist?"

"I just got home."

"Well, why? Damn it all, everything was so peaceful with you gone. Why?"

"I was quiet so I wouldn't disturb you." He could not tell from the hiccupy sounds she was making whether she was laughing or crying. "I'm sorry."

"What did she do?" said Marguerite. "Walk out on you?"

"What?" Feeling her lie back down, he got under the covers. "Who?"

"I hope she's nobody I ever met."

"What in God's name are you talking about?"

"You," she said, still making the hiccupy sounds. "You haven't come near me for months and all of a sudden you go away for the weekend, by yourself so you say, and then you sneak back early and grab me."

"Maggy," he said reproachfully, "please." He reached out for her. She was on her side facing him, all elbows and knees and shins. "Darling, there's nobody else. I went up to Mendocino to see a mathematician who used to be a brother at St. Anselm's but he got out of the order during Christmas vacation."

"Jesus, how insulting!" she cried and kicked him. "You don't even respect me enough to think up a story I could at least swallow enough of to keep one little shred of self-respect. Mathematician! God!"

He made soothing noises, and she shrieked at him to shut up and listen.

"The children," he said sternly.

"Abandon them's all right," she hissed, "but let us not disturb their precious sleep. Well, listen to me—they don't love you any more."

"Oh." He turned flat on his back, legs side by side, wrists crossed on his chest, face straight up. "They don't seem to be afraid of me."

"Why should they be? You don't even love them enough to spank them when they're naughty. They know."

The image of a beached whale came to him.

When Marguerite punched him in the arm, he became aware that she had said, "Are you listening?"

"I'm listening."

"Leonie's folks aren't going to be using their cabin up at Echo

Lake till August, and they're letting Dick and her have it till then. But he can't get away from the agency before August, and she doesn't want to be stuck up there alone with her kids, so today she asked me. Are you following me?"

"Go on."

"Well, I'm going to take the children and go."

She turned onto her side with her back to him, pulling the covers half off him.

"I hate the mountains," he said.

"Nobody asked you."

He was aware of her still unsteady breathing and of his own quick, shallow breathing.

"When?" he said.

"By Memorial Day if we're lucky. As soon as it's not too cold. We won't come back till August. If I come back. If you're here when I come back."

"I will be," he said.

"Hallelujah. Now go sleep on the couch where you're supposed to be. I've got to get up with the children by seven, remember?"

"I want to sleep here with you."

"Why? So you can hit me till I'm black and blue the way you did last week? I won't be able to go swimming for weeks yet."

"I told you I was sorry," he said in a remote voice. "I was having a bad dream."

"What'll I say when people ask me where I got all the bruises —my husband beats me in his sleep?"

" I didn't beat you. My elbow just happened . . ."

"Didn't beat me! Are you trying to weasel out of it now? Have you actually got the gall?"

"All right, Maggy, I hoped I wouldn't have to tell you but I guess I do."

"Who cares? She doesn't want you either, eh? Well, Buster, you've burned your bridges. Again."

"I participated in a dangerous scientific experiment," he said. "Yah."

"I wasn't supposed to tell anybody, but now I've got to tell you. I haven't really gotten over it yet, and that was January."

"So, you've been deceiving me all these months! You just admitted it yourself. How can I believe a thing you say?"

"I've got a bridge," he said. "You know my bridge with three false teeth? Well, I've got another just like it that fits on the wrong side of my mouth. It's down in the lab. I'll bring it home and show you."

"Are you out of your mind?" she yelled in a whisper.

"No. But I was." He was still on his back, still facing straight up. "Let me just lie here in the dark and tell you about it."

She twisted her head back enough to look at him. "It's late. Go to the couch." He did not stir. She pushed him. "You're not kidding? You really were in danger?"

"In a strange way, very much so."

"You're all right now, though, aren't you? Healthy, I mean."

"Physically I check out okay."

"It's something new?"

"Yes."

"Mental?"

"Or spiritual."

"God, now he's getting religious on me on top of everything else."

"The main thing I know is, I don't care whether I ever write another poem again in my life, I just want to teach; immortality doesn't mean anything to me any more, just living while we can; communion; poetry's all right but you have to wait so long to see if anybody gets it and you're not even there when it happens. I like teaching better."

"It's too late."

"I need you so badly," he murmured.

"You waited too long!" she cried and began half-hiccupping

again. "I don't want to listen to all that crap! If you don't go sleep on the couch, I will."

He remained rigid. She left, walking on her heels.

He thought, Failed again. If she won't listen to me now, she never will. It hurts too much; I won't ever be able to make the overture again. There's nobody else to say it to. It's all my own fault.

The next day he moved into a furnished room not far from St. Anselm's, leaving the car with Marguerite. She told the children he had to be away working a lot, and they arranged for him to come home every other day late in the afternoon to be with the children till their bedtime. He did not bring them little presents; they did not divert themselves much from their play to pay attention to him; he would watch them mutely, and every once in a while catch one or the other up in his demanding arms, saying how much he missed and loved them; he told them bedtime stories, but with a sinking heart. For he thought Marguerite was right, they did not love him. She was scrupulous in every arrangement, and as soon as the children had been tucked in there was nothing for him to do but leave.

The weather was so warm that the day after Memorial Day Marguerite and the children piled into Leonie's station wagon with Leonie and her two, and all their gear, and they took off for the mountains. Stuart stood on the sidewalk, like a dog left behind, watching them drive away. Two hours later he had moved back into the flat.

For ten days he spent as much time as possible at St. Anselm's, working, talking with any students who came by or whom he found in the coffee shop. He played poker or went to a movie every evening. The evening of the day he finished up at St. Anselm's, he prowled some dives in Oakland, nervous and lustful, half-meaning to pick up a woman for the night. He had never done it before; he was not sure how to go about it; the women he saw were repulsive. But then a couple of vulgarly pretty ones came in and glanced at him boldly. If they had been whores in a brothel he would have taken either one, but here in this bar he would not insult them by approaching them as though they were whores—how could he know? He went home glad he did not know where there was a brothel, for he would have gone to it, and repented. But then it occurred to him that what he would really have bought in a whorehouse, in the guise of assuaging his desire, was the not being rejected by a woman for a while. The remorse he would have felt from paying a woman to not reject him (and then to say some of the words and make some of the motions of love) would surely have been great. But it further occurred to him that he had been kept from a whore not because he could not find one—cab drivers pimp, as everyone knows—but because he had not dared. Reproach at his base impulse and shame at his pusillanimity combined to anesthetize his sex and guts, make his waking thick, and clog his sleep with unremembered dreams.

For four days he got out of bed only to go to the toilet, nibble at whatever he came on in the refrigerator or cupboard, collect the mail, which he left unread. The phone rang from time to time, the doorbell a few times; he did not answer them.

Late the fifth morning he was awakened by the doorbell's buzzing like a rattlesnake, on and on. When it quit, he went into the kitchen. The first things he laid his hands on were a box of ginger snaps and a can of corn. He had not noticed steps on the back stairs, but suddenly there was a banging on the back door and Brother Nicholas' face was at the top pane, shouting at him. Stuart frowned and shook his head. He finished opening the can, stuck a spoon in the corn, then shuffled into the dining room with the can in one hand and the box in the other.

There was the sound of breaking glass, then Brother Nicholas' loud flat voice, "Let me in, Stuart!"

If he just wouldn't make so much noise, Stuart thought, and

stared at the spoonful of corn trembling halfway to his mouth.

There was a fumbling and clicking, the door opened, Brother Nicholas called, "Stuart?" and came into the dining room. Stuart carefully put the spoon back into the can, and, smiling secretly, looked up into Brother Nicholas' worried eyes.

"Where's your family?" said Brother Nicholas. Stuart licked his lips. "It's stuffy in here, it doesn't smell good."

Brother Nicholas opened windows in every room in the flat. At the feel of the breeze, Stuart inhaled deeply, and stretched.

Brother Nicholas came back and sat at the end of the table. "You never answered my notes reminding you to come in for a six-month checkup. Didn't you get them?" Stuart shrugged. "Look, I'm sort of responsible for you. You're obviously not well. Where's your wife?"

"She left me here." His voice cracked—began high and tight, then cracked to a phlegmy baritone. He cleared his throat. "She and the children are vacationing." It felt strange, using his voice; he liked the feeling. "They went to Echo for two months."

"Echo Lake?" said Brother Nicholas, and Stuart nodded. "Any phone?"

Stuart wanted to see how well he could aim his voice. He aimed his "No" at a downward decrescendo in the middle range, but, though he found the range, what he hit was a piteous bleat. He was ashamed. "No," he barked.

Whereupon, to Stuart's surprise, Brother Nicholas grinned broadly, slapped his hands flat on the table, and pushed himself up. "Now," he said, and on his way to the door picked up the can and the box, "so this is what you eat," and held them out. "No wonder you look so scroungy." Laughing his loud flat laugh, he gave Stuart a friendly elbow in the shoulder and went into the kitchen.

Again with the secret smile, Stuart looked after him wistfully, and was still watching the doorway when he came back from rummaging through the cupboards and refrigerator.

"Now, come on, Stuart. I'll go get a steak and you take a bath.

Throw those goddamned pajamas into the laundry and take a hot bath."

"Do I smell bad?"

"Friend, you stink. And you've got lint in your beard!"

Stuart caught his lower lip between his teeth. The recurrent image of the whale stranded on a beach of gray pebbles came to him.

"Okay, Stuart?"

He turned back to Brother Nicholas.

"I'll be gone for half an hour or so. I've got to get my car filled with gas and the tires checked."

Stuart drew his chin in. "I've got a car."

"But we're going in mine."

"Where to?"

"Echo, of course."

"I thought you brothers couldn't own anything."

"Well, it's a college car legally, but I've got it."

"Why not go in mine?"

"So I can get back today."

"You're going to leave me there?"

"What else?"

"She doesn't want me." Stuart burst into tears.

Brother Nicholas held his shoulders for a little while. "Come on, come on now, maybe she'll have you. Did you tell her about what you've been through? The dynocryne?"

"Don't you dare tell her!" Stuart wiped his eyes furiously on a sleeve. "That's my business."

"Hers too, maybe?"

"Get out! Leave me alone!"

Brother Nicholas did a strange thing. He was heavy and strong, his features were gross and unlined, he was unshaped in his cassock. But he crumpled. In Stuart's astonished eyes, he collapsed and diminished just as he was standing there, hardly moving.

"Forgive me," he said.

"Aw," Stuart said, and some gentle tears flowed from his eyes without cracking him.

Brother Nicholas went into the kitchen and drank a glass of water. Stuart followed him.

"I'm hungry," said Brother Nicholas. "I'm going to get a three-pound sirloin and some tomatoes. You like tomatoes?"

"Sure."

"And some French bread, and some dago red."

"I like milk," said Stuart.

"A *little* wine?"

"Bread and wine. Yes. The body and the blood. Where two or three are gathered there am I."

Brother Nicholas ran his finger around the edge of the glass. "I wasn't necessarily thinking along those lines."

"No. It just manifests itself, doesn't it?"

"I was thinking you could use some relaxation."

"Relaxation!" Stuart started to laugh. He felt an uncontrollable convulsion of laughter beginning to swell in his guts, and choked it off. "I've been so relaxed I could hardly get out of bed."

"Well, toning up, then? Getting ready for a trip? Okay, I'll go off now for a while, so take yourself a hot bath and put on some clean clothes. You have some?"

"Sure, but I'd rather take a shower than a bath."

"Well, all right, take yourself a shower. In fact, that's better, you can sing in it. Sing, go ahead, it'll make you feel better."

"Will it really?"

"It really will. The steam will be good for your voice too."

"Good, I'll use up all the hot water."

"That's right." Brother Nicholas beamed. "That's the ticket."

He was still singing in the shower when Brother Nicholas returned, and he was so slow to trim his beard and dress that the steaks were half-broiled by the time he came out of the bedroom.

After they had been driving for a couple of hours and were

climbing the mountains at sixty miles an hour, Stuart turned off the car radio and said, "What's going to happen," then, his voice cracked up and tight, "when we get there?"

"I don't know," said Brother Nicholas. "I just know one thing. I'm going to tell Mrs. Stuart exactly what you've been through and then I'm going home."

"How are you going to go about it?"

"You tell me."

Stuart leaned his head against the doorpost for a while, letting the hot dry wind whip his hair and make the skin on the right side of his face stretch tight. At first he felt hopeless at the prospect of going to Marguerite, of how to introduce Brother Nicholas to her. But then he recognized the torpor into which he had sunk. It was not listlessness, tense stasis, despondency. It was the still readiness into which he usually immersed when sitting in front of a blank piece of paper about to set down the first word of a poem. All he had to do was let the alternatives swirl about helter-skelter in that immobility, and of itself the time would come to say. The time came now.

"We'll rent a rowboat and row out to a little dock a hundred yards from the house they're staying in, hidden behind the point. I'll stay in the boat with my sleeping bag, so the children won't see me and start anything. You walk across the point, there's a path, and find Marguerite. Take her aside and tell her whatever you want to tell her. Then come back to the boat. If everything's all right, I'll get out and stay. Otherwise, I'll go back with you."

"You understand," said Brother Nicholas, "I'm only doing this . . ."

"I understand," said Stuart, sitting up straight, "I understand." He arched his back and stretched his arms forward, curling his toes in his shoes, yawning. "I understand." Then he relaxed, happily relaxed, relaxed alive, thinking, I'm glad he just assumed I wanted to go back to her. I don't know what I'd have said if he'd asked me whether I wanted to.

Though the women went on and on about how cold it got at night and how much dew had often fallen by morning, Stuart just said, "I like to watch the stars," and unrolled his sleeping bag on the open porch. He did not ask Marguerite to join him there. He did not offer to kiss her good night, only touched her fingers with his when everybody turned in.

The cottage fell silent. Faint music, and once in a while laughter, came across the lake, and owl cries. He lay on his back with his hands clasped under his head, looking at the stars, nearly but not quite crying.

Then there were creakings, footsteps, the screen door opened, and Marguerite laid the pallet from her cot on the boards beside his sleeping bag, straightened the covers and got in.

"Stu?" Her hand found his crooked elbow. "Give me your hand, darling."

He started to take her hand, but she pulled his hand to her and put her cheek against it.

"Did you really understand what Brother Nicholas told you?"

"Of course not," she said, "but I believed him. I don't really understand all you said about communion and antiworlds and so on, but I don't care if you never write another line of poetry again, if you don't want to."

"It's so much easier with students," he said, "that kind of spiritual intercourse, I mean, talking. It's so hard with you, and Charley and Susie, after what I've put you through, everything you mean to me, more than talking, total. It's total. Bear with me?"

She unbuttoned her pajama jacket and shifted toward him a little. Then she took his arm under the blankets and snuggled it to her bare body, elbow in her belly, wrist between her breasts. He remained on his back.

"I'll bet you do, though," she said.

"Do what?"

"I don't really care, but I'll just bet you write another poem.

About those trips you took in the cold, or something. My poor, poor baby, you've been so cold."

He turned his head toward her, though he could make out only the ghostly aureole of her hair; he wanted to feel her warmth, and he wanted his silent tears to spill onto the pillow instead of running into his ears. She folded his large hand over her small one, which he pressed for a moment. He crossed one ankle over the other. They did not talk. After a while she dozed off, her lips still touching his knuckles.

His mind filled with the image of the black whale parching in the hot sun, beached at low tide, no breakers washing it, not even any spume reaching it, its flukes and tail giving a flop or two from time to time, gasping in irregular spasms, lungs crushed by its own heaviness.

He felt the sanctioned buzz of words again in his mind and watched them swarm and begin to settle around "the beached whale gasping."

Again!— But, he menaced himself, it's got to chant. If it won't chant, I won't write it.

Presently it occurred to him that whales can't gasp, they breathe through a blowhole. Maybe it whistles when they're dry? I haven't read *Moby Dick* for years, he thought happily. I've got to go read it and find out what I can do with this whale of mine.

An Hour of Last Things

1

Betty Hollander, a tall, lean, pale woman, found herself widowed at the age of thirty-eight by an automobile accident which killed both her husband and his father. Her husband, Winton, was a designer of rest homes, and his father was a retired optometrist with heart trouble. The father and son had been driving to Baltimore, where Winton was to look over three houses which a client of his planned to remodel as rest homes; Mr. Hollander had gone for the outing. It was raining and traffic was heavy. Winton was pressing to make an eleven o'clock appointment. On the outskirts of a town in Delaware a car swerved against him, whereupon he slammed on the brakes and skidded head-on into a furniture van. Mr. Hollander died in the ambulance. Winton lay in the hospital for five days, his liver ruptured, his forehead crushed, and his right eye penetrated by a sliver of glass. All three drivers had been somewhat at fault in the accident: the first driver had swerved to avoid hitting a dog, Winton had been going too fast for the condition of the highway, the truck driver might have turned aside in time had he not been lighting a cigarette at the moment Winton's car had slid at his left headlight. Betty was relieved to put blame and revenge out of her mind by delegating them to the insurance company.

She went into Winton's room at the hospital three times every day, except the day of Mr. Hollander's funeral, when she visited Winton only in the evening. He did not respond to her voice or the touch of her hand. Once he was mumbling fretfully, but she could not make out one syllable. His head was swathed except for his nostrils, mouth, and chin, so that he could not open his jaw enough to get out any words which he might otherwise have been capable of making. The noise he produced was more like whimpering than like speech. The last time she saw him his fingers were plucking at the bedclothes.

In the evening of the fifth day, well after visiting hours, Betty was sitting in the hospital waiting room with a popular magazine right side up in her hands. She had been glancing at a picture story of costumed dogs that had been trained by a boy in Minnesota to dance mostly on their hind legs but also on their front legs. From time to time she tried to understand what the pictures represented, but she could not make it out. A few pages further in the magazine, there was a picture of a gaunt woman, a Protestant missionary's wife, who had just been released from a Chinese Communist prison; the caption read RELEASED AFTER YEARS OF TORMENT; she could not understand that either. On the couch opposite her two shabby young women with blotched skin and miserable eyes sat not even looking at a magazine. The larger one looked as though she wanted to cry. Betty smiled sternly the two times they caught her eye. Confronted with them, she was grateful that she had troubled in the hotel room that afternoon to smooth out her gabardine suit with her traveling iron and that she was wearing shoes with heels instead of the flats she usually wore. The smaller woman kept glancing about, though her lips were moving and her fingers were telling the beads of a rosary. The larger kept wringing her handkerchief, and when a Puerto Rican nurse stepped in and glanced at each of the three, she stuffed her handkerchief into her mouth and cringed.

"Mrs. Hollander?"

Betty nodded, closed the magazine, and set it on the table beside her chair, put her flat purse under her arm, and stood up.

"Would you step this way please?"

The nurse took her behind a partition where there were two straight chairs and a small table and told her that Winton had died five minutes before. Betty had been afraid she would break down at this point, but she did not even feel like crying. She asked the nurse in a businesslike way whether there were any arrangements she should make. The nurse said they would wait till morning and asked her if she wanted a sleeping pill. Betty said certainly not. She would sit there behind the partition having a cigarette—if the nurse would be so good as to bring her an ashtray—and then walk back to the hotel.

As the nurse was leaving, Betty heard one of the other two women murmur to her and the nurse murmur in response. Betty suspected that the nurse was telling them that Betty's husband had just died. There was nothing to look at. She kept forgetting to draw on the cigarette. She became aware of sobs from the other side of the partition; then also of a muttering. She ground out the cigarette and set her mouth. When she strode out from behind the partition, she glanced at the two women on the couch. The larger ceased her sobbing and pressed the knuckles of her hand against her teeth; the smaller dropped her rosary and pressed her companion's right hand in both of hers. They kept that position, seeming to hold their breath, while Betty left the room.

2

Because Mr. Hollander had died before Winton, his only son, Betty inherited Mr. Hollander's property as well as Winton's. Mrs. Hollander, who had divorced Winton's father twenty years before and had lived in Florida since then, wrote Betty a letter condoling with her and congratulating her at once. Betty had inherited enough in insurance and stocks to live without having to work, and she knew that Mrs. Hollander, who had never remarried, was not well off. Betty offered to give her mother-in-law, whom she had known for one week nine years before, half of what Mr. Hollander had left. In the letter accepting this gift, Mrs. Hollander implied that Betty was to be congratulated for getting rid of half her guilt.

Mr. Hollander had lived in the same house in Staten Island for thirty years. After his wife and son had left, he lived there alone for a while, but in the ten years Betty had known him he had had a colored housekeeper who lived in and who came and went quite as she pleased. She had moved out of the house the day after Mr. Hollander's funeral, despite Betty's pleading with her to stay and take care of the house until Betty had decided what to do with it. The housekeeper, who had wept noisily at the funeral, refused, saying it would make her heart too heavy to stay on, for Mr. Hollander had been a good man.

Betty had had Mr. Hollander's body brought back to Staten Island for the funeral service and buried in a perpetual-care grave for which he had already paid. Winton's body, however, in accordance with both his and her own wishes, she had a local undertaker cremate without ceremony; the ashes she had disposed of inexpensively and without fuss. She had found Mr. Hollander's funeral parlor *cum* Methodist service repulsive. She more or less closed her ears to the words, so that the organ music stayed in the background; but the flowers obtruded upon her. She never wore flowers, and she and Winton had only occasionally permitted flowers in their severe apartment; they preferred a jagged branch with berries on it, or three plumes of grass against a bare wall. Despite these matters of taste, the loud grief of Mr. Hollander's housekeeper and her irrational determination to leave his house troubled Betty. She knew they were not meant as a reproach; nevertheless, she felt reproached; she thought of herself as being rational in her decisions and too emotionally repressed. Since the accident she had wept once, stranglingly, alone in the hotel room the evening after she had first visited Winton in the hospital. None of their friends or acquaintances blamed her by the least inflection or hesitation for the way in which she had disposed of Winton's body; on the contrary, those who mentioned the matter applauded her. After the Goodwill had taken away his clothes, she felt no reluctance, even when she would return late at night, to unlock the door and enter. Though there was a chair he had customarily sat in when he read, she had no impulse to move it, for its position was the most suitable one for the arrangement of the room. All the same, when she thought of Mr. Hollander's housekeeper she felt deficient. She could not relieve her sorrow by putting on noisy ways, and though she knew she was suffering intensely, she had no external signs to prove it, as the housekeeper had. She was half-consciously afraid she was not suffering enough. She felt vaguely that it would be better for her if she moved out of that apartment, in which she had lived with Winton for the nine years of their marriage, and even out of Brooklyn Heights, though many of her friends lived in that neighborhood.

She supposed that she would not be at such loose ends if she had had a child, but then reproached herself for her selfishness. She would have been leaning on someone whom, she agreed with Winton, they had no right to bring into so dreadful a world as this. Mrs. Hollander had made the gift of half of Mr. Hollander's money unsatisfying, so that Betty felt that to have given her the entire estate would have been no more noteworthy than giving ten dollars to the Community Chest. Betty thought of giving the other half of what she had inherited from Mr. Hollander to some such cause as the American Friends Service Committee; but she knew such a gift would not be a satisfying action to her at that time. Moreover, she began to want to quit her job, having worked in the same social welfare agency for seven years, and she feared that, because of her pervasive, unrelenting malaise, she might need money for further psychoanalysis.

After two weeks of perplexity and indecision, she decided to have another interview with the analyst to whom she had gone for four years but whom she had not needed to see for the past three years. She learned that he had recently moved to St. Louis. Because she had been raised in a town not far from there, she obscurely felt that his leaving New York for St. Louis was a retrogression as her doing so would have been and that he might have betrayed her. All the same, she wrote him asking if she might talk to him over the telephone. He replied immediately, setting a day and hour. She put in the call, expecting little but not knowing what else to do. He astonished her by the open friendliness of his voice. He seemed sympathetic with her for her loss and unimpressed by her symptoms, and they talked for nearly an hour. She had expected him to be elaborately cautious on the subject of Mrs. Hollander; instead, he asked for the practical details and then said she sounded as bad as ever. At that point Betty decided to communicate thereafter with her mother-in-law only through lawyers. She also decided, during that telephone conversation, to quit her job, move into her father-in-law's house, and see how she liked living there; if she did not like it, she would take a trip to Europe. As she suggested these plans over the telephone, she became aware of their ordinariness and apologized for it. The doctor, however, laughed at her apologetic embarrassment in such an indulgent way, telling her like a friend not to be silly, that gratitude warmed her. He also told her that her most threatening problem now was having too much free time on her hands.

When she had picked up the receiver to place the call, she had been sitting stiffly sidewise to the table, on which cigarettes, ashtray, and a cup of coffee were arranged, and the toe of her crossed foot had been pressing hard against a table leg. When she hung up, her shoulders were sagging and one bare foot was tucked under her on the chair. She shoved back the things on the table and laid her head sideways on her arms. The grief had worked its way out into her muscles. She could feel its pain coming up behind her eyes. Her relief at feeling in her very body manifestations of intense sorrow was so great that she did not resist it but let it shake her and course through her.

3

It was the custom at Betty's agency for the colleagues of a departing worker to give a going-away present. Since Betty now had much more money than the others and since they knew how "fussy" her taste was, they decided to give her a farewell dinner instead in the banquet room of a moderately good restaurant, one which the director of the agency seemed to have his heart set on.

The banquet was not as stiff as Betty had anticipated. Most of the three bottles of Scotch on the sideboard had been emptied by the time everyone sat down to eat, and at dinner the director's half case of champagne was matched out of a kitty taken up among the others on the spur of the moment. The food was good; the director's long toast was stuffy, but it was also sentimental. He even made a little joke about how "we are going to miss our Wasp, she kept us on the *qui vive.*" (Betty was the only White Anglo-Saxon Protestant in the agency.) Several others were emboldened to make speeches too.

At first Betty feared that she was supposed to respond in kind, but presently she realized that those who spoke were not speaking to or even about her so much as they were using the opportunity to enjoy themselves. She drank all the champagne she wanted, sank back in her chair, and smiled and blinked at people.

The party did not break up till midnight. Everyone agreed that the director was an amiable fellow when he let himself unbend and that the banquet had been a great success. Some of the women wept a little when they said good-bye to Betty, assuring her that they could not stand to think she was going to move out of town and never come back to the agency. She reminded them, eagerly, that she would still be in New York City, but they said—what she knew—that going to Staten Island was quite a trip, only two out of seven of them had ever done it except to go across on the ferry for the ride.

Francy Rugero, her department head for the past year, had maintained an official distance with Betty on the job and had not said much during the evening. However, in the hubbub of farewells, she suddenly loomed in front of Betty and grasped her at arm's length, a hand on each shoulder. She was even taller than Betty, and she was beefy; she was in her forties, and so far as Betty knew she had never been married. Her ebony, lumpy forehead was scowling. Betty, who was blurry with champagne and affection, smiled at her and patted her shaftlike arms. Francy kept staring into Betty's eyes as though searching for something, then hugged her close and kissed her on the cheek. "Good-bye, Betty, damn it," she said in a flat, furious voice, put on her trench coat, and strode out by herself.

4

That morning Betty's possessions, most of which had been selected by Winton, had been moved from the severe apartment to the Victorian house. She had been looking forward uneasily to that first night alone in the house, which she had not yet been able to think of as hers; but the mellow effects of the dinner stayed with her as she wove her little, upright foreign car among the pressures of Flatbush Avenue, across the Brooklyn Bridge, and to the tip of Manhattan. On the ferry, she stood outside so as to be alone and was conscious of the cool air in her nostrils and of the three-quarter moon. She drove along the streets of Staten Island, imagining that their quietness was an invitation and smiling at the silliness of her fancy. She parked her car in her garage and let herself into her house, which for some reason smelled good to her. She stood at the front windows for a few minutes, gazing out over lights which were all the prettier because she could not identify any of them. The weeding out, painting, and rearranging to be done had been preying on her mind, but they now appeared to her as agreeable offices. Doing them would make this house, which she felt awkward and comfortable in, so familiar to her that it would become an expression of herself. At first she had intended to get rid of nearly all of Mr. Hollander's furniture but now she decided to keep a good deal of it; taste or no taste, she liked it. The movers had put her bed, a single mattress on box springs to which legs were attached, in the cluttered guest room; it looked uninviting to her. The housekeeper had left Mr. Hollander's ornate double bed made up, with a fresh counterpane and ironed sheets. Betty did not much like the patterned wallpaper in the master bedroom. Nevertheless she decided to sleep there. Once in the bed, she liked having the headboard there to touch when she stretched out her arms, and the four spooled posts, which had seemed disproportionately tall when the lamps were on, towered about her in the diffuse moonlight both elegant and protecting. Through the open window the sound of crickets came in louder than the noise of the city.

5

At eleven thirty the telephone rang. She sat bolt upright in bed, startled and confused. By the time she had put on her slippers, cleared her throat, and gone into the hall, the line was dead. It seemed to her a bad omen not to have answered the first person to call her in her new house. She was eager for new possibilities. What opportunity had she just missed?

She arranged the garden furniture on the south side of the house, put some Mozart sonatas for violin and piano on her old record player, opened the windows, and took her coffee and toast out in the hot sun. She watched a squirrel in her elm tree. Four little boys in chaps went shooting across her lawn, paying no attention to her. Two cardinals were pecking orange-colored berries in a bush. Her neighbor to the west, a barefoot old woman wearing dark glasses, shorts, and a halter, invited her across the hedge to "come take a dip in our swimming pool any time." Betty thanked her but regretted that she did not swim. It was true that she did not swim, but it was not true that she regretted it at that moment. In her opinion, no one was less worth knowing than a false-young old woman, and nothing more vulgar than a blue cement swimming pool in the back yard of an eighty-year-old house in Staten Island. Her telephone's ringing again abridged this unwanted neighborliness.

It was Francy Rugero saying that she had an extra ticket to the Juilliard School of Music Recital Hall for the next Thursday night. "My cousin is singing there—she's a contralto—making her debut. How would you like to go with me?" Betty said she would like to. "You know, babe, her friends are sort of papering the house for the poor child. I understand she's not bad. I hardly know her even if she is my cousin. Actually, she's my mother's sister's daughter's daughter."

"My God, aren't there any men in your family?"

"Men! In my family we got parthenogenesis down to a science. The only use we got for men is to pleasure ourselves with them from time to time."

They joked awhile longer and then made arrangements to eat together before the recital. Betty was still sitting by the telephone, wondering whether there was something behind Francy's sudden friendliness, when it rang again.

This time it was Harold Garrett. He lived across the hall from Winton's friend Cedric in a dingy apartment house east of Greenwich Village. She had met Harold two or three times at Cedric's parties, without much liking him. Harold had told her once that he made a living by buying blocks of theater tickets and reselling them to groups but that he "also had a few other little things going on the side." He spoke breathlessly, like a gossip with a fresh tidbit.

He wanted to come see Betty right away because he knew she adored music so much she would be wanting a new hi-fit set tailored for her present needs. She was annoyed that he presumed to know anything about her taste.

"Are you selling hi-fi equipment?"

The sharpness in her voice halted him. "Not exactly."

"Because I'm not interested in any one brand. If I get one, I'll get the best and only the best."

He assured her that was all he had in mind.

She announced that she would drop by and see him Thursday afternoon at five, and hung up.

Her decisiveness with Harold, her all-but rudeness, made her feel good. It indicated to her that she had accepted these first two phone calls as omens and had already begun to act on them. She remembered the analyst's warning about too much free time, and realized that a weight of unconscious worry had disappeared from her mind, about how she should occupy herself in the unaccustomed leisure yawning before her. She would turn—with these actions she seemed already to be turning—to music. For many years she had not bought a new record and had not gone to as many concerts as she would have liked to. Winton's indifference to music had prevented her from satisfying her hunger for it. He had urged her to go to concerts alone and he had always spoken with genuine regret of what he called his "tone deafness." Nevertheless, when the time came for her to go to a concert, it had usually seemed "too much trouble" and she had, resentfully, stayed home with him. When she stayed home like this, he had not looked pleased so much as puzzled. Even so, she had blamed him for depriving her of music or at least of causing her to deprive herself of it.

Now she realized how badly she was treating him in her thoughts, and was ashamed of herself; she began thinking of the good things about him. He had been unfailingly courteous and considerate; she had learned good taste from him; he had rescued her (she always thought of it as a rescuing) from loneliness. But the main thing was her inexpressible gratitude to him for having found her eyes beautiful—nothing else, just her eyes, the only part of herself she could believe to be not drab or plain. All her life she had automatically rejected as flattery any man's praise of herself. But Winton had looked into her eyes in a special way the first time they had met—at the house of a mutual acquaintance for dinner—and again and again he had told her she had the most wonderful eyes he had ever seen. She had believed him.

All the same, she looked forward now to going to as many concerts as she wanted to.

6

As she breezed through the door pulling off her gloves, she said, "Hello, Harold." He called her Mrs. Hollander in a deferential voice. She had not recalled that she was quite a bit taller than he. Because she knew he was preying on her, his thin nose appeared to jut from his round fat face like an owl's beak.

He began a circuitous story about advances in electronics and getting things wholesale.

"You're a contact man, right?"

He said you could put it that way.

"On a commission basis?"

He began eagerly to explain that his "associate" was interested only in building the best set the customer could afford, brand was no consideration.

"You get five percent?"

He hunched into himself and nodded.

He began tentatively to tell her about the hi-fi equipment, and in fifteen minutes he had worked himself back up again. She rose, told him she wanted two thousand dollars' worth of equipment installed right away, watched him thank her, and left.

She had not expected money to afford her this sort of pleasure.

7

They strolled in Riverside Park before the recital.

"Her real name," said Francy, "is Delilah. Delilah Strong. So when she got a scholarship to Juilliard, this night-club cousin of ours said she had to change her name to something that would look more dignified in the public eye; you know, some name that didn't mean a thing about Strong. Rosetta, that was our grandmother's name and everybody thought that's what she was going to be, but when she came to register at Juilliard she just up and made it Julia without so much as how-d'you-do to anybody. Gratitude, she said. It's not too bad of a name, but her mother hasn't forgiven her, she says she reached right out of the family. She won't call her anything but Lila to this day, except once in a while when she gets mad she'll call her Juilliard to be mean. I wouldn't be too surprised if Rose-of-Sharon did not come tonight. She's a vengeful woman. She's a day worker, you know, cleans people's houses, and she certainly doesn't have to any longer. She does it out of spite. And she's a Witness."

"What? What? Go slower. I'm all confused."

"A Witness, a Jehovah's Witness. Rose-of-Sharon's a Jehovah's Witness. Humble and bleak, you know, and devastating. Well anyway, Julia—I don't know her so well but what 'Julia' comes easy to me—at least she don't have a father to contend with."

"Where is he?"

"He was funeralized," said Francy, modulating from a standard American into a Southern Negro accent, "in nineteen forty-three, courtesy of the United States Army. He died for his country in upstate New York. They stuck an unsterilized needle in him and he got the jaundice bad."

"Wait!" Betty held her hands over her ears and laughed. "Take it easy."

"I just wanted you to be prepared, babe." Francy chuckled.

"Don't be too surprised if she don't do full justice to the Nazis' sugarplum composer."

"What? Dear God, Francy, take it easy on the turns. Who?"

"Richard Strauss. I just want you to realize she wasn't to the manner born. I understand she's going to sing something by him and I didn't want you to hold the results against her too much."

Francy laughed largely. Betty would have understood a constricted laughter, ironic or bitter, but she was troubled by Francy's because it sounded expansive and free.

"Another thing," Betty said abruptly, "the tickets are free, so what did you mean the house was papered?"

"Why, it's counterfeit paper, babe." Francy staggered with laughter against a bench.

Out of contagion, Betty joined in. Her laughter sounded open in her own ears. However, she wondered if even Francy knew what they were laughing about.

Julia walked onto the platform rigidly easy, a slender, pretty, walnut-colored girl with a long neck. She wore a knitted, blue-white, sleeveless dress that made her thighs look thick as a mature woman's, but her shoulders narrow. The way she held her hands seemed to Betty at once artificially studied and naturally graceful. She nodded glacially at her accompanist, a pink girl in a black dress.

She sang three Schubert songs. The first two, out of nervousness and wrong expectation, Betty was unable really to listen to, though she knew the tones were rich and the control firm. The third, "To Be Sung on the Water," was familiar enough so that Betty, now confident of Julia's ability, heard it. Its loveliness infused her till she ached. She wanted to cherish her feeling inwardly awhile, not to behave like just another member of the audience. But to prevent questions or glances from Francy, who was clapping politely, she applauded and smiled like everybody else.

After a trio sonata and an intermission, Julia returned to sing Strauss's "Four Last Songs," which Betty had not known. The music took her over, and filled her with yearning feelings of tolerable despair and love. Because of Francy, she restrained her tears and shouted *Brava!* with a few others. Julia bowed like a queen-to-be.

Despite Francy's reluctance, they sought Julia out in the corridor. They stood to one side with Mrs. Strong, watching Julia. She was surrounded by congratulating friends; she kept clapping her hands and squealing and sometimes she hopped from one leg to the other like a little girl. When only a few remained, she broke away and came up to her mother, who kissed her dourly. Francy introduced Betty, who congratulated her, and then rushed the four of them out to a taxi and to a restaurant away from Julia's school friends. Mrs. Strong said little and watched like a badger. Betty promised to introduce Julia to some influential friends and said she believed in her. When Francy coolly asked who some of these friends were, Betty just smiled. Julia wore a bemused and dazzling smile.

Betty awoke at dawn from a dream of Julia singing. The tones of that dream voice faded so fast that in a minute or two Betty could no longer hear the lovely tune it sang but only a faint continuous chime. When even that had receded out of hearing, she shook herself severely and began to look for meaning in her dream. Finding none, she allowed memories of Julia's actual recital to rise in her mind, and indulged herself in a sensuous ease she had not felt for years.

She decided to give a housewarming party.

8

Harold showed up at five Saturday afternoon to see if the workmen had done a satisfactory job of installing the hi-fi set. He was eager to respond to whatever she said. He seemed to her without corners.

He had not been there ten minutes when Francy telephoned. Her brother-in-law and his wife had tickets to the Desegregation Benefit Ball at Delmonico's that night and they had both come down with the flu. Did Betty have some man she'd like to bring? It would cost nothing but the drinks.

"You can get to my place about nine fifteen and we can all four go from here together. Paul likes to get places not too late."

"Paul?"

"My husband."

Betty, who had been suspicious of Francy for calling again so soon, repeated "husband" with more relief than tact.

"Sure, he hates a big do like this but he has to go to two or three a year. He's a state senator, you know."

"No, I didn't know. An escort. Let me think."

She had worked all day; her hair hadn't been done for weeks; she didn't much like to dance.

"Formal, I suppose?"

"The best you've got."

The only man she could think of was Winton's college roommate, Cedric, and if she felt the slightest obligation to go to this ball, she would have called him up. She did not have to go if she didn't want to, she owed Francy nothing and wanted nothing from her. She realized that, not only did she not want Cedric, she had never much liked him and did not care whether she ever saw him again.

"Harold?" she called. He came to the doorway. She beckoned him over her head. "Do you have a tuxedo?"

He did. She told him about the ball and told him she'd like him to take her if he wasn't busy that night. He blinked; after he said sure, okay, he remembered to smile.

9

There were three hundred people, more or less, at the ball, most of them Negroes, few of them black. Betty had not felt so oppressed by good manners since her high-school graduation dance in a gymnasium lined with mothers. Paul was a man of frigid affability. At first Harold had made small talk, but after a prolonged laugh from Paul froze one of Harold's jokes to death, Harold said little. Couple after couple came up to their table to pay their respects to Paul, and it gave Betty a little amusement to watch Harold's eyes thrum. The main relief she found from the respectability was in observing the subtle pride of body with which some of the people, especially as they were dancing, moved about in their clothes.

After a while, the boredom, the two highballs she drank, the dancers, and the saxophones set up in her a sexual clitter-clatter. She deplored, but did not restrain, the erotic thoughts about Harold which rose into her consciousness. When Paul finally took Francy off to dance, Harold sighed, said what an impressive man Paul was, and invited Betty to dance. They danced together better than she expected, despite his belly and the difference in their height, which her highest heels increased. After one number, Paul and Francy returned to their table; Betty could see Harold yearning to rejoin them, but she was enjoying the dancing too much to want to stop. She enjoyed almost as much keeping him dancing till he was sweating. Three years before, she had had her left breast amputated for cancer. Now, she took a certain satisfaction in observing Harold's uneasiness when, from time to time, she pressed against him the mound of foam rubber which he would naturally take for that breast.

At the next orchestra break when they joined the Rugeros, they found at the table a man whom Paul introduced as Bob Flanders, a writer. Betty remembered that he had written a profile of Bartok in *The New Yorker* and several other pieces on musical subjects. With an animation she had lacked all evening, she took over the conversation, made herself pleasant, and invited everyone to her housewarming party, which she impromptu set for the first Saturday in August. She made Staten Island sound exotic and her house a curiosity worth traveling to see. They were to come any time from mid-afternoon on; it was quite a trip getting there; she had croquet and badminton. They were to plan on staying for supper. Paul declined; the *New Yorker* writer hoped he could make it; Harold of course was happy to come; Francy said she would be there with bells on. Betty urged everyone to bring a friend, she was sure everyone would have a good time. She casually mentioned to Francy that she hoped Julia could come, and Francy said she'd bring her.

Presently, to Betty's relief, she felt the erotic nonsense melt away. For the rest of the evening, her thoughts turned, whenever she wished, to Julia: not to the silly girl in the school corridor or the clumsily shy one in the restaurant, but to the young woman on the platform singing Schubert and Strauss. She especially enjoyed imagining Julia dressed in attractive gowns, and began closely observing the best-dressed young women in the hall. She imagined buying Julia an elegant, strapless gown which would set her off well. She had no reason to suppose that Julia could be especially graceful in her bodily movements, since in fact the evening of the recital Julia had walked with something of the gaucherie of a little girl wearing her older sister's shoes. Nevertheless, Betty put her doubts aside and imagined Julia the most graceful of the dancers, her body secretly free inside a stiff, bright gown.

10

Six days later the installation of the hi-fi set was complete; a wall had been taken out and the wound plastered over.

Next morning Betty went to a record outlet. There were thousands of records on the shelves; the catalogue listed thousands more. The aisles in the store were narrow and milling with customers and clerks. The clerk she kept bothering, a squat, pasty-faced man with an uptilted cigar in his mouth, finally stopped to look at her.

"Lady, how much you want to spend?"

"Up to a thousand dollars." She was sure of that much.

He nodded. "How many records you got already?"

"None, really. I've just had a hi-fi set put in."

"Come on."

She followed him across the street to the shipping room. He sat her in a corner, pulled up a chair beside her, and put his notebook and pen on a packing box. They paid no attention to the workers about them, tearing paper and shouting jokes.

"Now," he said riffling the catalogue, "all the ones you were asking about were classical. Do you want some popular too?"

"All classical."

"How about parties? Nothing light?"

"Well, yes, jazz."

"Uh huh. Half a dozen progressive, three or four Dixieland."

"No! Nothing but Dixieland. I know what ones I'd like to have too."

His ball point pen was cocked. There was a lack of responsiveness in his pale eyes waiting for her to speak. For a while she knew what she wanted.

He gave her clear choices, from a one-disc sampling of Gregorian chant or the full Easter liturgy, to *Wozzek* or *The Rake's Progress*. Usually when she said she didn't know, he would go on, but occasionally he would say such and such a recording was too good to pass up and write it down. In two hours she made and let him make a thousand dollars' worth of choices. She would have spent weeks thinking about the task, had she not relied on him. He sounded sure of himself, he was a stranger and cynical, he did it only for money.

"I paid him for the right to blame him for any shortcomings in my choices." She formulated this on the ferry returning to Staten Island, and with the thought she strode about the deck, as happy as though her conscience would be long appeased by her intellect's having made this obscure motive clear.

As soon as she had eaten a dish of cottage cheese, she put on the one record she had paid for in cash and brought home, a long-playing pressing of some old Muggsy Spanier pieces she remembered from her college days. She had brought that one along because Muggsy's had been the only good jazz band she had heard live; the term of praise for his playing had been "really dirty." The afternoon was soft; the windows were open to the sounds of birds and lawnmowers; her neighbor to the east, a gray-haired man with whom she occasionally smiled and nodded, was out weeding. When she put on the record, she expected it to revive memories of the dance hall in east St. Louis where she had been taken on a blind date to listen to Muggsy. Instead, the music left her right in her new large room which needed paint and curtains, slouched in an easy chair, her glasses off, a cup of coffee on the stand beside her, and recreated in her the special, sustained, "cool" excitement which she had cultivated in college for listening to low-down recorded jazz, one foot tapping time, eyes locked on a spot on the rug. Jazz somehow evened up sides within her and made the dirty combatants embrace in a struggle so taut that when the music stopped they fell apart exhausted and she dared to look at them for a while or even to play with them.

11

At four thirty a carload of five women social workers from the agency arrived. They wore dark glasses with outrageous rims, and even the one with fat pale legs wore Bermuda shorts and sandals. After they had exclaimed over the house, four of them went out to play badminton barefoot on the lawn. The fifth went with Betty into the kitchen and talked while Betty finished deviling the eggs.

There was a ham in the oven and a large beef roast ready to go in as soon as the ham came out. There were two green salads with different dressings; slices of avocado, carrot strips, celery, frilly radishes, and three kinds of olives; a potato salad, deviled eggs, and a tomato aspic, with mayonnaise she had made herself; sweet and salt butter, three kinds of rye bread, and rolls with hard crusts; smoked salmon and smoked oysters, four spiced sausages, and a hillock of black caviar and cream cheese; pickles and relishes of every kind; oranges, cherries, strawberries and powdered sugar, pineapple in kirsch, peaches; five kinds of cheese; two kinds of wine, ale, Scotch, and cognac. There were fresh flowers in every room.

By six thirty, over twenty people had come, including a man who worked with disturbed children in the Staten Island schools; he turned out to be a killer on the croquet court. By seven thirty, she counted everyone she remembered having invited but Francy. She felt the party could not really begin till Francy arrived. Perhaps Francy would bring Julia? She hovered within sight of the front door. At eight, Francy arrived with Julia, who was smiling eagerly but at the same time glancing around nervously.

Rather to Betty's surprise, Bob Flanders, the *New Yorker* writer, had shown up, though he announced that he had to leave by nine thirty. She rushed Julia into the dining room, where he had been ensconced for some time near the caviar. He lounged in an open window with a bottle of white wine precariously beside him on the sill, passing pleasantries with whoever came by inside or outside, kibitzing on the croquet game, whistling to the music from the record player. She introduced them and remained in their vicinity, getting tidbits for Julia to eat. She overheard enough to regret her arrangement-making. Flanders was asking Julia proper questions about her singing and she was properly answering. He kept tapping his foot and glancing out the window; she was the grande dame in a high-school play who knew nothing about the part but her lines. Betty cringed and fled.

She decided the party was ready for a Handel concerto grosso. The swarthy Staten Island school man came by with a can of ale in his hand and sparkling eyes. She asked him to keep an eye on the record player. He urged her to take a job in his department. She said she would think about it, and went to see how the food was holding out.

The beef roast was done. Francy wanted to carve it, but Betty brushed her aside, telling her that a man must do it. None of the men in the vicinity wanted to. She went outdoors. The older of the two men Harold had brought, a leathery painter named Ronald Turner, said he liked to carve. He made a little production of it, tying an apron high under his armpits, sharpening the knife till it cut a hair, dancing about the table for just the right position to carve in. Francy stood by watching, ready to carp at anything he did wrong, but his slices were thin, even, and straight against the grain.

Wherever Betty found herself, the faces told her that everybody was having a good time.

When she stood gazing out a window or when she went outdoors to watch the vociferous croquet game, she was aware of the curtains of her neighbors, who were home.

"Come on, kid, quit being a hostess," said Francy. "The party will take care of itself. Let yourself go."

Twice Betty came to herself leaning in a doorway staring at Julia, who liked to stand with one hip thrown out and back. Sometimes she would throw her head back in laughter, emphasizing her rather prominent Adam's apple; only the laughter was sensual and open, not her motions.

Both times when Betty caught herself trying to find more physical grace in Julia than was there to be found, she glanced about anxiously. No one had noticed her unseemly stares. She began looking for a dark corner from which she could give herself over to watching Julia as she ached to do. But she could not go far without being reminded of her duties as hostess, which would not permit her to disappear for long.

12

The croquet players came in and stood about in the dining room bragging in the guise of Scotch-and-soda toasts to one another. The next time Betty saw them they were seated around the kitchen table playing bridge.

Outside, she came upon Harold and five or six others seated on the grass at Turner's feet. He was in a lawn chair half-facing the light and was doing the talking.

"Betty Hollander! You must quit wandering around and begin enjoying a most relaxed and enjoyable party. Do sit here."

He stood and urged the chair toward her, but she disposed herself on the grass at the edge of the group.

"I was just trying to explain," he said, settling on the grass too, leaving the chair empty, "to some of these incorrigibly provincial natives of the five boroughs the only reason I ever come to New York is business. I'm here on a straight business trip—to see my gallery about my show this November."

"Ah," said Betty, "I noticed your boots."

He extended his legs and gazed at them. They were short cowboy boots made of soft dust-colored leather with a serpent design carved around the top.

"Hopi," he said with a note of deprecation, flicking the silver tips of his string tie. "I live on a ranch in Arizona, you know."

"All right," said Betty, making her voice sound pleasant, "I don't have any trouble seeing what's so good about Arizona. Just tell me what's so awful about New York."

"The hippopotami." His inflection, and his smile at the little stir of expectancy in his audience, seemed to her rehearsed. "I think of every man," he addressed himself to her, "as having a hippopotamus in him. A gross, hideous beast with a monstrous big maw. And when he defecates . . . Have you ever seen one defecate?" She said she had not. "There's one I know in the San

Francisco zoo that likes to bellow, and scrape his tusks on the wall, and blow in his pool awhile, till he gets a good crowd at the fence gawking at him. Then he turns his rear end toward them and lets 'er fly. His tail goes like a little fan and sprays water and dung for yards in every direction, clear out onto the spectators. There, my friends," he said, leaning back on his arms, "you have the ego incarnate." There was a general stir of laughter, during which Betty, watching him, nodded sardonically. He no longer addressed himself to her directly. "In a civilized community, the hippos are seemly about keeping themselves under water. About all you see of them are nostrils, eyes, ears, once in a while the maw. But here, in New York, in Gehenna, they're on the sidewalks, they ride elevators, they buy and sell, a cocktail party is a congress of nude hippos." The last phrase he threw away. He cued his audience with a chuckle.

Betty laughed politely, though she thought him a show-off, and went back to the house.

Someone had put on a Bach suite for unaccompanied cello. Betty came to the doorway to make sure nothing else so demanding was put on, and found Francy alone in the room, listening. When the music ended, instead of relaxing back into her chair, Francy leaned forward into herself.

"The face of one who listens to the space between the stars."

At the sound of Turner's voice at her ear, Betty turned, prepared to jump on him for fanciness. No one else was near, yet he seemed to have been addressing not her but himself. He went away.

She was looking at his ornate phrase to see if it meant something, when Julia came strolling along with downcast eyes.

"Honey," said Betty and blushed at saying the word. "Honey, do you ever listen to the space between the stars?"

Julia frowned and shrugged impatiently. "Not so's you'd notice," she said over her shoulder as she turned around and left.

Betty took this to be a reproof for the phoniness of her own question. She started after Julia to apologize, but before she had gone three steps she stopped, not knowing what to say.

13

Toward eleven Cedric yodeled to her from the open front door. His complexion was albinistic; one eye was pale green and the other pale blue. She had forgotten having invited him. She had forgotten he existed. He brought with him a dapper friend named René Stern, whom Betty had heard about for years; René was a gay seducer and a reporter for the UP. Cedric apologized for being late and presented her with two records for a housewarming present. She offered to make the introductions; they said they'd rather just circulate.

René, who had been peering about, put his fingers on Betty's forearm in a manner that looked friendly but felt intimate. "What a delightful surprise, Mrs. Hollander. It's been some time since I've been in a gathering of new people where I don't have to pass if I don't want to." He was olive-skinned and hazel-eyed, and his accent had Main Line in it. Before she could speak, he directed her attention out the front door. Julia and Bob Flanders were coming up the path. "Who's the chick with Bob?"

"Julia Strong. She is a promising young contralto."

"Fabulous."

She moved ahead of him and spoke to Bob. "I thought you had to leave at nine thirty?" The voice in which she uttered this rudeness was friendly enough. "Well, it's nice you could stay after all." She took Julia's hand and patted it, paying no attention to whatever Bob was saying.

As René closed in, she started to draw Julia aside.

"You know," said Julia, "I got to go to the little girls' room and put some of that cherry-red on my lips."

Betty winced at the gross coyness of this and at the vamp

swagger with which Julia walked away; but when Betty glanced at the three men, she was surprised to see that not even Cedric looked disgusted and that the other two were ogling Julia up the steps. With intense relief she felt that she had been wrong to see Julia as vulgar and gauche; Julia really was as desirable as she had found her to be.

The corner of her mouth twitched when she looked at the labels of the records Cedric had brought, sweet tunes played by a conventional band. She would have put the discs away with a thank you, had René not taken them from her and gone to put one on the turntable.

She turned to Cedric. "Is he part Negro?"

His eyes sparkled. "Why do you ask?" He laid his boneless finger on her wrist. "Did he hint?"

"He said he didn't have to pass unless he wanted to. Not that I care. But why did he bring the subject up?"

"Darling," said Cedric, almost breathing into her ear, his eyes flicking about as though for eavesdroppers, "everything about him is so deliciously louche." He lingered over the *sh* sounds.

She restrained her impulse to back away from Cedric. "You know him well?"

"How old is he? Has he ever been married? Is he part Negro? Does he publish poetry under a pseudonym?" Cedric leaned back, his eyes became liquid, his voice lowered in pitch. "He is my closest friend since Winton."

René came up, rescuing her from Cedric's complicitous smile, invited her to dance, and would not accept her refusal. She had disliked him on sight, mostly for the calculation in his gonadotropic glances. She knew she did not dance well, and she intended not to enjoy dancing with him. He did not exactly lead, yet he did not let her lead. Somehow, in a way as blurry yet steady as the music, he managed to make her dance better than she could ever remember having danced.

14

As she approached the door of the laundry room, which was a sort of lean-to added on the rear of the house proper, she saw Julia and René not quite touching noses, their heads moving gently up and down. She stood at the screen door watching.

"See?" he said in his smooth ironic voice. "It's much better than kissing. What did I tell you?"

"Oh, go on." Julia began laughing again.

"I'll prove it."

He held her close and kissed her a long time.

They were dimly illuminated by reflected light, and Betty was close enough to be able to see every detail of their embrace. She thought of going away, but decided that it would be rude of her to do so, for the noise of her moving might interrupt the kiss. After all, it was just young people kissing at a party. As long as chance had stationed her there, she would watch. She could not help watching. When René's hand moved lower down Julia's back and pressed her body hard against his and when their joined mouths opened to one another, Betty experienced an erotic excitement more intense than she had ever felt when she herself had been embraced by a man. Even as she gave herself over to their kiss, she felt a terrible resentment that no man had ever excited her like this.

The kiss slowly ceased. Without letting go of one another, René and Julia began not quite rubbing noses again.

"What did I tell you?" said René. "This is much better than kissing, Julia baby. No? Or shall we do it again till you are really convinced?"

His words struck Betty as being utterly insincere and Julia's laugh mere flirting.

Julia turned in her laughter, saw Betty, and pulled guiltily away from René.

"What gives?" He glanced over his shoulder. "Ah, Betty Hollander, the cause of all this joy. I was just demonstrating the power of nose-rubbing *à la Chinoise*."

Glancing in embarrassment, Julia hurried past Betty into the kitchen and then out of sight.

"Mr. Stern," Betty said. She was set to attack, without having decided where to attack him.

"Yes?"

She noticed the crow's feet at the corners of his eyes and recalled what Cedric had said about his age.

"How old are you?"

"Twenty-seven."

"In a pig's eye you're twenty-seven."

"What gives?" he was saying as she left him there. "What gives around here?"

She poured whiskey into a tumbler, drank it down, shuddered hard, put on the Muggsy Spanier record, and went up to her bedroom. She lay on the bed in the half-dark alone, come what would.

At first the images of caressing Julia that rose in her mind were erotic, but without emotion. "This is wrong" kept ringing in her ears. She clenched her jaws and set out to insult tomorrow's conscience. She tried to make the images deliberately lewd, but they all melted into a kiss. They had no emotional power over her until they became a kiss. She gave up trying to insult her desire, and lay on the bed, dry of throat and rigid from head to toe, imagining herself and Julia embracing in a dark place, kissing and being kissed.

15

She found Julia and René outside in the lawn chairs, leaning toward one another, their feet touching.

"There are only two ways to prevent the destitution of overpopulation," René was saying, "more war or less love. I don't mean less sex. I mean sterile sex, fewer and smaller families, and loveless institutions."

She made the two acknowledge her presence by asking if they needed a drink. Julia pushed her question aside.

"You know, René, you sound like a Witness," said Julia.

"Oh?"

"Except you're more intellectual. You know, they believe the world came to an end in nineteen fourteen."

"Yes?" he said. "They were just one war off, and this is hell nor are we out of it."

Betty could not keep from looking at him, though she thought him insincere in every word he said.

Julia put her hand on his arm. "My mama's a Witness. Tomorrow there's a big rally."

"In Yankee Stadium."

"Well, the main part is, but we live near the Polo Grounds so we're going there with the overflow. Mama doesn't care too much about seeing. As a matter of fact, she'd just as soon stay home and listen to things on the radio, only she's got it in her head she wants to sit in the stands right back of first base. She says she'll never get another chance to sit at first base in the Polo Grounds, so she's going to sit there in a five-dollar seat free and enjoy the word. Why don't you come with us?"

He grinned. "Oh, I'll come. I'll be there observing and observing. I spy for UP. Want to come up to the press box with me?"

"Mama," she complained.

Cedric called René from the living room window. René waved dismissively, but Betty gave him a little shove.

"Go on and see what he wants." Her heart thumped. "I've got something to tell Julia. Go on."

He smiled at her ambiguously, kissed both their hands, and left.

Julia was frowning a little.

"You know the 'Four Last Songs'?" Betty said urgently and stepped close to Julia. "I have a record of them you must hear."

She began chattering without following her own words. "It's a wonderful version. You must listen. It would mean so much."

"Yeh? I know the Della Casa record." Julia moved toward the house. "She's great. Why don't we go inside? It's starting to get chilly."

It was nearly three o'clock. Some were dancing again.

16

Betty sat in one of the chairs, tears streaming from her eyes, racked by an enormous wanting.

Harold came by. Because she was sitting with her back to the dim light, she did not bother to wipe her face. Nevertheless, by the double glance he cast at her, she saw that he was aware something was wrong. She was setting herself to hate him.

He spoke of Turner. "He's one of us," Harold kept repeating. "He's a great artist and a great man, yet he's one of us."

This awe struck Betty as soggy and she doubted, without evidence, that Turner could be much of an artist. Yet what Harold said, and a quality in his voice, got to her.

She realized that she did not believe it possible for anyone to be like her and yet wonderful. Harold, whom she thought less than herself, was more than she if only because he believed in the possibility of being more. She squeezed his hand without minding its pudginess. He went away.

Thoughts of Julia returned and fell to wrenching her insides so cruelly she could hardly sit still. Her grief at Winton's death had been purer, but this yearning engulfed it. She longed to have him back, for if he had been alive, he would have safeguarded her from these passions that were boiling up in her, threatening to burst out into actions.

But a surge of the other sorrow made her longing for Winton fade and left her with one desolate thought: having lost her protection from wanting, she could not keep from wanting Julia, whom she did not really like.

17

When the record was being changed, she heard splashing sounds from her neighbor's pool, then a man's voice and a woman's giggle. She clapped her hands to her jaws at the thought of the pool lights going on and disclosing Julia and René swimming naked. Even while she bulged with this image, she recognized a low anxiety: let the swimmers be whites. She stalked the pool.

There were a man and two women swimming, all three whites. When she hissed at them, they came out, goose-pimply in the breeze and slapping themselves, their underwear sticking to their flanks. They were the Staten Island school man and two of the social workers from her former agency. They were amiably drunk, and kept whispering to Betty, as they dressed in the bushes between the two houses, that this was the best party they had been to in years.

As she went into the empty kitchen, she smelled smoke. One of the curtains at the window above the sink was blazing and the other was starting to burn. She gave a little scream and stared at the flames without moving. René was the first to run in; he filled a pan of water and doused the fire in a moment. The wall and ceiling were stained with smoke but not even the curtain rods were injured. Nevertheless, she felt shaken, especially at herself for not having stirred to put out the fire.

There was much talk. No one could imagine what had started the fire. No one admitted to having been in the kitchen for a long time. Betty was uneasily aware of Francy's watching her. Two thirds of the party had gone home. Betty did not look at anybody. She found herself staring at Julia's yellow shoes.

"Come on," Francy said in a loud clear voice. "It's past three o'clock. We've had enough fun and done enough damage. Now let's go home—everybody."

People looked at Betty, and she looked at Francy with open gratitude.

Once they had assembled their things and stood relaxed in the hall, reluctant to say good-bye, Betty felt better disposed toward them. René cracked a little joke about a fireman, and Turner had something to say about swimming holes. People became aware of Julia's voice; she was telling Bob about her recital at Juilliard.

Julia addressed herself in turn to each of the men and to Francy and Betty. Betty, seeing the others smile with unabashed pleasure at Julia's languid flirtatiousness, felt such a pleasure stir in herself. Julia was confident and humorous; she made fun of herself for having been so scared and stiff, and she spoke of her singing teacher with admiration. When two or three of the other women social workers, as agitated as though they were wives, began to rush about emptying ashtrays and making sotto voce remarks about gaudy little bitches, Betty enjoyed their spite as proving Julia's power. Julia kept up her little star-performance for three or four minutes. At the first sign of masculine defection, she turned everything into thanks to Betty for the party, and the others joined in.

18

When Betty got into bed she shivered for a while. She did not want to sleep off her melancholy; though it pained her, it was intense.

Her consciousness went out like a light.

She was agitating a pan full of cherry jelly. As soon as the liquid was no longer turbulent, it would set, and she must avert this. There were thirty-eight wasps flying about, making a melodious violalike drone. One of them dived into the liquid jelly. She was worried about him, but he seemed to swim about happily, most of the time under the surface. She kept agitating the pan with one hand and fishing for him with the forefinger of the other hand. When she got him out she held him on her finger while he flapped the liquid off his wings. Close up, she saw that he was a tiny hippopotamus with wings. He opened his mouth, uttered a high-pitched bellow, and flew off thrumming as though nothing had happened. Then all thirty-eight flying hippos hovered over the jelly, formed the word FREE in the air, and, holding the formation, flew away from her very fast, till presently all she saw was the tiny word receding, though the viola sounds remained as clear and loud as ever. She awoke in tears, for she had not kept the liquid sufficiently agitated and the jelly had set; no little flying hippos would ever be able to bathe in it again; hereafter they would have to walk on the tough, sticky surface.

Her consciousness clicked back on.

If the hippo was the ego, the jelly would be the id. And then? How dull. She lay in bed listening to the birds and thinking of the party. She writhed under a pang of sadness sharp as a stab of pleurisy, and breathed irregularly through her mouth.

Her mind was taken over by an image of Winton in the hospital bed as she had last seen him. She wanted him back. She could hardly bear not having him. She writhed, and chewed the pillow.

19

She put on brown walking shoes, a beige skirt, and a white blouse, and carried a flat brown purse and a black umbrella. She went by bus, ferry, and subway, because she wanted to be with ordinary people; also, she did not trust herself to drive.

Twenty minutes before the announced starting time, she emerged from the subway west of the Polo Grounds. As she hurried down the hillside she caught a glimpse of part of the shadeless temporary bleachers out beyond left center field; they appeared to be more than half filled already. A helicopter hovered over the stadium.

On the path leading to the grandstand she was paced by a stout colored woman who waddled stiffly and who was closing a tasseled violet umbrella as she went. Two Negro and two white smiling men in badges and arm bands blocked the ramp to the stands. One of the men wore a straw hat on the black band of which was printed in phosphorescent pink letters: PRAYER WORKS. The woman just ahead of Betty waggled her parasol and cried in a well-controlled shout: "Glory, brothers! I've had the spirit all day! First thing I got up this morning, I felt the spirit and it's just been getting stronger as the hours roll by! It's in my heart." Betty saw she was wearing a badge; the men waited till Betty had gone on a way down toward the field and then let the woman, who was steadily shouting, through to the stands.

On the descending ramp a young white woman and two small girls lay in the shade with their heads against the wall in the postures and with the unresponsive eyes of those who are being allowed to die in public places. The three were in pink frocks with white bobby socks and black leatherette shoes. The mother had a large costume-jewelry diamond clipped onto the top of her left ear. By each chewing child stood a box of Crackerjack.

Betty emerged onto the field intending to go straight for the grandstand behind first base, but the sight of the vast crowd stunned her. An usher asked her in a kindly voice if she didn't want to sit, there were still some seats down front. She let him seat her, so that she might have time to take her bearings. She was on a folding chair in the sixth row, in the full sun, slightly infield from third base.

On the field beyond the rope were batteries of loudspeakers trained on the congregation. From them came blurred music of the kind which gets housewives in supermarkets to buy more than they want of things they do not need. When the helicopter went away, music and crackle from the speakers pained her ears. In the clearing were sprays of flowers, upright palm branches, electronic equipment, persons bustling, and a cluster of Witnesses dressed in costumes of other nations. The music stopped, and a little man went up to the microphone on the speaker's stand out beyond second base. In a Scandinavian accent he introduced visitors from other countries, especially a long grinning man from Ghana in bright robes. The little man announced the next number, which turned out to be an arranged hymn. Betty could not decide whether the singing came from a record or from Yankee Stadium. The Polo Grounds did not join in.

She tried to recall when she had last sung a song with any group on any occasion. The most recent one she could think of was "Auld Lang Syne" at a New Year's Eve party the year before she had met Winton. She did not remember that a couple of times she and Winton and Cedric had spent part of New Year's Eve in front of a television set watching the celebrators in Times Square. On those occasions she had joined the two men in shaking her head at all that grim fun, though secretly she had liked it a little for those others to sing "Auld Lang Syne" for her. Now she looked contemptuously at these who were having their hymns sung for them.

Far over in right field she saw a white-sweatered figure leaping before a section of the grandstands and waving its arms. She got up and started to move in that direction, circling in front of the grandstands, in order to see what it might be doing. On the way she was distracted by a sign up in the stands: DEAF AND DUMB —HARD OF HEARING. From where she stood, there seemed nothing odd about the people in the vicinity of the sign. She stared up into the packed stands in which, even if she had access to them, she scarcely had the heart to go looking for Julia. She felt like crying. She had never seen so many people in one place.

Another hymn started up. The white sweater out in right field was flipping again. She moved toward it. It was a blond athletic young man cheerleading a couple of busloads of white and Negro young men and women strung out behind a streamer which identified them as the Jesus Ralliers of the Ozarks. They wore white sweaters with red JR's on the chest. Betty could not make out what their cheers said. They accompanied every stressed cry with a short hard punch held close to the belly, left, right, left, right. People in the vicinity beamed at the Ralliers.

She became aware of a different sort of motion. A tall man looking down into a reflex camera backed into her.

"Watch where you're going," she said.

He apologized. Then, seeing that she was not a Witness either, he said, "I'm trying to find some place to stand where I can get them all in."

20

In a flat reasonable voice the loudspeakers greeted the multitudes and announced that the government of the United States, like every other government, had failed to do God's bidding but was doing the devil's work by hastening Armageddon. A ripple of applause started in Yankee Stadium but died out before it got far into the Polo Grounds.

It excited Betty to hear the obvious wickedness of governments spoken of in public to scores of thousands of ordinary people, even in the language of stale apocalypse. She had not heard words of such a kind mass-spoken since before the war; but that message, which had seemed so fierce then and now seemed so tame, had been no more than that one government did better or worse than another.

The rule of nations was ordained by Jehovah-God not to succeed and Jehovah-God's kingdom had already come, beginning in the fall of 1914. If you'd read your Bible correctly, especially Ezekiel and Revelations, you would see how affairs were fulfilling God's world-scheme. The H-bomb fitted in; it was the devil's invention. Each announcement was greeted with applause.

If the speech had been reasonable, Betty would have argued against it. Because it was hopelessly absurd, she did not resist the satisfaction it made her feel; but because she thought this satisfaction degenerate, she quit following the speech. Without the words, the noise of the loudspeakers swarmed all over her mind like hysteria. She clutched with her eyes at the people near at hand.

A young man in the nearest row was contemplatively eating grapes and spitting the seeds at a post. A mother clapped her hand over the mouth of a child who had leaned against her to ask something; the child did not squirm. Betty realized she had seen no child running around nor heard any child laugh or cry. Nobody either met her eye or seemed to avoid meeting it. Nobody seemed to want much, except the end of the world.

21

In the press box, which was not half filled, she sat on the first available chair and did not engage by word or glance with any of the others; René was not there. She scrutinized as from an eyrie this field full of those who called themselves the other sheep. After a time she found her eyes sliding across the crowd indifferently and resting on the vacant gazebo of a speaker's stand; she sat back in her chair and closed her eyes.

"You know," one reporter said, "the President's mother is a Witness."

"Poor woman," said another, "her son is a minion of Satan."

All bad men are going to kill each other off in Armageddon, which will take place within the life span of many now living. The other sheep will survive and, together with a flock of resurrected sheep, will spend a thousand years cleansing the earth of its ruins and planting the earthly paradise.

Betty thought: They cannot think about last things nor leave them alone. Neither can I. Last things are my murk. Those who think best, the scientists, do not speak about last things. Yet they are the ones who pushed the Last Thing into everybody's mind.

René's smooth voice said in her ear, "You look like you're having a good chiliasm."

She opened her eyes, intending to say something rude, or to glance at him balefully and turn her back on him. Only his lips smiled; his eyes were fearful.

"Come look through the binoculars. I've spotted a couple of beautiful grasshoppers for you. It helps a person forget there's a plague of them."

The high-powered glasses swiveled on a pivot. René carefully focused them and then gave his place to Betty. She saw a girl adorned with vermilion, green, violet, and phosphorescent orange; her coiled bleached hair had glass fruit in it. Beside her leaned a man in a short-sleeved Hawaiian shirt, whose right arm was only slightly longer than its sleeve; from the stump grew three processes with which he was stroking her arm. He nudged her nigh breast with the stump. Frowning coquettishly, she batted her eyes, lifted his arm, and rubbed the processes against her cheek.

Betty looked here, then there.

The speech was naming Jehovah-God's enemies. The most important were the Communist party, the Protestant and Catholic clergy, and every government of any kind.

"*Illegitimati non carborundum,*" said René.

"What does that mean?"

"Don't let the grasshoppers eat you down." He trained the binoculars on a spot above first base. "Here's another one for you."

It was Julia beside her mother. Betty felt the blood rush to her heart. Her ears rang. She dimly resented René for prying into her so deviously, but he had found Julia for her. Resentment of him, like the rest of her turmoil, was blotted out by a surge of desire to be with Julia. A touch of dizziness closed her eyes for a moment. Watching again, she saw Julia say something to her mother, and then pass down the row to the aisle and go down the steps toward the nearest exit.

"What's the matter?" said René.

Betty avoided his eyes. "I've got to go to the john." She was aware, as she hurried out, that he was looking for Julia through the binoculars. On the stairs she heard him call after her.

22

Just as Betty was going into the women's toilet nearest first base, someone came out of the exit door, and she heard Julia's voice cry, "René!" Betty immediately came back out, and was aware of René's lifted eyebrows when he glanced at her.

"Betty, you too?" said Julia. "It's quite a coincidence, isn't it?" She was flipping the tip of her nose with her forefinger and looking from one to the other.

"Not a bit," said René. "You said you'd be at first base. I'm reporting, Betty's slumming. Didn't you know, sweet stuff, you're the flypaper and we're the flies?"

Julia kept glancing from under raised eyebrows. Betty's throat aborted a word.

There were several people standing around in the large corridor, most of them munching, licking, or drinking. A little squirrel-voiced woman near them was telling an usher she was afraid she would lose her way home.

"So you couldn't stand it?" René said to Julia.

"Well, it's pretty hard to take. All that gobbledygook. I told Mama I'd wait for her down here."

"Now you just listen to me, lady," the usher said in a rough, emotionless voice. He looked like a train conductor. "We'll get you home after the meeting. We'll get you home. You just don't worry."

"The subway scares me, the subway scares me. That's the thing and I'm far away from here. Oh."

Julia took her finger from the tip of her nose and leaned toward René familiarly. "You remember what I told you last night?"

"What did you tell me last night?" He made as though to rub noses.

She let him get close, then with a pulling hand pushed his head to one side. She said something Betty could not hear, and rolled her eyes.

René caught Julia's hand, then looked at Betty. "She said she betted you would remain true to the memory of your husband. That's a rare thing, you know."

Julia ducked her head away. "I just mean."

"It was a tribute," said René.

Betty nodded. Her heart clenched.

"I got the name of the place in my purse, mister," said the little woman. "I'll show it to you."

"Now you don't need to do that, ma'am," said the big man roughly, restraining her arm.

"It's a number," she said. "I was wrong, it isn't a name, it's a number. One of the brothers got it for me. He just buzzed and asked. They're Jews. I prop my chair against the door of my room at night. Isn't that all right? They don't make me pay anything. They don't want the word. They asked me to watch their TV with them. I don't. What do you think?"

"Listen," said the usher sternly. "You just listen."

"I'm to go home tomorrow."

The speakers issued loud, Yankee Stadium applause; fainter applause came down directly from the Polo Grounds above them. Ushers shook hands. The countermen slapped spatulas, lined up paper cups, and wiped counters. The alarmed woman searched her usher's face, smiled, and gave out squirrely chirps. The applause went on much longer than any other had done.

"Do you know why they're so happy?" said René. "Because they are so many. Betty, did you hear how many they claim are in attendance? Two hundred and fifty-three thousand. They won't fight, they won't vote, all they want is to have the earth scorched so they can take over." He was keeping an eye on Julia, who was looking at the first hurriers coming down the tunnel.

René suddenly stepped in front of an elderly couple walking down the corridor. They apologized to him. The man took the woman's arm and guided her around René. René cupped his hands and shouted upward, "You are a plague of locusts!" The woman looked over her shoulder and nodded pleasantly to him. Julia bent with laughter.

"What are you going to do about them?" René said to Betty. "There are nine hundred thousand of them. The sun never sets on them. What are you going to do?"

"Nothing. What are you?"

"Love them of course. I'm not much on churchgoing. I'm just the Golden Rule type. I'm going to love them as I love myself. Okay?"

Betty turned to Julia and asked her the question; but her voice was so urgent that Julia took a half step backward.

"Well," said Julia, addressing herself to René, who took her hand again, "I'm going to go home and work on 'The Trout' tonight—that is, after Mama calms down enough to leave me alone. I'm going to sing the best I can and have me a ball once in a while, that's what I'm going to do about it."

Betty told herself many things. She had as much right to touch Julia as René did, but at the moment she ought not to try because she could not do it casually. Another time. There were many little plans she could make to see Julia often, reasonable plans, friendly gestures: a weekend at the Tanglewood Festival of Music, a picnic with Francy, dinner and a play, who could say what all? There was much to hope for. Patience, caution, restraint. Her heart paid no attention to her head and began voiding its desire.

Julia let René not quite rub noses. When he brushed lips, she stretched away to look for her mother among the throng debouching sluggishly through the exit tunnel.

Betty looked at them coldly. This mere flirt who happened to be able to sing well, and this desperate seducer—they both used sex as it were to immunize themselves against trouble. But in the land of the sick, Betty thought, it is shameful to be well; they were carriers, criminally negligent, cowards who dared not face the world unless inoculated with sex.

They became aware of her gaze on them. René raised a finger, then went over to the squirrely woman. Julia, eyes flicking over the emerging crowd, leaned against Betty, shoulder to shoulder, arm along arm, and said something in a friendly voice. Betty did not listen to what she said. The touch she had longed for, Julia's voluntary touch, was making its way into the muscles of her arm and shoulder, and she watched to see if it would spread to her heart. She was so confident it would not she did not even move away.

René led the little woman up to Betty and assured her that Betty was a social worker who knew the city well and would see that she got home safely. The woman said she didn't know and looked at them suspiciously. She said there were so many. She came from Milwaukee but the last forty-five years she had lived in Ontario. Her husband died last winter of blood poisoning; stabbed his foot with a pitchfork.

"There's Mama!" cried Julia and began waving.

With irony, fury, and gratitude, Betty said thank you to René, who winked and followed Julia. Betty took the little woman by the elbow.

The woman peered up into Betty's eyes.

"Why, you're crying, miss. It's because it's too much. There's so many. Come along."

Betty dashed the tears from her eyes and let the little woman let her help her. On their way out to a taxi, a middle-aged Texan with pop eyes and a mole on his Adam's apple asked them if they were saved. The little woman chirped that she was. Betty refused the leaflet he was handing out by keeping her head bowed.

A white young man and a black young woman passed hand in hand, gazing into one another's eyes.

23

On the ferry to Staten Island she gazed for a while at the Statue of Liberty, that ugly thing standing for a thing once beautiful. It occurred to her that she had better begin looking for something to want, for there was not much time, though as much as always. Meanwhile, till she found it, she had better do what would keep her conscience clear. She would take at least a part-time job with the Staten Island schools. This was no more what she really wanted than was the end of the world or a love affair with Julia, but it was what she could do and it was worth doing. For the time being she might as well try wanting what she had left.

✺✺✺
✺✺✺   Sandra
✺✺✺

A few years ago I inherited a handsome, neo-Spanish house in a good neighborhood in Oakland. It was much too large for a single man, as I knew perfectly well; if I had behaved sensibly I would have sold it and stayed in my bachelor quarters; I could have got a good price for it. But I was not sensible; I liked the house very much; I was tired of my apartment-house life; I didn't need the money. Within a month I had moved in and set about looking for a housekeeper.

From the moment I began looking, everyone assured me that I should get a domestic slave. I was reluctant to get one, not so much because of the expense as because of my own inexperience. No one in my family had ever had one, and among my acquaintances there were not more than three or four who had any. Nevertheless, the arguments in favor of my buying a slave were too great to be ignored. The argument that irritated me most was the one used by the wives of my friends. "When you marry," they would say, "think how happy it will make your wife to have a domestic slave." Then they would offer, zealously, to select one for me. I preferred to do my own selecting. I began watching the classified ads for slaves for sale.

Some days there would be no slaves listed for sale at all; on Sundays there might be as many as ten. There would be a middle-aged Negro woman, twenty-two years' experience, best recommendations, $4500; or a thirty-five-year-old Oriental, speaks English, excellent cook, recommendations, $5000; or a middle-aged woman of German descent, very neat, no pets or vices, good cook, recommendations, $4800. Sensible choices, no doubt, but none of them appealed to me. Somewhere in the back of my mind there was the notion of the slave I wanted. It made me restless, looking; all I knew about it was that I wanted a female. I was hard to satisfy. I took to dropping by the Emeryville stores, near where my plant was located, looking for a slave. What few there were in stock were obviously of inferior quality. I knew that I would have to canvass the large downtown stores to find what I wanted. I saw the ads of Oakland's Own Department Store, announcing their January white sale; by some quirk, they had listed seven white domestic slaves at severely reduced prices. I took off a Wednesday, the first day of the sale, and went to the store at opening time, nine forty-five, to be sure to have the pick of the lot.

Oakland's Own is much the largest department store in the city. It has seven floors and two basements, and its quality runs from $1498 consoles to factory-reject cotton work socks. It has a good, solid merchandising policy, and it stands behind its goods in a reassuring, old-fashioned way. The wives of my friends were opposed to my shopping in Oakland's Own, because, they said, second-hand slaves were so much better trained than new, and cost so little more. Nevertheless, I went.

I entered the store the moment the doors opened, and went straight up to the sixth floor on the elevator. All the same I found a shapeless little woman in the slave alcove ahead of me picking over the goods—looking at their teeth and hair, telling them to bend over, to speak so she could hear the sound of their voices, stick out their tongue, like an army doctor. I was furious at having been nosed out by the woman, but I could not help admiring the skill and authority with which she inspected her merchandise.

She told me something about herself. She maintained a staff of four, but what with bad luck, disease, and her husband's violent temper she was always having trouble. The Federal Slave Board had ruled against her twice—against her husband, really, but the slaves were registered in her name—and she had to watch her step. In fact she was on probation from the FSB now. One more adverse decision and she didn't know what she'd do. Well, she picked a strong, stolid-looking female, ordered two sets of conventional domestic costumes for her, signed the charge slip, and left. The saleswoman came to me.

I had made my decision. I had made it almost the moment I had come in, and I had been in agonies for fear the dumpy little shopper would choose my girl. She was not beautiful exactly, though not plain either, nor did she look especially strong. I did not trouble to read her case-history card; I did not even find out her name. I cannot readily explain what there was about her that attracted me. A certain air of insouciance as she stood waiting to be looked over—the bored way she looked at her fingernails and yet the fearful glance she cast from time to time at us shoppers, the vulgarity of her make-up and the soft charm of her voice—I do not know. Put it down to the line of her hip as she stood waiting, a line girlish and womanly at once, dainty and strong, at ease but not indolent. It's what I remember of her best from that day, the long pure line from her knee to her waist as she stood staring at her nails, cocky and scared and humming to herself.

I knew I should pretend impartiality and indifference about my choice. Even Oakland's Own permits haggling over the price of slaves; I might knock the price down as much as $300, particularly since I was paying for her cash on the line. But it wasn't worth the trouble to me. After three weeks of dreary looking I had found what I wanted, and I didn't feel like waiting to get it. I asked the saleswoman for the card on my slave. She was the sixth child of a carpenter in Chico. Chico is a miserable town in the plains of the San Joaquin Valley; much money is spent each year teaching the people of Chico how to read and write; "chico" means greasewood. Her father had put her up for sale, with her own consent, at the earliest legal age, eighteen, the year of graduation from high school. The wholesaler had taught her the rudiments of cooking, etiquette, and housecleaning. She was listed as above average in cleanliness, intelligence, and personality, superb in copulation, and fair in versatility and sewing. But I had known as much from just looking at her, and I didn't care. Her name was Sandra, and in a way I had known that too. She had been marked down from $3850 to $3299. As the saleswoman said, how could I afford to pass up such a bargain? I got her to knock the price down the amount of the sales taxes, wrote out my check, filled out the FSB forms, and took my slave Sandra over to be fitted with clothes.

And right there I had my first trouble as a master, right on the fifth floor of Oakland's Own in the Women's Wear department. As a master, I was supposed to say to Sandra, or even better to the saleswoman about Sandra, "Plain cotton underwear, heavy-weight nylon stockings, two dark-blue maid's uniforms and one street dress of conservative cut," and so on and so on. *The slave submits to the master:* I had read it in the FSB manual for domestic slave owners. Now I find it's all very well dominating slaves in my office or my factory. I am chief engineer for the Jergen Calculating Machine Corporation, and I had had no trouble with my industrial and white-collar slaves. They come into the plant knowing precisely where they are, and I know precisely where I am. It's all cut and dried. I prefer the amenities when dealing with, say, the PBX operator. I prefer to say, "Miss Persons, will you please call Hoskins of McKee Steel?" rather than "Persons, get me Hoskins of McKee." But this is merely a preference of mine, a personal matter, and I know it and Persons knows it. No, all that is well set, but this business of Sandra's clothes quite threw me.

I made the blunder of asking her her opinion. She was quick to use the advantage I gave her, but she was very careful not to go too far. "Would you like a pair of high heels for street wear?" I asked her.

"If it is agreeable with you, sir."

"Well, now, let's see what they have in your size. . . . Those seem sturdy enough and not too expensive. Are they comfortable?"

"Quite comfortable, sir."

"There aren't any others you'd rather have?"

"These are very nice, sir."

"Well, I guess these will do quite well, for the time being at least."

"I agree with you, sir."

I agree with you: that's a very different matter from *I submit to you.* And though I didn't perceive the difference at the moment, still I was anything but easy in my mind by the time I had got Sandra installed in my house. Oh, I had no trouble preserving the proper reserve and distance with her, and I could not in the slightest detail complain of her behavior. It was just that I was not to the manner bred; that I was alone in the house with her, knowing certain external things to do, but supported by no customs and precedents as I was at the plant; that I found it very uncomfortable to order a woman, with whom I would not eat dinner at the same table, to come to my bed for an hour or so after she had finished washing the dishes. Sandra was delighted with the house and with her quarters, with the television set I had had installed for her and with the subscription to *Cosmopolitan* magazine that I had ordered in her name. She was delighted and I was glad she was delighted. That was the bad thing about it—I was glad. I should have provided these facilities only as a heavy industry provides half-hour breaks and free coffee for its workers—to keep her content and to get more work out of her. Instead I was as glad at her pleasure in them as though she were an actual person. She was so delighted that tears came to her eyes and she kissed my feet; then she asked me where the foot basin was kept. I told her I had none. She said that the dishpan would do until we got one. I told her to order a foot basin from Oakland's Own the next day, along with any other utensils or supplies she felt we needed. She thanked me, fetched the dishpan, and washed my feet. It embarrassed me to have her do it; I knew it was often done, I enjoyed the sensuous pleasure of it, I admired the grace and care with which she bent over my feet like a shoeshine, but all the same I was embarrassed. Yet she did it every day when I came home.

I do not think I could describe more economically the earlier stages of my connection to Sandra than by giving an account of the foot washing.

At first, as I have said, I was uneasy about it, though I liked it too. I was not sure that as a slave she had to do it, but she seemed to think she had to and she certainly wanted to. Now this was all wrong of me. It is true that domestic slaves usually wash their master's feet, but this is not in any sense one of the slave's rights. It is a matter about which the master decides, entirely at his own discretion. Yet, by treating it as a set duty, a duty like serving me food in which she had so profound an interest as to amount to a right, Sandra had from the outset made it impossible for me to will not to have her wash my feet. She did it every day when I came home; even when I was irritable and told her to leave me alone, she did it. Of course, I came to depend upon it as one of the pleasures and necessary routines of the day. It was, in fact, very soothing; she spent a long time at it and the water was always just lukewarm, except in cold weather when it was quite warm; as they do in good restaurants, she always floated a slice of lemon in the water. The curve of her back, the gesture with which she would shake the hair out of her eyes, the happy, private smile she wore as she did it, these were beautiful to me. She would always kiss, very lightly, the instep of each foot after she had dried them—always, that is, when we were alone.

If I brought a friend home with me, she would wash our feet all right, but matter-of-factly, efficiently, with no little intimacies as when I was alone. But if it was a woman who came with me, or a man and wife, Sandra would wash none of our feet. Nor did she wash the feet of any callers. I thought this was probably proper etiquette. I had not read my *Etiquette for Slaves* as well as Sandra obviously had. I let it go. During the first few weeks, all my friends, and particularly all my women friends, had to come to observe Sandra. She behaved surely and with complete consistency toward them all. I was proud of her. None of the women told me that Sandra was anything less than perfect, not even Helen, who would have been most likely to, being an old friend and sharp-tongued. After the novelty had worn off, I settled down with her into what seemed to be a fine routine, as one does with a mistress. To be sure, it was not long before I would think twice about bringing someone home for dinner with me; if there was much doubt in my mind about it, the difference in Sandra's foot washing alone would sway me not to bring my friend along, especially if my friend was a woman.

When I would come home late at night she would be waiting for me, with a smile and downcast eyes. I went, in October, to a convention in St. Louis for a week. When I came back, I think she spent an hour washing my feet, asking me to tell her about the physical conditions of my trip, nothing personal or intimate but just what I had eaten and what I had seen and how I had slept; but the voice in which she asked it. One night I came home very late, somewhat high, after a party. I did not want to disturb her, so I tried to go to my room noiselessly. But she heard me and came in in her robe to wash my feet; she helped me to bed, most gently. Not by a glance did she reproach me for having disturbed her sleep. But then, she never reproached me.

I did not realize fully how much I had come to depend on her until she fell sick. She was in the hospital with pneumonia for three days and spent six days convalescing. It was at Thanksgiving time. I declined invitations out to dinner, in order to keep Sandra company—to tend to her, I said to myself, though she tended to herself very nicely. I was so glad to have her well again that the first time she could come to me I kept her in my bed all night—so that she might not chill herself going back to her own bed, I told myself. That was the first time, yet by Christmas we were sleeping together regularly, though she kept her clothes in her own room. She still called me sir, she still washed my feet; according to the bill of sale I owned her; I thought her a perfect slave. I was uneasy no longer.

In fact, of course, I was making a fool of myself, and it took Helen to tell me so.

"Dell," she said over the edge of her cocktail glass, "you're in love with this creature."

"In love with Sandra!" I cried. "What do you mean?"

And I was about to expostulate hotly against the notion, when it occurred to me that too much heat on my part would confirm her in her opinion. Therefore, seeming to study the problem, I relapsed into a brown study—under Helen's watchful eye—and tried to calculate the best out for myself.

I rang for Sandra.

"More Manhattans," I said to her.

She bowed, took the shaker on her tray, and left. She was impeccable.

"No, Helen," I said finally, "she does not make my pulses race. The truth is, I come a lot closer to being in love with you than with Sandra."

"How absurd. You've never even made a pass at me."

"True."

But Sandra returned with the drinks, and after she had left we talked about indifferent matters.

As I was seeing Helen to the door, she said to me, "All the same, Dell, watch out. You'll be marrying this creature next. And who will drop by to see you then?"

"If I ever marry Sandra," I said, "it will not be for love. If I have never made a pass at you, my dear, it has not been for lack of love."

I looked at her rather yearningly, squeezed her hand rather tightly, and with a sudden little push closed the door behind her. I leaned against the wall for a moment and offered up a short prayer that Helen would never lose her present husband and come looking in my part of the world for another. I could have managed to love her all right, but she scared me to death.

I thought about what she had told me. I knew that I was not in love with Sandra—there were a thousand remnants of Chico in her that I could not abide—but I could not deny that I needed her very much. What Helen had made me see clearly was the extent to which I had failed to keep Sandra a slave. I did not know whether it was her scheming that had brought it about, or my slackness, or whether, as I suspected, something of both. Some of the more liberal writers on the subject say, of course, that such development is intrinsic in the situation for anyone in our cultural milieu. It is a problem recognized by the FSB in its handbook. But the handbook advises the master who finds himself in my predicament to trade his slave for another, preferably some stodgy, uninteresting number or one who is deficient in the proper qualities—in my case, as I thought, copulating. The trouble with this sound advice was that I didn't want to get rid of Sandra. She made me comfortable.

In fact, she made me so comfortable that I thought I was happy. I wanted to show my gratitude to her. After she had straightened up the kitchen that evening I called her into the living room where I was sitting over the paper.

"Yes, sir?" she said, standing demurely on the other side of the coffee table.

"Sandra," I began, "I'm very proud of you. I would like to do something for you."

"Yes, sir."

"Sit down."

"Thank you, sir."

As she sat, she took a cigarette from the box, without asking my permission, and lighted it. The way she arched her lips to smoke it, taking care not to spoil her lipstick, annoyed me, and the coy way she batted her eyelids made me regret I had called her in. Still, I thought, the Chico in her can be trained out. She's sound.

"What can I give you, Sandra?"

She did not answer for a moment. Every slave knows the answer to that question, and knows it is the one answer for which he won't be thanked.

"Whatever you wish to give me, sir, would be deeply appreciated."

I couldn't think of a thing to buy for her. Magazines, movies, television, clothes, jewelry, book club books, popular records, a permanent wave every four months, what else could I get her? Yet I had started this offer; I had to follow up with something. In my uneasiness and annoyance with myself, and knowing so well what it was she wanted, I went too far.

"Would you like freedom, Sandra?"

She dropped her eyes and seemed to droop a little. Then tears rolled down her cheeks, real mascara-stained tears of sadness, of profound emotion.

"Oh yes, sir," she said. "Oh my God, yes. Don't tease me about it. Please don't tease me."

So I promised her her freedom. I myself was moved, but I did not want to show it.

"I'm going for a short walk," I said. "You may go to your room."

I went for my walk, and when I came back she had prepared my foot bath. She had burned two pine boughs in the fireplace so that the room smelled wonderful. She had put on her loveliest dress, and had brushed her hair down as I liked it best. She did not speak as she washed my feet, nor even look up at my face. All her gratitude she expressed in the tenderness with which she caressed my feet and ankles. When she had finished drying them, she kissed them and then pressed them for a time against her breast. I do not think either of us, during these past few years, has ever been happier than at that moment.

Well, I had my lawyer draw up a writ of substantial manumission, and Sandra took the brass ring out of her left ear, and that was that. And that was about all of that, so far as I could see. She was free to go as she wanted, but she didn't want. She got wages now, it is true, but all she did with them was to buy clothes and gewgaws. She continued to take care of the house and me, to sleep in my bed and keep her own personal possessions in her own room, and to wash my feet as before. The manumission was nothing in itself, only a signpost that there had been some changes made. Continually and slowly changes kept being made.

For one thing, we began to eat together, unless I had guests in to dinner. For another, she began to call me Mr. Oakes. It seemed strange to have her go where she wanted, without asking me about it, on her nights out. I became so curious about what she could be doing that finally I asked her where she went. To night school, she said, learning how to type. I was delighted to hear that she had not been wasting her time at public dances, but I could not imagine why she wanted to learn typing. She had even bought a portable typewriter which she practiced on in her room when I was away. "Why?" she said. "My mother always said to me, 'Sandra, they can't fire slaves.' Well, I'm not a slave any longer. That was one nice thing about it, I wasn't ever afraid you'd fire me."

"But, my darling," I cried, "I'm never going to fire you. I couldn't possibly get along without you."

"I know it," she replied, "and I never want to leave either. All the same, I'm going to learn how to type." She had her own friends in to visit her; she even gave a bridge party one evening when I was not at home. But she never called me by my first name, she never checked up on me, she never asked me the sort of intrusive, prying question which a man hates answering. She kept her place.

Then she discovered she was pregnant. I immediately said I would assume all the financial responsibilities of her pregnancy and of rearing the child. She thanked me, and did not mention the subject again. But she took to sleeping in her own bed most of the time. She would serve breakfast while still in her robe and slippers. Her eyes were often red and swollen, though she always kept some sort of smile on her face. She mentioned something about going back to Chico. She began serving me canned soup at dinner. I drove her off to Reno and married her.

Helen had been right, I had married Sandra; but I had been right too, it wasn't for love. Oh, I loved her, some way or other, I don't know just how. But I married her simply because it was the next thing to do; it was just another milestone.

Nothing much happened for a while after we were married, except that she called me Dell and didn't even take the curlers out of her hair at breakfast. But she hadn't got to be free and equal overnight. That was to take some months of doing.

First of all, as a wife, she was much frailer than she had been as a slave. I had to buy all sorts of things for her, automatic machines to wash the clothes and the dishes, a cooking stove with nine dials and two clocks, an electric ironer that could iron a shirt in two minutes, a vacuum cleaner, one machine to grind the garbage up and another to mix pancake batter, a thermostatic furnace, an electric floor waxer, and a town coupe for her to drive about to do her errands in. She had to get other people to wash her hair now, and shave her legs and armpits, and polish her toenails and fingernails for her. She took out subscriptions to five ladies' magazines, which printed among them half a million words a month for her to read, and she had her very bathrobe designed in Paris. She moved the television set into the living room and had a tear-drop chandelier hung from the center of the ceiling. When she had a miscarriage in her sixth month, she had a daily bouquet of blue orchids brought to her room; she had to rest, and pale blue orchids are so restful. She became allergic to the substance of which my mattress and pillows were composed, and I had to get a foam rubber mattress and foam rubber pillow, which stank. She finally insisted that we go to visit her family in Chico, so we finally did, and that we go to visit my family in Boston, so we finally did. The visits were equally painful. We began to go to musical comedies and night clubs. Helen had been right: my friends did not drop by to see us, and they were apt to be sick when I invited them to dinner. Still we weren't all the way.

One night I came home late from work, tired and hungry. Dinner was not yet started, because Sandra had been delayed by her hairdresser. She fixed pork chops, frozen green beans, and bread and butter, with canned apricots for dessert. I had done better myself. After dinner, after the machine had washed the dishes, I asked her if she would bathe my feet. I was so tired, I told her, my feet were so tired; it would be very soothing to me. But she said, in an annoyed voice, that she was feeling nervous herself. She was going to go to bed early. Besides, the silence she left behind her said, besides I am your wife now. She went to bed and I went to bed. She was restless; she twisted and turned. Every time I would shift my position or start to snore a little, she would sigh or poke me. Finally she woke me clear up and said it was impossible for her to sleep like this. Why didn't I go sleep in her former room? She couldn't because of her allergy, she had to stay in the foam rubber bed. So I moved into her room. And then I knew that she was my equal, for most of the equal wives of my friends lived like this.

Another night, I came home wanting very much to make love to her. She had avoided my embrace for a long while. She was always too nervous, or too tired, for the less she worked the tireder she became; or she was busy, or simply not in the mood. But tonight I would admit of no evasion. She was beautiful and desirable, and I knew how well she had once made love to me. Finally, I held her in my arms. She knew I wanted her, and in a way as odd as mine she loved me too. But there was no sensuous pressure of her body against mine, no passion in her kiss. She put her arms about my neck not to caress me but to hang like an albatross against me. She pressed her head against my shoulder not for amorous affection but to hide her face, to shelter it, in loneliness and fear and doubt. She did not resist me, or yield to me, or respond to me, or try to avoid me. She only went away and left me her body to do with as I pleased. And then I knew that she was free, for most of the free wives of my friends were like this with their husbands.

I had four choices, as I saw it: divorce her, have her psychoanalyzed, kill her, or return her to slavery. I was strongly tempted to kill her, but I was an optimist, I thought she was salvageable. Besides, who would do my housework for me? I made her a slave again.

It is a wise provision of the law that says no slave may be completely manumitted. Even substantial manumission provides for a five-year probationary period. Sandra had not passed probation. I had the necessary papers drawn up, told her, an hour before the men came, what was happening, and had her sent to the FSB Rehabilitation School in Colorado for a month.

She came back with the ring in her ear, saying sir to me, and the very first night she washed my feet. Furthermore, she made love better than she had done for a year. I thought we were to be happy again, and for a week we seemed to be. But the machines are still there to do most of the work, and she still has her allergy. She does what a slave is supposed to do, but it is an effort, she has to will it; it exhausts her.

One evening six months ago, I came home to find no dinner

cooking, no foot bath waiting for me, no sign of Sandra in her room. I found her lying on my bed reading *McCall's* and smoking with a jewel-studded holder I had given her when she was my wife. She flicked an ash onto the rug when I entered the room, waved a languorous Hi! at me, and kept on reading. I had my choice; she had clearly set it up for me. I hesitated only a moment. I went down to the basement where I had stowed away the three-thonged lash which had been provided along with the manual of instructions when I first bought her, and I beat her on the bed where she lay.

I think I was more upset by the beating than Sandra was. But I knew I had had to do it. I knew I had neglected my duty as a master not to have done it long ago. I think now that all this trouble could have been averted if formerly I had only kept a firm hand, that is to say, had beaten her when she had risen too presumptuously. For the truth is, Sandra is happiest as a slave. That beating did her good, it kept her in place, and she knew where she stood. It is no doubt all right to free exceptional slaves, but not one like Sandra who is happiest when hoping, when wheedling and pleasing, when held to her place.

But the beatings I should have given her formerly would simply have hurt; she would simply have avoided getting them. Now, I am not so sure.

For she repeated the offense, exactly, within a month, and I repeated the punishment. It wasn't so bad for me the second time. She began seeing just how far she could go before I would bring out the lash. She cooked more and more badly till I gave her a warning one evening. When I had finished speaking, she sank to the floor, pressed her forehead against my foot, looked at me, and said, "Your wish is my command." The irony was all in the act and words, if irony there was, for there was none in the voice or face. The truth was, as she discovered the next evening when she served me corned beef hash and raw carrots for dinner, my lash is her command. She seems happier, in a way, after these distasteful blow-ups, comes to my bed voluntarily and with the welts still on her back, does her work well, hums sometimes. Yet she falls back into her old stubborn mood, again and again. There seems to be nothing else for me to do but beat her. The FSB manual supports me. Yet I find it repugnant, and it cannot be good for Sandra's skin. I had to lash her a week ago, and already, from the dirt she is allowing to collect on the living room rug, it looks as though I'll have to do it again. This was not what I had wanted. Of course, I have learned how to make the lash perform for me, how to make it sting without really damaging, how to make nine blows lighter than three. But it seems a pity to have to resort to this, when it was all quite unnecessary. It's my own fault of course; I lacked the training, the matter-of-fact experience of being a master, and I did not set about my duties as a master so conscientiously as I should have. I know all this, but knowing it doesn't help matters a bit. Sometimes I think I should have killed her, it would have been better for both of us; but then she will do some little act of spontaneous love, as now bringing me a cup of hot chocolate and kissing me lightly on the back of the neck, which makes me glad to have her around. Yet tomorrow I shall have to beat her again. This is not what I had wanted, and it cannot be what she wants, not really. We were uneasy and felt something lacking when she was a slave before, though we were happy too. We were altogether miserable when she was free. Yet this is not what either of us had ever wanted, though we are both of us doing what we must.

The Well and the Bulldozers

During the next to last spring we lived in Cajalco, my father said one Sunday, "Son, we must dig a well this summer during your school vacation."

I groaned, but he was right. There was one well we used, but it was on the Ramsey property and it was going dry. For the muscats, we needed a lot more water than the Ramsey well gave us.

Father went to Elsinore in May to get a water witch to tell us where to dig. The water witch came on a Sunday for ten dollars. He walked all over our land with a forked hazel switch held tightly in his hands, pointed straight up. When he came to water, he said, it would flop straight down. He found two places; one was on the hill where we couldn't possibly dig a well, but he said it was a strong stream. The other place was in a little hollow at the lower end of the grapes. The water witch said it was a fair stream; his switch trembled and trembled in many spots, but there was one where it flopped over hard. It was there we were to dig.

I tried being a witch all that week after school. I walked around with forked sticks made out of juniper, cottonwood, carob, orange, lemon, but none of hazel because I couldn't find any. They flopped over all right, but never in the same place twice.

The water witch was a very wonderful man, and my little brother Jimmy had nightmares about him.

Then we dug the well.

At first it was easy, just shoveling and a little picking. For twenty feet down it was dirt and decomposed granite which needed a casing to hold it back. We cased it with two-by-twelve redwood planks, and the well was four feet square.

When we hit harder granite, we had to pick all the time. First Father would pick awhile; then he would call for me to lower the bucket for him to shovel full of dirt; I would wind it up on the windlass, dump it out, and wait for the next bucketful. After a couple of hours I would go down and pick awhile, and Father would rest on top, windlassing the full bucket up.

At forty feet we had to blast. Father would go down and drill holes, put sticks of dynamite in, attach a fuse and a cap to each one, pack them in tight, and light the fuses. Then he would climb up the ladder as fast as he possibly could while the fuses burned down to the caps. It was always terrible when we couldn't hear a separate explosion for every stick. That meant either that two had gone off at once or else that one fuse had died out, so that if one of us hit the pick point right on the cap the stick of dynamite would blow up in his face.

This harder granite began to sweat as we went down through it, but not more than a bucketful of water would collect overnight. Once, after a day's work, Father climbed out of the well and stood fanning himself with his hat and looking at the hills for a while. "My boy," he said, and I knew he was going to tell me something important because he said "my boy," "they're wonderful things, the strata. They're as old as the dry hills there; in fact they're a part of them. And yet they bear water for us, and they always will. Our well is a part of them now. It will outlive us a hundred years."

I used to dream of the well, down where it was gloomy and damp, and the acrid smell of dynamite hung around. I was constantly afraid of things dropping down on my head, though nothing very big ever hit me. Sometimes when I was resting, I used to tap on a shovel just to have something to listen to. Old-timers said if the well was deep enough you could look up and see the stars at noon, but I never could from our well; of course, it was only sixty feet deep.

At fifty feet we had a trickle of water. Then we had to drop a pipe down and run a horse-and-a-half gasoline engine to keep it pumped out while we worked. We dug for ten more feet, and had more than enough water for the grapes and an acre of alfalfa. He was a good water witch.

That very winter there was a terrible cloudburst, the worst in forty-seven years. It lightninged and thundered, and rained four inches in two days. The gullies roared with water and the goats shivered and bleated. It was glorious. But many gophers had dug little tunnels up to the casing of our well. (We had caught three thousand gophers in the first year we were there, and hung their tails around the rabbit hutch in a fringe.) Our well was in a little valley, and the cloudburst went down the gopher holes, making them larger and larger and carrying the dirt with the water down into our well. After the cloudburst the dirt around the well was all gone on the upper side, and the well was filled up to the casing with solid mud.

When my father saw it, he slapped his thigh with his hat, and stamped the ground; he cursed before me, a thing he did only when tried beyond his strength.

We had to dig out the well again that spring. The dry, hard mud was almost worse than the granite, because we had to pick instead of blast. Something had happened to the well, too, because there wasn't as much water this time as before. We finished it, though, before the Ramsey well went dry, and had enough for the alfalfa and muscats, and for anything else we should ever be able to grow on our land.

That same spring the surveyors began to come.

They came in spiffy-looking station wagons and went about driving stakes in the ground at various places for miles around. One of them would look through a little telescope on a stand at a black-and-white stick which another one was holding up a long way off. They would yell and wave at each other and write things in little books.

Everybody in Cajalco was upset; all we knew was that the surveyors said it was going to be a reservoir.

"Right of eminent domain," said my father; he had worked for a railroad company once, as a fireman, so everyone had great respect for his knowledge. "A big company will come and we'll have to move. I've seen a railroad line laid right through a graveyard," said my father ominously, "and there was nothing the church could do to stop them."

All spring the men surveyed, leaving only their stakes to show for it; and in June, notices came to everyone explaining about the reservoir, how it was the terminal reservoir for water for Los Angeles and we would all have to move. *The Southern District Metropolitan Water Corporation.*

"You see," said my father, "and they won't pay a cent more than they have to."

It wasn't so bad, though, because only one man in Cajalco made a living off his land anyway.

That fall, when we all had to move away from Cajalco, the bulldozers and trucks and power shovels came. The bulldozers were terrible. They were huge and noisy; when they started on a cold morning, they sounded like machine guns. They could uproot huge trees. They could go up steep mountains. They moved hills, whole hills they moved to form a dirt dam: they took the Bottom and moved it two miles to make a long dam. They paid no attention to fences or roads or gullies. They dug great troughs. They laid waste the land till you never would have known it.

But to our well they were worst. Our well was sixty feet deep, yet they dug a trench a hundred feet deep and half a mile wide right through our well and into the side of the hill back of where our house had been. To them, our well was just another gopher hole. They didn't even know it was there. Our well was four by four and sixty feet deep, a hole in the ground, and suddenly the bulldozers fixed it so there wasn't any ground for the hole at all. I don't know why they dug this ditch into the hill and then stopped; maybe the Metropolitan Water Corporation knows, or science.

I should like to think of our well still there in the desert, maybe starting to fill up with dust and weeds and ground squirrels and lizards that fall in; or at least, since they built a big reservoir, at least our well could be a deep place in the reservoir. But it's gone completely: there isn't even any ground for the well to be in, and now where the well and the ground were, there is water. The whole landscape is gone under water. And even if you drained the water off, still the bottom of that lake is not the countryside where I lived seven years. The hills would be different; and the sagebrush and grapevines and cactus and carob trees and tamarisks, the fences and houses and barns and roads and windmills and our reservoirs and water tanks would be gone, and now some sort of slimy underwater plants would lie there in the middle of the desert in that unrecognizable landscape where I lived for seven years.

ೋಕ್ಷ್ಣ

ೋಕ್ಷ್ಣ   # Invasion of the Planet of Love

ೋಕ್ಷ್ಣ

One thing surprised us about the stormy surface of Venus, and that pleasantly—the temperature. It was as low as ten degrees centigrade at the poles and not over seventy at the equator. We saw several active volcanoes, and no signs of water. It was in the southern temperate zone, sheltered by a range of mountains about twenty thousand feet high, and a couple of hours ahead of the nearest tempest, that we finally landed. Rossi and Bertel, armored and cautious, began to explore the vicinity of the ship; Dr. Pound and I covered them with depressor-gun and solvator.

There was nothing to discover but granite. A mountain of granite, a plain of granite, granite boulders, seams of granite. And granite dust, everywhere granite dust. We got back into the ship and moved on ahead of the approaching storm. We stopped in the middle of a plain as vast as Africa. Granite.

After seventy-two hours of fruitless exploration we were all in a state of acute disappointment, especially Rossi, who, being the expert on this part of our expedition, seemed to feel slightly apologetic at the state of affairs on the second planet. Bertel went off to sleep, and I, as I always do in such a case, kept eating too much. Dr. Pound no longer prayed; he even gave up that smile which it has taken three centuries of Anglican conquest to breed; he sat glued to his periscope, peering at granite.

For at the back of our minds was the dread of failure. Five expeditions to Mars had failed: they had approached, begun to land, and had never been heard from again. So we had been sent to Venus, and we too were failing. Though we had arrived and though we could probably return in safety, yet we were failing: we had not found that which it was necessary for us to find.

We were out of communication with Earth because of the tempests; I think we were all glad of it, for had it been otherwise we would have waited till the three hundredth hour, as we were supposed to, to use our last and most desperate resource. We had five hundred hours in all; if we stayed longer than that we would be dangerously far from Earth for safe return.

We could not use the crater of one of the extinct volcanoes as we had hoped, because the craters were all filled with sand. We agreed to do it in a temperate zone, and near a mountain. We returned to the place where we had first landed. A standard Venus supertempest was on when we got there. Rossi said that would be fine for clearing the gross radioactivity fast. We dropped the bomb at the eighty-second hour; at the ninety-sixth hour we returned, fully protected, expecting to find merely a few more variations on the granite theme. And found instead, we thought, what we had been looking for: natural resources and rational beings . . . riches and enemies.

The cavern which the bomb had scooped out was hundreds of feet in depth. In it were evidences of many mineral deposits, including, Rossi said, a large vein of gold and considerable pitchblende. But his enthusiasm at the minerals and water was lost presently at our discovery of the evidences of life—burrows issuing into this cavern. Not many and not large—about four feet in diameter—but regular and clearly artificial.

"There!" cried Dr. Pound, his eyes at his periscope. "There! One of the holes over there disappeared!"

It was of course quite dark in there, and he was not the most reliable observer imaginable, but he swore that as he had been looking at one of the openings it had closed up. In less than ten seconds, it simply became not there, but a part of the wall of granite. Sand could not have done it. We armored ourselves, and got out of the ship.

We approached the nearest hole slowly. Rossi carried a solvator, Bertel a Murdlegatt, I two depressors, and Dr. Pound, who was old-fashioned, a submachine gun in one hand and a cross in the other. We reached the hole safely, and saw nothing, as far as our lights penetrated, but a sort of tunnel dug for four-foot miners. The air issuing from it was relatively cool.

We started, and turned around. There was a scraping sound going on behind us somewhere. We could hear its clear and special noise under the echo and howl of the blasting winds outside. And then, as Dr. Pound had said, the entrance of a hole, which none of us was looking at at the moment but which all of us knew had been there, suddenly was not there. We ran over to where it had been, and found what at first seemed to be a sandstone plug in the entrance. But Rossi, investigating it, found it to be a highly intricate light-metal filter or screen. He got rid of it with his solvator turned to 7.7, and we entered the tunnel, stooping.

It was not quite pitch black in the tunnel—we don't know yet how they managed this—though it was very dark all the same; you couldn't see your hand in front of your face, but you could tell you were *not* seeing it, which is more than you can tell in pitch darkness. There were no irregularities in the surface of the tunnel and no turnings, so we saved our lights. We walked a very long way, always slightly uphill.

Dr. Pound, the last in line, said, "Stop!" in that tone of voice which stands the hair up on the back of your neck. It seemed to be silent in the tunnel at first, just as it had seemed to be black; but presently we knew that there was a padding sound, which was more than the beat of our hearts in our ears, coming from

behind us. (How could anything have got behind us?) I snapped
on my light.

Twenty feet away, blinking in the sudden glare, stood a bent,
large-eyed, grinning, two-legged creature. He was nude, his entire body seemed to be without hair or wrinkles, and he had the
white color of underground life; he came toward us with claw-
hand outstretched; he was more like a human being than like
anything else. Dr. Pound warned him to stop, with word and
cross, but the Venerean did not stop. His claws were very sharp;
he grinned too much.

Dr. Pound shot him down at five feet. We watched him clutch
his belly and shriek in pain; but when he was clearly about to
die, his features relaxed into an expression of peace, and his last
act was a smile of joy for Dr. Pound; he died with that expression on his face. Dr. Pound knelt, made the sign of the cross over
the corpse, offered an ejaculation for the soul it might have had;
and we went on our way.

It was not three minutes till we saw light at the end of this
tunnel; a dim pinpoint far ahead. Then the pinpoint became
obscured; we heard a calling sound; another Venerean was approaching, no doubt to investigate the noise. I blinded him with
my light; Rossi solvated him (at 2.1); we stepped over the
puddle, and approached the entrance cautiously. The tunnel permitted only two of us at a time to look out; Rossi and I crept forward on hands and knees, guns ready, till we could see into a
great cavern.

There were warmth and moisture in the cavern—exactly the
right condition for going about unclothed as the Venereans did—
and it was so large we could not see the opposite side of it. The
sides were sheer and high, there was soil on the floor, and the
huge stalactites covering the dome glowed where they hung.
From our vantage point some hundred feet above the floor, we
could see a profusion of pale vegetation and large numbers of the

pale little people. They were doing something or other—jumping about and hugging each other, disappearing under the leaves, calling in guttural voices.

"What's going on down there?" I asked Rossi.

He shrugged. "They're lunatics. Dancing lunatics."

But Bertel and Dr. Pound were tugging at our shirts and whispering to us to give them a turn. We gave way to them.

Both of them were so excited as to be incautious in their zeal. They craned their necks out and began arguing in intense, carrying whispers that rose to a considerable pitch.

"There's no reason," said Bertel, "to suppose any eccentricity in what they are doing."

"Come," said Dr. Pound, "look at them, man."

"What do we know of their motives? We are merely guessing what we would mean if we were doing that."

Dr. Pound stared at him with amazement.

"And what," he said, "do you psychologists ever do, with primitives especially?"

"Bah," said Bertel, avoiding the question. "If these fellows are human, I'd say they're pre-sapiens. Observe—"

"No!" said Dr. Pound. "I detect a pattern in their movements. I am willing to wager that this represents a dance propitiating the gods for the terrible explosion of our bomb."

"Not a bad idea," said Bertel. "But to me it looks too random. I'd say they may be seriously disturbed by the effects of our bomb. The inner ear maybe."

The argument did not pause, but I ceased to pay any attention to it. I began speculating on what my task would be if these Venereans did turn out to be equivalent to human pre-literates. I had helped develop the Kräse system of reducing primitive languages to a sort of Basic that greatly facilitates education. There had been a couple of Brazilian tribes whose languages seemed not to respond to the Kräse method, and I was very anxious to see what I could do with the Venereans.

"Come on," I said to the wranglers, "how are we ever going to get down there?"

Rossi laughed. "It'll take a ladder to civilize those babies."

We could see that our tunnel opened, like all the others in sight, a hundred feet sheer above the floor, without paths or mechanisms of any visible sort for getting us down. But even as we watched, we saw gliding among the stalactites, like a launch on a calm lake, the means of transportation: a sort of shallow skiff floating through the air. There were two Venereans in it; they directed it toward another tunnel opening, warped it into position, and then pushed their cargo into the tunnel. It was a plug such as we had solvated. One of the men disappeared with the plug, pushing it, and the other sailed away. We did not know what to do.

Our tactics and strategy had been laid out for us in complete detail years before; if we found intelligent beings (as we obviously had), we were to isolate a small number of them, communicate with them so as to learn as much as possible about their life-system and educability and the planet's natural resources, and be absolutely honest about our intentions though not about our powers; but above all, we were to *trust no one.*

Our problem therefore was: how to get to the floor without trusting ourselves to one of these little boatmen? Bertel suggested that we hail one, get him to teach us how to operate the boat, and then throw him overboard. But the rest of us agreed that that was too risky a procedure. We could see no alternative to trusting one at least for the one trip. And so, with grave misgivings, the next time a boat approached to deposit its load, we shouted and waved till the boatman saw us and came toward us.

He came smiling and open-armed up to the mouth of our tunnel, making little throat-noises, not at all astonished at our appearance. Before we could make him realize that we were repelling his advances, he had touched us a number of times trying to embrace us. But finally he got the point; smiling no more, he let us enter his boat apart from him. We pointed straight down, and in graceful spirals we descended.

The boat was metal and had no visible controls in it. The Venerean seemed to do nothing to guide it. We were all mystified (and still are) at how it worked. Dr. Pound, who could be very embarrassing, painfully so, half-muttered that maybe it was only a grain of faith that moved the boat. I think Rossi at that point would have traded Dr. Pound for a shot of good Scotch; I know I would have. When we landed I depressed the boatman, so as to insure our safe return.

Bertel, who had been keeping his eye on the floor of the cavern, called to us to be prepared against an assault. The Venereans were capering toward us by the score, leaping and chortling as they came. There was no natural safeguard of any sort for us, only the flaccid, pale-green, humid plants with their huge, ginkgolike leaves. And there was no time—the Venereans were approaching from every direction, with no sign of hesitation. They were armed, some of them, with what looked like shovels and hoes.

With our backs toward the cavern wall, forming a semicircle against their semicircle, we shouted at them to stop, but they did not stop. Then we opened fire. We must have eliminated fifty in the first round, but I do not think the others behind them understood what had happened for they kept on coming. Again we opened fire—all our weapons were effective on them. Again. And this third time the remainder stopped at about fifty paces.

All but a child, who came toddling on toward us by himself, beating his little claws together and chortling at us. His mother came clucking after him. Dr. Pound shoved him over with the point of his submachine gun; the mother picked him up and comforted him by giving him suck; then, smiling, she extended an arm with the brutal claw at the end of it *(Trust no one)* and leaned at Dr. Pound. He shot her down; like the first one he had shot, she died smiling at him. All the other people ran away.

We decided that they were afraid of the noise; the baby, paying no attention to his fallen mother, ran after them with his claws over his ears, wailing his guttural loss.

We solvated the dead and resuscitated some of the depressed, and set about the long tedious process of safeguarding ourselves, communicating with them, and exploring the physical resources of their world. Rossi went sailing off with the boatman and the Murdlegatt for 150 hours, and came back with some mighty tall tales about mineral deposits. I managed to establish what seemed to be telepathic rapport with the Venereans, though we were never sure how they understood us. Dr. Pound had no success whatever in his attempts to convert them, and Bertel is still trying to make coherent sense of their thought-ways from such psychognosis as he was able to perform.

However, for reasons of National Security, I am not permitted in this public narrative to enter upon a detailed discussion of any of these aspects of our expedition. What I can say is that this gusty, populous planet contains such wealth as can be expressed only by statistics, and an enemy that isn't worth a good epidemic of measles. We did not even discover to our satisfaction whether they are highly enough evolved to be able to learn the advantages of having books and clothes and machines and wars—whether, in short, they can be brought up to a decent level of civilization.

It can be said that for over two hundred hours we subjected a dozen random but obviously typical specimens of Venerean man to every experiment which ingenuity had devised beforehand and which necessity imposed upon us now. I would point to my eyes —they had eyes like ours—and then my mind (and Bertel's and Dr. Pound's also) would fill at their suggestion with the image of a chain of lakes under a clear sky or of a garden of roses in bloom. I would rub my skin and pinch it, and my mind would be occupied with the sensation of a warm bath or of fresh smooth sheets. I pointed at my belly, and was made to think of roast turkey (there are of course no turkeys in Venus); at my ears, and heard birds at their dawn-singing (no birds, no dawns). It was as though they had once lived in a world like ours and had been driven underground by earlier invaders, preserving among themselves the memories of that pleasant life. Bertel, who is more realistic about it, says they worked on our emotions, and our own minds formed the specific images. When I found myself weeping after I had pointed at my fingers, Bertel said it indicated their pity for our not having claws. Sometimes we were suffused with the desire to embrace them in friendship (we had to depress them once in order that we might conquer this impulse); and sometimes our minds were overcome with sexual images so voluptuous and indecent, though never perverted, that it was as much as we could do to keep from solvating the whole batch of them.

They were either incredibly simple-minded, or else extremely clever. Indeed, if they had been the species Homo sapiens, Bertel would have called them dangerously neurotic. For nothing we could do aroused their hostility; or, to put it perhaps more accurately, no matter what we did they would give no indication of their hostility. They cried when we beat them. They learned to run when we chased. One we starved; he just died. Another we blindfolded and hobbled and stuck head-first into a hole; after struggling for a while, he seemed to croon to himself till we pulled him out.

It was Rossi, after he had returned from his expedition, who suggested we torture one of them. I was in favor of it, though Dr. Pound opposed, for it seems to me you can discover a good deal about the level of a being's culture by the way he handles pain; one of a low order merely cries or endures it, whereas a highly developed type will be able to turn his pain to some good use.

We began by betraying him. We would proffer him friendship and love, which he would always be happy to accept, and then as he was all ready to receive it we would hurt him, slap him, or knock him down. Again and again and again, and he never learned. We overwhelmed him with hostile thoughts; I think they projected successfully for he seemed to feel a sort of bewilderment and pain at them. We submitted him to physical torture, and then a monstrous thing happened. At first he cried in pain, but shortly he seemed to understand that this treatment was what was in store for him and he *smiled* at us. Very dimly, but very certainly, as we burned the soles of his feet or gouged his eyes out or twisted his arm off, we felt ourselves invaded with his tenderness and affection; in me it took the form of wanting him to forgive me.

We were baffled and defeated; for how can you expect to civilize beings so unable to handle pain as these smilers? What worthwhile accomplishments could be expected from such fellows? We were about to give up when the greatest danger of all threatened us.

We were knocked to our knees.

We did not know how or whence, but suddenly we were knocked to our knees by an onslaught of joy. In all four of us it became a surpassing joy to breathe the oxygen from our capsules, it was new and strange to feel the backs of our hands thrill against their gauntlets, we liked intensely being on our knees and being aghast at ourselves. I think Dr. Pound was right: it was awe we felt. I am not sure. I know very little about awe.

Only Rossi regained even partial control of himself, but it was in time to save us. With the visage of an angel of annunciation he told us to get into the skiff; tranced like those for whom miracles are worked, we obeyed. He undepressed the boatman and we rose. As we went up, we observed, as far as the eye could reach, a multitude of Venereans facing us and pursuing us with their love. Rossi had to depress Dr. Pound to keep him from joining them by jumping overboard.

We returned to our tunnel, which Rossi had previously marked with a slash of the solvator, and went into it. The power of those rejoicers diminished, but we did not feel safe and free from it till we had reached the outer end of the tunnel. They had put a new plug in; we solvated it and stepped into our bomb-cave, welcoming the hot noisiness of outer Venus.

It was the 380th hour; we had plenty of time. We felt like performing some sort of ceremony to mark our escape and the success, however slight, of our mission, but no celebration was possible under the circumstances. Rossi explored to the inmost extremity of the cave; he reported that he found almost no sand there, only a layer of dust. He guessed that the cave would never be filled, nor even completely closed off. None of the rest of us cared.

After we had entered and sealed the ship, we sat in the control room eating and philosophizing a little, reassuming, as it were, our roles as extensions of Earth.

"I would say," said Bertel, "that we've failed."

"Why?" I asked. "We've discovered—"

"Yes, yes," he replied, "we've discovered, and we've discovered. But who the devil would bother to make war on these nincompoops we've discovered? They'll never be up to it."

But Rossi was more helpful.

"There's always Mars," he said. "We can plunder the strength of Venus to wage war on Mars. Mars seems to be enemy enough for anybody."

"May they both last," said Bertel, "till man's nature has changed."

"That," said Dr. Pound, "is unthinkable."

Bertel looked at him contemptuously, but he saved his arguments till we should be out in space. It was time we took off.

As we were emerging in the ship from the mouth of the bomb cavern, Rossi remembered that we had neglected a part of our duty. The President had particularly admonished us to see to it when he had bid us Godspeed so many hours before. We agreed that the best place to put it was on the rear wall of the cavern. So we went back in, disembarked again, and fastened the bronze plaque high on the wall. It read:

THIS PLANET WAS DISCOVERED BY AUTHORIZED EMISSARIES OF
THE UNITED STATES OF AMERICA

PERMISSION TO EXPLORE MUST BE OBTAINED FROM
THE GOVERNMENT OF THE UNITED STATES OF AMERICA

ALL RIGHTS OF EXPLOITATION ARE RESERVED BY
THE UNITED STATES OF AMERICA

TRESPASSERS BEWARE

Rilla

One of the reasons I went back to driving a cab was to steer clear of the fair sex. Driving a cab, you don't have to come any closer to women than "Thanks for the tip"—unless you want to. However, as my wife used to say, "Bert, you were born in the wrong house." She was talking about Scorpio and Gemini and the planets and such like, but you could get her meaning without too much trouble. That was before she was put away. Well, the main person I had to deal with in the Spee-Dee Taxicab Service was the expediter of course, and the swing-shift expediter was Rilla.

The afternoon I went on the job I didn't really pay too much attention to her. Emory introduced me to her, naturally, but the main contact I had with her was, she came out when I was wiping off my cab and gave me my record sheet.

"Here you are, Bert," she said as friendly as you please. "Did Mr. Emory tell you the clutch is bad on this Plymouth? Don't get stuck on a steep hill. You'll have to back down."

"Thanks, kid," I said. "The way the old man talked, the governor of California would be honored to ride in a limousine like this."

She had a nice laugh, a real nice laugh. In fact, she was well fleshed and I liked the way she dressed and I liked her coloring, so it's surprising she didn't make more of a first impression on me. I think it was the way she batted her eyes. She had nice eyes, shiny as a squirrel's, and long dark eyelashes. But she used them too much. She batted them at me when she wished me luck, and she looked at me up from under, sort of. Anyhow, when I got down to my stand at Twenty-second and Broadway, I didn't give her a second thought. I honestly didn't anticipate any more trouble from that quarter than I would from a waitress in a cafeteria.

When I was driving cab during the war they didn't have these two-way radios, so it was three or four days before I discovered I could listen in when the other drivers were gassing with Rilla. Mostly, she hadn't talked to me much. "Bert," she'd say, "go to Bonita Avenue," or some such place; and I'd say, "Okay." You don't get much of an idea from scraps like that. But one night about quarter to seven when everybody was holed in for dinner and not ready to step out any place yet, I snapped on the radio to tell her I was going to cruise for a while, I was sick and tired of the blinking neons, and I heard this conversation going on.

"Hey, Chester," Rilla was saying, "have you had a fare yet tonight?"

"Yes, from the Leamington to the SP station. It came to a dollar even. He didn't tip me a thing."

"Well, here's a woman that wants to be down to the San Francisco airport by eight forty."

"Hot dog!" Chester said. "I get a break. Where is she?"

Rilla told him the address, and then I heard another voice, I didn't know whose it was.

"Hey, Rilla, I just had me a customer."

"Mm-hmm," she said, very nonchalant, the way a person will when they think you mean more than you're saying.

"He was sloppy drunk and he kept saying he had a broken heart."

"Who was it?" said somebody else, but Rilla didn't say anything.

"He was wall-eyed and he had a mustache," says this same voice.

Then everybody else that's listening in, four or five, yell in chorus, "Percy Glasscock!" And Rilla makes a funny noise and clicks off the radio. She can click anybody and everybody off the radio any time she feels like it.

Well, naturally I didn't know all the ins and outs of the matter, but it seemed pretty rough to me to have the whole bunch of them jump on her at the same time. So she had broken Percy Glasscock's heart maybe; so she probably felt bad enough about it already without everybody jumping on her. That's the way I was figuring it, but still I didn't want to get mixed up in anything.

What I did was, when I clicked back on, I told her in a nice way I was going cruising, and when she said okay in a dispirited way, I asked her would she like a milk shake. Her voice perked up a lot at that, and she said she sure would, vanilla, and it was really lonely there in the garage by herself from four thirty till one. So I took one by for her and gassed awhile as she drank it. She was friendly as could be and I noticed how well built she was, and she kept tucking her blouse in more than I could see any call for, and she kept batting her eyes, which wasn't so good, and I went back onto the streets.

I went down to the Twelfth and Broadway stand and it was empty. Now mostly the other drivers hadn't been too talkative with me, which is what I wanted as much as anything else, so this time I just sat there having a good time watching the people walk by and playing my imaginary trombone. That was a habit I got into, left over from the days when I played in big bands, till the drink and my wife's trouble got me and I never went back to playing. So I was really surprised to see another Spee-Dee cab pull up behind me and this human ape step out with a forehead so low his cap sits on his eyebrows.

"Hello," he says, leaning in the window, "you're the new man."

This was the joker with the Percy Glasscock story. I recognized his voice, and I didn't like him already.

"Yep," I said, "Bert's the moniker." I got out to be sociable. We shook hands, only he's got a grip like a vice.

"Ormie's mine," he said. "Pleased to meet you."

"Sure, Ormie," I said. I was feeling better. A guy like that, it would be a pleasure to call him Ormie ten times a minute.

"Well, how do you like the job?" he says.

Well, what does anybody in my situation say to a lead like that? You like it fine, Ormie, fine. Only I like to appear good-natured and peppy, as I appreciate such features in others; so what I did now was, I sort of tipped my hat and bowed a little and I said with such a fleet of cars and such fellow workers I was honored to be a member of the Spee-Dee Taxicab Service. Maybe I laid it on too thick, because he just stood there and hitched up his pants and looked at me sour. His little black eyes were so far apart you were surprised to see them work together.

"Say, Ormie," I said, "those are really nice socks you got there."

That was a little better. He hitched up his pants again to look at them and he puffed up like a kid. That's what they were, kid socks, red and yellow diamonds of that neon color they have now-adays that glows like it was alive. He looked like a pig that some-body had painted his ankles so they could catch him in the dark.

"Sure," he said, "I like 'em. Rilla gave 'em to me."

"Is that so?" I said. I couldn't feature it. Besides, if she really did give them to him, I couldn't see the way he'd laughed at her on the radio.

"Yes, that's so," he said, tough. "Rilla's a nice kid, only you got to know how to handle her."

"Like you?" I said, really pleasant.

"What do you mean?" he said, suspicious as all hell.

When one of those guys begins pawing the dirt, what you've got to be is fast on your feet.

"Who's Percy Glasscock?" I asks, so he won't get up too much momentum.

"Percy Glasscock was a driver, see?" Ormie pokes one of those chopped-off cigars he wears for a finger against my chest. "He thought he could make some time with Rilla but he didn't get nowhere, see?" He keeps punching at the same place, very painful, only he's five inches taller. "There ain't nobody gets nowhere with Rilla so you'd might as well not try, see?"

"Sure," I said. He had me up against the window of the cigar store, and I don't mind saying it, his breath was not of the best. "Sure, she's a nice girl. That's what I always thought."

"I just don't want you to forget it, that's all. You and your milk shakes. She's poison."

Frankly, right then I'd just as soon I'd never met either one of them, so I just stood there. I won't say I wasn't sore, inside and outside. Ormie goes into the cigar shop, and from the way the guy waited on him it was clear to the naked eye it was just for the business and not for the friendship. Ormie cracks a couple of jokes, but the guy doesn't even crack a smile. I like the cigar man better from that minute on, even if he does wear a toupee.

The next afternoon when I came to work, who should be laughing and kidding in the office with Rilla but my old pal Ormie. You'd have thought they were bosom friends from the way they were laughing and pushing each other, and I can't deny it, she was as set up as he was.

"Hey, Ormie," I says behind my hand, only out loud, "ask Rilla if I can have my stuff."

"What's the matter, Bert?" she says.

"Yeh," he says, "what's the matter?" Little Sir Echo.

"You told me last night it'd be just as well if I didn't speak to her any more."

I winked at Rilla when I said that, so she'd be sure to see it was just a joke. Only nobody took it as a joke. Ormie got so mad he wanted to push me through the floor. He couldn't because Rilla was there, so he just went out to clean up his cab. And Rilla was mad at him too, but she was sweet as pie with me.

There were a couple of things I wanted to find out about her, how sweet was she really with me, and who wasn't she sweet with? You can have too much of a good thing.

"Say," I said, "those are sure loud socks Ormie's got on."

"Yes?" she said, and she put on lipstick, only she didn't need any more lipstick that I could see.

"Did you give them to him?" I said. "He said you did."

"Sure," she said, "don't you think they're cute?"

"No," I said, real mournful. "I've got to be honest with you. I don't think they're cute. The least I can say is, they're not cute."

"Well, Ormie likes them," she says, and she straightens a shoulder strap. One thing about Rilla, if you're around her she sees to it you have a hard time looking at anything but Rilla. Of course she's got something to look at. "Ormie likes them and he's the one that's wearing them." She was as pert as you please and I liked her for it.

"When's your nights off, kid?" I said.

"Wednesday and Thursday."

"How about going out with me Thursday?"

She didn't even pause a second, and the way she said, "I'd love it," I really thought she meant it. In fact it worried me a little how much she meant it, me being practically a stranger as you might say. About that time Chester came in, and she was as friendly with him, batting her eyes and all, as with anybody else. The truth is, I didn't have her figured out.

This Chester now, he was a good enough fellow, but nothing out of the ordinary that I could see. He wasn't any taller than I am, which isn't tall enough, but he was thin and sort of frail looking. He had a big voice which he was always using real deep; in fact, it sounded flat most of the time it was so deep, like a kid playing grown-up. Now what would a woman see in a flat-chested little guy like that?

That same day I was just telling about, I found Chester standing in front of a pawnshop with his hands in his pockets and staring at the guns. He was such a sad sack I couldn't keep from trying to buck him up a little. It was a slow day, so I thought I'd tell him about some of my experiences as a hunter. But by the time he'd said a few things like "I've never gone to Trinity County" or "Me, I never even shot a thirty-thirty," I was dragged down so far I couldn't even finish the story I was on. That man just made me *tired*.

It was a good story too. My father and I went up on the Trinity Alps the summer I was fifteen, deer hunting. The first five or six days we didn't see more than half a dozen doe and not a buck, so the last day we lit out from camp early for a little valley my father had heard of, where practically nobody ever went; it wasn't too far from the Oregon border. Well, the long and the short of it is, we scared up as big a nine-point buck as I've ever seen and cornered him in a pocket of that valley where he couldn't get out. The way he came at us when he saw how we had him at bay, you wouldn't believe a deer had it in him if you didn't see it. My father told me I should never trust a deer at bay no matter how they act, and I believe him. I went back to that valley by myself once, a few years later, and I cornered me a doe in the same spot. Only I let her go. In fact I think even if I could have shot her legally I'd have let her go. She was a nice fat doe, scared to death, but she was game. The feeling it gives a man to let a creature go like that, it's worth it.

Well, how could I tell a story like that to a character that probably never even saw a damned deer outside of a zoo?

"Say," I said, "Chester, I just remembered I promised to take something over to Rilla. I'll see you later."

He quit whistling. He'd been whistling between his teeth, "Do not forsake me, O my darling," and naturally I hadn't been too overjoyed talking to a whistler.

"Rilla," he says, "Rilla." He sort of snorted. "Just watch your step."

I was downright sorry for him, and it occurred to me that that was the way Rilla felt about him too. All the same it isn't pleasant to see a man be so hypocritical, talking with a woman and laughing real friendly with her but then speaking against her behind her back. So I didn't even answer him. I just drove away. I didn't even go to see Rilla. I thought I'd let it ride till Thursday and then we'd see what we'd see.

So that Saturday afternoon I'm lying on my bed reading a mystery and I hear the landlady showing a guy the next room and he takes it. There's a locked door between my room and his but you can hear through it pretty well, if you're so inclined. I go out about four and who should be walking down the hall ahead of me but Chester himself. You can just imagine how my pulses began racing at the sight of him.

"Hey, Chester!"

He sort of jerks and looks around at me. "Where'd you come from, Bert?"

"I live here, next door."

"Well, by golly, let's go have something to eat before we clock in."

"Those were my sentiments exactly. Do you like chow mein?"

He liked chow mein. While we were shoveling six-bits' worth of it into our mouths, he said to me, "Have a good time Thursday night?"

"Sure," I said, looking at him sharp. "What were you thinking of?"

"Rilla. Ormie seen you coming out of Sweet's Ballrooom with her."

"So what?"

"So nothing. Don't get sore at the drop of a hat. I just thought I'd let you know Ormie saw you."

"How do you know he did?"

"He was mentioning the fact."

"I suppose I've got to make an account of myself to Ormie every time I want to take Rilla to a damned dance and buy her a drink. Well, by God."

"Don't get so excited," he said, with a sort of little grin on one side of his face. "He's got nothing to go on."

"So he hasn't. What difference does it make? And how does he know he hasn't?"

"Look, Bert," he said and reached for his wallet. "Here's a ten-dollar bill. I'll lay it against a one-spot that you can't make any time with Rilla between now and Monday night."

I had a sneaking feeling I was being suckered into something, but by the time I saw his money I was so mad I didn't give a damn. I laid a dollar beside his ten. "Will you take my word for it?" I asked him.

"Oh, I'm next door to you," he said. "Get her into your room. I'll hear."

The way he grinned at me I felt like a heel, but I didn't back out.

Still, when I was alone in my cab and had time to cool off, I began to think it would be the decentest thing to Rilla to not go through with it. For one thing, we'd had a good time all right Thursday night, but that wasn't all there was to it. When I was driving her home after the dance, she kept holding hands passionately. Can you imagine a man like me that's been married once for four years wanting to hold hands passionately? Anyway, she did, and she got me pretty well steamed up. I stopped the car and put my arm around her to kiss her but she ducked. I kept on trying and she kept on ducking, till finally I brought my other hand into play and she gave me a left jab in the ribs I could still feel Saturday night. So we didn't part on the best of terms, but I still wasn't mad enough at her to want to hurt her reputation. I just wanted to keep out of trouble, but here I was sucked into it. Besides I wasn't sure I could make the grade with her.

Still and all, I like to get along with people, so when she clicked me on about eight thirty and told me in that low-pitched, friendly voice of hers that I had a pickup, I couldn't be anything but friendly back with her. When a person likes you and likes to laugh a lot, there's no point in trying to do anything but like them back. At least when you're with them.

The address she gave me turned out to be an ice-cream joint, so I knew what she wanted. I decided to make peace and I took her up a milk shake.

Ormie's cab was parked out in front of the garage and when I opened the door to the office there he was coming out looking like the wrath of the Lord, with the finger marks on his cheek where Rilla had slapped him. I held the door open for him and took off my hat and bowed. He grunted like a hog and hit the milk shake up so it splattered in my face. If Rilla hadn't been there he wouldn't have stopped with a little tap like that.

She was crying, and by the time we'd got me mopped up and her calmed down we were pretty good friends again, and when she kissed me on the cheek good-bye I'd really decided to let Chester have my buck.

But just as I was going out she flips on Chester's radio to give him an order and there's Ormie's voice.

". . . *any* where you see him."

"What do you mean?" says Chester.

They'd obviously been having a conversation with the microphone left on.

"Look," says Ormie and you can just see that King Kong scowl on his face from the way he's roaring, "all you've got to do is find him and trail him. Let me know where he is, get it? Leave the rest up to me."

"Okay, Ormie," says Chester quick as he can. "Okay, anything you say."

Rilla snaps them off again and comes running over and grabs me by the arm.

"I'm scared of him," she says. "He's mean. Don't go out there, Bert. Go home. He'll calm down."

Those were my sentiments exactly, and if she'd let me alone I'd have done just that. But here I was put on my mettle by a woman.

"No," I said. What else could I say? "It would take a better man than that moron to scare me out." By God, for a minute I felt up to my own words.

I pulled her up against me and kissed her. It wasn't the best kiss in the world, I guess she was too upset to put her heart into it, but at least she didn't stop me. It's a good thing she wasn't too reciprocal with me right then because if she had been I think I'd probably have begun falling in love with her and that would have been a hell of a note.

I cruised up and down Foothill Boulevard, where nobody would be likely to look for me for the good and sufficient reason there isn't any business out here. They're not rich enough to not mind the money for a cab, and they're not poor enough to get a big boot out of riding in one. But about midnight a colored sailor hails me on the corner of Seminary; he's been up to Oak Knoll hospital where a friend of his was dying, and he wants to go to a place down on Fifteenth Street. Okay.

I avoid the main arteries as much as possible getting him there, but I hadn't any sooner than dropped the sailor and driven up a couple of blocks than I see a Spee-Dee cab leaning around the corner and heading straight down the block at me. Of course it may be one of a dozen but then it may be Ormie, and this is a damned dark street, Sixteenth or so down near Cypress, where the cops walk in pairs. He's coming like a bat out of hell, that's for sure, and I don't know his intentions. I would have had my radio on, only Rilla told me she was keeping me off the air so no one could find me. What I figured was, if this was Ormie he was going to block the street and try to grab me before I could back away. So just before he got to me I ducked up a double driveway onto the sidewalk. There wasn't anybody on it so I gunned her down to the corner, bumping on the driveways and walks and running over a toy that went pop, and dropped off the curb and got away without any trouble. But Ormie was trying so hard to catch me he swerved to hit me; he swerved too sharp and caught the rear fender of a parked car with the left corner of his front bumper; it tipped his cab over onto its right side. I laughed fit to kill as I drove away.

I didn't laugh long. As soon as the sirens began verging down there toward Ormie on his side, I began to get riled. When I passed a prowl car with its red lights winking I really got mad. It could have been for me. In fact it had been supposed to be for me. By God, thinks I to myself, that Ormie and his stooge Chester, who do they think they are? They think they can scare me off, do they?

It was twelve thirty and Rilla quit at one. I was supposed to stay on till two, but I drove straight to the garage and told Rilla to close up for the night. She didn't even argue a minute. She just said Ormie wasn't hurt bad and came along. When I told her what he was trying to do when he got hurt, she got so worried and upset that I had to quit being mad and try to kid her out of it. Besides, it had its humorous side all right, and I like to laugh as a rule. So by the time we'd had a couple of drinks in a place called the Bar None, she was over being scared and I was over being mad and we were both laughing, all keyed up like.

Rilla had such a throaty, hearty laugh it was a pleasure to watch her throw her head back and let her rip. In fact, in about fifteen minutes with her, she was so friendly and sexy and full of fun it just slipped out of my mind the run-around she'd given me two nights before. I kept her laughing. I told her about my grandmother that used to hear angels sing, and used to hit me on the head with her ear trumpet when she got mad, and died at ninety-seven. I told her how my brother and I ran away from home when we were about ten and a bull chased us to the top of a haystack where we had to sleep all night till the farmer came and rescued us. I had plenty of stories for her and she liked them. When she began wanting to hold hands again, I began to get real wrought up. I couldn't believe, holding her hand under the table and listening to her laugh and feeling her roll over against me once in a while, that she was only flirting with me. All the same, I avoided the direct approach.

I told her a story that happened to me when I was playing with Charlie Shaw's Chanticleers. It was a slow evening in a night club, and I'd tickled the vocalist with my trombone slide in the middle of a number so she'd jumped and taken a pratfall. She'd gotten so mad she'd started a free-for-all and Charlie had fired me.

Rilla laughed, but not too much. "You're kidding me," she said. "You never played with Charlie Shaw, did you?"

"You're darned tootin'," I said. "For two years. I made 'Smoke Gets in Your Eyes' with his outfit. Best record he ever made."

"Don't kid me," she said.

"Who's kidding who?"

"Why did you quit?"

"It's a rough life." I shrugged and spread my hands out. "The war came along. Look, I'll get that record on the juke box."

They had one of those machines in the Bar None where you put in a coin and tell a woman, who has hundreds of records to choose from, which one you want. I'd had her play Shaw's rendition of "Smoke" before, but this time she said she didn't have it any longer. She had five other recordings of it though, wouldn't one of them do?

I was pretty sad. But I didn't want to show it. If I looked hard enough I could find a copy of it in some secondhand store in town, but I wanted it right now for Rilla. That was bum luck.

"Too bad," I said when I sat down in the booth beside her, "they broke the record. It's a collector's item."

"Oh," she said, really sympathetic, "that's a dirty shame."

"That's the way the ball bounces," I said and laughed, sort of.

Then, by God, she did something I couldn't figure out. She took me and pulled my head down on her shoulder and patted me like I was a baby. I can't say I didn't like it.

"Say," I said, "Rilla, I've got that record. You want to hear it?"

"Where?" she said.

"Not too far," I said. "I just live a few blocks away."

I don't know what came over her to fall for a gag as old as that. I figured she'd changed her mind about me, or else she was drunker than I thought.

"Sure," she said, only not sexy any more, "sure, Bert." Not sexy at all; in fact, she sounded like she was talking to a baby.

She kept patting my leg while I was driving to my place. When I stopped the car, I guess I was drunk because I sort of flopped over with my head in her lap. She took advantage of me, and rubbed my head and kept calling me Bertie in such a way that I couldn't tear myself away, but I really resented it, lying there enjoying myself like that. You give a woman an inch and she'll take all you've got.

When I had her in my room with the door closed behind her, and turned on the light so she could see I didn't have a record player or a record even, or nothing but a chair and a bed, I really felt good for a minute. If Chester's home yet, thinks I to myself,

I've won my ten bucks. So I kissed her first thing, which was like kissing a corpse.

"Where's the record, Bertie?" she said.

I started to laugh, but I saw tears in her eyes and it wasn't funny. "I don't have it any more."

So what does she do? Does she yell at me or hit me or run out or laugh at me or freeze up and order me to take her home or anything you'd expect? No. She lies down on my bed with her face to the wall and doesn't make a sound. Here she is, at bay like, and she doesn't fight or anything. She just lies down as much to say, Kill me if you want to. What satisfaction is there in that, I ask you? She wasn't even going to let me leave her go in peace. In fact, her dress was riding up above her stockings in one place, and I was so embarrassed for her I pulled it down. She was so helpless that I couldn't do a thing, and naturally I thought she couldn't be dangerous. I thought she'd given up. I went over to make some coffee on the hot plate.

I was quite a while at it because I wanted to give her a chance to pull herself together. I heard her stirring a little on the bed and I felt better. But when I turned around with the cups in my hands, there she was reading something. I got close enough to see it was a letter, and then I recognized the handwriting. It was a letter from my wife I had left under the pillow. She didn't write often, and I'd just got it the day before. She always signed them upside down.

Dear Bert,

Yesterday the candy came that you sent and it was all eaten up in an hour everybody liked it so much I only had three pieces to myself but two of them had cherries. I felt so good I fixed myself up a little when we went to the movies last night and Dr. Smardon said I was looking very attractive. I didn't know where to look when he said that and after the show Winnie Stuart told me I was better looking than the movie star herself even, that was Ava Gardner.

She meant it too because she told somebody else and they told me she told them. Of course she's a Capricorn.

I just thought you might like to know.

Your wife,
Celia L.

Well, when I saw Rilla had read it, I was so mad I spilled the coffee putting it down. I grabbed the letter from her hand so hard it tore. I really hated her then. "Get out," I said. "Goddamn you, get out." I could have hit her too. I hadn't looked at her I hated her so much, but when she didn't even stir I looked at her face. She was crying and looking at me.

"I'm sorry," she said. "I wouldn't have done it if I'd known. I wouldn't have done it for worlds."

"But you've done it," I said. "I don't want to see you any more."

"I was just evening things up," she said.

"Now they're even—so get."

"You had no right to trick me to come here."

"So I didn't," I said, "so get going."

I'll say this for her, she had a lot of poise. She sat up and fixed her face so she'd look presentable and adjusted her clothes, not sexily but just put them in place, and then she said in a very dignified way, "You will drive me home, Bert."

Two minutes before if she'd said that I'd have felt like kicking her downstairs, but now she'd won me over again, and I said okay, I'd drive her home.

She hadn't any more than got her hand on the knob than we could hear somebody climbing the stairs and whistling in a special way, "Do not forsake me, O my darling."

"Wait a minute," she whispered.

He let himself into his room, next door of course, still whistling. Rilla looked at me puzzled.

"It's Chester," I whispered. I thought it was only a grim joke so I wasn't in the least prepared for what she did next. She turned white as a ghost.

"He could have heard me," she whispered. She looked at me. I nodded. "He would have told Ormie." Her eyes got big. She really looked betrayed, and I never felt like such a heel in my life. "You knew it too."

She didn't say a word all the way home, and she wouldn't let me walk her from the car up to her door. I waited a good minute for her to let herself in the apartment house, but she seemed to just be standing there all hunched over. I went up to find out what was the matter, and when I saw she was crying and her hand was trembling so hard she couldn't fit the key into the lock, I just plain loved her.

"Rilla," I said, "Rilla—goddamn it all, honey."

So I hugged her and kissed her tears away, and she shivered for a while up against me. This time when I kissed her it was a real kiss—a real, real kiss, and the way she leaned back and looked at me I thought probably she loved me too. I was afraid for a minute she was going to talk, which would have been a mistake at a time like that, but she didn't.

The only time I've seen her since was in a restaurant where I heard her laugh in a booth toward the rear. It warmed me up to hear her, and I started to go back to say hello. It had been a couple of months and there didn't seem to be anything she'd done which was particularly unforgivable any more. But then I saw her batting her eyes up at some zootie character with a goatee, and I changed my mind and went back by my lonesome to my hamburger steak.

Better to Burn

1

FEBRUARY 19.

I have the suspicion that I am driven to take up my pen by womanish cowardice. It comes to me sidewise whispering that I dare not follow to its end the straight way I have taken, that I stop instead at the furthest extreme of the ordinary, still in bounds. I fear that these many words will serve only to bewilder my heart, in its sickness, into believing it is whole again and well.

I should be ashamed to linger to death when I might have burst like a star.

But if I do not reduce the whirl of my mind to some sort of order I shall go mad of it; the least I can do is to understand the laws that govern the whirl's fury; I may go under, but it will not be from the boredom of watching the same impure notions whirl and whirl and mean nothing. I have lain for twelve days in the box of this room, and all I have learned is that the man on the other side of the wall gets up at 6:45 and that oatmeal is best if you cook it for two or three hours. I have memorized the procession of my whirl, and I have scratched myself when I itched, and that's that.

The truth is, I thought I had buried myself in this stucco tomb, this Oakland motel, either to die or to gather the strength for going back to life. But I have done neither. I have spun between till I can spin no longer. Because I am too cowardly to help myself die, I must crawl back out into life again.

FEBRUARY 20.

Another truth is, I get pleasure from this difficult putting of words together. One tires of oatmeal.

FEBRUARY 21.

I must start at the beginning; everybody knows you must start at the beginning. But I do not know where the beginning is.

FEBRUARY 22, Washington's birthday.

Happy man! He was the beginning of something and he knew it. Well, I was the first woman business agent in UPA 32. Maybe I could begin there.

But politics have nothing to do with what I am looking for. I have devoted the best years of my life to left-wing politics; it was all irrelevant.

The father of his country wore false teeth. Where is he now?

FEBRUARY 23.

I try to run the rabbit down; but there are swarms of rabbits, they proliferate as I chase them. Worse, their warrens are all connected below ground. At least they seem to be. I chase my feelings about Lloyd into their holes and follow them as best I can—and discover myself in my tenth year shouting at my mother that I will never wear Mary Janes again no matter what. I try to describe my physical appearance, and find myself envying the Greeks who could make sense of the outsides of people as I cannot. I set out to describe the house where I was born, and discover myself suddenly in the maze of History.

Perhaps my whole quest is for the beginning. Perhaps I should seize on anything and work back as I can. I am not a map maker. I shall have got where I am going only when I have discovered the point from which I should have started.

FEBRUARY 24.

I slept sixteen hours, from seven last evening until eleven this morning, not being sleepy, and woke exhausted from incessant dreaming. I remember nothing of what I dreamt, and the left side of my face was slashed with white wrinkles from having pressed so long against the pillow. I can concentrate just long enough at a time to keep my nails trimmed.

FEBRUARY 25.

This journal is of no help. It goes round and round stirred, like my dreams, by the whirl of my mind. I must do something.

There was a figure about millstones of tedium, a mill of boredom, the fatigues of ennui, the great creaking coarse stones of the tedious, which I have been trying to fit into what I am saying; but I cannot get it into any shape. I have sat for three hours on a straight wooden motel chair trying to shape this notion into something expressive. I cannot hold the idea in my mind long enough to do it.

FEBRUARY 26.

Nine years ago today, about five miles north of here, I was married, by a justice of the peace.

I should have married oftener.

FEBRUARY 27.

It is cold weather. If I run the gas heater the room stinks: everyone has the right to an air-conditioned tomb. If I lie in bed for warmth, sleeping or waking I have dreams. I'm being driven back to life. All I need is a way to get out of here.

FEBRUARY 28.

Whirl is king.

MARCH 1.

What I have against the whirl is that it is all present. There is no past any more. My dead parents and the first man I went to bed with proceed in my flat, gray parade exactly like, and equal to, the smell of oatmeal in this room, unordered, in a useless present, unjudgeable. I cannot live without a sense of the ways in which the past differs from the present; otherwise the samenesses between them mean nothing.

Without a past there can be no judging.

Without judging there can be no choice.

Without choice there can be no future.

Without a future I have two alternatives, the Now of the senses and the Always of death. Perhaps my solution is death by way of the senses.

This is the logic of too much whirling present. It is no beginning.

MARCH 2.

Today I have something to talk about. I don't think the event is of any importance, but at least it has set my blood to circulating again.

I was lying in bed at ten thirty this morning memorizing the pattern of the wallpaper. It has trim, epicene youths blowing clarions, alternating with pastel pumpkins. How well I know them! Yet a week after I leave this place I am sure I will not be able to recollect these figures. They are the sort of things that come into your mind months later while the lumpen waitress in a bare café is telling you about her hay fever. I was lying on my right side facing in from the windows, trying to decide to get up. There was nothing to do after I had got up. Still, it is shameful to stay in bed all day doing nothing. The clarion blowers, they of the flirting jackets and the saucy buttocks, shamed me.

Solid, female footsteps approached, and someone rapped solidly on my door. I had paid my rent for a week in advance. I paid it when the woman brought clean sheets and towels. We communicate through the half-opened door. She has never bothered me. Once a boy came offering to wash my car for fifty cents. Once a drunk at the wrong door. That was all. The woman of these footsteps was different from those others; it was obvious from the way she walked and knocked.

I think the only reason I answered was to shock her with my appearance. My face was creased and puffy, my hair was wild, my nightgown was soiled, and my feet were bare. It was Anna. She was shocked.

"My dear!" she cried in a strangling sort of voice.

I too was astonished. "How did you ever find me, Anna?"

My voice must have been as wild as my appearance, harsh with resentment and disuse.

"Oh Julia," she said, "you must help me."

I was prepared to slam the door in her face, but I noticed that she had extended her hand in through the opening—as though in appeal and kindness but really to keep me from closing the door. Besides, her bogus appeal to me to help her aroused my curiosity more than my suspicions. She could not possibly need my help, so what did she mean? I stood staring down at her.

"Let me in," she said. She was standing on the step, the wind whipping her coat about her legs. "We can't talk like this."

"You didn't answer my question," I said. "How did you find me?"

"Oh Julia." There were tears in her eyes. "I am cold."

I stood for a moment longer looking at these tears, which were probably bogus too. But I was not sure they were bogus; it is hard to know about Anna, who does not know about herself. The wind was cold on my legs. I stepped back, and went over to turn the steam radiator on.

"Just don't cry," I said. "I can't stand crying. I only cry in my sleep."

I don't know why I said this last. I had not intended to. I had intended to keep myself strictly removed from whatever she talked about. But I was out of practice. Except for my three unimportant callers, I hadn't talked for two weeks to anyone but the enemies in my dreams. I glanced at Anna to see if she was going to use this advantage I had given her; but she was very smooth—she seemed not to have heard me. I got back in bed and lay watching her.

In ten minutes she had aired out the place, emptied the ashtrays, emptied the garbage, hung up my clothes, straightened the bathroom, and put coffee on to percolate in a clean pot. I cannot say I didn't like it. I cannot honestly say either that I didn't enjoy the smooth job of chattering that went with it—smooth if a little forced.

She began telling me about her boys and about the pneumonia she had just got over, and about my poor complexion, and even about political matters. She was very clever—she tried to choose precisely those topics which would interest but not arouse me. It was only gradually that I became aware of how she was getting behind my guard—by answering every family question I might have asked, by taking my side in issues that concerned me, by leaving me myself pretty much out of it. But by the time she had poured the coffee for both of us, smiling knowingly over my fondness for sugar, I had aroused myself.

"You said you wanted my help. What can I do for you?"

Her equanimity was disturbed by my coldness, but not for long.

"It's just this, dear. Beverley would so like to know the address of your friend Lloyd, and I told her I would find out from you next time I saw you."

I confess I was nonplussed. Not by an inflection did she suggest that I was reprehensible to be forcing my own daughter to get in touch with me through her aunt, and in order to get the address of her mother's lover. Not by an inflection, yet I knew she thought it was vile of me. I thought it was vile myself, but I could not let Anna know this.

"What does she want to know for?"

"He sent ten dollars to her at school as a birthday present and she insists on returning it. The letter was postmarked Memphis, Tennessee, but there was no return address."

"I don't know his address," I said, staring at her unblinking. "I didn't even know he was in Memphis. Tell Beverley to give the ten bucks to the Community Chest. I'm sleepy," I said turning over on the bed away from her. "Leave me alone."

Not even Anna, now that her excuse for having bothered me had been used up, could persevere after that. She put her hand on my shoulder so warmly I almost touched her in farewell. She is sentimental beyond belief. But I stuck to my guns and did not move till she had closed the door. Her footsteps diminished solidly down the walk.

It occurred to me that she had not told me how she had found me. I yelled after her, "Anna, Anna, how did you find out where I was staying?" But she did not hear me, and it wasn't important enough for me to go running out after her in my nightgown.

I took a shower, and spent hours fixing my nails. I am not sure what I should do. I am almost certain she will come back.

2

MARCH 4.

On the third night of March I slept well. I do not know how many weeks it has been since I last had a good night's sleep. In these past weeks I have slept as much as twelve to fourteen hours for night after night, and have awakened as fatigued as though I had been working in a factory. More fatigued, because I had nothing to look forward to after the night shift but a different sort of fatiguing, the weariness of waking. I would wake feeling that I was not all there, not completely myself; as though some strangling part of myself had been oppressing me all night, had forced me to an exhausting defense, and now that I was awake had gone off to some dark place—with what malignant motive?—to wait till I was too weak again to hold him off. Yet last night I slept a whole person, not on guard against my strangler because he was sleeping too. All my circuiting thoughts, racing about the elaborate orbits they have devised for themselves, going nowhere ever faster, stopped. All night they stopped. The muscles of my throat are free and at ease; last night they did not constrict with crying or shouting, or worse, with restraint of crying or shouting. In a word, I slept.

I read this over, and am ashamed of myself. It sounds as though I have been reading one of those magic mystics full of big cloudy theories and fine Latin terms, say Paracelsus or Jung. All this does not become a materialist. Yet that is how I feel, and I take it I would do well to find out what I am actually feeling before I try to judge it or correct it. A theory about things prevents you from seeing the things as (you think) they are. This is obviously true of others, say Christians. Maybe it is true of me as well. Which, I suppose, is another way of saying I no longer know what I believe.

But then—I will begin with the event. I did sleep well last night. Why?

Because Anna aroused me two days ago. Stirred me to some sort of action.

Because I got some exercise yesterday packing up and driving down here to the ocean.

Because I was within sound of the breakers.

Because I said in a loud clear voice last evening on the beach, "I will never do anything for any member of my family again."

So what?

Two weeks from now I'll be right back where I was, only lower. I'll be flat broke, and not even Anna will be able to find me here.

My God, where is the beginning?

MARCH 5.

Still nothing.

I did not even go out and walk by the sea, today, but lay in bed.

MARCH 6.

I am going to take my own advice and quit looking for some way to organize my confusion. That, I think, is one of my troubles, too much organization. I thought, or tried to think, like a Marxist for so long that I am looking now for a dialectic for unhappiness. In the depths of my sadness, in the recesses of my swirling sleep which is no sleep, I have known that the reasoning part of my brain was never quiet but was clicking away: thesis—antithesis; the graver my distress, the faster it clicked. Around and around, like a calculating machine set to divide 100 by 7 and never stopped: 14.2857142857142 . . . For there was no synthesis. I would give up all I have, the Party, Lloyd, Beverley, just for the security of knowing that my feeling and my knowing were a part of the same whole.

A vain sacrifice, since I've left the Party, lost Lloyd, and neglected Beverley. Perhaps the security I think I want is a vanity like the sacrifice.

No more of this morbidity. Logic is a snake with its tail in its mouth.

MARCH 7.

I am sitting in a sort of diminutive wing chair writing on my lap. The alternative is to sit at the kitchen table, which is a board hinged to the wall; but it is covered with the remains of my lunch—oatmeal, honey, canned milk, coffee, and raisins. The room is small, and proportioned like a box. It is stuccoed, and heated by one of those panel-ray businesses. The bed is unexceptional, reasonably comfortable with a sway on the side next the bathroom, where heavy people have sat scratching and yawning in the morning and put on their shoes; the head- and footboards are sheet iron painted to look like mahogany panels. There is a hook rug on the floor—the homey touch. The bathroom has a shower, and about two dozen clothes hooks. The cooking stove is electric, and where you expect the oven to be is a small refrigerator. According to the bill I read when I rented the place, there are seventeen kitchen utensils, dishware, etc. I have not counted them. There are cream-colored Venetian blinds at the windows, and outside the west window, on the other side of a parking area, is the pounding sea.

Now what do I know? What question am I posed by these articles of knowledge, these outsides of things, their conjunction here and now?

Wisdom, I was told, is asking the right question at the right time. I shall press on. Maybe the question will occur to me.

I am thirty-six years old, five feet seven inches tall, and I am usually a little overweight. I am physically strong, but not masculine looking. I have always enjoyed the employment of my body. My face, like my figure, is usually called striking rather than beautiful. My hair is my best point. I enjoy brushing it, and I enjoy having it praised. I have never felt that praise of my hair was praise of me, but I have learned that other people, men that is, do not make this distinction. Lloyd never praised anything about me but my hair and my work as a business agent; yet he loved me. I have rather too much hair on my body and limbs for modern taste; I scorn to shave it off, as I scorn to pretend that I do not sweat. I have all my teeth. I have a sort of birthmark behind my left ear.

What then?

How antique *wisdom* sounds.

All the while I have been writing about these outsides, I have been wanting to describe an unimportant memory. My formal analysis gets me nowhere; neither will this anecdote, but at least I'll enjoy writing it.

The morning two months ago when I woke up knowing I had to leave Lloyd, I turned over to look at his face on the pillow next to me, and found him already awake and gazing at me. Just before I was going to speak, he reared up on his elbow, pulled my hair very hard for a moment, and said in a flat voice, "I'm getting out." We were strangers. I could not look at him any longer. I dressed in the bathroom with the door shut so he should not see me, and sat in the kitchen while he packed his suitcases. I stood by the doorway as he left, hoping he would not kiss me. Nor did he. He wanted to go without a word, but I could see he felt that would not quite do. He put down one suitcase, gathered the hair at the nape of my neck in his hand, and pulled it again. Involuntarily I leaned my head against his hand. "I'm leaving town," he said. The last thing I said to him was, "The car's in your name." He shrugged as he walked down the hall, and was gone.

MARCH 8.

I awoke in the black of the night—there are no city lights in the sky here but only stars, which are not enough—and I found my fingers lost in the cool reaches of the sheets; I drew them back beside me, and quieted them. They paid no attention to me when I told them Lloyd was gone, but lay obedient only because I was awake. I told them, He is gone, gone far away, I made him go, I don't know where he is, he won't come back, all gone. Yet I was not asleep before I found them slipping out again, like women onto a battlefield, to look for the hard still body of their love.

I had not realized I missed him. I drove him off, for I hated him. I did not even like him, he is a sort of lout, and I was glad to see him go. And yet today I feel that if I were with him again I would be well again. He is my health. Why did I drive him away?

I must not think about it, or I will not sleep again. Where is he? I shall never be able to find him. I must put him out of my mind.

MARCH 9.

I was walking in dejection on the beach today, climbing over the rocks, feeling the cold spray on my skin. Yet not completely in dejection either; I think I could never be completely dejected by the sea. There is some excitement in it which has nothing to do with happiness or misery. It makes me feel that I am living, experiencing, being, more intensely than I usually am. Yet that is not right either. It's not that I feel the usual emotions more intensely, but that what I feel is some power within me like the power of the sea. It is not a human sort of power, so I do not have human feelings about it. It is greater than I, more than human, and it goes on and on so long as I am by the sea; a sort of boring ecstasy. Yet along with it one can feel happy, or dejected as I felt today thinking of my family.

My family. I know I am part of it, yet this knowledge has no reality for me. I do not even know the names of my great-grandparents, and if I did I would have no sense of them. Grandparents, parents, brother and sister, child, all are strangers, accidents surrounding me like this motel. And like this motel they were not long before me and will not be long after me.

I have no past, I am my own present, I shall never be anyone else's past. I am particular and therefore inscrutable. I am alone and I hate it. I have more in common with the surf than with my own daughter.

Yet what a skein of family entangles me. It is from Anna that I am escaping now, though to a better thing than Oakland. It is

Beverley who ties me to the world, so that I mailed her a letter yesterday against my better judgment; I love her, stranger though she is. The bleating sheep I bludgeon in my dreams has my mother's face.

I push my way through these family, struggling toward a shadowy figure in the form of Lloyd, in which is contained all I want. But they close behind me, and deceive me, so that when I approach Lloyd, I no longer want him.

Yet the sea is mine. It they have not touched.

My brother has not touched it, who would devise some wrong, substantial metaphors for it. Nor my father, who would stake the tides and count the comings of the moon. Nor my sister, who would call it pretty, or worse, inspiring. It's mine, quite mine, mine to see as I will and to mean what I will and not to be if I will.

One image of the sea stays in my mind from my walk today. A long line of breaker heaved itself up, like a shrug of will flexing itself in the exuberance of its own power—one of those breakers slightly translucent and with its undersurface a sheer bending plane veined with foam, enormous, jade green, taloned. And at its perfect height I saw—immobile, slanting a little to the right of vertical, pure of form—the dark outline of a fish. The wave crashed to froth and the fish was thawed from its moment's freezing; no one saw it but me; it has occurred countless times before and will occur countless times again; yet it exists only in my memory and shall cease to exist when I will.

There is so much of the sea that I can do with it what I will. I can make or change, rejoice in it or hate it, destroy it; and yet there will always be all of it left. It is safe for me. It does not care.

MARCH 10.

I woke up last night in tears. I had been dreaming. I dreamed that I was walking with a friend, a woman who seemed to be somewhat older than I. We were walking in a very large public square such as one sees in paintings of Paris; this one was called La Place de la Vie. The buildings were old, rococo, dingy and tall; they were identical on every side of the square. I became aware after a time of a disturbance in the center of the Place. It had been going on for a long while before I noticed what it was. There was a high wall running for perhaps two hundred yards down the center of the Place. In the middle of the wall was a gate, but the ends of the wall were not attached to any buildings; my friend and I had been walking past the ends of it freely. Yet, on one side of the gate the most recent girls were clamoring to be let in and on the other side of the gate the most recent boys were clamoring to be let in, and each group was pushing with hard but equal force on its side of the gate so that neither could get what they both wanted. None of them thought of walking around one end of the wall and joining hands freely in the clear spaces. When I became aware of this absurd situation, I began to laugh wildly. My friend was weeping, but she tried to console me. She took me by the arm and helped me over to a bench under a tree, saying in a quieting but sobbing voice, "That's all right, my dear, they're already in, that's all right, you don't need to laugh any more." Yet when I woke up, it was I—I in the bed in the motel—I and not my anonymous friend who was crying.

I am not myself even in my own dreams.

MARCH 11.

Last night the black dog sat outside my window again, staring between the slats in at me. He has snuffled his way along my trail from that stucco motel at the edge of Oakland to this stucco motel at the edge of the sea. It has taken him a long time to get here. And now I shall be afraid not to sleep for hours upon hours every day, and all night: the moment I acknowledge by so little as a gesture or a glance that I know he is there, I am at his mercy. He will violate me. I am afraid he will come back.

MARCH 12.

Sleep.

MARCH 13.

I am alarmed at myself. Today, at three in the afternoon, by the purest act of will, I dragged myself from bed, made coffee, ate cold oatmeal, and dressed. I had a ferocious headache, and my joints operated just well enough to keep me from falling into a heap. I had to keep myself by main strength of will from going back to bed. I was not capable of walking along the cliffs. What was I to do?

I read over this journal. At least it revived me.

Two things struck me about it. One is that in a way I am not as bad off as I sometimes think I am. In what I have written there is almost always, I feel, some note of mockery at myself. There is always some hard, sharp-toothed, indestructible little laughter left in me. He got me out of bed today. I am glad of him.

But the other thing that struck me is that I am worse off than I ever think. What is all this stuff I get wound up in about quests and the whirl and fingers that crawl around by themselves? I know better than that. It's morbid self-indulgence. I can too easily allow myself to think in such mad vivid ways, and I always justify myself by saying that nothing is really what it seems to be. I must think of things as they are.

And the main thing that is, I know now, is Lloyd.

3

MARCH 14.

I am thankful that I did not know Lloyd before I had left Sid, for if I had left Sid because of him I might never have been sure of the purity of my love for him. But I left Sid because he was Sid, and I went to Lloyd because he was Lloyd, and the two were never mixed up at all.

I had known for years who he was, had seen him around, known he was a person of some importance locally in union politics. I had not liked him much then, from what I saw of him; he was arrogant and uncouth and paid no attention to me. But after I had become business agent for the UPA and had been a delegate at the Alameda County CIO Council for a while and had served on some committees with him and we had felt each other out, it finally dawned on us one night that we loved one another.

We had both arrived at a committee meeting—without previous arrangement—about a quarter of an hour early. The room was of medium size, dusty and not well lighted. There were a couple of gaudy old union banners on one wall and a photograph of President Roosevelt in his younger days on the other. The windows were seldom opened. We talked for five minutes with great animation about how bad fluorescent lights were on the eyes; we fell silent; I stood up as though to go over to the bookcase; he stood up; we looked at each other for a moment, with mutual desire; and we kissed. I knew immediately, from the strength of his embrace and the assurance of his arms about me, that this was no frivolous pass on his part. I knew from my own profound disturbance at this one kiss—a somewhat awkward one at that, in which I was conscious of his jawbone pressing against my chin —that we were not just flirting with one another or with the possibility of a night or two of love-making. No, it went a long way down. I do not think I have ever been more excited, consciously, than I was for the next hour.

The rest of the committee came. Lloyd was chairman. We did two hours' work in less than one. It was easy, we let the other side win every time. It wasn't very important business—who the delegates to the state CIO convention should be. The five of us walked out of the building together. I left Lloyd on the sidewalk. All he said was, "See you later." Yet I had hardly got to my apartment when he rang the buzzer. I had not bothered to tell him my address, nor was my number listed in the telephone directory. I had simply known that by then he would have found out where I lived, and he had. He did not say very much, no wooing and smooth words, but I could feel his knees trembling. He took no delight, as some men do, in undressing me or seeing me undress. He wanted me naked in bed, and there he had me soon enough. Before we went to sleep, we made love three times, like gods perfectly.

Our bodies have always been like gods—captious, beautiful, powerful, maggoty, always right. Yet, if there are dozens of ways of loving physically, there must be hundreds of emotional ways, all of which but one we used and knew. Which one is the final trust—the trust of giving yourself up finally to another, or to something through another. It must be true that there is such a last way of loving; it was what we were after in all our positions. Our kissing mouth to mouth was a praying: *Surely we are one: who were surely two.*

Well, we settled down to being lovers; that's what it amounted to, though it was several months before we admitted it to ourselves. Not that we were skittish: we slept together as often as we wished. But we did not talk to each other in lovers' language. I said that he was my petcock, what kept me from exploding. He couldn't say anything about love at all, not for months; just "My God, my God, how I want you" or "What hair, what beautiful hair." Instead, he kneaded me. Almost for hours on end, he would rub and bend and knead my body. A sort of amorous naprapathy. At first I thought he did it because he knew that I liked it. But that was not the reason, at least not much of it. The truth was that the strength of his feeling for me struck him dumb —he didn't even know what to call it, though he finally settled for "love"—so that he had to handle me, to discover if he could the potent mystery my flesh contained. Once he said that he would have got into me if he could: "I wish I could put you on." And though this did not affect me at the time, I have sometimes longed to be able to take into me more of him than I can. He will never have had me completely until I completely have him.

I write in the future tense. But he has gone off I do not know where. I drove him off, and when he left I knew I would never see him again. I know that for me there is nothing left of him, except memory and understanding memory. I know it, but I don't believe it. For it was not Lloyd I loved but the daemon in him. The daemon I still love, and he the daemon in me. Our daemons will see to it that we meet again.

They're in no hurry. Their time is not as our time. Perhaps time is irrelevant to them, as it is to gravitation. They are irresistible.

There is not a great deal more to be said about our love affair. There were five years of it between the first uneasiness and the break. We tried to cut it off many times. We became expert at lying. We were unfaithful to each other, without joy and with much shame. We assumed the all-but-one stances of love; and as our fear that we would never learn the final one grew upon us, our asseverations of love grew solemn and huge. And false, utterly false, for what does the vocabulary of Oaklanders have to do with the loves of daemons? But our bodies were always right and we knew it.

I doubt if we would ever have changed, really, if I had not done what I did two months ago. We would never have got married, I am sure. We talked about it sometimes, or rather I talked about it. Lloyd always said it wasn't for him, he'd tried it once; I never made much of the issue. The truth is, we should not even have tried living together. Love is the stronger for being secret and fitful. Anyway, we bored one another.

We developed an odd custom after we had lived together awhile during this past year. We could never get to sleep if we were touching at any point. It became our last ritual after we had said goodnight to lie on our backs side by side, his left arm and my right one stretching down the center of the bed between us like blades. After a few minutes of this we could turn over on our sides, facing away from each other, and go to sleep.

There is nothing important left to think about now but why I did what I did.

But I am very tired. It is three o'clock in the morning and I have earned a rest. Not that I didn't sleep enough yesterday. But I feel that today I have done something. I am better off than I was. *It's three o'clock in the morning*—that reminds me of the sentimental song they used to sing when I was a child. *We've danced the whole night through*—that was supposed to suggest all sorts of high living and dark wickedness. Could they have been so childish? What I have done, what I am, is wickeder than they could imagine, they haven't even a place for it on their spectrum, just bottomless black.

MARCH 15.

I got up at nine thirty, anxious to go on, as though I did not know what was coming next. But the truth is, that while I do know what happened, I don't know why it happened; and why is all that matters.

I have to go back to the week of my father's death. When Anna came by to tell me about the funeral Lloyd was furious. She found us at home after dinner and stayed half an hour; and however uncomfortable I felt, caught between her intrusiveness and Lloyd's wrathful silence, still I could not tell her to get out. I had promised—not promised, assured—Lloyd that I would get rid of her if she ever showed up again; but when I came right down to it, I couldn't demand that my sister go away and not tell me about the death of my father.

When she had left, Lloyd said, "I don't ever want to see her again." It was an order, and a cold order.

Now I did not want to see her again either. Nor was it my doing that she had come or that he had died. Yet when Lloyd gave me that superfluous order, I instantly emptied of all emotion except a dull resentment, a sort of dogged feeling that I would not obey him. It had been my decision to make, not his to make for me.

I poured a full cup of coffee and threw the contents of it straight at his face.

He was across the table from me, in a kitchen chair, watching me. When he saw it coming he leaned aside, easily and gracefully; he wiped the back of the chair with his napkin, and laughed at me. Now I am not given to throwing things, much less hot coffee at a man's face. And Lloyd had not been as rude as all that, no worse than often indeed.

I railed and shouted at him for half an hour. I emerged from my resentment and apathy flaming hot with anger, and said to him all the bitter and nasty things I had felt for years and been afraid to say. I said that he was selfish and cold, that he had never loved me but only used me because he needed me. I called him a bully and a coward, and reminded him of the time he had refused to let his pickets fight the cops; I said he had done it because he was afraid for his own skin (though I knew it was for discretion's sake). I called him depraved and debased and lazy. I said he had bad taste, and to prove it I looked around for something to smash. But I wanted to smash something that he liked and I did not. My eye fell on a table lamp he had given me, a phony antique with a long white bottle neck and with golden leaves embossed all over it; it seemed expendable. I threw it at him, but I had not unplugged the cord; my aim was deflected and the lamp fell onto the floor in bits. I said I hated him and loathed him. I said I wished he would die. But all the while that I was prancing and railing, I knew that I was not saying the right things. Either they were as true of me as of him, or else they were the meaningless extravagances of anger. No, what I knew I must do was to find the unforgivable thing to say and to say it as harshly as I could. I remember the pleasure I felt when I thought I had found it, the joy of leaning across the table toward him saying it in a cold clear voice. "You bore me. You are stupid and dull and an oaf. Talking with you is like cutting cork with a razor, tiresome and useless and dulling. You can't discriminate between ideas closer together than truth and winning, or beautiful and pleasing; and like a proper oaf you can't stand it that anyone else should try. 'Get something done,' you say, and go off to a meeting or take me to bed. Two things you know—how to run a union and that cats are not gray in the dark. That's something. But it's all." I stopped, thinking I had got down to the unforgivable itself. I remember the sense of danger I felt as I watched for his reaction. I felt that if he should take it I could never respect him again, but that if he should leave me I would not be able to live without him.

He had not said a word. Now he stirred himself. "Are you through?" he asked. I only glared at him. I could not wait to see what he would do—say nothing like a cowardly martyr, look hurt and make me apologize, just walk off like a pompous man, shout back, affect indifference. But I did not know him; I was judging him, as I have so often done, according to the standards of the other men I have known. Actually Lloyd has always been capable of surprising me and he surprised me now.

"You haven't said anything we haven't both known for a long time. All that stuff hasn't got anything to do with what's the matter with you now."

"Is that so? Well, what *is* the matter?" My rage was petering out. My words sounded silly in my own ears.

"I don't know, and I don't think I want to know. Go home for a few days. I'll come around when I want you again."

I had no idea what to do. My cannon had shot a pea; he was not leaving me, he was not taking it, he was only brushing me aside. I just looked at him awhile; I sank back into my chair. My anger drained away. Only a sadness was left; a new sort of sadness that I had not known before, the sadness that has driven me here by the sea now. I didn't care what I did. I thought that what he had told me to do was probably very sensible. I took some clothes and drove back to my apartment.

The next day at my father's funeral I cried. I cried, more or less, every day that week, waiting for Lloyd to come get me.

So I had said the unforgivable thing, and not so much had come of it after all. *It's what we'd both known for a long time.* Well, knowing such a thing is very different from saying it. Hypocrisy is six of the seven virtues in matters of love; the seventh is heat.

He came and got me, and we were strapping fine hypocrites for a while. But I had changed. I discovered that, for having said what we already knew, I was not to be forgiven after all: by Lloyd perhaps, but not by myself. I could no longer abandon myself to him, not even for the moment of love-making; I feigned it.

Within a week after I had gone back to live with him, everything I did was feigned. I could not get to sleep at night until I was sure he had already dropped off: he might strangle me, I felt, if I went to sleep first. I would pretend to be asleep, breathe deeply and regularly, perhaps make a sudden start with my legs, like one who has just dropped off. I do not forget the night I woke up not long after having gone to sleep myself, secure that he had dropped off, only to find him reared up on his elbow looking down on me, his hand already slipping over my shoulder. I nearly screamed with fear; he sank back and said I had been having a bad dream. But it became clear to me then that he had been outsmarting me; he had been outpretending me at my own pretense, and had caught me sound asleep. I would be safe only if I stayed awake all night on the watch.

So I did stay awake, all night every night. And by Christmas I had to quit my job at the plant so that I could sleep in the daytime. Yet, even as I would lie there beside him (was he asleep or awake?), I sometimes knew that I was being absurd and extravagant. If he wanted to strangle me, he would do it without all this rigmarole. I offered myself, in the course of the desultory monologues with which I filled the dark hours, every conceivable argument against doing what I was doing; leave him at least. None of it had the slightest effect on my actions.

I had done all the deeds of love so often, had said all the words, that now I had little enough trouble pretending. But finally I had to feign even the heat. Cold hypocrisy is very tiring; therefore one takes short cuts. One says I love you instead of giving all the circumstantial evidences of love: it's so much easier. One acquiesces in everything, becomes a slave and a flatterer: it comes so coldly.

As cold, as easy, as tired, is the flattered one, the slave's master, the false-beloved.

By January we were silent and restless with each other, except for the short-cut hypocrisies and exigent love-making. For as one by one every other reason for our staying together disappeared—common concerns, with work or politics, pleasure in each other's company, conversation, love—we forced the physical acts of love to assume burdens they could never bear. A wordless violent politics of flesh. Or perhaps an ethics of love: if you do good things, some say, finally you are filled with good; therefore, if I do love things, finally I am filled with love.

We had been excellent in our making love. Now it was without heat, and as we felt the cold creeping in we pushed our words and deeds to the shrieking limit. All our fine-edged instruments of passion on and on became husks, limbs, organs, mere laboring agents of will, abandoned temples, flesh empty to the brim with ferocious sense.

During these three or four weeks I could not fall asleep while in the same bed with him, but slept only after he had gone off. On weekends I scarcely slept at all. If he was with me I did not dare, and if he was away I was afraid he would return before I had awakened. I was losing weight; my face was sallow and spotty. Lloyd became so irritable he had to go out every evening I was home; he couldn't sit in a chair reading for ten minutes at a time. One night, Lloyd was not sleeping well. I lay quivering, overfatigued and nervous and full of dread, listening to his whimpers and starts. He sat up and said, out of his dream in a declaiming voice, "Let the fliers beware!" I was so terrified of him that I crept out to the kitchen, got the butcher knife, and held it in my hand down by my leg all night ready for him. Nothing happened. He had never hurt me physically. He never did.

On the evening of my birthday, January 12, we went out to dinner in the city, at Jack's, an old good restaurant. As we sat bored at the table waiting to be served our soup, I looked in the mirror across the room and saw the profile of a handsome man with a heavy sensual face and dark hair. His hand on the tablecloth was large and not appropriate to the businessman atmosphere of the restaurant. It was several seconds before I realized this man was Lloyd. When I turned to glance across the table at him, I felt a sudden little spasm of genuine affection for him.

"My dear," I said, and reached across the table to squeeze his hand, "your profile in the mirror was so handsome I didn't recognize you."

But this, which I meant, must have sounded falser than the feigned speeches, for he said in return—what I did not deserve—"Of course, dearheart. It's the profile I keep for special occasions like your birthday."

He had taken to calling me dearheart. I don't think there's a term of endearment that offends me more, unless it's lambie pie, which Sid started calling me once; I cut him off.

"Where shall we go after dinner?" Lloyd said, smiling at me.

"Wherever you'd like," I said.

"Oh no. It's your birthday, dearheart. You get to have anything you want."

But I hate to make decisions like this and he knew it. He had always been the one to decide what restaurants we should go to, what plays. There were a couple of movies I would have enjoyed seeing that night, or a play, or I would have liked to go to the night club where Louis Armstrong was playing. But since Lloyd was tormenting me like this, I decided to get even with him.

"Wait till we have our coffee," I said.

He touched my ankle with his, and we relapsed into our boredom.

At coffee, I did what we had often done before we had got used to each other, talked in conversational tones like any diners, about love-making.

"What I want to do," I said, "is go to the same hotel we went to the first time we spent the night together. Do you remember which it was?"

"We could find it. Is that all you want to do?"

I pretended to be hurt.

"Are you so tired of me, Lloyd?"

"My God, I thought we were going to have an outing."

"I'd rather have an inning."

He laughed, as though I'd cracked a fine joke.

"All right, dearheart. It's your birthday."

"There's nothing so new as the very old, you know."

So we went to our hotel again, a murky one in North Beach. It was rather exciting going into the place, and by chance we got the same room we had had five years before. Everything in the room was as it had been before, only shabbier.

We were keyed up. We were spoiling something by going back there.

I am unable to make myself write down some of our extravagancies. They were the truest desecration.

We heard the church bells strike midnight.

"Have you had a happy birthday?" he asked me in a gentle voice as though he meant it.

"Oh yes," I said, "the best ever. I have never been happier." I buried my face in his shoulder in shame at my lies. "My love, my lover, my wonderful wonderful body. Body I love. You will never die."

"Never die?" he said with a sort of animation. "Never die? We are dead already. Rotting." He lay on his back, rigid. I felt his forehead and it was, or seemed to me then, cold. "Kiss me," he said. "You will feel the slime."

It was no joke. I kissed him and I felt the slime. My God, but he was dead. And slime was mine too. The slimes of love. I lay as still as he, but my eyes were open. A terror held me. I did not know what was going to happen. Perhaps he would suck my blood as vampires must; but I was as much corpse as he. Perhaps, I thought, we had both some fatal disease and would die together. The thing to remember was, that we were bodies and dead.

He pulled his lips back as far as they would reach, exposing his white dead slimed teeth, grinning like a skull. I pressed my face against his neck that I might not have to look at him, and held him tight about the body that I might feel his warmth, and said, "Lloyd, Lloyd." But he did not stir. I drew my head back from his neck, laying it on his shoulder, and looked with one eye at his face; my other eye was pressed shut. But I was too close to him; his face was huge, and waxen like a polished apple, and masklike.

I think I fainted. The next thing I remember is standing at the door of the room, dressed to go out, looking at the body on the bed. It seemed dead to me. Wrapped about with my fears, I rushed out into the thronging night.

I peopled the night with my enemies. A woman standing at a bus stop had a submachine gun beneath her coat. Spies lay in ambush up every alleyway; I could hear their cracklings. A man in front of a bar had to clutch his hands behind his back to keep them from beating me. I saw a creature huddled inside its overcoat lying in a doorway, perhaps asleep, perhaps contagiously dead. It occurred to me that the body I had left on the bed in the hotel room looked dead because I had killed it.

And all the rest of that night, and all the next day, and until ten thirty the next evening when Lloyd came home, I stayed in our apartment dull and immobilized with the fear that I had killed him and left him there. I did not call his office for fear of giving myself away. All I could think about was that grinning death's head. Whatever I might be doing, lighting a cigarette, heating some canned soup, trying to read a magazine, staring—suddenly the memory of it would assault me and make me quiver along the very bone as with a high fever. The death's head has not left me yet; for last night it rang down my memory to me here where I am, as rings down a corridor of prison cells a howling from the dead of sleep.

I do not think I was quite sane that day till Lloyd came home. We said almost nothing but how did it go today? and how about a glass of beer before going to bed? It was the next morning that I awoke to find him already awake and looking at me. I had slept that night, out of pure fatigue, I suppose. Or maybe it was that I had nothing left to fear from him. He told me he was getting out and he got out and here I am.

4

MARCH 17.

Yesterday I went mad again. I think that if it happens once more I shall not be able to come back. Anna had to drag me back as it was.

I was mad for a couple of days after Lloyd walked out on me, with the madness of exaltation. Because of such madnesses angels were thought of. It is very fine up there, finest of all is forgetting that devils wait for you in the madness below the bottom.

When Lloyd left, I was free. I walked through a door that wasn't there, straight out of time and doing into eternity and the rules of doing—out of loving *you* into Love, out of the world of streetcars and grandfathers into truth, out of what is and was and will be into the whatness itself. But I found it a chilly world and very glaring. I came back before long, and closed the door behind me. I think I caught a cold there which I am only now shaking off, having caught something worse where I was yesterday.

There is another way out of time and doing: into the freeze of fear. Yesterday I was there again.

The whole trick is to stay within the sequence of events. The danger is that you may cease to love, and so yourself become a sequence of events like a character in a naturalistic novel. Anna seems to know the trick. I must ask her how she does it, how to love by the clock.

Yesterday I awoke early, refreshed and easy in my mind. The day before, I had walked for an hour or so by the sea. Tired, and full of the feel of the waves, I slept well the night before last. When I awoke, I lay on the bed listening to the foghorn miles away and the breakers at the foot of the cliff below me. I could smell the fog and the sea, and the air was cool on my arms outside the covers. My belly rumbled with hunger—a considerable event since I had not been conscious of hunger for a long time; I had stoked my stomach at regular intervals as a hired man stokes the furnace of a house which does not belong to him but in which he rooms. This morning, feeling good, I wished I had something better than raisins and oatmeal to eat. My scalp itched, and I had the urge to wash my hair. I stretched, a full, indulgent stretch, and yawned. But in my stretching and yawning, I had turned toward the window, and I had come to know that the black dog was staring in between the slats at me again.

It was not fair. I lay on my side half curled up, the covers half off me, facing the window but not daring to look at it; and I thought to myself: It is not fair, I have earned a respite. As I lay there, having to disguise my actions and the expressions on my face, I worked at a couple of blackheads on my left knee. Cunning at their task, the muscles of my face held my face, and would hold it so long as I was being watched, in a mask of ease. And all the while I was saying behind the mask: It is not fair, I have come very far for a little rest, I have no more strength.

But the breeze was cold on my skin, and my blackheads were soon enough squeezed. I got up, put on my robe, turned on the heater, and closed the other windows (not the one facing the sea), washed my face in a rag so that I might weep safely for five seconds, and stoked my stomach. Then I washed my hair, not because I wanted to but because I had wanted to once. After that there was nothing I wanted to do, and nothing I could remember having wanted to do. Furthermore, though it was still early morning, I was exhausted. As I sat in front of the heater fluffing my hair, my arms were so weary I could scarcely keep them from falling into my lap. But I forced them to their task till my hair was quite dry. I could not force them to put it up in curlers. I was just able to haul myself to the bed and collapse on it. I passed out; it was not exactly a sleeping. Nearly passed out —there was one furiously busy part of my mind that knew I was in danger and kept trying to raise the alarm throughout the rest of me. There was no plan of escape or defense, just the panic crying, *Do something! Do something!*

I do not remember what my feelings were after I came to, only what I did and the sense of urgency with which I did it. I must have lain there no more than half an hour, though it seemed to be hours, for when I came to I heard the children walking and shouting up the highway to school. I think that small messenger of panic, so busy as I lay there for half an hour, had accomplished his purpose. The backs of my legs, my knees, my ankles, were ready; the muscles across my shoulder blades, over my shoulders to my biceps, down my forearms, onto my hands, to my very finger joints, all were ready. My eyelids opened suddenly and alert; I moved to the window as efficiently and smoothly as a cat; my actions were all prepared ahead of time.

The windows in the motel were the kind that are cranked open and shut. I had left the crank at the kitchen window. I got it, and closed the front window. I did not close the blinds. What might he not do if I did that? My problem, of course, was to keep him from coming into the room. The only way I could do that was to pretend he wasn't there, and certainly to pretend I didn't mind having him come in if he wanted to. I unlocked the front door. "I wish I could open it," I said half-aloud so that he might hear me, "but there's such a chilly breeze." I poured myself a cup of cold coffee and drank it. I was in my nightgown, barefooted, my hair still uncombed and about my shoulders. I turned off the heater: I wanted to fight on even terms.

"And that chest of drawers," I said, "it blocks things off. It should be over here." I pushed it up between the foot of the bed and the wall. There was a little box-shaped place now, bounded by the wall on two sides and by the bureau and the bed. But a side of the box was open under the bed. I did not know how to close off that open space without arousing his suspicions. Once I was in it I would be perfectly safe. I could hardly pretend to make the bed. That would be too obvious. I could not do it in one quick act. He was too fast. Nor could I leave that space open. He would get at me from under the bed. There was nothing for it but to challenge him openly. I had never dared do that before, but until I did it I would not know precisely how great his powers were. He made up the rules as we went along. "Now," I said, "I am going to lay the blanket on the floor and up alongside the bed." I did it, and he did nothing. Perhaps he's stupid, I thought, and doesn't see what I'm up to. Then I lay on the bed as though to rest, but suddenly I rolled over and fell onto the floor, stretched myself out flat on my back, folded my arms over my chest, and closed my eyes. Outside the window I could hear what sounded like a low snarling.

He would get tired and go away. I lay there for a long while. My body got stiff and cold.

Outside, from time to time, there were the sounds of fangs and anger. I knew I could outlast him though he should stay all night and it should turn cold.

I did not open my eyelids once while I lay there, nor shift my position on the floor. I was not relaxed. The rigor that held me was dark and cold. I seemed to have locked out even fear.

But then there was a shuffling on the gravel outside, a mumbling, a breathing at the door, and a knock. There was nothing I could do that I had not already done. If I was not safe then, I would never be safe. Another knocking. Another. Then the door opened a little, and a contralto voice called out, "Julia?" I remained perfectly calm, being safe.

Footsteps, and "Julia?" again, and then a loud shrieking. The chest was moved away and my body was being handled by warm hands. But I did nothing till I heard the words, "My dear, my dear, what has happened to you?" Then I opened my eyes and allowed myself to be hoisted up on the bed. It was Anna.

I watched her as she fussed over my body. She kept talking as she worked, explaining what she was doing and why she was doing it. She kept calling my body "you." "You're terribly cold, from lying there like that. I can't imagine why anybody should want to go and do such a thing, Julia. You're actually blue around the lips. I must get some heat into you." She put steaming hot towels under my knees, at my feet, along my sides. "There, you'll be better shortly." The intolerable thing is that in her blundering way she turned out to be right: it was not just my body that she affected.

She went outdoors. I heard her talking to someone. A car door slammed. She came back in and rummaged through my purse, looking, she said, for the keys to my car. She went out, and I heard her get into my car, grind away at the starter for a while, and finally get it going. She drove off, but came back within a minute. I was not curious. There was more talk with someone, and the other car drove off. Anna came back in.

She began to change the towels, warming them in hot water. But as she bent over me to take away the towels from under my knees, I noticed her hat. She wears absurd hats; this one looked exactly like one of those very old-fashioned, gingerbread hats

that the Queen Mother of England always wore in newsreels.
Our own mother used to have one like it. It was so silly on Anna
that I began to laugh. My laughter felt free and easy to me, but
I could see by the look on Anna's face that it did not sound so
to her. I quit laughing.

It was then I noticed how cold my body was. I lay noticing
with interest how waves of shuddering would stir themselves at
the small of my back, gain power, spread and crash into spasms
that shook me all over. They had a rough rhythm; not a regular,
clock rhythm but their own, as waves do. Every ninth one or so
was very fierce.

The next thing I remember is finding myself in my car with
Anna at the wheel. It was night, and I was very tired. I did not
let her see that I had awakened. I was slumped down in the seat
but I could not see out. We were in a flat countryside. A great
many low posts went flashing by us. Huge mounds of white substance appeared in the fields to my right, and finally an illuminated castle, tall, piled high, delicate. This would be the salt plant
near the road coming off the Dunbarton Bridge. She was taking
me home.

I rolled my head a little and looked at Anna. Her face was
thinner than I could remember ever having seen it before. There
seemed to be some sort of blotch like a cold sore on her upper lip;
but I could not be sure of it because of the imperfect light. She
was intent on her driving; she gripped the wheel with both hands
firmly, sat up straight, and peered at the road as though she expected something to leap out onto it at any moment. It occurred
to me that she had always made a point of not being able to
drive. I was sure that she did not know how to drive and never
had known how to. Yet here she was driving quite well enough
for anybody. Perhaps, I thought, this is only an hallucination
that Anna is taking me home: a detailed and realistic one, not
very imaginative in any way, but an hallucination all the same.
Perhaps I was really in bed with Lloyd waking up from some sort

of confused dream. All I would have to do would be to reach my hand and touch his body, just press the backs of my fingers against his hard side, and the hills of salt would be mounds of sheet, and Anna's face would be Lloyd's face, and what seemed to be a rocking, vibrating car would really be our steady bed; the infirmness would be inside myself. I played with this idea for a while. This is the best hallucination, I thought, that I've ever heard of, but the thing about any hallucination is that some detail or other will give it away. Like Anna's being able to drive. It would analyze out, I thought, that Anna is actually the manifest disguise for someone else, my mother probably. Another good detail of this hallucination is that I am able to speculate about it as it goes along. A clever way to keep myself from waking up. Of course my mother couldn't drive either.—We were approaching the lights of a little town. I did not want to stretch my powers of dreaming too far. I did not want to see the neon announcements of THE RENDEZVOUS—COCKTAILS, and the soiled, smiling Coca-Cola girl; nor did I want to look at the movie marquee, as I always did, for the twin attractions and a bowl for every lady. Therefore I felt it was carrying things too far that when I reached out to touch Lloyd beside me it was Anna's tweed coat my fingers felt. I pinched her leg to make sure, and so startled her that she careened us all over the road. I was scared, and sat up. She stopped the car, and we sat for a moment staring at each other, neither believing what she saw. I called out, "Anna!"—I do not know with what emotion in my voice. She sobbed; we fell into each other's arms, and both of us cried.

"Anna, it's really you, Anna?"

"Yes, my dear, of course it is. How do you feel? Just lie back and take it easy now."

"I thought, somehow, this was all a dream. You know? I don't know what I thought."

"It's not a dream at all. Where you *were* was a dream."

"Where are you taking me?"

"To Permanente."

"Permanente? What's that?" Yet my union belongs to the Permanente Health Plan.

"Why, the hospital, dear."

"It's mine too."

"Yes, dear, but I want Ham's friend to look after you. I was there for two weeks with pneumonia, at New Year's. I had *such* a good rest."

And she went on and on about her stay there, how they treated her and why it took her so long to get well, how she wasn't completely back to normal yet, the first time she'd been so sick for twenty years, it was tiresome and a waste of time, but Ham had been so kind and loving to her. We had got to the Oakland airport on our way in, before I remembered to ask her how it happened she was driving.

"I had to," she said.

But she said it in such a tone of voice that if I were to continue to ask her about it I would know that I was encroaching upon her, teasing her. I did not have the strength to tease.

"How did you get down to where I was?"

"Flo Wishnevetski drove me down."

"How did you find me anyhow?"

"Your letter to Beverley. I just looked in all the motels around Half Moon Bay."

"But I told her not to tell *any*body I'd even written to her."

"She was right and you were wrong."

Anna was not impatient or irritable, only sure of herself and very strong. I leaned against the door, gazing out at the industrial gloom along the speedway. My cheek was cold on the metal strip of the door, and I felt like crying again.

As we were driving up Broadway, I saw a way to assert myself.

"Anna," I said, "I won't go to Permanente."

"Oh Julia," she cried, "please don't be stubborn."

"I'm not sick. I'm just unhappy."

"Julia, please."

"Just unhappy."

"How can you tell the difference? Doctors can't always."

"All I want to do is to cry."

I don't know what had got into me, to say such a thing.

"Yes, my dear, you shall have a private room."

"I won't go to Permanente, Anna."

"Julia! I don't know what else to do."

Anna was biting her lower lip and her eyes were shiny.

"Take me to your house. I'll lie in bed and cry and cry."

She seemed to be relieved at the idea, and brought me here and put me in the large bedroom where I now am.

That was last night.

I woke up this morning early, feeling light as a dandelion puff. Anna brought me hot chocolate and toast and two soft-boiled eggs. My arm drifted the food to my mouth. I bathed in the long tub. Ham's friend, Dr. Hanse, detached and courteous and probably right, came to poke at me and tell me to rest and take vitamin pills. For lunch I ate cottage cheese and cold roast beef and milk, a good lunch.

It has been painful and exhausting, writing this last installment. But as all this slips away from me more and more I will become less and less willing to think about what has been happening. What have I learned? I know three things.

I am sick.

Only when I am with Lloyd am I really alive.

The cure for madness is hot towels.

MARCH 19, 4 A.M.

I am damned: the proof of it is I shall die. So shall they all; the difference is this, that I know it. Knowing it, I shall see to it that I am well damned.

5

JUNE 20.

Last evening at nine o'clock my old life came to an end. Anna left, and no one from Oakland will ever seek me out again.

When I found Lloyd here a month ago, I knew an end was in sight. It wasn't hard to find him; he had written one friend he was driving an armored truck, and I took the birthday present to Beverley as an invitation for me to come to him. But that Lloyd Cotruvo should have holed himself away from responsibility in as slimy a chink as capitalism provides, transporting cash, that fact when I found him assured me that a life was ending for him as well as for me.

I dare not ask him why he has given up for fear he will spout me some line about taking cover, about the death throes of a decadent society, about the corruption of American labor; spout it in that speaker's stance, eye on the rear of the hall, which he assumes when he is lying to himself most furiously. The truth is, having lost his nerve with his faith, all he gave up was his job.

I have not got a job. We have no friends. We will certainly not get married: ghosts needn't bother. I no longer feel obliged to brush my hair in the morning. I do not even write to Beverley. I think I shall not change much again, just erode a little, year after year, like a gulch.

Yesterday afternoon I had come back from the store with a bag of groceries. It was so hot I couldn't make up my mind whether to go to the library and get a book or just to lie it out in the room. There was a knock on the door. I opened it. There was a short woman in the hallway but it was so dark I couldn't recognize her.

"Who is it?" I asked.

And then I heard Anna's sentimental voice: "Julia!"

"Oh my God, family," I said and went over to the table with my back to her. "You might as well come in." Her mere silence made me conscious of the grimy room, of my bare legs and slovenly hair. "I found him. See? Is there anything else you want to know?" I heard her sit down, but she still didn't say anything. The air was clotted with disapproval. I turned back onto her. "Well, are the medicoes having a convention in Memphis? Or are you just passing through on your way to New York? Toodledoo, sweetheart, it's been so nice seeing you." Even this didn't do it. She just looked at me, so sad I relented a little. "Quit just staring at me. Say something. What do you want?" I poured myself half a glass of whiskey with water and drank it.

"I came," she said, "because I was worried about you, my dear."

So it wasn't disapproval; it was pity. I pounded the tumbler down on the sinkboard and said with as much hostility as I could, "Will you leave me alone?" But to get at Anna you have to play her game of politeness. "I have to go out for a while. I was just leaving. Why don't you come back in an hour for tea? Lloyd won't be home till five thirty. You clear out before then." I picked up my purse and stood at the door waiting till she stood up. "I don't want him to come home on an off chance and find you here alone. Well, Anna, there was something for you to worry about, wasn't there? How do you like it?"

On the sidewalk I asked her which way she was going.

"That way," she said, pointing left.

"Too bad. I'm going the other way. So long." I didn't look back.

I thought she would not return, but Anna does not give up easily. I met Lloyd at his work and we went out to dinner. I did not tell him about Anna's visit.

When we came home, I lay in my bunk and he sat in the armchair at the foot of the bunk, his feet up on the table, listening to the radio account of a prizefight. Our room is immediately to the right of the outside steps to the house; because it was hot our windows were up, so that from where I lay I could see anyone entering the house. Lloyd was barefooted and had taken off his shirt; I was wearing a slip. I had a glass of whiskey in my hand, but I was by no means drunk. It was just that the alcohol, the chronic, flat excitement of the announcer's voice, the heat, the lying flat on my back in the lower bunk, all succeeded in suspending me in that state in which one neither feels nor thinks nor acts nor dreams—an enviable condition, an inconsequent happiness, pure being.

The fight ended; he turned off the radio; I opened my eyes. The first thing I saw was Anna's face just outside the window, rather dim in the street light, looking in at us appalled. I didn't care. I neither cared what Anna did next nor did I care about myself; but I knew what Anna saw—me in a dirty room with a man in his undershirt, flat on my back with my hands at my sides, in a bed like a coffin, with my right foot sticking out, holding a glass—I knew she was seeing this and I nearly smiled with the knowledge.

Lloyd got himself a drink and sat down again. Idly he reached out, took my foot and waggled it a few times, and tossed it back inside the bed. It was an ordinary gesture, ordinary for a working man on a hot night after listening to a fight, certainly ordinary for Lloyd. But I saw Anna raise her hand and press the back of it against her mouth, and I knew how she had seen it; he had picked my foot up as a butcher picks up meat to display to a customer, he had waggled it like meat, he had tossed it back like meat.

Her face disappeared. I heard her go down the stairs. I heard her steps diminish up the sidewalk. When I could not hear her any longer, I knew that my life had ended.

My life has ended. I have survived myself. This is life after death. How peaceful it is, how unchanging except for the erosion, for which one is prepared. We do not quarrel any more or watch one another suspiciously. I never think of the future, and I have forgotten the past: the present is my always, as eternity requires. I love and am loved, as we prove night after night after night. I can lie for hours without an emotion or thought in my head, without needing to do anything, not dreaming, not even itching. Is this not peace? If not, what is? Happiness—what else?

What else?

Is He Dead?

1

As he coasted up in front of the little white house, wood among its stucco companions, he heard a piano cheeriness of Haydn's coming through the open windows; it was Rachel playing while the potatoes were boiling; he knew her touch. He got out of the car without slamming the door, walked on the square little well-trimmed lawn to the tulip bed at the corner of the house, and stood legs spread, staring at a striped tulip, listening: he became the music, the flower, and a stone. He was a large, square-hewn, grizzled man in a business suit, his eyes were deep-set and fierce, and he had powers of concentration like a magnifying glass. A child a lawn away gazed at him with her finger in her mouth; when the music stopped, he shook himself and spat like an ordinary man, and the child ran behind a bush.

"Dad! Dad!" cried Rachel and met him on the porch. "How long have you been standing out there? Why didn't you come right in?"

"I could have stood out here till dusk, listening to you play, and never got tired. How is my grandson? Where is he?"

"Oh, he's out in the back yard turning somersaults. He turned one this morning by accident and now I'm afraid he's going to wear all his hair off tumbling around on the grass and rugs. Teddy!" she called. "Teddy Bear! Grandpa's here. Oh Dad. I'm glad you got here before Dick. He has me upset."

"That's why I said I'd rather have come for lunch. I think Dick isn't liking me these days."

"More than that. Watch him, Dad, try to figure out what is happening. Do you have to leave early tonight?"

"Teddy boy!" he cried, and leaned down with his arms wide.

"Grandpa John!" the child shouted. "I can turn somersaults."

"Turn me one then."

He did, and John picked him up and squeezed him. Teddy showered his grandfather's rough face with fists and kisses till Rachel tried to stop him and they all three hugged each other, laughing and shouting, "A hug-it, a hug-it!"

"Tell me a story when I go to bed?"

"All right, one story."

"*Three* stories, Grandpa."

"Just one, honey, just one. I have to go away early tonight."

"You never tell more than one," said Teddy, his face puckering toward tears.

"Here's a stick of gum if you'll turn me another somersault," said John.

"Where do you have to go tonight, Dad?" Rachel asked. "Stay with us."

"The party bigwigs are meeting to select candidates for the primaries. I thought I'd drop by about nine or so."

"But, Dad." She was surprised at what he'd said, but she was a steady woman: she did not, as she might ordinarily have done, blink her eyes or shake her red hair and lean forward at him; she gazed steadily at him, balanced, alert, relaxed. "But, Dad, there's no question about it, is there? They'll put you up again?"

"Yes. That's not the question. I have a surprise for them. For you too, dear. I've decided to retire."

"Retire!" she cried, and clutched Teddy up to her bosom. "You're not sick?"

"No, my dear. I'm not even exhausted. I've simply decided that I want to go fishing for a while. I've been attorney general for the people of the state long enough. There's too much title to it and not enough smell of fish and marsh grass and coffee at daybreak. Teddy Bear, do you want to go fishing with Grandpa?"

"Yes! Yes!" Teddy yelled. "Tell me all about it."

"I don't know," said Rachel, passing Teddy to her father. "Come out in the kitchen and talk while I string beans."

And as his grandson listened wide-eyed and prompting, and as his calm-seeming daughter snapped green beans into a pot and listened for whatever she could hear behind the words he said, he told of casting for trout at sundown in a cold stream and of running up a flat beach in the moonlight for grunion in the sand between waves and of game wardens counting your catch in your basket and of beer in country stores and of a leaky rowboat on Lower Lake; and especially he told, till both of them were sharp-eyed and still as mice, of wading in hip boots into the Eel River in the pearl mist of dawn, casting for salmon, cold, strong, the breathing center of a still world.

"I'm going to get you a pole, Teddy, if your father and mother will let me, and teach you how to fish so you'll love it. And when you'll be going on sixty and think you've been busy enough in the world long enough, you'll have something better to do than tourist around and play cards all day or watch TV. Teddy, I'm buying a little house near the mouth of a river and whenever you want to come see me I'll want you to come."

But Dick broke the spell.

He banged the door behind him; he walked, though a slight man, on heavy heels; his face had no expression even when he winked at Rachel or chucked Teddy under the chin or nodded at John. Presently they heard him in the living room tuning his viola. Motioning to John to stay where he was, Rachel went in to the piano. Then, as they sometimes did when Dick came home, they played a duet; this time it was the close of a sonata by Franck. They had first met at a party of young musicians, and Dick had had his viola in one hand and the bow in the other when he had asked her to marry him, and it was only in music, now during Dick's strangeness, that they came together any more.

John, listening to this bookkeeper, his son-in-law, play with such sweep and surge, shook his head at what seemed to him the perversity of some men: Dick now, keeping books for an automobile dealer, when he might have been playing, if he didn't run open-armed toward unhappiness, at least with some good symphony orchestra. John had never played a musical instrument, had never, that is, known how impulse and decision and execution can be all the same gesture, and moreover he had not in his life seriously lost confidence in himself. Therefore, when Dick had said (what was not true) that he wasn't good enough to play with a symphony, and had refused to say anything more, John had thought him perverse and had thought Rachel forbearing for not pressing Dick onward. It had no more occurred to John that he might lose his nerve—politics is less risky than music—than that he might forget how to walk. Yet Rachel, whom he respected, had asked him not to press Dick on the matter.

"Dick," said Rachel when they had sat down to dinner, "Dad has to leave early. He has an important meeting to go to." Her voice was just a little more cheerful than it needed to be. "Dad's going to retire."

Dick, staring at John intently, laid his knife and fork down, clenched the table edge, and said in his flat voice loudly, "What about Brock?"

"Catching Brock's murderer is a matter for the police, and prosecuting him is a matter for the district attorney. I am neither."

"He had enemies," said Dick ominously. "Plenty of enemies. They were out to get him."

"Well?" said John. About his official duties, about his probity, he had little humor.

"You know who he was attacking when they shot him in the back. You know who the alley rats were he was dragging out into the light for everyone to see."

"I know," said John sharply, "that he was denouncing dishonest politicians. I do not know who killed him, and neither do you."

Rachel busied herself over Teddy's plate. Her red hair hid her face. Neither of the men paid much attention to her.

"He's been dead three days," said Dick. "They tied his hands behind his back and shot him in the back of the head in an alley. Is that any way for the sacredest man in the world to die? Is it?"

"It's no way for anyone to die," said John. "But I shall retire all the same."

"Honest John," Dick muttered, and muttered down into incoherence. "Honest John Haffner."

"What's that?"

"I mean," said Dick sullenly, "the only man this state has to be proud of has been killed, and you're the only politician the people trust, and you're quitting."

"You mean," said John, but it was time for Rachel to interrupt and veer them away, "that I'm afraid?"

"Now," said Rachel, "it'll be several months before Dad'll even be out of office and I'm sure everything will be straightened up by then."

Teddy began to wail.

"You're not afraid of the politicians," Dick said at John. Suddenly with an altered gleam in his eyes he leaped to his feet like a batman whose colonel has just entered the room. "I know that and the people know it too. But you're afraid. For a good reason." He made a grimace like a smile, kissed Teddy repentantly, and left the room.

Teddy leaned toward his mother, who took him into her arms. Absently, John patted the baby.

"What did he mean?" John asked.

"Tell me," said Rachel.

"Exactly what was he talking about?"

"That's what I ask myself again and again."

"Was he a follower of this Brock?"

"He's never talked to me about it," said Rachel, "but he went to some of the meetings. Particularly after Brock began denouncing the politicians. What was there about this man?"

"How do you know Dick went to the meetings? Did he tell you?"

"No. He would just go out. I would find throwaways in the wastepaper basket. Do you know what they always said?"

" 'You don't have to die,' " said John in a brooding voice.

"Dad! *You* weren't interested?"

"I am interested in any religious man who can get two hundred thousand people in one week to come listen to him talk, and who can raise enough money from his followers to buy three hours of television time every Sunday on six stations, and who gets himself murdered. 'You can die if you want to, but if you want to you can live forever.' A single-minded man. You know where you are with a fellow like Brock. An utterly single idea, with a little bunting to flutter out behind it."

"Didn't he ever break the law?"

"The law is the will of the people and the will of the people about crackpots is: leave them alone. We could have harried him. He wasn't that important."

"Are you sure?"

"Well, not until he got himself killed."

"What are you going to do?"

"I don't know because I don't know what's going to happen. Nothing, I hope. I've got to leave for my meeting now."

He kissed the baby good night, and left through the living

room. But Dick was on the dark porch waiting for him.

"I don't want you to think," Dick whispered at him, "that we doubt your honesty." The oval of his tilted face swam up at John. "It's just that we like to have someone we can trust."

"What's that?" said John in a stalwart voice. Feeling Dick's hands clutching his left arm, he drew back thin-lipped. "It's a case of murder. Justice will be done."

"You know yourself there's many a murderer walking the streets today unapprehended. Unapprehended."

"We solve half our homicides. That's better than the national average. I've got to go."

"You're a strange man," Dick whispered.

"Am I?" said John. "I'm due at a meeting."

"Someone," said Dick in a whisper, "has got to be punished for the killing of Mr. Brock."

"Someone," said John, "will be. Speak out. I can scarcely hear you."

"I don't want anyone to overhear; it might alarm them. Do you have any suspects?"

"I'm not a policeman, Richard. I don't know whether there are any suspects or even any leads. But I doubt it. This is the sort of case where some lunatic comes wandering into a station five hundred miles away and says, 'I did it,' and then we've got to prove he did it if we can."

"If a man says, 'Punish me for what I have done,' why do you doubt that he has done it?"

"Experience," said John, and pulled away.

But Dick ran after him down the steps. "John," he said in a low voice, "John." He plucked at John's elbow. "Do you know what we are going to do with Mr. Brock?"

John stopped. "What do you mean? He's dead."

"Dead," said Dick pityingly, shaking his head. "He did not believe in death. You know that."

"Then what is all this stuff," said John, dropping his voice to

Dick's intense pitch, "about arresting his murderer? How can you be murdered if you can't die?"

"It's the others," said Dick. "Those who do not know yet. They must not be confused. We are going to have him especially embalmed and put in a glass casket. His own Universal Church will be his tabernacle. There will be pilgrims. Do you know that, John? There will be thousands and hundreds of thousands of pilgrims."

"My God," said John, "either the man's dead or he is not dead. Can't you leave his body alone?" Even in his own ears his voice had the harsh impatience of a Puritan who is, as usual, in the right.

"But it will not decay. Do you know what we call it?" asked Dick. "The visible wonder. He is the visible wonder. Long after you are the dust you think you will become, he will remain the visible wonder of the world." At the door of John's car he whispered again in at him. "Are you running, John? I used to run. What do you fear? Do you know what you fear?"

2

When he entered the anteroom, two women looked up at him. One was Miss Robertson, the governor's secretary; the other he did not recognize till she smiled and said his name in a gentle voice. She was Mrs. Freeman, the wife of the bishop; he saluted her and went to Miss Robertson.

"Will you tell them I'm here?" he said.

"I'm sorry, Mr. Haffner, they don't even want me to take minutes right now."

"Well, just go tell them I'm out of the running."

There was not so much as a flicker in her eyes. "They locked the door," she said, "and besides, I don't think they'll accept your withdrawal."

"Won't they though. Just give them my message, Miss Robertson. I'm leaving."

"Oh Mr. Haffner, I know they'll want to see you. It's very important."

"They will, huh. I'll give them half an hour."

He sat down beside her to talk. It was not that he liked Miss Robertson particularly. Her soul had been for a long time as smoothed out and hobbled by girdles and high heels as her body; her personality was as blank and brown as her gabardine suit; her mind was exactly good enough to take down 240 any sort of words a minute without error, without boredom, without wincing. But she could talk idly in a bare room like this well enough; he remembered that she liked science-fiction; he drew her out. Besides, she was not Mrs. Freeman. Mrs. Freeman was a good woman; that is, she did good, and did not resent those who did bad but pitied them. For example, now: she was knitting alone while the other two talked, neither trying to join them nor, as John actively knew, making them uncomfortable for not having included her; and she was waiting for the bishop, who for reasons no one understood, hated to drive at night without her. John liked good people—no, he respected them above everyone else, above the powerful or beautiful or rich, whom he knew well, the gifted or learned or even the wise; indeed, he was rather in awe of the good, but their actual sweet presence made him uncomfortable. Mrs. Freeman there: with her hair drawn back straight to a bun, she sat in a steel-tube, leatherette chair, against a beige, fire-resistant, sound-absorbent wall, knitting in that ambient, indirect light socks for the mad. He knew quite well that if he should go over beside her she would talk with him in her gentle voice about whatever he wished to talk about; that she would have firm views which, however, she would never declare harshly against his should they differ; that she would tell him, if he asked about her work with the insane, what she had accomplished and what failed to accomplish; that she would make him acutely uncomfortable. He felt himself deficient not to be living, as people like Mrs. Freeman seemed to live, in an altogether moral world, but more especially he was reluctant to come near such people because he did not want to know more than he could help knowing of their motives; he did not trust motives; he was a lawyer. Therefore, though it was all but rude of him, he sat with Miss Robertson till the door opened.

It was the little AFL man, Dell Monahan, who poked his head out and nodded for Miss Robertson to come in. He was obviously surprised to see John, and without greeting him said, "John Haffner."

Governor Stahlman's big voice boomed down at him: "What's that, Dell?" The AFL head disappeared and there was another shout inside; Stahlman's claim to fame was never having had to use a public address system. "Honest John!" he belled. "Bring him in, Dell." The door opened wide, and John, annoyed, stepped inside. As he entered, the thirty people in the room, all looking at him, stood.

Stahlman, a big, loose-jointed halfback in a loose-fitting, handsome suit, strode over toward him smiling, put his arm across John's shoulders muttering, Good to see you Glad you got here Couldn't have picked a better time, and led him through the odd silence to the chair at the head of the table. "Ladies and gentlemen, your next governor, Honest John Haffner!" John glanced up at him in disbelief, but Stahlman had put on the face of sincere congratulation; John heard the dinning of sixty fists on the table; he looked at the thirty faces, some of them smiling, all familiar to him; and he realized they meant it—they were putting him up for governor. Why? As he looked at these representatives of people and of power, not one of whom was there because he was himself but only because of what he represented—Farmers, Oil, Negroes, Women, Lumber, Civil Liberties, Local Party Machines—it occurred to him that he was not there either because he was just himself, just Haffner who had got in on a reform ticket twenty years earlier and had had no more to do with the machine than he could help. No, he was Honest

John—he was the representative from Honesty. It was not himself they had chosen; he could see that in every face; if it had been himself only, he could have declined easily. They had chosen, in a tight year, Honesty; he was profoundly touched. The drumming had stopped; he suddenly realized he was supposed to say something; but tears blurred his vision and his throat choked. He knew by all the eyes that his emotion was misinterpreted; it would be too much trouble to explain what he felt; he waved his hand a little and sat down.

But he recovered from his sentimentality after ten minutes of listening. "Get out the vote. Anti-Communist. FEPC. Loyalty oaths. Gasoline tax. Bookies. Highways. State Board of Equalization. Local option. Schools. Housing." It was not Honesty they were nominating in him, but a winner. They would have preferred, if it was necessary to play thus irregularly, a conquering, golf-loving general to put up, but there were none left over; Haffner for four times running had fetched more votes as attorney general than any governor of the state had ever got; he was a winner, not quite reliable, not quite a general certainly, but also not a loser; and it was a tight year. Honest John, good old Haffner, you can bank on Haffner, a vote getter, a solid man. . . . Well, if they got him, he said to himself, it was honesty they'd get whether they liked it or not. Church, Labor, Minorities were for him; together they could elect him. The machine was not happy; its hostility could make him lose. Farmers and Money were against him; but they were not likely to bolt the party— and certainly not for Brock's Universal Party.

"Ladies and gentlemen," he said in the first crack in the talk, "I came here tonight to tell you I wasn't going to run again for attorney general. I wanted to go fishing." What a wit! "Well, now you tell me you're going to nominate me for governor. And I still want to go fishing." Who would have guessed old John had a sense of humor like this! "Just tonight I was telling my daughter, and my grandson Teddy, about fishing." All right, we

can afford to beam at the doting grandfather; it won't take long.
"I tell you, if you've never felt the tug of a fish on the end of
your line, that line tying the two of you together so you can't
think of anything else but that fish, you haven't really lived." All
right, he wants to get it off his chest. Besides, the sporting ele-
ment is something to bear in mind; they'd like a fisherman. "I
tell you, sometimes I think I'm not only closer to Nature when
I'm out by myself fishing, I'm closer to mankind too. Speaking
for myself—most of the time anyhow—I've found that a few
miles between me and my nearest fellow man doesn't make it any
harder for me to love mankind, especially when I've got my
attention fixed on a fish." We've really got a speaker here; by
God, who'd have thought it. What a wit!—But John was sorry
he had trimmed the statement of his truth to suit their humor.
Sorry, though he liked their laughter and attentiveness. "I don't
want to run for governor, I don't want to serve as governor. But
if you can persuade me I ought to, I will."

Now there was an odd little bomb to toss out amongst them
spluttering.

"Honor. Prestige. Fame. Something to make your family proud
of."

"If my family aren't proud of me as I am, I don't give a damn
what they think of my titles."

"Power. Power. Power."

"I have saved the lives of some men and sent others to their
death. That's as much power as governors have. Give me a
reason."

"The state needs you. There are always abuses to be remedied.
The people need leadership."

"Why me?"

"The party needs you. We need you, to stay in."

"That's your reason: it's your party. What's my reason?"

"Duty."

He took the trouble to look each one of them in the eye.

"Why should I do what I don't want to do for people I don't much like?" The way he spoke, the animal spread of his nostrils, the unpolitic unequivocation of what he said, all were wrong for this board-of-directors' suave and well-joined room.

Bishop Freeman, who had been slumping in his seat, struggled upward at the slap of silence, as one nearly asleep emerges struggling at a rap at the window.

"John," said the bishop, speaking for the first time, "John, you can't be tempted. I know that. But you can be driven. These Brockmen, I think they call themselves—what if this Kroger of theirs does in fact run for governor as he threatens?"

"How does my duty enter into it?"

"It's hard to say how many votes he can attract. What do we have to set against him?"

"Nothing but old John!" cried Stahlman. Heartiness glossed his corruptness like the glister on decaying fish. "You're our strongest point—Honest John. You'll cross-file and win both major parties on the primary."

"Not everyone in this room," the bishop continued, "is happy to have you as a candidate. But everyone in this room, yourself included, John Haffner, agrees that a Brockman victory would be disastrous. And you will be more assured of winning than any other politician in the state." There was a general nodding and grunting. "I think you will be driven by the facts."

The bishop, a worried expression on his plump ruddy face, looked at his watch, shook his head, and perched on the edge of his chair.

"Besides," said Stahlman glisteringly, "we'll see that you get in the limelight in this Brock murder case. Honest John—he upholds the law to defend the victim he hates."

There was a stir of appreciation at the governor's perception. The bishop rose, mumbling that it was late, and left. But the door had scarcely closed behind him when he re-entered, followed by a reporter with a flash camera in hand.

"Get out of here, Bishop!" roared Stahlman. "You know damned well," he shot at the reporter, who rode like a tank through the patter of the pellets, "that this is a closed meeting. How did you even know where it was?"

"Governor," said the reporter, "I've got news. Brock's murderer just confessed. He was one of Brock's own followers." And with a flash bulb he froze their astonishment.

"Who is he?" "What's his name?" "Why did he do it?"

"His name is Richard Horton." He poised his reloaded camera again. "John Haffner's son-in-law." And he blanched them again. "Any statements, Mr. Haffner?" But the halfback drove him from the room.

"I must go," said John, "I must go to Rachel. Dick must be out of his mind." He stood bemused a moment, alone at the end of the table, stared at. "One thing, naturally—I will not accept the nomination. If you want to, you may have another five days to see which way the wind blows, or else just forget the whole business. I'll be glad to forget it myself."

"No, no, John," cried Stahlman, as though it were principle he was upholding. "You know we're behind you. Of course it's too early to make any final decisions yet. We all appreciate that. But we're right behind you. You can bank on us." He put his arm across John's shoulder as though it were affection he was offering. "Now, go find out how bad things really are. You know how we feel about this thing."

John without a word or gesture went. As he was closing the door, he heard a voice (Oil or Lumber) saying, "We'd better stand ready to meet again on . . ." And Mrs. Freeman looked up from her knitting to extend him a sympathy as plain as the way she wore her hair and as serene as her eyes; she was too tactful to speak of his sorrow. He left the anteroom with head hanging, unable to respond to her offer of sympathy; it was not sorrow he was feeling so much as the turmoil and rage of the not altogether good when the screws are on.

3

She came back to it again and again.

"But Dad, you think your husband is sitting on the front porch and then Anna telephones and tells you he's confessed to murder—it's terrible, it's just too much. And how did she learn it? From a radio station fifty miles away. I can't get used to it. I just don't know what to do. Sometimes I have the feeling I'm falling behind. I don't care where I am any longer. And I thought he was right out on the porch. I thought I'd heard his chair squeak and I didn't want to bother him. Teddy was asleep of course. I was reading. Isn't it terrible?"

"Do you want to see him tonight?"

"No!" It was almost a cry. "No!"

"Why does he say he did it?"

"I don't know, I don't know. It's as though I should go out to hang up the clothes and find a deep pit suddenly at the bottom of the back steps. I just answered the phone and there it was."

She ran into Teddy's room, to make sure again that he was all right.

"Rachel," said John, grasping her by the shoulders, "if Dick is released, you must not take him back."

She dropped her eyes; she had thought of it already.

"He'll need me."

"He's harmful. You don't still love him?"

"Love him?" At the wave of the wand of that word, tears spilled from her eyes. "But I did."

"He's harmful. He will be able to harm Teddy."

"Leave my husband when he needs help most? How could I?"

"He is not the same man you married."

She raised her head and looked at him full in the eyes. She spoke with that thorough, gentle bitterness of which those are capable who could never be cynical if they wished but who are learning how it is that others find cynicism easy.

"Oh, but he *is* the man I married, and I shall be loyal to him. Don't tell me, Dad, that you never remarried after Mother died just because you never found another woman to your taste."

It was his eyes that lowered.

"It's easy to remain loyal to the unchanging dead."

"But more important to be loyal to the living," she answered. "The dead are so dead. He is the same man, only lost, terribly lost. Can I blame him because he has lost his way?"

He put his hat on. "Good-bye, my dear. Call me whenever you need me." They embraced; she laid her head on his chest and sobbed two or three times. "I hope with all my heart," he said, "that the doctors decide he is insane."

"I doubt if they will." She was staring at the telephone like a bird at a snake. "I think there's only one thing wrong with him really, and I doubt that they'll think him mad because of it."

"What's that?"

"He believes he will never die."

"Is that all?"

"A great deal follows from that. Oh, a great deal. I've been thinking about it."

"Well, take me to him, anyway," said John. But the turnkey didn't move. "I had hoped he would see me voluntarily, but I've got to talk to him in any case."

"Mr. Haffner," said the turnkey, "he's mighty peculiar. If you don't mind I just think I'll stick around while you're in with him."

"Bah," said John. He saw a straight chair on the other side of the room, went to it, knelt, grasped one of the front legs with his right hand, and raised the chair steady and level above his head. "I'm not as old as all that."

"I'm responsible for you, sir. That's all."

"What do you mean? I'm his father-in-law."

What it lacked in logic his statement gained in conviction.

"Okay. But you won't get anything out of him. He'd turn his back on Jesus Christ Almighty."

"Maybe," said John, and watched the fellow. "But would he turn his back on Brock?"

The turnkey's voice reeked with scorn. "That turd."

Dick, when John entered and stood beside him, looked as far as John's shoes and then buried his face back in his hands.

"Dick," said John. He was startled at the tone of his own voice; it was ordering a dog. He tried to speak more neutrally. "Dick." But Dick did not respond. "I've read your confession. Listen to me. At about eight or eight thirty in the morning, the detectives will come to work. Most of them will be put on your case because Brock is hot. By noon they'll be certain you're lying." That was a strong word, "lying," in any tone of voice. Apparently he couldn't even pretend to be impartial; well, he didn't really want to. "By three o'clock if they can manage it, by four at the latest so they can knock off work early, they'll have proof that you never killed Brock. So you'll be turned over to doctors. And I doubt if they'll think there's much point in locking you up in an asylum. So you'll be released. Dick, by dinnertime tomorrow you'll be loose. What then?"

"No, they won't," said Dick anxiously, shaking his head. "They mustn't. I'm guilty."

"You never killed anyone," said John. "What're you going to do when you're turned loose again?"

"Leave me alone," said Dick. He looked up. His face seemed smaller to John, pinched together, wan. "I confessed. Isn't that enough?"

"You drip with lies like a sponge," John said full voice. "What I want to know is, do you intend to bother Rachel any more? Don't."

John found his fist doubled and arm flexed. He knew that he had better leave the cell at once.

"But you can't," cried Dick. "You can't let a murderer go

free. It's terrible. Why, what kind of justice is that? I want to be translated." He looked at John's fist. "Are you so afraid of what I may say that you are going to beat me?" He buried his face in his hands again. "Go ahead. It won't do you any good."

John had to leave. "You leave Rachel alone." He reeled to the door. He was half-blind. "May God damn you." It was a true curse, the curse of a man who believes in God.

The turnkey guided him out. John did not even say good night to him.

He sat in his car till three o'clock in the morning before he drove home, thinking of Dick's lunacy, of Rachel's stubborn loyalty, of the danger to Teddy. But not one of these things, not even all of them together, accounted for his sudden, total rage in the jail; not least of what he thought about, chilly in the car staring at the dark jail wall, was what it was that had been able to entice him, twitching like the tail of a lion, to the barbed frontier of violence. He kept feeding himself reasons; that it was the impatience of age, that he must retire soon because he was losing control of himself, that he was overtired. But he knew better than these.

The detectives did come to work at eight thirty, and by nine they were out on the Brock case, and by noon they did suspect that Dick was lying; but not that day nor the next nor the next could they prove he was lying. In fact they could prove nothing at all. Dick was armored-plated, bullet-proof, and relentless. "I won't say why I killed him: he is not dead. I lost the gun I shot him with. Execute me: I shall not die." He was afraid of their harshness and suspicious of their gentleness. He refused to see his wife, he ate bread and water, he kept demanding trial. He spoke in a diminutive, reasonable, unnatural voice, like a voice from a dictaphone, its issuing intelligence now five miles five days away. Yet the doctors refused to set everyone's mind at rest and pad him off in a hospital; he kept giving right enough answers to their questions; they did not bring up the question of dying, for they were not sure what the right answer was.

John, during these days of Dick's stubbornness, attained a celebrity no one had suspected him capable of. He had been honored and widely known, as an upright man in American politics can be; he was that sort of embodiment of civic virtue whom voters, when they are permitted to, vote for, unless the times are most lunatic. Yet he had had no dash, no sparkle, no casual appeal to the people, and the times were lunatic enough. For three days he was front-page because of Dick: "I will combat Brock's ideas and influence in every way open to me, but Brock's murderer I will see prosecuted even though he is my own son-in-law. . . . I do not think my son-in-law guilty of this crime, but demented by that demented spellbinder. . . . I have no notion why my son-in-law has confessed, or why he might have committed the crime if he did commit it, or why I should be expected to know. *Why* is a question of shaky legality." On the fourth day, however, he made his own fame.

For weeks he had been appointed to speak at the state convention of the Veterans of Foreign Wars. He had looked forward to the occasion with a sense of dull duty, for he had never done well at speaking to large audiences. Committee work was for him, or conferences where authority was clear and there was a job of work to be done, or interviews with suppliants. But to groups as large as this he spoke worthily of worthy causes; they, liking from time to time to be reminded of their duty, from time to time invited him to speak to them; the bolted warehouses which he knew lay wasting behind his listeners' boredom, he had never known how to open. The hall was filled: notoriety, and the topic he had already written his speech on, drew all the delegates; John, believing strongly that it was better for ten guilty to go free than for one innocent to be locked up, had chosen to speak at the first evening session on the topic "When Justice Miscarries." Now some of these veterans were Brockmen, and they came with blood in their eyes.

They booed when he was introduced. Early in his speech when he said, "We must enlarge our idea of justice: justice is more than correcting injustice," one of them yelled, "How would *you* know?" When he had finished his first example, a worthy, yawn-making story of a man who had been executed on insufficient evidence, the same Brockman yelled, "That's not the point. Did he *want* to be executed?" Even then John would have ignored the fellow, but as he was starting the next sentence, the man—a large blond one-eyed smiler in a turtle-neck sweater—strode up toward the platform and shouted: "Answer my question. Did he *want* to be executed?"

Without the amusement of incredulity, John said, "I forgot to ask him. Go sit down."

"It's the duty of the government," said the one-eyed man, "to execute anybody who is ready to be translated." There was a gust of indignation from the audience. The men in the front row started to rush the fellow out of the hall, but as they were shoving him he reared himself up so that his radiant head rose above the others and shouted straight at John, "What are you afraid of?" John lost his temper.

"Let him go," he ordered them; then to the fellow: "It is the duty of the law to punish the guilty."

"How," said his taunter, "can you tell when a man is guilty?"

"When I can prove he did such and such a thing."

"Shouldn't the guilty man know more about it than anyone else?"

"What he says hasn't much to do with it one way or the other."

"Honest John Haffner," said his taunter to the whole assembly, "he has the nerve to talk to us about 'when Justice miscarries' and he is afraid to execute his own son-in-law. Do you know why?"

One of the others yelled, "He thinks he's going to die!"

There was a roar from the crowd, "Throw them out! Get rid of the bastards!" And the blond Brockman was thrown out.

But no sooner had John begun speaking again than another

one yelled, "Is it true you're going to run for governor, Honest John?" The crowd rumbled, but they wanted to hear his answer. "I haven't made up my mind yet," he answered.

"You'd better," said the Brockman, "so that when Richard Horton is condemned you can give him a pardon. After all, he's in the family."

The meeting nearly broke up into roars and throwing out Brockmen and orders like thunder over the public address system and flash bulbs like lightning in every part of the hall; but John in his anger took the first opportunity to order the crowd's attention. And during the next forty-five minutes he did what he had never done before and what no one had suspected he could do: made a mass of men feel what he wished.

Forgetting his written speech, he grabbed the microphone and wielded it like a weapon. He leveled the Brockmen with scorn: the crowd approved. He warned full-voice against excess in religion and politics: the crowd bellowed approval. And he reminded them, with all the passion he had never before been able to use, how the law is above us all, how we need the law for our safety and peace of mind, how we must never pamper ourselves with the law, how we must allow harmless lunatics to go their own way but not let them pervert the law as they would like to do; the crowd bellowed as joyously as though he had been inciting them to slaughter the enemy across the way. And even as he was riding like a sea god the billows of their turbulence, which he could like a god arouse and allay as he wished, he knew that he liked this power better than he had ever liked anything else. This was to fame as fame is to knowing you are right.

4

John did not realize it, the crowd did not care, but the reporters knew it: the campaign for governor had begun. The four of them pushed him into the quietest corner of the Townhouse bar and worked over him. Unfortunately, desiccated of passion, what he had to say sounded like platitudes of worthy sentiment. The reporters liked him, they liked a good candidate: they revered a good story. One of them, a bland Iowan with kind eyes and a slight stutter of earnestness, pulled out a shiny little question, the sort that cuts you to the bone before you know you've been touched. "Is Brock dead?"

"Of course he is dead," said John.

"Then you don't believe in God?"

"What? What has God got to do with it?" It was hard to hear accurately over the juke-box music.

"If man is mortal then there is no God. Many people say so."

"I believe in God," said John in that sort of voice, like a lion's, which pricks up ears to the limit of its reach, "and I know that every man is going to die, and more than that it is none of my business." But the story transcribed badly. "Questioned by newsmen at the Townhouse after the opening session of the state convention of VFW (Veterans of Foreign Wars), John Haffner, State Attorney General, averred yesterday evening that he believed in God. He also gave his opinion that . . ."

The next morning at four John and Rachel and Teddy had driven off to the house he had bought by the sea, so that by the time the morning edition had been delivered and read no one could find him. Friday, when he returned to his apartment, he found Miss Robertson there waiting for him; she made two telephone calls while he shaved and dressed; and a limousine with a state patrolman before took him sirening to the governor's mansion. Stahlman in a dressing gown, reeking with cheer, poured John some coffee, hoped that he'd had a relaxing day off, and told him never to commit himself in public again on the subject of mortality. John, who did not know whether he could do again at will what he had done on Wednesday night with that crowd, guessed that he needed the party machine; he did not answer. Stahlman said he had talked to key people about the matter; they all agreed. Nothing else stood in John's way to the candidacy; he was handling the son-in-law business very astutely; he was becoming a popular figure; he would do a fine job; he was entering the national political arena now; but he had to be careful. John took the discipline.

He greeted the reporters awaiting him at his office with a formula from which none of their needling could make him deviate. "Is Brock dead?" "Biologically yes." And to all the questions washing in its wake, "No comment."

He drove across town to Rachel's after work.

"Who was the fellow in the gray suit?"

"Didn't he catch you? He wanted to see you."

"I sat in my car watching him leave," said John. "You look alarmed."

"Do I?" said Rachel, and uttered a snort of laughter; her face was drawn and her eyes stared at him febrilely. "He was an insurance man. He wanted me to sign something."

"Did you?"

"No, I told him to see you about anything, as you said I should." She laughed again. "It had something to do with Dick."

"He carried fifty thousand dollars' worth of life insurance. The Universal Church was his beneficiary." She began laughing harder; he thought, sitting wearily in an armchair with his head thrown back, his eyes shut, that it would be good for her to have a good laugh. "Furthermore," he said in a tone of mock despair, "one of the companies Brock owned was the Universal Casket Corporation."

She laughed all right, too hard, painfully. He looked at her sharply; this was a seizure of laughter; this was her Janus-face of calm; her eyes were desperately not laughing. He jumped up, grabbed her by the arms, and shook her. "Rachel! Rachel!"

"I'm sorry, Dad," she said, hiccuping. "I don't even dare to laugh. At night I cry." She glanced up at him when she said this, wanting to make sure that what she had said was all right.

John had never seen her so; as a child, even till she was six-teen or seventeen, she had given way before difficulty and turned to him for the support he always offered; but now she was in far worse trouble than anything else she had known, and she was not yielding herself to him as he wanted her to; she sat huddled in her chair encapsulated in misery. She was trying to be self-reliant, as a wife and mother should be; and at the same time that he admired her for her courage he resented her separateness. He wanted her head on his knees; he wanted to stroke her long red hair and say, "Daughter, daughter, I will take care of you." But he could say nothing to her of all this, though he wanted to and though he was sure that at least a part of her wanted him to; John was of the "Let's not talk about it" school of family troubles; he thought, whom temblors of doubt had never shaken to the base, that he did not need to tell her how much he loved her, that she knew it without being told, that saying it would be sentimental.

The jatter and flick of the television set caught his conscious-ness; he strode over toward it.

"No, Dad!" cried Rachel. "Kroger is going to be talking."

"Kroger," he said with scorn and snapped it off.

"You must find out what he's like," she cried, and ran over to turn it back on. This was dreadfully important to her; she had planned something; he must not refuse her. "You must know, for the big meeting tomorrow night. There will be some Brockmen there. I just thought," she suddenly collapsed, "it would be a help."

"Of course, honey, sure." How could he reject this offer? "It's just that I can't stand that fellow Kroger. He's as bad as Brock was."

"But it will help you if you see him. Won't it, Dad?"

"Of course, honey, sure. Now sit down here." He pressed her hands warmly. "There's something I've got to tell you."

"Oh," she cried, shying involuntarily from the danger behind his gravity, like a horse from a snake's rattle, "I forgot to tell you. Bishop Freeman phoned. He wants to talk to you."

"All right, Rachel. I'll telephone him. Now . . ."

"He sounded urgent. I think he wants to talk to you right away."

"I will, Rachel. First I want to talk to you."

"Do you want to talk to me about Dick?"

"Yes. The police have satisfied themselves, finally, that he's not guilty."

"No, he's not guilty."

"But now they are sure enough of it to set him free."

"Set him free." She spoke in a very little voice, without emotion.

"Yes, this evening. I asked them to hold off awhile, till I'd seen you. Now what I want you to do is this: Put Teddy in your car, asleep as he is, and drive down to my cabin. Here's a hundred dollars. Stay there till I get in touch with you."

"In touch."

"Yes. I'll take care of Dick. When it's all right for you to come back I'll let you know. He doesn't know where the cabin is. Practically nobody does. You'll be alone. Now he won't be home for a couple of hours. Do this for me, dear."

"No," she said in the same little voice, her eyes yearning he could not tell for what.

"No? You must." She shook her head. "Why not?"

"You know. I told you."

"But he is mad."

"Are you sure?"

He was not even angry. He could have wept. "Well, well, who knows what is best?" He knew she would not yield.

"Don't blame me, Daddy," she said.

"No, my dear." He spoke brusquely, having given up. "I'll phone the bishop now." He walked brusquely from the room.

But Rachel followed him into the unlighted little hall, tagged along after him as it seemed to him, stood by him while he sat dialing the number. He turned in annoyance to tell her he would be through in a minute, but the sight of her dumb and slumped and immobile beside him was more than he could bear. "Honey," he said and held out his arms, "baby, I love you." And now finally that he had given way she too gave way, and threw herself on his lap and hid her face on his shoulder. Here at last was his daughter begging him with tears to take care of her, and he was, for a moment, happy comforting her.

But only for a moment: she was too big. She was a good-sized woman, heavy on his legs and awkward leaning against him, and he inadvertently pressed one of her breasts with his hand, trying to comfort her. This was no daughter yielding and altogether trusting, but a sexual woman (once his daughter) who would stand by her husband. Yet, when in a moment she stood up, they were not uncomfortable with one another. It was as though this genuine interchange of love, which yet failed of that retrograde satisfaction they had both wanted, had by its very failure and yet true warmth forced them to reassume their proper roles.

He dialed his number again, and she went to the kitchen to make coffee.

She brought him a cup where he sat watching Kroger.

"Did you talk to the bishop, Dad?"

"No. He'll be home about eleven. I'll go by then."

"I'm out of cream. Will milk be all right?"

"Sure, dear." He smiled at her easiness and smiling. "Is there a match around?"

She glanced at the television image of Kroger's flat, furious face, and looked at John. "You're a fine man," she said. And if they had turned off the television set then, they could have sat together in a silence of peace.

Kroger was leading four thousand in a stomping hymn of universal love. He was square-faced and glowering. He kept shooting his cuffs and adjusting his hand-painted long silk tie. The coat of his suit extended nearly down to his knees and he wore rings with flashing stones. He walked up to one of the huge sprays of iris on the table behind him and brushed a leaf with the back of his fingers. He went over to a couple of men at a side table, like a fighter to his trainer and towel boy, talked to them a moment, and tossed off a glass of water. When the song was over, he prayed at God with doubled fists to bless everyone on earth Protestant Catholic or Jew it made no difference so long as they were good Christians who believed in His universal love. The text for tonight, he said, would be taken from a talk of the greatest man of the twentieth century, who set an example to the whole earth—Protestant, Catholic or Jew. Fortunately there was a tape recording of this talk, and it was also printed in *The Brocklight*. It is so beautiful. Isn't it? (YES) It is so good. Isn't it? (YES) It is heavenly music. Isn't it? (YES) There is no death. Is there? (NO NO NO) While the great television audience was hearing this inspirational message in Brother Brock's own voice Kroger said he would accompany with the electric organ, using the printed version as his score. He set the open magazine on the music holder and began chording out night-club entertainer clichés; the words appeared on the screen in montage over the image of his face, just as Brock's voice swam in Kroger's mood music.

Brock's message was this: Don't put any value on things of this world; give what you have to the Universal Church, where it will do the most good by carrying the truth to others; television time is mighty expensive, and so is building churches, and so is printing and mailing half a million copies of *The Brocklight* every week; so line up and pin your folding money sins on the clothesline of redemption now.

Kroger approved of these sentiments, but since he was going to run for governor he applied them to himself. He pointed out (and shed his coat as he did it) that he would make a good governor because he was indifferent to things of this world. Half an hour later, as he was pulling off his tie, he introduced a second idea, which was that every good Christian whether Protestant Catholic or Jew should vote for him to keep the state free of Communism and Reds and other subversive low-down sneak thief elements. At the end, with his sleeves rolled up and his hair in his eyes, he was enjoining the blessings of God down onto every loving mother's son in the world; he was cut off regretfully by the station announcer.

Rachel, who feared as the gentle do experience of anarchy, shuddered before this confident anarch, this destroyer, this un-creator who had not even the humanity of hypocrisy. "Dad," she said as she went to turn the set off, "what can you do about him?"

"There is nothing I can do," said John, "but ignore him. You can't argue with him."

A voice from the doorway to the little hall hit them from behind: "Right!" It was Dick laughing. "He's got the best argument in the world on his side."

But Rachel, of surprise, exhaustion, relief, anxiety, half-fainted against a chair. They laid her on the couch, and she waved their attentions away while she recuperated. She watched Dick's undeviating eyes as though she would never understand what they hid.

"You were afraid to punish me," said Dick to John. "You got them to set me free. I suppose it had something to do with the gun. What do I know about guns?" He was animated with a strange force. "Do you know what we must do? I have it. Here." He pulled out a wrinkled, soiled envelope. John, for Rachel's sake, did not oppose him. "I'm leaving this for Mr. Kroger. He must know our best approach. Do you know what that is?" John shook his head. "I wrote it all out in jail. The government must execute the guilty." He was whispering, intensely. "The machinery is all set up for it. It must be used. The guilty know who they are. They must be translated when they offer themselves. I have been ready to be translated. You have not done your duty. This must be the first plank in our platform. No?"

John took him by the arm. "Let's leave Rachel alone."

"Let go of me!" said Dick, with a sort of authority in his voice. "This is my own house. Don't you like my idea? We'll make it a law. Then it will be all right for you, won't it, John? There are a lot like you who hold by a thing just as long as it's the law. Honey," he cried, and darted over to Rachel, who had groaned. "How are you? I didn't mean to scare you, but I heard Mr. Kroger's voice when I came up outside and I was so glad to see you listening to him I just came in the back way. I thought it would do you both good to watch him. The truth works in strange ways. Oh honey, did you hear his message? Did you let it touch you? John," he said, turning, "you're going to run for governor too. Well, whichever one of you is elected there's going to be a new law about sacrifices and I know you will respect it. Think of the example. Sometimes twenty or thirty or even fifty guilty people executed for one crime. They are ready to be translated. They are guilty. I must set an example now. It's the least I can do. You have made it hard for me. But I'll do it. Think, when one bomb is dropped on a city, how many are guilty—all the men in the airplane, all the men that ordered them, all the men that made the bomb, that designed it, that shipped it. I've thought about it all. I know. I was a bombardier. How many are guilty of murder? No no, how many are *not* guilty, that is the true question. The government must help those who are ready to be translated. It can be good for that much at least. John," he said, and his voice deepened, "you think that Mr. Brock is dead because you have seen his body in the casket. But he is not dead. Who," he paused and looked triumphantly first at one then at the other, "who do you think is talking to you now?"

Rachel sat up and John began to appeal to her, but Dick stopped him. "I'm sorry, John. I've nothing more to say to you. I have something to tell my wife."

"Rachel," said John, "do you want me to stay?"

She spoke with her eyes on the floor. "No. I'll call you in the morning, Dad." She stood up, and he saw a kind of strength in her eyes that gave him assurance enough to leave without speaking.

Dick opened the door for him, a little ceremoniously, and closed it after him.

For an hour John sat in his car, alone on the dark side of the moon.

"Will you have some sherry, Mr. Haffner?"

"Thank you." (Why not?)

"The bishop will be down very shortly." She smiled knowingly at John. "Diocesan meetings are usually tedious."

"I'm sure."

"My husband is very upset about the followers of this Brock person. Could you tell me, Mr. Haffner, what there is about them to excite him so?"

"Well," said John, "they don't seem to keep politics and religion apart as they ought."

"Really? I'm afraid I know very little about their doings. What is it that they are noteworthy for?"

John did not like her, and he was too worried to pretend to himself that he did. "Their leaders, Mrs. Freeman, Brock himself and now this man Kroger. Beyond that, the most notable thing about them is, they are mad."

"Mad? Oh dear."

He saw the prepared concern light up her eyes, and remembered that helping the mad was her avocation. "Not insane, not the sort you lock up, but old-fashioned mad, lunatic, horn-mad, the kind in whom cowardice and fear are so diffused that they no longer know the difference between things. They are morally a slush in which vileness taints everything decent, they are brutal run-down tag-end Christians, the sort that slaughter whoever won't be converted, the sort that live forever."

"John," said the bishop from the door; he spoke in a courteous, steady voice, not a voice that one would have expected after such a tirade, "John, I'm glad you could come. My dear," he said to his wife, who looked troubled, "thank you for entertaining Mr. Haffner until I could come down."

"Willard," she began.

"My dear," he said, helping her rise, "Mr. Haffner is a busy man. He is being considered as a candidate for governor, you know. We have a little business to talk over. It is late."

They said their good nights.

"I gather," said the bishop as he stuffed his pipe, "that you were disburdening yourself of confusion and trouble upon my wife. I think it is a tribute to her that she is so good a confessor. People find it safe to heap not just their words of confession but their turbulence as well upon her. You are one of many."

It was a conscious rebuke, which John, deserving it, swallowed.

"I understand," said the bishop, watching his fingertips carefully two by two press against each other, "that your son-in-law has been released."

"This evening."

"How is your daughter?"

"Extremely upset."

The bishop allowed his fingertips to interlace; he tapped his chin with his thumbs. "You realize, John, how the Brock people will use this episode of your son-in-law against you."

"Claim I pulled wires to get him free?"

"Yes."

"I think you know my opinion of them."

"There is no way you can beat them in argument, John. If you withdraw from the running, it's because you are afraid of them. If you stay in, you will be exploiting the notoriety of your son-in-law. If you are publicly friendly to him, it will prove you are expedient. If you are hostile, it will prove you are not a good family man."

"I know it. I shall ignore them."

"Can you?"

"Yes."

"We are old friends, John. I admire you. We have got along together well. You know how I support you. But John, I must tell you, I am having trouble with my people. Only tonight, for example."

"But you church people hate Brock and Kroger as much as I do!"

The bishop leaned over and filled John's wineglass as he spoke. "Well, perhaps we don't disagree with him quite so wholeheartedly as you. Not in so many particulars. Your statement Wednesday, for example—I hope very strongly, as a staunch friend and supporter, that you won't be tricked into making one like it again, not publicly."

John was stuffed to the gullet with Stahlman's warnings, but he tamped this one down on top of the others. "No," he said dully, "I know I won't be tricked again."

"The pity is," said the bishop, "that such an entirely personal matter as a point of religious dogma should ever get mixed up in politics at all."

His wife opened the door. "Mr. Haffner, your daughter is on the telephone. She sounds very distressed."

He returned from the telephone to find them both waiting for him. "The police just told her," he said bitterly, "that Dick— that's her husband—threw himself under the wheels of a truck half an hour ago."

"Heavens," cried Mrs. Freeman. She put her hands to her mouth. "How horrible. Why did he do such a thing?"

"He told us this evening why." John was set to attack these two who did not disagree with Dick quite wholeheartedly. "To punish himself for Brock's murder. Is that mad enough for you?"

"John," said the bishop, putting a kindly hand on his shoulder, "your daughter needs you. Go to her."

"Yes," said John, ready to flare up again.

"If there is anything we can do to help," said Mrs. Freeman, with warmth, with tears.

"Thanks," said John brusquely. But those were wet, human tears on the cheeks of this mask of mercy. She deserved a genuine answer. "I am going to send my daughter and her little boy down to my cabin by the sea. I will take care of the disposal of the body and deal with friends and so on."

"Willard," said Mrs. Freeman, "can't we help by arranging the services?"

"Hardly," said John, his voice tempered by rudeness again. "In the Universal Church they are translated, which requires no funeral. The body of their dead . . ."

"John, this is a tragic misfortune to you," said the bishop, giving him his hat. "We understand one another? I wish you all success in your political life. I only hope you will not make it necessary for my people to turn from you. Your way would be made very difficult without us."

"Anything at all," murmured his wife through the closing door.

5

John was to speak Saturday night at eight, but by quarter to seven it was obvious that the hall they had hired in which to listen to the worthy attorney general could not possibly hold all that were coming to hear the headline candidate. At state conventions of the AFL normally, those who were not off drinking on Saturday night or watching dancing girls undress were deciding the policies of the year in hotel-room caucuses. But John, marrying in his person by whatever accident unshaken virtue to sensational and religious crime, was the biggest attraction since General MacArthur had flown home from the East asking for hot dogs. On the spot they hired the biggest auditorium in the city and nearly filled it with delegates and friends and persons of political importance; the three or four hundred seats left over at the top of the gallery were opened to plain union members.

John had written his speech the weekend before; the title was supposed to be humorous, "When to Break the Law," but reading the speech over he found it intolerably dry; yet he had no strength to change it, and he was afraid to walk up to the speaker's stand empty-handed.

All day he had drunk coffee and had been able to eat nothing. Only Monahan's pleading and Stahlman's cajoling—the good of the party—had brought him out tonight at all. Monahan introduced him fast.

John went to the speaker's stand and opened the manuscript of his speech, and suddenly all the lights went out except for a circle of glare of which he was the center. He glanced up and back: he was alone. He felt small. A roar assaulted him, that rhythmless total many-mouthed single roar of the crowd. He had heard it a thousand times before, but this time it was for him. He felt weak. He peered out into the quivering darkness, seeing nothing. He did not smile; there was nothing to smile about, in himself or in that huge sound which was neither welcoming nor affectionate; this was the tribe eons before reasoning, asserting its power and oneness. But reason was his faith; he was utterly alone in the spotlight, wanting to tell them they were wrong, he was not what they thought; after three full minutes of the roar he could not even have said that. Yet he was not exactly afraid. He felt a profound disquiet, a total, inexplicable disquiet. Trying to see faces in the crowd, needing individuals to exchange a glance of intelligence with, he looked at the dim faces of the roarers in the front seats; the glare was in his eyes but he peered, and thought he made out Mrs. Freeman in a black hat not shouting, Rachel smiling proudly, his assistant, a judge, a neighbor, but he knew better; yet if he did not find someone who would remind him he was himself, he would become that reasonless leader the crowd wanted him to be; he saw then (he was a man with weak visual memory), saw with utter and reasonless clarity impassive on whichever of the crowd, the face of Dick as he had seen it stone-stare up that morning from the coroner's slab. He had to have light.

With all his strength, he walked composedly over to the left side of the stage, beckoned the light man, and asked him to turn up the house lights. There were some muttered objections; John commanded. Light diminished the roar and also his disquiet from the roar. Light made for him faces that were not creations of his fantasy, faces that were more than orifices of tribal force, faces that reminded him of reason. These are but five thousand, he said to himself, and there are millions of voters.

The crowd quieted. He said, "My friends," in a steady, reasonable voice; yet he felt a quivering in his guts. He thanked them. And because he could have done nothing else in the world at that moment, he began to read his moral, mildly humorous, desiccated speech. At first he was encouraged by their laughter and applause at nearly every pause. But the further behind he left the obvious, easy jokes—"The best time to break the law is about four in the morning when the police are asleep"—the less the audience applauded. And it was not only their applause that he was losing, it was their enthusiasm as well; they didn't care a damn about the niceties of moral decision forced upon the just by unjust laws. The further into reason he withdrew, the less (as he knew) he advanced the public cause of reason. He read the last sentence of the tenth paragraph with a sense of arid desperation: "For there is, surely, a law superior to anything written on the statute books." What next? Who cared?

Then a voice from the back of the house yelled, amiable, but demanding an answer: "John, is he dead?" That's all there was to it: "John, is he dead?" That's all they wanted to know, all of them: "Is he dead? Is he dead? Is he dead?"

He kept shaking his head and saying, "I don't know, I don't know." But they wouldn't listen to that. "It's better not to think about it." But they were thinking about it.

In the front row looking up at him motionlessly there was a

little woman in a black hat, grave as Mrs. Freeman would have been here, who knew the answer; behind her, there was a shouting barrel-chested man in a hand-painted tie, who knew the answer. Leaning over the rail of the balcony to his left, there was a blowsy, tousled, middle-aged woman making urgent gestures at him friendlily, and a big-bellied man beside her giving the finger to a hand-painted tie across the hall: they knew the answer, the opposite answer.

"How should I know?" his voice boomed over the public address system. "What difference does it make anyhow?"

But their quaking roar would not let him off.

There were these three:

Expediency, and all his political advisers, holding him back: No.

Rachel, and his deepest belief: Are you sure?

Truth, as it seemed to him then, as the crowd wanted it then, just the truth: Yes.

For a moment John grasped the edges of the stand; he was dizzy with the fumes from decision-making. When his head cleared he pulled himself up and looked out at the whole crowd, now its master. They knew it by his eyes and fell silent.

"Yes. He is dead." He spoke in the tone of voice they wanted. "Of course he is dead, and my son-in-law is dead. They're both as dead as doornails, and it won't be long till I'm as dead as a doornail." They roared and they roared. And he thought it was what he had said that had won them again, forgetting that Wednesday when he had won that other, identical crowd, he had said no such thing as this. "We're all doornails, every last one of us, and it's too damned bad." Ah, but his voice was inciting to war on The Enemy. The disapproval on the face of the woman in the black hat, her quickly leaving by a side door, told him that. He didn't care. "But you're not going to do anything about dying by saying that it isn't so. If there's one thing I hate it's a coward. No, there's something worse—cowards that don't even

know they're cowards. They squeal in the dark. I've heard them."
The Brockmen did not roar for him; he saw their sullen faces
glancing about them; they were fearful of opposing him now.
"It's a damned shame we're all going to die, but I heard something worse over television last night: there's a man in this state
named Kroger who squealed for an hour that he was *never* going
to die. Imagine that. A permanent Kroger." The crowd's raging,
contemptuous, laughing will billowed up under him.

For an hour he walked on water.

"Mommy, where's Grandpa?"

"I've told you, honey, you can't go fishing after supper." She
did not turn around from washing dishes.

"I don't want to go fishing. Where's Grandpa?"

"I'm not sure where he is, Teddy. But we've got to leave him
alone some of the time. Grandpa is awfully tired."

"There's this man, Mommy."

"I couldn't help hearing what you said, Mrs. Horton." It was
a bony young man standing in the doorway between the kitchen
and the living room. "My name is Rossiter."

"Newspaper?" she said, leaning on the edge of the sink, exhausted and afraid.

"AP. I just wanted to talk to Mr. Haffner."

"How did you find us?"

"Luck. Let me put it this way—in terms of public service I
feel justified in . . ."

She could have cried, she could have cringed in a corner from
his hard polite energy, she could have crept into bed and curled
up under the covers and whimpered; but Teddy was there to
keep her a woman. "Honey," she said, taking him to the back
door, "run down to the river and see if you can find Grandpa,
and if you do find him tell him to come right home."

"Why, thank you," said Rossiter with surprise. "This is very
kind of you."

"Be careful!" she called after Teddy. She walked into the front room and sat where she could look over the misty little valley. "My father is in his fifties," she said, gazing at the gray boulders on the green hillside across, "but he is very strong. He'll drive you away."

"Mrs. Horton! He is a public figure. He belongs to the people, in a sense."

"That's a lie." She spoke abstractedly, her attention outside the window. She craned her neck a little to look at the stretch of riverbank she could see. The river was swollen with spring and dark with the rich loam it bore down from the hills. "You climbed over our locked gate without permission. You walked into our home without permission. You are remaining here against my will."

Her indifference to what she was saying—which was really not indifference but a withdrawal from feeling again more than she could bear again—worked strongly on Rossiter.

"Mrs. Horton," he said rapidly, "there's a story behind that press release he gave out. That's the story I want to get. The people deserve it. Now nobody can help me as much as you can. You know yourself he's not old and feeble. Why did he withdraw right when he was getting up momentum?"

"He likes fishing."

"So? He also liked talking to the masses so they'd listen. He liked handling them. You could tell by watching him."

"He'd antagonized the churches; that's enough."

"That's enough of a political reason. But it's the story behind that I'm after. Why did he antagonize the churches? That's the human story."

"It wasn't his intention to antagonize them. It was because of the crowd. That's what he told me: 'I was with them.' " One of those boulders perched on the hillside was John with a rod in his hand. She had seen him squat there when he had gone out after supper, but the light was too milky with evening for her to be able to tell which one he was now. "Do you really want to know why he quit?"

"Yes."

She herself, her voice remote, was going to find out. Only this peacefulness, disturbed just as much as this man had done, not dangerously, could have made her talk thus. She wondered, dimly, what she was going to say.

"The law was his life, and he believed in the people. He was the servant of their will. When he discovered he could be the master of their will, he no longer knew what was right or wrong."

"You mean John Haffner lost his nerve?"

"No. I mean he was tempted from behaving justly and resisted the temptation."

"Well, tell me this—was there any question of a deal with the Universal Party? With him out of the running their chances are certainly improved."

"Mr. Rossiter, he began to feel—he told me he felt, as he stood before crowds, that their welfare depended upon his power over them. What he did Saturday night was his sin against the Holy Ghost; but when he led that crowd into the wilderness of his own will, he did it in such a way that he should never be allowed to lead them back into the land of law again."

"Then why did he answer that question as he did?"

"What question?"

"*The* question—Is he dead?"

She stood, still not looking at Rossiter. "My father will be here before long." Her voice, with refusal to feel, was small and thin. "If you tell anyone else where we are staying, or if you print any of this interview, or if you ever come bothering us again, my father will make you regret it."

He left.

She sat down again, weak and remote. But she was glad that she had found the strength to resist the outside world; perhaps she had found it because she was protecting John. This little valley, John, and Teddy were her world now. She saw the dot of Teddy running along the shore. He had got his feet wet, no doubt, crossing the river. Perhaps he would spot John and bring him home. It didn't matter, so long as Teddy didn't stay out too late. John was content now. He usually stayed near the mouth of the river, but she did not think it was because he caught more fish there; his line trailed where it would most of the time. Actually he seemed just to stand or sit for hours like a rock, as now, deaf to her halloos, turned in from doing, her father, that private citizen her father whom she loved, smoking from time to time and shifting position a little when he got stiff, watching the river proffer its wealth to the unappeasable sea.

Miracle Play

In my sixth year I learned to my wonder that there was an invisible world perfect with the one I saw.

I awoke on the morning of my sixth birthday, not to the strains of "Happy Birthday," not to my mother's kiss, not even as usual to the sound of my dad in the bathroom singing as he shaved, "Where is the child? for I am Herod thy king"; I awoke alone and late, hearing Granny's heavy foot in the hall and the clank of basins in the bathroom. When I came out, she told me in a cross voice to hurry with my dressing and then go outdoors to play. When I asked her why, she told me not to bother her, Mother was not well, and she gave me a whack on the bottom that wasn't for my birthday. All I had for breakfast was an apple. After breakfast I went out, and found tadpoles in a bucket. I took one up to Granny to see, but by the time I'd reached the first landing of the stairs she'd run down to me; she made a hissing noise when I showed her the tadpole, and cuffed my ears and said I was bad. A cuff is only a cuff, but I'd never been cuffed on the head before, or if I had been, it hadn't made much difference; I went into the parlor to be alone and lick my tears. I vowed not to go out till they came for me, and if they never came I'd die there of hunger on the horsehair sofa where I had no business being. I hadn't been bad, or good, or anything else.

I'd just wanted to see my mother, and wanted to know what was the matter that I couldn't. I sat on the slick sofa quite straight; I thought for a time of putting my feet up to spite Granny, but I decided I wouldn't for fear the spite would hurt Mother more. The blinds were not quite down, and through the cracks I watched the sun go out and the heavens darken for a summer storm.

And then—I'm not sure when but a little before the storm broke—I heard Dad humming on the porch. When he opened the front door he was singing in his deep voice, "For I am Herod." Mother had told me he was practicing to be Herod in a Christmas pageant at church; but since I did not know what she meant by a pageant or by Herod I just listened to the songs he sang. He worked on the railroad at that time and would be gone for long stretches; he'd never been home so early in the day as this. I ran to the parlor door ready to jump to him in the hall, but then I heard Granny call from the kitchen, "Henry?" and I remembered where I was. I watched them, through a crack I made in the doorway, as Dad asked her in a low voice all sorts of questions I could not grasp. Granny was steaming and billowy, wisps of hair lay on her left cheek, she kept rolling her hands up in her apron. Dad was Dad.

"And where's the boy?" he said.

"I haven't been seeing him around for a while," she answered. "He was getting underfoot."

"We mustn't leave him out. He's afraid of thunder and lightning."

"Oh Lord, he is," she said impatiently.

"And besides," said Dad, "it's his birthday today."

She threw up her hands, sighed, "With all I've got to do," and went back to the kitchen.

What was there for me? As soon as she was gone I flung open the door and caught him with one foot on the stairs.

"Daddy!" I cried. "Daddy! I want to see Mother!"

His hands were raspy on the backs of my legs as he picked me up, and his beard hurt my cheek, and he smelled of sweat and pipe smoke. "Just let me go say hello to her, my boy, and see whether she can have you."

She couldn't. He told me she was dozing. But then, whatever Granny might say to the contrary, he carried me up to Mother's door and let me peek in at her with the white sheet up to her chin and her hair all loose on the pillow.

He held me during the storm, singing to me.

A doctor came while it was still hailing and stayed for a short time.

I thought two or three times I heard Mother cry out; Dad didn't seem worried enough. Then, once during a lull, I knew I'd heard her and began crying myself. He told me that she was not sorry to be in pain, so we must not cry. But I thought he was just comforting me, and as I lay in his arms crying, I gave myself over to hating Granny with all my heart. I was sure that she was responsible one way or another for Mother's hurting and that Dad simply did not understand. To myself I called Granny the Old Hag of the House, and I wished passionately that she would get locked up in the closet under the stairs till she was dead.

As soon as the storm had passed, Dad took me to the barber-shop and for a birthday present had my hair cut for the first time by a barber; I was very proud. Then he took me to Aunt Rebecca's to stay till he should come for me; I couldn't go back home till a big surprise should be waiting for me; he winked as he said it; I wondered why. When he kissed me good-bye I told him I loved him.

Aunt Rebecca was Dad's older sister, very tall, and I'd heard people say she was afraid of men because she had a purple birth-mark on her face and throat. Maybe she was, but that day a dandruffy, out-of-town man named Nathan, with whom she laughed, came by in a touring car and drove us into the country for a picnic. They were kind to me, but their real talk was only to each other. He kept saying what a character she was, and though I didn't know what he meant I knew she did not like being called it, and I loved her jealously. The grass was wet. They were stretched out on a blanket in the sun. I went off by a brook to play. When I was squatting behind some bushes, they kissed. I was astonished to see them do it, for Nathan's feet didn't go much farther down than Aunt Rebecca's knees. I stood up to watch but they kept on kissing and laughing away. I was ashamed of their rudeness and went off by myself. Yet, on the ride home, Aunt Rebecca held me in her lap and talked only to me, or sang under her breath a song I'd been hearing her practice, "This babe a crown doth wear"; when she said good-bye to Nathan, she did not shake his hand or even look at him, but thanked him "for the nice time" in the way you don't mean it.

After a while she took me home. On the front steps we met the doctor again.

"Well, Harvey," he said, "how do you like the idea of a twelve-pound baby brother?"

He smelled of medicine. I didn't know what he was talking about.

"How is everything going?" Aunt Rebecca asked.

"Fine, everything's fine and dandy." And he pushed a lemon drop into my mouth.

There was a baby in the house all right; I could hear that squeaky noise babies make. When Granny said so, Dad carried me up to Mother's room. Mother was very pale but she smiled at me and held out her hand; Dad leaned me over and she kissed me on the forehead and patted my hair.

The baby was asleep, tucked under her arm. His name was Jimmy. I thought it particularly outrageous that he should already have a name. Granny said I must get out and leave Mother in peace with the baby.

Some time later I was again sent off to stay with Aunt

Rebecca, this time because Granny was sick. Next morning Dad came for me, took me on his knee, and told me that Granny had passed away to a better world and that I must be very careful with Mother. Aunt Rebecca said she would bake a spice cake for our dinner, she had to do something. As soon as Dad and I walked in the door of our house, Mother grabbed me and burst into sobs that alarmed me into tears.

Next afternoon I was told to go alone into the parlor to look at my grandmother for the last time. In the parlor, it felt chilly on the hottest day; the casket was sleek as a piano and lined with pink satin; the air was dripping with the odor of flowers; I was very solemn. Her face was not the same: broader, smoother, pinker on the cheeks. I would not have known her but for the mole on the side of her nose. I touched her hand, and nothing happened.

It occurred to me that, if this was really Granny, though she looked so changed, then Jimmy might be changed too from what he really was. Maybe he was really a little pig; he looked as much like a pig as this Granny looked like the Granny I had always known. Mother had said that God had given us Jimmy and now she said that God had taken Granny; yet here Granny was; so where had Jimmy been before God had given him to us? Probably in a pigpen. Mother and Dad had both told me that Granny was happier now than she had been in life, in this vale of tears, Dad called it; but neither of them acted as though they believed what they'd said, especially Mother, and the expression on Granny's face was very stern. I tried to make my face as stern as hers, but as I stood there stiff as a soldier I began to feel my heart beating in my neck, and I was seized by the fear I might blow up if I didn't start breathing again. I panted till I was dizzy.

Only one thing was I clear about: I felt the opposite of what everyone else was feeling; just as I was sorry Jimmy had been born, I was glad Granny had died. I felt neither proud nor guilty about this, but only wondering; to be sure, I hid signs of my contrary, imprudent emotions.

Aunt Rebecca sang at Granny's funeral. She wore a long black dress with a white lace collar, and she sang "Nearer My God to Thee" and "The End of a Perfect Day." She stood facing the casket as though she was singing to Granny; but I knew that Granny was in heaven listening to the angels' music; perhaps the angels sounded like Aunt Rebecca. Afterward, everyone said how beautifully Aunt Rebecca had sung and how lovely she looked. The way she was standing we could see only the right side of her face, the unafflicted side. I hardly knew her.

By December life seemed to be getting satisfactory again. It's true Mother paid me much less attention than before, most of the time, and often she looked sad, when she was thinking of Granny; but since I was off at school a lot, it wasn't so bad; besides, Dad had taught me to read already, and I often read Bible stories while she was ironing. Jimmy improved; he was fun to play with once in a while; he laughed at me and liked to grab my nose; he began to look less like a pig and more like Mother. Dad was Dad.

Then the Sunday before Christmas Dad went off right after supper, and Mother took Jimmy next door to stay with old Mrs. Shipley, and she and I bundled up and went off to church. I had never before been to church in the evening; the only light was from candles; where the pulpit had been stood a tall plush chair; on the other side, in front of the choir seats, was an old-fashioned cradle and a stool. The piano was not in sight, but from behind a curtain of sheets on a wire came piano music. Nathan was sitting in front of us, by himself; he didn't notice me and I didn't tell Mother I knew him. The church was full.

The three wise men came out and sang how far they had come to see the child that was to be born. Someone came and told

them the king wanted to see them. I was very excited because
these wise men were really members of the church whom I saw
every Sunday and often around town during the week; the thin
one was our mailman. Yet they seemed taller than usual, larger
in every way, and their beards astonished me. The next thing I
knew they had gone to see the king on his throne, the tall chair,
and the king was my dad. "Herod!" they sang. I gasped. I leaned
against Mother, who put a finger to my lips and said it was only
Daddy. It was as much as I could do to keep from crying out
to tell him to become my dad again, but Mother's hand was
right on my shoulder ready to clap over my mouth; I made no
noise.

For he wasn't only my dad, he was Herod too. His voice was
deep, he wore king's robes, he was taller than all the rest, his eyes
were dark and fierce. Dad was trusting and warm, but Herod
was full of suspiciousness and hate. Dad was kind to any dog or
cat, but Herod said with a dreadful sneer, "Thou cur," to a
servant. Dad loved me, and spanked me only when there was
nothing else to be done, but Herod ordered all the first-born men-
children to be put to the sword. After he had sung this order to
his soldiers, there was a thunderous drum roll from behind the
curtain.

I was used to the thought that everyone had a soul, and I was
used to God as I was used to loving and being loved; I had
always more or less assumed that, though I'd never seen a soul or
God, in heaven souls and God would all see one another. Nothing
unimaginable was.

For several minutes I was a jelly of terror. Mother knew
nothing of it, for she only patted me idly from time to time,
watching the play.

The next thing I knew, Aunt Rebecca in a long white gown
and with sparkling jewels in her hair was singing to Mary that
her babe should be crowned the Savior of the world. The robe,
as I knew, was really a double-bed sheet which Mother had been

helping her sew on the day before, but when she stretched her arms out to Mary on the stool, I was sure this was how the angels appeared. I heard Nathan sigh; he shook his head a little; I liked him better; he didn't think she was a character now. There was an invisible violin playing the melody along with her as she sang.

Yet, though she was standing so we could see her whole face, birthmark and all, she was—everything was—so beautiful I had a falling-away feeling in the stomach.

My terror awoke while the shepherds and wise men were adoring the blessed doll, for I remembered that Herod's soldiers were at that very moment looking for this first-born to kill him. Then, at the end as I listened to the invisible angel, visible Aunt Rebecca, warn Mary and Joseph to flee to Egypt where the child would be safe, I realized that it was far more important that these people had done what they had done, and that God had wished it so, than that actually they were church members and my family. The beauty was as great as the terror. All of us sang "Noël."

Words Words Words

The words were ready: "Our marriage will be a contract of equals freely joined." He had decided upon them two weeks after leaving port, in a rolling sea. Everything else he'd thought about for the past four months, everything of importance to him, had been adornment, explanation, preparation for the delivery of those words. He had not written them to her, for he felt never so stiff as with a pen in his hand; written, that sentence said everything he meant; yet he knew that, uncircumstanced, it would be impotent upon her. And he intended it to bind; he meant her never to forget it so long as they should be married.

Words, as he believed, bind only when delivered with ceremony, and here was his problem. Their love being free from authority, Jane and he were deprived of ceremony; indeed, once when they had talked about two of her friends who were living together, they had agreed that marriage itself was a social convention to be deferred to only for convenience' sake and the sentiments of relatives; they had therefore never talked about getting married. But off the coast of Venezuela outward bound, he had decided to propose to her. He needed, atavistically, a profounder tie than New York lovers were bound by. They would be bound to freedom, that must be absolutely clear, but bound. He had had to invent his own ceremony.

His plan was this. He would phone her at her office as soon as his ship docked; he would have air-mailed her a letter from the last port so that she would know which day to expect him; she would be sure to have kept that evening free for him. He would go to her apartment a little after six; they would talk for a while, till the flush of reunion should have subsided; he would take her to the Captain's Table, where they would have shrimp cocktail and broiled lobster; then, over coffee and, he hoped, at the same table from which she had first accepted him for her lover, he would say what he had to say. It was a ceremony of sentiment, he knew that, wholly private, devoid of sacrament; but he knew no other way to freight the words of his proposal with the gravity he wanted them to bear. No words repeated to a justice of the peace in a courthouse office could bind them more than legally, and an altar would make liars of them. The Captain's Table; shrimp, lobster, and white burgundy; her left hand in his right at the edge of the table, as it had been when she had said, "Come make love to me"—he would ask her to wear the same green dress and her Toledo earrings.

The ship arrived on a Tuesday; good, the restaurant would not be crowded. It was berthed in Brooklyn by nine thirty in the morning; he was second only to the first mate in getting to the pay booth. Jane's "Darling, you're here at last" greeted him in the accents of every sailor's dream of welcome; she had been waiting for him; she adored him.

He got to his hotel-rooming house in Greenwich Village by five. His room was made up and his clothes were hanging pressed in the closet. There was his father's invariable card waiting for him: the old man's leg was bothering him again, they'd had the coldest March fifth in thirty years and the gas north of Syracuse had failed for eight hours, thank God nobody died of it, business was about as usual but every year the new cars got harder to work on, come home for a good long stay. And there was another envelope from Syracuse too, in a hand and with a return address he did not recognize, postmarked more than three months earlier.

The letter was a short paragraph, signed, "Very sincerely yours, Rosannah," and the salutation read, "Dear Mark." Well, good. She'd never called him Mark during the time they'd known one another. He'd sent her a picture postcard from Beirut, where her father had gone to medical school, a neutral greeting which he'd signed Mark and sent in care of her father at his hospital. The May before, waiting for his mate's papers, he'd substituted at The Drumlins for the golf pro, who'd sprained his ankle; Rosannah had taken lessons three afternoons a week; in the midst of the last lesson they'd had a spring half hour at the sixth hole; she was engaged; he got the impression that she wished she weren't; he did not even kiss her; she said, "Good-bye, Mr. Birch," and ran off with her head bent; he'd cried before going to sleep; and thence to sea. "Dear Mark, It was so nice of you to send me that card. It made Daddy quite homesick. I am living away from home now, as you can see by my address. I'm teaching first grade in the poorer section of town and loving it. At least I love my children, every one of them. Our acquaintance (I guess that's what it was) came to an end so fast, I didn't have an opportunity to thank you for everything. I hope we meet again." Well, well. Such girlish handwriting. He was at least six years older than she and felt six more than that. She'd shown promise of becoming a good golfer. "I hope we meet again." No more engagement. Well. Too late now, kid, you had your chance. He wondered whether she'd let her hair grow as he'd told her she should.

Jane's door opened as he came down the hall, but she was not in sight. The room was dimly lit. "Jane?" He stepped inside. In the fireplace two logs were flickering softly. "Darling," she whispered behind him and pushed the door closed. She held her arms out to him. She was wearing the silk dragon coat he'd sent her from Saigon on his first trip, held by a gold cord at the

waist; her feet were bare; she wore no make-up. He tossed the
yellow roses he'd brought onto a table and took her in his arms.
She had perfumed herself heavily, as she did only when they were
about to make love. Even so, he might have had fortitude to
resist her, for the moment, as he had planned, were it not for
the Scotch and ice already poured and waiting. "Not yet," he
said as she reached one to him.

"I thought you wouldn't want to," she answered, "but it
wouldn't be loverly to make me drink alone, now would it?"

"But I wanted to talk."

"Of course, darling, we'll talk till dawn if we want to. I don't
have to go to work tomorrow."

What could he do? Good whiskey, four months' abstinence,
her perfume, her white shoulder bare where he'd pushed the coat
askew, her lips after kissing tumescent between pain and invitation till gradually they closed back to the little smile which meant
she was content, her voice of dreamlike welcome—what could
he want to do? The words would wait. He lost the wish to say
them.

"How brown you are, darling. Look how wintry pale I am
beside you. Aren't I revolting? Take off your shirt." Well, she
was exactly as she had been, as nearly perfect as she could be.
The room and the rug, her straight hair helmeted to her head,
her somewhat stubby legs, the just audible chamber music from
the record player, all the same. "I have been faithful to you, you
third mate you. You'd better make it up to me, good good good."
So he was not able to delight her first off with Madagascar as
he had planned, nor to learn whether she had been made head
of the domestic workers section of the agency as she had hoped;
he was not able to do it and could not will it; her dreamy perfection, which had won him in the first place and which at sea
he had wanted to crack, englobed him now again belly, brain,
and members. The ceremonies they performed were those of
sailors' dreams.

The *I love you*'s with which he bejeweled her lost their luster as the fire burned down.

Also, by nine he was hungry beyond crackers and blue cheese. "Let's go out for dinner."

"How thoughtful, darling. I didn't want to cook, even for you, not tonight. Where shall we go?"

"The Captain's Table."

"Marvelous. You know everything I want. I was there a couple of weeks ago for lunch and had the best oyster stew in the world. It was the best."

Instead of entering her game, he said rather gruffly, remembering his plan, "I want shrimp cocktail and lobster. A two-pound lobster. Don't you?"

She looked at him with an expression of worry about the eyes, an expression that had always annoyed him; for the concern, which seemed to be for him, turned out to be for herself, anxiety for fear he should attack her, apology for having displeased him, displeasure at his ill temper. "You have something on your mind, Markie."

"Love."

"Love on your mind? Now?" She laughed with relief. She had never said she loved him. "You got to wait, sailor boy. Which dress do you want me to wear?"

"The green one with the full skirt."

"Oh, you remember! You're my favorite lover ever."

"And those earrings Mike gave you." Mike had been the friend from whom he'd taken Jane.

They sat at the same table all right; she obviously did not remember it; perhaps she did not remember the event either. Perhaps she did not remember that two weeks after they had first become lovers, just before he had sailed on his first voyage, she had told him, in this same room, that she would not go around with other men while he was gone. He must remind her. For so sentimental a ceremony to have any force at all, each step in it must be recognized and savored. He decided to wait till they had finished their lobster before speaking; they were hungry; there was plenty of time; he was not in the right frame of mind. It was so comfortable inside her globe of perfection that only the memory of his resolution and the knowledge that his dissatisfaction was sure to resurrect itself had power to move him on.

Yet even as he began to speak of love he felt the weakness of his words. She was able to treat what he said as mere tenderness, and to preen. He said, intensely because he was angry, "But I mean it," and knew that to say *I mean it* at such a moment meant *I want to mean it.* "I want to marry you," he said, of momentum.

"Oh darling, so fast?"

"We've known each other since last June. You gave up other men for me. You were faithful while I was gone. I think of you all the time. I love you."

"Grim grim grim." He had the impulse to smile with her because he loved her mouth, but he repressed it.

"Our marriage would be a contract of equals freely joined." And they were even holding hands in the same way too.

But *will be* had become *would be*; he had forgotten to remind her of what had happened here before; the ceremony lacked even sentiment. He felt hermetically sealed. "No," she said, "you know I am not sure. Marriage must be all thought out. No, darling, not now. Don't you like what we have?"

"You know I do."

"Then let's don't spoil it by rushing things. It's so wonderful that you're a sailor. I don't think I'll ever get tired of you. The perfect solution!" Solution to love? Very well. He would play her rational, esthetic game of solving love problems. She had defeated him. Or else, not really wanting to be bound even by free and equal marriage, he had capitulated to her.

"Okay, Jane. I just wanted you to know where I stand."

"I do, darling, I know so well and I adore you. So. And if

you don't keep scaring me like that maybe I'll let myself love you. Huh?"

"Okay. Say, who did you come here with anyway a couple of weeks ago?"

"Oh, I was afraid you weren't ever going to ask me that. Good boy." She settled down to curry him sleek with jealousy; he relaxed and enjoyed it.

For five days they were, perfectly, lovers. Only when he was alone and quiet—not often—was he discontent. Ceremony in a restaurant—what had he expected? He was disgusted with himself. Yet he could not help reflecting sometimes that even when they were sharing her pillow with the breath of her repose warm against his neck, he said nothing to her that he might not have said in a Village restaurant in the same tone of voice, nor she to him.

On Sunday he left for Syracuse to visit his father, his Baptist father. Jane cried a little when he was about to leave and laughed at herself for crying, and just before he put his hand on the door handle she brusquely ordered him, "Good-bye."

Two weeks became two hours; the coast of Venezuela became the shores of the Hudson, and the rolling sea a landscape bleared by the sleet and the train window; words of a marriage proposal became a nostalgia. He supposed their love affair would dream along, artificially stimulated by his absences, without rupture for a long time; he should think of it, as Jane did, as a sort of refuge or nocturne, an experience of its own genre, signifying nothing. That is, insignificant. He damned his father for having polluted his childhood with religion; religion's lies he had worked to cleanse his mind of, but its residual sentimentality was harder to purge. He wished he felt emotionally, as well as he admitted intellectually, that Jane was right about their love affair.

The sidewalk and path of his father's house were swept clean. There was smoke from the chimney. When he opened the unlocked front door, the odor of baking ham welcomed him. At his call, his father, beaming and hand outstretched, came from the kitchen in an apron. "Well, son, I'm so glad to see you. It's been lonely without you here." They embraced; Mark's hand avoided with the practice of years the hump on his father's shoulder. "Come in and warm yourself by the fire. I saved some apple logs for this occasion, son. I hope you're good and cold. And hungry. Your letter came yesterday and the first thing I did was go down to the A&P and get a ham, the best that money could buy." Mark said he was grateful, and he was; but also he wished that just once his father would celebrate with something besides ham. The moment this thought irritated him, he was ashamed of it, for he knew that his father worked nine hours a day in the shop and knew how much labor it was for him to cook a big meal. "I called up Calvin and Mona to tell them I wouldn't be out to dinner today. This will make three Sundays in a row I haven't seen them."

"I'm sorry, Dad."

"It's all right, son, Mona's been feeling sort of drug down recently. The winter's been hard on her, no sun for so long. She's not as young as she used to be." The cheeriness which expressed itself on Mr. Birch's face opposed his tendency to look on the worst side of things; the result was neither cheery nor dour, but dry. Mark got the fidgets—the Sunday-afternoon fidgets in his first fifteen minutes at home.

He had not had to stay on the ship the night before but had lied to his father about it—lied so that he could arrive on a Sunday afternoon when there could be no question of his father's suggesting, however despondently, that he go to church. "Dad," he said, "what was the sermon about today?"

Mr. Birch had been Sunday school teacher, deacon, and elder in the same church for twenty-five years, but he would never call a minister by his first name. "Dr. Walker spoke on the text from John, 'And the Word was made flesh and dwelt among us.' He threw light in a dark place." Mark could not imagine what

Walker, who leaned toward homely stories and bad metaphors, could say about the Word; but Mark cared enough to ask his father to go on; he knew that an evening of watching TV giveaways, gags, and ads yawned before him; he would rather have the Word.

In the beginning was the Word. How did God create the world? He *said* Let there be light and there was light. He *said* Let us make man in our image. When God said Let there be a man who shall redeem all men, that man existed. His name was Jesus. He was the Word of God. Mark sank into a sermon-listening apathy under this; I don't care what you're talking about, I don't understand it, I don't think you do either. But suddenly, in a burst of irritation no doubt at his apathy, his father said, "Jesus said, 'Why do ye not understand my speech? Even because ye cannot hear my word.' " And Mark appreciated abruptly that Jesus' feeling and his father's were the same as his own had been with Jane; each had been cut off by the very words which were meant to bind. For a moment he and his father cast a look of recognition across to one another. But he knew that his father would not rest content with that look.

"I'm getting hungry, Dad."

It occurred to him at ten next morning, staring out the window at the patches of snow in the shade, that the only person in town he would actively enjoy seeing was Rosannah; she would be teaching till three thirty or so. Strange, he'd seen her at nine lessons, then once downtown in Grant's, and for the eleventh and last time at the tenth golf lesson; he had touched her only in the ways a golf teacher must touch his pupil, for the grip's sake, for the swing's sake, and embracing her thus formally had not excited him at all; yet he remembered the intensity with which they had talked on the sixth green, just beside it near a bush, not even holding hands. He had seen her, three days before that, at the stationery counter in Grant's intently choosing among address books; on impulse he had stepped up immediately behind her, bent over so that his lips were at her ear, and said, "Keep your eye on that ball, Rosannah." Her head toddled in a way that unmistakably meant emotion; he stood straight, and her head for a moment touched his shoulder as she looked up at him; in her eyes there was no questioning about whose voice that had been, nor surprise exactly, but only for that surprised moment an unveiled warmth. He responded instantly. Then they dropped their eyes to the address book in her hand. They talked inanities about address books. When she'd paid for the one she picked, she said that his would be the first address to go into her book; it was supposed to be a little joke, but when he did not smile at it her mouth fell; he gave her his address and told her that he would be gone to sea in less than a month, and her mouth ohed in a dismay as pleasing to him as the pressure of her head on his shoulder had been. Then they'd gone to Schrafft's for ice cream and coffee, and he'd told her how dull civil engineers were and how he'd be coming to Syracuse hereafter only to visit. Thinking of this encounter now ten months later, he wondered why he had stolen up behind her in the department store and why, three days later toward the end of her last lesson, he had told her he loved her; for he had not even tried to kiss her, though he knew she returned his feeling in some kind. It occurred to him now that it would be interesting to find out what so tenuous an infatuation could have left behind it, and to compare it to his relationship with Jane, anchored substantially in sex.

He telephoned the Board of Education to find out what school Rosannah was teaching at, and discovered instead that schools were closed for spring vacation. Splendid, he'd have lunch with her. Her name was not in the phone book. Well, he had her address. The unexpected chance excited him to action: he would surprise her. He put on his dark red sports shirt, light gray slacks, and tweed jacket, and walked the couple of miles to her place, swinging his arms in the sunshine.

But the look he surprised onto her face was not of the sort he had had in mind. Her hair was in a bandanna, her jeans were rolled up to her knees, she was wearing a half-buttoned man's shirt with the tails hanging out, her bare feet were grimy. Her wide eyes of astonishment became raised eyebrows of disapproval. "You should have phoned me."

"Your name isn't listed in the book."

"Anybody who can find out where I live should be clever enough to find my phone number."

"But," he was aggrieved, "you put your return address on the letter you wrote me."

"Hmph," she said with a flourish of the nose. She had not admitted him into her apartment. "I'm cleaning."

"*I* don't care. It's nearly time for lunch."

"Lunch? Very well. Come back in one hour. Okay?"

"But I don't have anywhere to go!"

"Oh yes, you do, sir. Syracuse is full of places for you to go to. Good-bye." And she closed the door. He was offended and left with the intention of not returning. Why, she'd given him her address herself and then said he'd cleverly found it! But the voice of her good-bye, slightly angry and yet warm, lingered in his ears; he had forgotten how sensual her voice was and how bright her eyes; she had been inviting him to return even as she was punishing him good-bye. Well, he would go back and see what came of it.

Jane's "Good-bye," her parting word, was resurrected in his memory—abrupt, timed so as to mean, "I'm glad to see you go," with a sort of drill sergeant's emphasis, in a voice devoid of affection. He flushed with postponed anger. To be sure, she had warned him that she would hate him every time he left on a trip, that each time he went from her he would be deserting her though she knew better; but that gave her no right to spoil his leavetaking. On the other hand, Rosannah, having scolded and punished him, had forgiven him in the very inflections of her reproof.

And having forgiven, she forgot: she greeted him upon his return as though they'd had this date for a week, stood aside as she opened the door for him, shook hands, and excused herself to put on the finishing touches. Her living room was conventionally feminine; there were doilies on the stand, and the pillows on the couch had ruffles; he smiled indulgently. She came out in the same sort of clothes she had worn at the golf course, blue pullover sweater, brown skirt, the same dirty white tennis shoes; but her eyelashes were blackened, her lips and cheeks rouged, and her bangs in front and pony tail behind were flawless. (And she had let her hair grow.) He had, without thinking about it, rather expected her to have fixed lunch for them in her apartment, but she went directly to the coat closet and pulled out a trench coat. She made a small, imperious gesture with her head, and he held her coat for her, delighted by her arrogance. They walked to Meltzer's and ate hot pastrami sandwiches and cole slaw. She told him about her first-graders, and he told her about Madagascar. She did not seem very keen to play golf next day, when he suggested it, but she let him persuade her—"if the weather held." At a slushy crossing he offered her his arm but she did not take it. Nor did she invite him in when they returned to her apartment.

Yet as he walked along the streets home from her place, he understood why he had said to her that he loved her: she was at once desirable and chaste. He was opposed to chastity on principle, but in her he respected it; still it was clear that the yearning he had built up for her he had translated into infatuation; a simple case of frustration and wish-fulfillment. So he laughed her out of his mind for the rest of the afternoon. The phone rang at dinner: a wrong number. "I forgot to mention it to you, son, but a young lady telephoned me one evening some time ago. Maybe it was around Thanksgiving. Anyway it was after the first snow, which was toward the middle of November this winter. What she wanted was your address."

"Thanks, Dad, she wrote me."

"The same one? She had a funny name."

"Tavolga? Rosannah Tavolga?"

"That sounds right. What is she, a Jewess?"

"It's a Russian name. I don't think she's Jewish. I never asked her." So, for the tedious hours till his father went off to bed, she was back in his mind most of the time, her name especially. It occurred to him that he had always remembered her name from the time he'd first met her, whereas he'd had the devil's own time remembering Jane's name. Jane Mercer—an ordinary name. Nevertheless, he found it odd that he had taken so long to get the Mercer stuck in his head; well into his second voyage he had been able to write her address on the envelope far more readily than her last name. But Rosannah Tavolga—the words fell together as though they were meant to, like Eleanor of Aquitaine, or Kubla Khan.

"Oh, my Lord, you're not the girl I was teaching."

"Why do you say that?"

"Your drive. You've got it down beautifully."

"Thank you, Mr. Birch."

"Oh, come off it."

"I had to use all my courage to put Mark down when I wrote to you. You had signed your card Mark, so I thought I should. But here on the golf course again, I feel like calling you Mr. Birch."

"Is that why you didn't much want to come out with me today?" She nodded. "Are names that important to you, Rosannah?" She nodded again and walked aside while he teed off; then she started ahead of him down the fairway. He caught up with her. "I was thinking last night how I had liked your name the very first time I heard it."

"I'm glad somebody likes it."

"Don't you?"

"Not particularly."

"Do you like my name?"

She gave him a complicated look. "Fishing, Mark?" She made the second hole in par.

"Did you take lessons after I left?" he asked her.

"No, I'm just lucky today."

"You must have played a lot last summer."

"I did. Nearly every day. Hollis liked golf."

"Hollis was the fellow you were engaged to?" She nodded. "Hollis," he repeated. "Now there's a name I could do without."

He decided that at the sixth hole he would remind her of their parting here. He would make a little burlesque of gallantry so that they could laugh together over it, so that she would not feel threatened again. They were both silent at the sixth tee waiting for a party of four middle-aged women to divot their progress up the fairway; the women insisted they play through, so that when they got to the green they were conscious of an admiring audience. The occasion was spoiled; Mark's anger cost him two strokes on the green, but Rosannah sank a twenty-foot putt slant-wise up a slope. As they were walking to the seventh tee they passed the bush beside which he had spoken to her of love. "We've been here before," she said without stopping, in a low voice. "Do you remember?" There was no joke in her voice, but intimacy and shyness.

"I remember," he said.

"You were so silly."

"I meant it."

"No, no," she said, "you meant something but not that. You were sweet. You kept banging the toe of your shoe with your putter."

"Your eyes sort of crossed, or wandered around, one of them."

"You noticed that?"

"Sure," he said, "I was watching you so hard I still remember everything you did."

"It's so humiliating; sometimes when I get all excited my eyes won't stay focused."

"You're not engaged any longer?"

"Oh no! You don't think I'd be— Say, are we playing golf, or aren't we?"

As they walked from the clubhouse to the car he held her hand, and she sat close to him on the way home. But she would not let him see her to the door. She had a date that evening, dinner and dancing; "a new doctor in town, an acquaintance of Daddy's, an internist, a dreamy dancer."

"I thought," said Mr. Birch during the first commercial of the evening, "that we'd drive out and see Calvin and Mona tomorrow night, right after supper."

"Sorry, Dad, I've got a date."

"A woman?" said his father heavily and scratched his hump.

"The girl we spoke of last evening, Rosannah Tavolga."

"You never used to mention her."

"No."

"You don't go see your old friends any more. You'd rather spend an evening alone with your old man than go see your oldest school friends, but here a new girl jumps up out of nowhere and off you go."

"Her father's a doctor, a skin specialist."

"And a Jew for all you know. You're a sailor all right, my boy. A sailor, God help me." Mark could think of nothing but where Rosannah and the internist might have gone on a Tuesday evening and whether they would neck. He was thankful that being with Jane had relieved him of any simply physical impulse to make a pass at Rosannah; as it was, he could play at having a love affair with her, hurting nothing, serious about nothing, just hold hands and talk, kid stuff.

Next day by noon he had the jitters bad. He felt imprisoned in his father's house, yet there was absolutely no place in Syracuse he wanted to go to, no one he wanted to see except Rosannah. Their date was for five thirty. He felt encapsulated within himself; he thought of breaking the date and flying down to New York so that Jane might tease him out of it, or tease him at

least out of thinking about it; Jane was a fellow captive whose
art it was to make him not mind his captivity, and sometimes
even to enjoy it. He telephoned Rosannah. He knew that his
own voice was more intense than was required to ask a girl
whether she wanted to play golf; nevertheless, he was quite put
off by the brisk, arrangement-making roughness in her telephone
manner; she said she would play, not that she would like to play
or looked forward to it, just that she would; he wondered if his
manner had affected her.

She chattered with him brightly, as though he were a friend's
cousin who had to be entertained for the afternoon. The pro
caught them in the clubhouse and jawed for half an hour. As
they were approaching the fourth hole, a one-armed fellow
shouted, "Coming through," at them, and came through without
so much as a nod. She sliced her next drive off into a gully. And
he blew up. "I've told you a hundred times not to do that," he
scolded, and holding her head rigid made her swing correctly
three or four times.

"Is that all right, Mark?" she said, mocking his fierceness a
little but at least he was Mark again.

"Yes," he answered in a remote voice, "it's all right." He was
thinking that he must get to her at this moment or he might not
have another chance like it. He decided to risk a high trump.
"I'm going back to New York tomorrow morning."

"Why?"

"My ship is sailing before long."

"You won't come back before you sail?" Her voice was
gentle and sensual again, and a little alarmed.

"No, I won't."

"I'm sorry."

"I'll miss you, darling."

She turned to put her driver in the bag. "Don't call me
darling."

"Why not?"

"Oh, it's sort of a New York word, the way you pronounce it. I'm not going to be anybody's New York darling."

"All right, Rosannah. Anyway, I *will* miss you." She strode angrily.

"Then why," she said without looking at him, "did you come look me up? Just to get everything all churned up again?"

"Why, I don't know what to say. I like you."

"Hmph."

He wanted to pull her back into shallow water. "How was your doctor last night?"

"Sick," she said miserably. "He got drunk and told me that he hates God. Very sick, very sick." Mark suddenly thought of Jane's light way of saying three monosyllables quickly together, especially sick sick sick, and he realized that Rosannah, who could not take another person's sickness lightly, would not toy with her own emotions; nor should he do so.

"I'm sorry."

"Sure." In a few minutes he saw her blow her nose on the other side of the fairway, with her head averted from him; his vanity was tickled that he had made her cry a little, but he did not want to do it again. And apparently she believed in God. But maybe she didn't go to church.

Until they got to the sixth green they spoke only of the game. There were no players in sight behind them. They both shot the hole in par, and laughing, arm in arm, did a victorious little schottische around the pole.

"Why did you go to sea?"

"Hey," he answered, pretending to stagger, "it's not fair to hit a fellow when he's off-balance."

"Couldn't you get a job as an engineer?"

"Sure. I just thought it would be fun to go to sea."

"Was it?"

"Yes."

"Were you ever married?"

"No, but what on earth does that have to do with anything?"

"Nothing." She was looking off at the trees in a preoccupied way. She glanced at him for a moment, and a secret smile appeared on her lips. "So you're going back to your New York darling tomorrow."

"What? I said no such thing."

"Oh yes, you did, Mark Birch."

"I did not."

"Is she prettier than I am?" He trembled inside; he did not know where she was leading him. He gave her her bag and they started strolling toward the seventh tee.

"No, about the same as you, in prettiness, that is."

"Do you know why I think you went to sea?"

"No, why?"

"Women. You're afraid to get too much involved with a woman."

"Oh, I am, am I."

"I think."

"What am I doing here with you right this minute?"

"Playing golf. Sort of flirting. Do you have to go back to New York tomorrow?"

"No. I'm not due back on the ship till Sunday morning."

"I want you to stay."

"Well." Everything she'd said seemed to him true.

"I dare you," she said.

"I won't rise to that bait," he answered. She dropped her clubs by the bush and pulled a budding branch down so that she might caress a downy bud with her lips. "That is," he said, "I could stay if we had a chance, you know, if you liked me so that . . ."

"Oh, don't be stupid. You know perfectly well I like you. You're even afraid to say the word, aren't you? Listen, Mark." She put her hand to the side of his throat. "The question is whether you will let yourself find out if you love me. And let me find out too. I had hoped we would."

"I'll stay till Saturday," he said, and even as he spoke he argued that at least he would have Saturday night to spend with Jane. He did not touch Rosannah. Her hand caressed his hair a moment. She had not paid much attention to his words.

She said, "I still hope we will."

He was sure she had not planned this; yet it seemed to him ceremonial of her to say this by the same bush, the two of them alone after he had scolded her again like a teacher. And the words: of course the words were unprepared, just the words which the occasion brought forth from her, not, as his words to Jane had been, rigidly memorized; they were as nearly exact as words could be about such a matter; they were true. Yet, he thought, their power was not just in their truth nor in their spontaneity nor in the unconscious ceremony of the time and place, but in all these together and in his assent to all these. She was smiling a little, in innocent triumph, he supposed, at having got him to stay for three more days, but her eyes, meeting his, were unwavering and affectionate. It was time to kiss, his lips were ready to kiss; but his mind, the IBM machine in his mind, was ticking away at a great rate sorting out the ways by which he could tell her how well she had handled him. What his ears and thence his reaching hands heard his lips say was this:

"Rosannah, you have opened my heart."

Tourist and Pilgrim

As soon as Chaim was asleep, Sheila began.

"You know I haven't asked anything for myself, Walter. You wanted to send your parents to Miami for the winter. They went to Miami. God knows they deserve a vacation while they can still enjoy it, after all they've done for their children. They went. You wanted to come to Paris. Here we are."

Already he looked annoyed, and got up and began walking around the room.

"Here *we* are," he said, "not just me, you too. You act like I'm putting something over. Here *we* are, Hy too, little good it's doing him, but he's here. This is the capital of civilization, honey, that's why we're here, this is *it*. You know that. You agreed."

"Agreed! I loved the idea. I'm so grateful to you. Am I complaining? In Paris, my first time abroad . . . Bringing Hy was a mistake maybe. Notre Dame scared him. He doesn't like the food, it's too rich, it's different. He's only eight, he gets bored. Why don't you take him to the circus? You remember what June said, the Cirque d'Hiver is pretty good. He'd like it."

"Why don't we all go? You too. I'm willing. A person can sight-see just so many hours; then fun! Sheila, please, come with us."

Six months before, Walter had bought—against Sheila's wishes

—five one-dollar tickets to the new state lottery and won $5,000. The week after winning he had bought fifty dollars' worth of tickets and won $3,000 more. Sheila had been so upset by his luck that he had promised never to gamble on the lottery again—a friendly game of poker with a quarter limit, sure; the horses, even, if absolutely irresistible; the lottery, never.

"No," she said, "I want you to take him, just the two of you, father and son, something special. For me, Walter? Do it for me? You know I haven't asked anything for myself, unless you count those ten visits to Dr. Rosenblum."

"Eleven."

"Eleven counting the first one where nothing happened; get acquainted."

"It's not that I mind, Sheila, you know that."

"I know that."

"But facts are facts. The check said two hundred and twenty dollars. That's eleven."

"But it wasn't for me personally, Walter. The lottery was too much, I felt a nervous breakdown coming on, he helped me."

"I know, honey, I know. I appreciate it. I'm not blaming you. So tell me what you want. For me and Chaim to go to the circus together? That's it?"

She was a round-shouldered little woman with pop eyes behind heavy glasses, and a flexible, sensual, unsuspicious mouth.

"Yes," she said, and then made a long upper lip like a Puritan with ill-fitting false teeth. "No. That's not *just* what I want."

She was gratified to see him beginning to get angry. He'd warned ahead of time that from the moment they got on the ship in New York, he would refuse to quarrel; and in fact the trip had been giving him such pleasure she couldn't find it in her heart to let him know how unhappy she was feeling sometimes. Here in this little hotel room, she couldn't forget the thin wall separating them from Chaim. They would have to keep their voices down. When he stopped pacing and turned on her, she realized she was still standing, and she sat on the edge of a straight chair. He liked to waggle his finger in her face when they argued; but he could not do this satisfactorily unless he could bend over a little, and he was no taller than she. There had been a quarrel when she did not give him the advantage by sitting, the one after his second lottery prize. It was not that she wanted to win that one: she did not dare lose it. She had learned this sitting-standing business from watching her parents, and she was pretty sure Walter was no more aware of what she did than her father had been when her mother had done the same thing.

Walter stopped, bent over her, shook his finger in her face, and looked as though he were about to shout; she put her finger to her lips and he whispered instead.

"What do you want? Dr. Rosenblum told you, always begin with what you want. Here you are in the middle of something already and you haven't said."

"I wish I'd never mentioned he told me that. You use it against me."

"Does it work, doing what the doctor prescribed?"

"It works," she said. "Pretty well."

"So, do you want to go to temple?"

"In Paris, Walter? Imagine saying '*Bon jour*' to a rabbi."

They both giggled.

"Anyway," he said, "we won't hit any holy days."

"I appreciate that very very much."

For their trip, Walter had been careful to pick weeks during which they would be free from religious duties.

"So," he said, "what is it you want?"

"I want to go to Chartres."

He drew back a little. "Cathedral?"

"Of course."

"All right, we'll go. Hy should see it. Maybe he'll like it."

"Walter, I want to go alone."

He drew back some more. "By yourself?"

"After breakfast I take a train down. I go look. In the afternoon I take a train back. The desk clerk found out for me; he telephoned in French. You and Hy go to the circus. We all meet back here, then we go eat dinner together. It's not so awful."

"Go. I didn't know you'd developed such a taste for churches, but if it's churches you want, Chartres is the best."

"You saw it, honey, you said it was."

"It was. Even a dumb GI like me could see that. Now, Sheila, you know what *I* want, right now, this very minute? I won't beat around the bush, I'll tell you. I want to go to the Folies Bergère and I'm going."

"Without me?"

"Sheila, don't be silly. Hy wakes up and the baby-sitter talks French to him. That would be the last straw."

"So, Walter, nude women. I'm surprised."

"Did I say I was going to stay all night? I haven't gone to a dozen floor shows in my life. Why shouldn't I see the floor show to end all floor shows? Beautiful costuming, beautiful stage sets, gorgeous dancers, first-class choreography."

"Nude shiksas."

"Am I prejudiced? This is Paris."

"Walter, don't you even want to know why I'm going to Chartres?"

"Look, do me a favor. That doctor of yours gave you a good prescription. Follow directions. Take one before every meal and a double dose before going to bed. Do I ask people that want to sell me transistor radios why they want to sell them to me? If a man says, 'Gutman, I want to buy your transistors,' do I ask him why? I buy, I sell. You want to go to Chartres? It's famous, it's beautiful, it's one of the high-water marks of civilization. I've seen it, I don't care how soon I see it again, not this trip, we only got two weeks; Hy won't like it, all he wants is peanut butter sandwiches with soft white bread. So go. Now," he said, putting on his coat and hat, "I'm going to the Folies Bergère. Don't ask why; I might tell you."

Because he was right; she did not argue any longer but stood in the middle of the room listening to him go down the steps, planning to lie on the bed and cry—into the pillow so as not to disturb Chaim—as soon as she heard the front door slam. But as she waited, holding her glasses upright, a shaft in each hand, she noticed she was tapping them in a pleasant rhythm against her chest, and she realized she did not really want to cry, she was going to do it just because she ought to under the circumstances. What was so terrible about going to the Folies Bergère anyway? They were beautiful, sure, she'd enjoy going herself sometime maybe. Besides, he'd told her he was going, that's what mattered. Let him go in health, it was only to be expected, as long as he came home at night. After all, tomorrow she was going to do something much riskier than go to a girlie show, and she wasn't even telling him. Who could say, maybe it was time they should have another child; a boy, of course, preferably. Hy (God forbid she should have such thoughts but there they were) was a whiner. A mama's boy, wouldn't stand up for himself, a disappointment even to his grandparents. Maybe when Walter came back from the Folies Bergère tonight, he would want to. If he did she'd let him. Wasn't this their second honeymoon? Chaim from the first one to Niagara Falls; what did God have reserved for them this time? Or no, Walter deserved a little punishment for walking out on her—she wouldn't let him till tomorrow night at the earliest.

She tiptoed in to see if Chaim was all right, and when she straightened the covers he flopped over onto his back, his face turned toward her. In the faint light from the other room she could make out his full rosy lips, slightly parted. She could not help bending down and kissing them tenderly. His eyes did not open, but one hand rose as though of its own accord and patted her on the cheek. She turned her head so that she might kiss the soft, moist palm, then she tiptoed out.

"God forgive me," she muttered, staring at herself in the mirror. "He's so sweet, he's so lovable, I love him so much. God forgive my thoughts no mother should have. I'm an owl." Her face was round; the horn rims of her glasses were round and black; her hair was disheveled; her pointed little nose stuck out like a beak. "All right, I'm an owl, then I should be a good owl."

She sat down and began studying the book on Chartres Cathedral she had bought in New York—had ridden bus and subway all the way in from 206th Street in Queens just to buy at Brentano's. The best; the clerk assured her it was the best there was; he was a gray-haired man with rimless spectacles and a precise way of speaking that indicated he should know. She'd only read the historical part at home—she hadn't left the book out where Walter would notice and ask questions too soon. Now she skipped the technical chapters on architecture, stained glass, and so on and so forth, and tried to get down to business: what things were supposed to mean, the Christian part. But the light was so dim and the writing was so dry that after three or four pages she put the book down and went to bed. To bed but not to sleep: she was still awake, though she pretended to be asleep, when Walter came home.

Her father's parents had been killed in the Ukraine by the Tsar's Cossacks. In Poland, her mother's mother and many cousins, aunts, and uncles had been killed by the Nazis; her mother's father had survived the war and now was in a rest home in New Jersey, not in his right mind. She had been born in Poland, and her parents had got out with her a month before Hitler invaded. They still lived in an apartment in the Bronx; her mother kept the door locked three ways and took tranquilizers; her father was all right, busy, made a halfway decent living driving a taxi. Walter's family was luckier; they'd all got out of

Austria in time. His brother Harold, however, when he was ten and they lived in Brooklyn, had been beaten up on the way home from school by some Irish boys, two of them sons of a policeman, and he'd been kicked so hard in the Adam's apple that for the rest of his life when he talked he would croak like a frog. Not only that, he was full of fears. He still lived at home at thirty-two; he had changed his name to Chaim and served as the shamus at the local synagogue, his only occupation; he never went on dates. Unfortunately, he not only sounded like a frog, he looked like one, and had always been timid enough; so no one could tell for sure how important the beating had been. The Gutman family was not very religious, though of course both boys had gone to shul; but Chaim was only content praying a great deal, puttering around the synagogue, looking after holy things. (They had named little Hy after one of Sheila's uncles she never saw, though just between themselves they knew they were *really* naming him after Walter's brother. But Sheila had wanted it for a reason she kept to herself: it was a name which had never been contaminated by Christians.) One of Walter's uncles had been killed by the British during Israel's war of independence. As Sheila's father put it, "He died like a man"; as Chaim muttered (just for her to overhear) when she repeated this comment, "At least they let him die like a man."

At City College, all twenty-three of the students in her second-year German class were Jewish except for one Negro girl, and the professor was a priest (then how could he be a teacher too?). Father Stahl was thin, dark-haired, quick of gesture; he smoked too much, and he had what was almost a tic of a way of tossing his hair back; his nose was large and hooked; he spoke English with an accent that reminded her a little of her grandfather in New Jersey. At first it froze her to be taught by a priest—not only a Christian, not only a Catholic, but a priest, and a German priest at that. (She often wondered in class why she had taken German in the first place, especially the eight o'clock section, such a bad hour. Fate?) In a couple of months she was half in love with him, as were the other two girls in the class she'd made friends with. He never said or did anything in the least flirtatious; sometimes he would reminisce, in a voice at once sad and happy, about the great days of German literature. In the second semester a boy, a Communist of some sort, belligerent yet deferential, asked Father Stahl if it was true that Hitler had been a Catholic. Father Stahl gave him a keen look, which Sheila interpreted as meaning he understood very well what mischief the boy was up to but would take the question seriously anyway. For the rest of that class period he talked about anti-Semitism. Listening to him, Sheila told herself that everything he said was in books already —where else would he have gotten it? But even as she was telling herself this, she was sure that she would never be the same again. Of course, by the next day she knew she just had a school-girl crush on him, and by the end of the term she was more glad than sorry to have to get a job and leave college, never to see him again. Yet she felt that she was in truth not the same as she had been. His arguments as such faded out of her mind; they were full of theology, people and places she had never heard of. It was all the Christians' fault. That is what she took with her. Anti-Semitism was invented by Christians. Nothing Jews did justified or even explained it, not really. Throughout history, the pure Jew-killing has been done by Christians and by totalitarians who were raised as Christians. Otherwise it's just neighbor-hating, which all men are good at, including Jews. Why else would Our Lord have commanded us to love our neighbors if it were not our nature to hate them? Father Stahl did not in any way exonerate himself or his Church from what he said—the most terrible words she ever heard uttered, uttered by him. Anti-Semitism is the worst crime in all the world, and fathers of my Church devised it. She had little enough resistance to him, and less to what he said. No word ever thrilled her so much as his word "devised": it slunk around in her mind for days, and as she lay in bed thinking of the wickedness of Christians, it would uncoil off her tongue in the dark.

Her girl friends, after that eventful hour, speculated on why he had ever become a priest and why he remained a priest now. Sheila decided in her own mind that the Church was holding him in captivity. (By the Church, she meant a hodgepodge of which the main definable ingredients were Ivan Karamazov's Grand Inquisitor, fat Irish bishops in Cadillacs, and nuns.) She could tell by the pain in Father Stahl's eyes and by the way he occasionally ran his forefinger under his collar that he wanted his freedom but that the Church would not give it to him.

He was the only Christian she had felt close to, and the one conversation (in the hall after class, bluebook in hand) she had with him began, "Sir, why did you only give me a C?" and ended two minutes later, "Thanks anyway, I just wanted to know."

None of the Crucifixions or Annunciations or Last Suppers or Ascensions or Madonnas or Adorations she had seen in museums or art books meant anything special to her. She knew a picture could have special meaning. When she was a little girl first going to shul, studying Hebrew because she insisted she had to know it, her grandfather had given her a book of illustrated Bible stories, and one of the pictures had been of Jacob wrestling with the angel at the foot of a ladder reaching up into a cloudburst of glory. (She never got the story straight; nothing of it remained with her but the picture. Imagine wrestling with an angel all night! Does he think he can make an angel give up? Suppose by mistake the angel did give up, what would Jacob do then? It meant nothing to her that in the morning the angel gave Jacob a new name, some sort of funny symbolism; she forgot it. Hy's middle name was Jacob; she never told why she wanted it, just said she liked the name; fortunately Walter liked it too.) *Paradise Lost* said nothing much to her, and she got bored with

Dante halfway through *The Inferno*. The New Testament was better, but what did it tell her that meant anything she didn't already know? Dostoevski, that anti-Semite, could be argued about, but not too much. What made him wonderful was his grasp of psychology, and since when did Christians have a monopoly on psychology? The B-Minor Mass shook her for a while; it affected her even more than The Ninth Symphony or *The Magic Flute;* in fact, more than any other music. But then she thought, How would I know it was Christian if the record jacket didn't say so? *"Agnus dei, qui tollis peccata"*—they might as well be singing *"Ein Vogelfänger bin ich ja"* or *"Freude, Freude"* for all she cared. "Joy, joy"; "A birdcatcher am I yes"; "Lamb of God, who taketh away the sins of the world"—what a lot of nonsense.

Yet here she was coming out of the Chartres train station in a light drizzle, huddling in her trench coat, her gray, helmet-shaped hat pulled down over her ears, going to see the most Christian thing she could find. She had been inside only two or three churches in New York, to musical events, and she had no special feeling for architecture, but she hoped and trusted she would find Chartres Cathedral beautiful. It really was magnificent, so if it left her cold, she herself would be at fault. What she wanted was to find it marvelous but meaningless, like Bach. A great artist couldn't help it if he was born a Christian. It seemed unfair to her that so many great artists had been Christians and so few of them Jews. But as Father Stahl had said one day in class, why should the Dutch have had great painters for a couple of centuries and no great writers ever? the Russians great dancers for a century and no great sculptors? If only the cathedral would turn out to be a beautiful place of worship built by an architect who just happened to be a Christian, then she would be able to see Father Stahl, say, as a good man who just happened to be a Christian; and she could go back to hating Christianity (though of course not people who just happened to be Christians) with a clear conscience, as she had not been able to for over ten years.

Nobody else on the train had looked like a pilgrim. The man she saw going up the cathedral steps ahead of her looked like an ordinary tourist, camera around his neck. Once inside, she saw some others gawking about, nobody kneeling. "What kind of a holy place is this? *I* am the pilgrim?"

By the time Walter came out of Chaim's room from sitting by him while he fell asleep, Sheila was in her bathrobe rubbing cold cream onto her face.

"So, honey," he said, "we told you all about the circus and what we did, and you told us some of your little things—rain and sunshine, omelette for lunch, getting lost on the Metro coming back. What about the cathedral? Was it worth the trip?"

"I never saw anything like it," she said in a matter-of-fact voice.

"You said."

"It's too much to talk about."

"Why so mysterious?" He began undressing, unbuttoning his shirt, reaching inside it, and scratching. "You've been acting like a cathedral is something we shouldn't talk about in front of Hy. Well, he's asleep. You can talk now. Please. Why not?"

She thought resentfully of Dr. Rosenblum's advice. Now, right this minute, how could she begin by saying what she wanted? She was all mixed up. She didn't want to think about Chartres. She didn't even know whether to put her hair up in curlers. In fact, she wasn't even going to try; she'd just brush it.

"It's Christian." The instant she said the word, she regretted it.

"This is news? We should protect the baby from such a dangerous fact?"

"I don't want to confuse him."

"He goes to Notre Dame and that's all right, but he mustn't even hear about Chartres. Sheila, you've flipped."

"Maybe it was a mistake to take him to Notre Dame."

"Sure, he was bored. We might as well take him to the main public library and show him books in French."

"What I mean is, Notre Dame is just a big church like any other. It's got its own style of architecture, naturally, and symbols, and so forth and so on, and Christians use it. But *it* isn't Christian, the way Chartres is. You know what I mean?"

"Keep on talking," he said. "Maybe I'll catch on."

She looked at him gratefully. He could be so patient with her at important times, like now. He wasn't pretending to understand the little woman, the way Irving could make June cry sometimes by pretending to understand her when she got all wound up in something.

He patted her shoulder. "Tell me, what was the main thing? The windows?"

"No," she said. "When the sun came out, they were wonderful, I'm not denying it. But I expected them to be, everyone talks about them. It was the statues."

"Statues? Of saints?"

"Do you realize, Walter, I never saw a really good statue in my life before? I was unprepared."

"Oh, now," he said, "in the Metropolitan Museum of Art they've got lots of statues, even some medieval ones, from churches."

"Yes, but a *museum*. They're just art in a museum. I mean great statues. How can you tell anybody? Nobody told me."

"What about the Museum of Modern Art, out in the garden, all those wonderful statues?"

"Nude women! Walter, all you got your mind on is nude women!"

"Why not?" he said. "Wipe your face so I can kiss my wife who isn't nude."

"Walter!" She wiped. "There." He kissed her. "Big fat nude women made out of lead."

"All right, honey, so tell me about your beautiful saints made out of stone."

"Not beautiful. Yes, beautiful. I mean, they have real faces, worried, mean—they aren't all saints, plenty of sinners too—wise, dumb, who knows what-all kinds, every one has their own face, human. But still they are beautiful. Mostly they're in those arches over the doors, going up, sort of streams of them going up, all alike if you don't look at each one separately, like flames, like streams of flames going upward, yet people. No one mentioned it. There are other statues too, but those going up over the doors are the ones that mean so much."

She felt on the verge of losing control. How had he got her to talk about this when she had resolved not to? He tended to be wishy-washy about Christianity. Live and let live. All right! But would *they* live and let live? No, they were monsters. How could it be that the worst people in the world should make such beautiful things? Impossible to talk about it. Something was wrong.

As she took off her bathrobe, she caught sight of herself in the mirror. She was wearing a light-blue baby-doll sleep suit which her mother had given her for the trip. It was supposed to disguise her dumpy figure and be alluring, leave her arms and legs bare. Her thighs in the mirror were fat and shapeless, and so was her short body, which the frills and froths didn't do anything for really. Could a sleep suit give her a waist? Make her bosom voluptuous? It was only a glimpse that she caught, but she immediately snatched off her glasses so as not to be able to see herself again; and she got into bed intending to lie with her back toward Walter. How could he love her, even under the blankets in the dark? But just as she was settling herself he spoke.

"All right," he said musingly, "I understand a little bit maybe. I see what you mean about the statues, but I don't understand the Christian part any better. I know I'm not too smart about artistic matters, I only went to college one semester, the same as not going, you've even got that book on Chartres you study. So, honey, tell me, I want to know."

He was standing at the foot of the bed, looking at her, his pajama top in hand, too far away for her to make out the expression on his face, but from his voice she was pretty sure he was serious. She decided not to lie with her back to him after all. Wasn't he putting on weight himself? His stomach wasn't disgraceful yet, but if he didn't watch it he was going to be in trouble before long, a bay window like his father. It wasn't his fault, really, that she'd said more than she should have. Now she was started, it would be rude to quit just like that, bang.

"It's so complicated, Walter, I'm not even clear in my own mind." She told him generally what she had gone to Chartres hoping to find, but even as she was talking she wished she could be telling him about Father Stahl too. Not that Father Stahl meant anything to her any longer—God forbid, a married woman and a mother, and him a priest! But it would be the easiest way to explain to Walter if she could mention her school-girl crush. Walter unfortunately had shown signs of jealousy; he might not see it in the right light. Besides, suppose he didn't understand even after she told him this secret? What would she do then? Now, somehow, not noticing, she had got onto heaven, Christian heaven and Jewish heaven. What did she care about heaven? She didn't even believe in it, though of course many did believe, Jews as well as Christians. Let them. What harm did it do? Yet here she was talking about heaven, the face of God, Elijah, eternity.

"Good Lord!" Walter interrupted her without warning. He pulled down the covers and turned off the light. "Why didn't somebody tell me nine years ago I was marrying a rabbi!"

"A rabbi?"

"A Talmudic scholar, then, he makes every comma mean something."

"It does, Walter!"

"To him, it does."

"In the Talmud it does! Everything means something!"

"Pardon me, Reb Sheila." He groaned. "By you every little comma means something. You've got the glasses already; where's the long forked beard you should be wearing? Why are you disguised as a woman?"

"Walter!"

Her outrage was all on the surface. When he called her Reb Sheila, she felt a spurt of secret pride, and then a gush of gratitude to him.

He got into bed and reached out to touch her. Before she could tell whether he only had it in mind to pat her in a friendly way, as he had done the night before when he got back from the Folies Bergère, she threw herself onto him.

"Darling!" she cried. "My angel!" She hugged him, she bit his neck, she struggled on top of him.

"Baby, my God, hey, not so loud! What's got into you? Remember Hy."

She could hear the shock in his voice, and in a dim way she knew she would be just as shocked at herself if she stopped to think what she was doing—she had never done such a sexy thing in her life. She pounded him with her fists and squeezed him with her elbows, she panted, she whispered hotly in his ear. Presently he fought back, and they strove without words, grunting, sweating. She did not yield for a moment, but he wrestled her over in a tangle of sheets and their night clothes, and he kept her under no matter how she threshed and rolled her head back and forth and dug her nails into his sides and back, at the same time calling him her angel, her lover.

❦❦❦

The Boy with U-V Eyes

The fall I was nine years old my father left Mother and me, and that was my childhood trauma. In nursing school two years ago, they gave us lectures on abnormal psychology, and the impression I got about traumas was that they were mostly unconscious; they sort of go underground like one of those rivers and keep coming up later in peculiar ways. Well, my trauma was conscious and I've never forgotten it a bit. Maybe that's because it happened in an airport where there are lights on everywhere and all that soothing music.

We walked over to a seat where we wouldn't be bothered. It was midnight, so there weren't many people around. He made a little motion with his hand, and Mother turned and walked off. Her heels clicked a lot louder on the floor when she was going away by herself than they did when we had all three been walking together.

He sat down and stood me between his knees. "June," he began, and stopped.

He only called me June on serious occasions. Otherwise he called me Junie or June-Bug, or even Junie-Buggy if we were laughing and playing around. Of course I knew this was a serious occasion. For two or three weeks I'd been hearing them talk about Saudi Arabia and oil wells and so on, and they quarreled;

besides, now I was staying up till midnight to see him off. So, it was all right for him to call me June. But he had tears in his eyes and he couldn't say anything else. I didn't know what to make of that. If I had begun to cry, I think he would have too. But I wanted desperately to hear what he had to say, and I just wiggled my hands inside his to make him feel me. He smiled and began talking and the tears dried up after a while.

He told me he had to be gone for two years, working. Mother was going to need a lot of help from now on; she would be working in the office all day, and I must help around the house and keep my room tidied up. When he came back I would be so big he would hardly recognize me, maybe, and he would be as brown as an Indian from all that desert sunshine he was going to be in. Then he took a deep breath and licked his lips, and he told me that when he came back from Arabia he would not be living with Mother and me. He wanted to, but he simply couldn't. He would see me as often as possible and he hated the whole thing but it had to be.

"Are you getting a divorce, Daddy?"

He nodded and closed his eyes.

It's a terrible thing to admit, but the truth is that what I instantly thought about was, now I could queen it over my friends. One of them, a new girl in school the year before, had parents who had gotten a divorce when she was a baby, but nobody I knew had parents who had gotten one when we were old enough to know about it. Marrying was what people did, but a divorce was a thing people got, sort of like measles. That's what we kids decided among ourselves; but now, I was thinking, I would know what it was *really* like.

He talked a good deal, but the main thing he kept saying was that there wasn't anything in the world he hated more than to not be with me but he couldn't help himself, it had to be. I kept twisting around, and once he clamped my hands so hard I almost yelled. He was so strong he didn't realize what he was doing, and

I didn't yell because it would make him feel bad to think he had hurt me at a time like that. I'm little and small-boned like Mother, and he always treated us as though we were as frail as we looked. It was my secret that he had hurt me, and I never even told Mother, though I meant to.

The reason I did not tell her was that she was so nasty about us staying to watch his plane off. He and I didn't have more than ten or fifteen minutes alone till he had to go get on his plane, and Mother walked with us down the long hallway to the gate. But after he had kissed us good-bye—he kissed Mother too, in a stiff way—and gone out the gate, she just wanted to pound right out to the parking lot and go home. I had to raise such a terrible ruckus to get to go up to the observation platform, even if it was windy, and watch his plane taxi and take off and disappear in the dark, that I put her in a really atrocious mood. Driving home, she kept snapping mean things, at me, at other cars, at stop lights, but she didn't speak against him.

By the next evening she was in a better temper. When she put me to bed right after supper, she sat by me for a while talking and brushing my hair, and she asked me what we had talked about there in the waiting room while she had gone to the ladies' room—that's why she said she had disappeared, to go to the ladies' room. I told her what we had talked about. She gave a snort, sort of. "So he says he can't help it. Well, honey, just remember one thing. I didn't leave him, he left me. Don't you ever forget it—he's the one that's divorcing us."

Occasionally over the years she would say something about him in a poisonous tone, but that was the only time she ever said a really bad thing about him. I believed her, but I believed him too. There must be some secret reason why he had to go away, and she did not know what it was. Neither did I, but I was sure he had the good reason. I couldn't argue with her since I didn't know what his secret was. Besides, if she didn't believe he had one, there was no way I could prove it to her. I'd been through that before, seeing things she couldn't see. So, we just didn't mention the subject and got along fine.

It was a traumatic experience, all the same. I kept thinking about it. Every once in a while around the other kids I would give a knowing look, and when they asked me what the big secret was, I would play innocent and say, "What secret?" The truth was that there *was* a secret, only I didn't know the answer to it any better than they did. My only advantage was that I knew where the secret was located.

Over the next months I kept thinking about these things all the time—I didn't do well in school that year—and somehow, in the illogical way children do, I got the fact that I was born on the day Pearl Harbor was bombed mixed up with everything else. I'm sure I don't know what my being born had to do with a treacherous attack on my country, or what either of these had to do with a Reno divorce for mental cruelty, or what anything had to do with the lighting in an airport and looking into people's eyes when saying good-bye, but they got all mixed up so tightly at that time that they seemed to belong together. At least, in my head they fit together—which is the kind of head I've got.

Gradually a firm resolve shaped up in my mind: I would never have children. That meant of course that I could never get married the way everybody was supposed to. If we had been Catholic, I would have become a nun, but of course Catholics don't divorce so the whole thing would have been different. But I didn't know about nuns yet, and I decided to become a nurse. If I couldn't have a family, I would help people who were in pain and needed comfort.

For eleven years I never swerved in my resolve and never even told anybody about it. I went on dates once in a while just not to be too different, but even when a boy would kiss me nothing would happen between us. Boys knew. In my high-school sorority my nickname was Mona, short for Mona Lisa because of my smile. I got through nursing school without temptation, and I was first in a class of seventeen. Then a year and a half ago I came to Mercy Hospital, a brand-new registered nurse, and met Lou, a brand-new resident. And now, here I am married, with a stepson, Ian, and eager to get pregnant. It's all because I can't stand the U-V in Ian's eyes.

U-V means ultraviolet, and I can see it. The reason I know about it was my high-school physics course, where I was the only girl in the class. Somewhere I heard that physics taught about light, and the one thing I really learned was all about the spectrum. I had read about bees in the Sunday supplement and how they could see infrared light but violet was black to them, and I went around for a year or two thinking I was like a bee and feeling very mysterious and special. But in physics I found out that what I could see was ultraviolet and some red is black to me—just the opposite of bees.

I got the teacher to give me an experiment all by ourselves and promise not to tell anybody. He was a nice thin guy getting his Ph.D. at the university and teaching half-time in our school. He took me to his lab at the university and tested me. He wanted to tell everybody about me, but I held him to his promise. He begged me to let him at least put me in a learned journal, so I let him, if he wouldn't use my name. I helped him with a U-V experiment of his own, in exchange. In June as soon as school was out, he tried to date me, but I wouldn't even go to his lab with him after that—he was my teacher and he knew my secret. I happened to run into him with Lou when we were on our honeymoon in Niagara Falls, and he gave me such a smile. I don't know what he was doing there, he was alone at the time I saw him, it was just in a movie theater lobby after the show. But I sincerely hope I never see him again.

The reason I kept it such a secret was because of the circumstances of originally finding out about it. That was the spring when I was nine years old, and I smashed my left big toenail roller-skating—I ran into a pile of bricks where they were repairing the Methodist church. It turned black and blue. That's just an expression, of course, because actually it was all sorts of fascinating colors that went up from my toe onto the top of my foot too. People are so funny about colors you wouldn't believe it, unless you are an artist or somebody like me who has a special reason to notice. Green, for example—the things people call green! Well, I'm no better than anybody else except I've become cautious about what I call things. Because, with my toenail, when it turned dark, Mother said it was black and I said no, it was blue, dark blue like the sky at twilight. At first she pooh-poohed me, but I got indignant. It was *my* toe and *I* knew what color *my* toe was. Of course I didn't have the right name for the color, since there isn't a name for it, except U-V, which isn't a name so much as a scientific expression for scientists to communicate with. Anyhow, she got madder and madder, and I began to cry and wouldn't back down. She said I had to learn to quit being so stubborn and admit to the truth. Well, for her to call me stubborn because I could see a color she couldn't see, even if I didn't know the right name for it, that was too much for me to take. So I screamed at her that she was color-blind like Bruce— he was a boy at school who was color-blind about red and green and she detested him. That was the straw that broke the camel's back for Mother, and she not only whacked me, she really gave me a tanning, the worst one she ever did. What I realize now— I had years of experience to concentrate on her—is that the one thing in the world Mother can't bear most of all is to be left out of things. But naturally I didn't know it at that time. Mainly what I got out of that licking she gave me was to keep my secrets to myself. I asked several kids and my Uncle Otis what color my toenail was and they all said it was black. So I just kept my U-V sight to myself. Besides, there actually aren't all that many things that have U-V in them, and it's not any more beautiful than any other color. My favorite color is green, especially putt-ing-green green. Sometimes I go around with Lou when he plays golf on Wednesday afternoons or Sundays, mostly for the greens.

Thus, up until Lou, the only person who knew my secret was that physics teacher, and actually it was U-V, in a way, that brought Lou and me together.

We both came to Mercy at the same time, not knowing another soul, either one of us, and I was given special duty on a heart patient he fell heir to when one of the older doctors had a stroke. So it was only natural that we sat together over coffee a good deal. We're both sort of retiring with strangers, and anyway we just plain got along well in the way you can't explain—friendship, not sex.

One thing about people in the medical profession, they talk a lot about sex. I never had any trouble talking about sex, because Mother had told me all I needed to know when I was little and they had a course in family relations in high school and later the picture was filled out for me in nursing school. What you have in sex, the way one professor put it, was a few main themes and lots of variations. Yet the way some of the doctors and older nurses talked about it at Mercy, you would think it was terribly mysterious and funny even to them with all their experience. I had always thought that once I got through school and out of adolescence I just wouldn't be bothered by coarse jokes and sniggles and so on. But no, there's a bald old orthopedic surgeon at Mercy who's as bad as anybody I ever knew in high school.

I was complaining about him to Lou over coffee one morning. I sort of sensed that Lou was as matter-of-fact about sex as I was, and he was too.

"He acts like there was a big secret," I said about the orthopedist. "What in the world's the matter with him? Here he's had three wives and the nurses say he's still a threat in a way if you let him be. He knows there's no secret."

"Oh, now, Junie," Lou said. He already called me Junie

sometimes and I let him. It was like family. "Sex is the secret everybody's in on."

I laughed and laughed. I laughed so hard that other people in the coffee shop glanced at us, in a friendly way, smiling.

"What's funny?" he said. "Is that so silly?"

"No no," I said, "it's witty, that's all. I just never thought of it that way. I didn't realize you were so witty."

So we chatted a little while longer about how doctors and nurses talk about sex, which was a nice roundabout way for us to get to talking about sex without getting personal. Naturally he liked to have me think he was witty since he isn't really. He's never said anything since that was half as witty as that about sex —which really isn't all that witty anyway, though I thought it was at the time.

Well, the next day I was on Emergency, and Lou happened to come by and stop for a chat, when the ambulance brought in an old man who had hanged himself and been cut down at the last minute. You couldn't tell for sure whether he was alive, just to look at him. He lived nearby and he must have been hanging in his kitchen for a long time. It was worse than a car accident. His tongue was swollen and dark. I was terribly upset, and so was Lou.

"Lord," he said under his breath, "it really does turn black."

"No no," I said before I thought. "It's getting some color. He's coming to."

Lou looked again and then he looked at me. Of course I realized my mistake: the old man's tongue was getting a tinge of U-V to it. I clapped my hand over my mouth.

"Nothing," I said. "No no, it's black. I was mistaken."

The whole little occurrence didn't take but a few seconds. In that time Lou realized that I had some sort of a secret to do with color, and I knew he realized it, and he knew I knew it. But he did not take advantage—he never once mentioned it to me or referred to the matter. Which is what did me in, in relation to him. How could I resist that? He respected my secret, which nobody else had the wits to even know I had, and if they *had* known they wouldn't have respected it, like that physics teacher.

The next week Lou asked me out, and when we held hands something happened. I was afraid of it, and I made up my mind I would avoid him from then on and never go out with him again. But in the car, parked in front of my apartment house, holding my hands very very gently, not squeezing them like he had captured them but just lightly and warmly touching so I was always feeling him there, he told me about his wife and little boy and how she had run off with a dental surgeon they had met at a resort. He wanted custody of Ian but she wouldn't give it to him. He would have sued, except he would have to prove in court that she was guilty of adultery and even then he couldn't be positive of getting custody. He couldn't bring himself to do that to his son's mother, so he agreed to a Mexican divorce. The breakup of his marriage was why he'd come to a strange city to do his residency.

Well, the next date he kissed me, and I thought I was going to die. Three months later he asked me to marry him. I explained everything to him about why I couldn't, and he said we certainly didn't have to have any children. We both had busy and useful lives, and what he wanted was *me*. If I could have found just one thing wrong with him more important than the way he sniffs a lot—which is certainly annoying, almost a tic—or the fact that he's as short as I am, I could have held out. But as it was, I couldn't find any excuse to say anything but yes. One of the things he knew better than to do was to talk about love. He probably said the right words—you just about have to—but what we talked about seriously was how we could help one another in so many ways.

Then, two months ago, his first wife and her husband were drowned in a motorboat accident and Ian came to live with us.

Lou was notified about the accident that very same afternoon, because this was the resort where those two had met the previous summer and a man was there who knew where Lou was. Actually, he was Lou's professor of neurology, and he was the person who had introduced the dental surgeon and Lou's then wife. He felt bad about the upshot of that introduction and went to a lot of trouble to help Lou get a good position—Mercy is a model hospital in many ways. So Lou had mixed feelings about him.

Anyway, Ian was in summer camp in Vermont at the time— he'd just turned seven—and had not been told about the accident yet. The neurologist thought maybe Lou would want to fly to Ian and tell him himself, which was thoughtful of him and a nice way to give Lou a plan of immediate action. A person needs a plan at a time like that, and Lou carried it out gratefully.

We could scrape up just enough cash among the people we knew to pay for a one-way ticket that night. I had to telephone Mother—she lives twelve hundred miles in the other direction— to wire me money first thing next morning, and I wired it on to Lou. He was gone five days, what with finding the bodies and attending the funeral services and getting Ian's belongings and seeing a lawyer to get the will business started. Lou phoned every day and I talked to Ian a couple of times. I had never seen Ian, of course, any more than Lou had met Mother, since we had been too broke to take unnecessary trips like that, and Lou's first visitation with Ian since our marriage wasn't due to take place till Labor Day weekend. I couldn't tell much of anything about Ian over the phone, other than that he sounded like a scared little polite boy talking to a stranger, which was the case.

Lou, though, sounded more and more excited every day. At the beginning, that evening when he caught the last plane out to go to Ian, he was mostly upset and worried. Of course he liked the idea of having Ian come live with us, but this was an awful way for that to come about. I wouldn't be the least surprised if he had wanted to kill his wife and the dental surgeon at the time she left him. In fact, he told me he'd wanted to kill them, but he said so in such a kind of quiet way, with a shrug, that I didn't take him seriously. Anyway, all that was past and gone. He no longer hated them so much, I'm sure of that. Still, to have them dead was for him to get Ian, and I *know* Lou is a better father than his former wife could have been a mother. What he kept saying, before he left on the plane was, "What will this do to Ian?"

But it transpired that Ian was inheriting all their property. The dental surgeon had a former wife but they'd had no children, and he and Ian's mother died simultaneously in the eyes of the law. So there was no question, Ian would get his stepfather's life insurance and property. There were other relatives but the lawyer assured Lou that there would be no trouble. (As there hasn't been—we've got the $25,000 insurance already.) The estate is worth upward of $60,000, enough so we could borrow from it to pay off Lou's debts left over from medical school and his expensive first wife, and put a down payment on a home of our own; we would sock the rest into a trust fund for Ian's education, and what we borrowed we could pay back into the fund over the years as Lou gets established in a practice, so Ian could have a start in life in just about any field he wants within reason. Well, with all this, and with Ian behaving so perfectly, Lou's voice over the phone got more and more vibrant every time he called. The accident had been the fault of a crazy kid in a speed boat, but Lou didn't have to get involved in that part of things in any way. After the initial shock, there just wasn't as much for him to be sorry about as there was for him to be happy about, and his voice showed it. He couldn't up and say how well things were turning out, considering, but I felt it in his voice. The result was I more or less lost track of Ian's situation and feelings.

Also, though I was glad for Lou that Ian was coming to live with us, for my own sake I was not exactly overjoyed to be having a child to look after, even a stepchild. I would probably have to quit working for a while, just as I was getting the hang of things at Mercy. I even had some resentful thoughts about Lou for having promised me the sky to get me to marry him. No children ever—and here in less than a year he presents me with a son! Whose mother was not even a nice woman! Still, I had pretty well got those thoughts under control by the time Lou and Ian were due to arrive back. I believe in fate to a large extent, and besides, Lou's excitement was infectious. And there was all that money.

So I went to the airport to meet them with my thoughts going every which way except toward Ian, as they should have done. I was prepared for nothing more than a nice little boy. And that was all I saw of him when the two of them came in the gate together. He had been taking a nap on the plane, and he was looking sort of puffy around the eyes and generally sad. Anyway, he looked so much like Lou that what I saw really was Big Lou and Little Lou. They both have long thin heads with delicate little soft mouths and a sensitive way of moving, like a deer, self-assured but at the same time somehow shy. All my misgivings vanished.

We walked up the corridor toward the main part of the building, with Lou and me each holding one of Ian's hands and chatting back and forth over his head. I had given Ian a little hug and quick kiss first thing, of course, but I hadn't wanted to push matters, under the circumstances. When we started up the corridor I just held my hand where he could take it if he wanted to but didn't have to. He put his hand in mine in such a natural, trusting way that I felt everything would be all right, and so did Lou. Lou and I had both been a little stiff when we had first kissed, because of Ian, but now we were happy and looked at one another as we walked along with real relief in our eyes and hearts.

When we got to the waiting room, Lou found a seat in a corner where there were not too many people around and told me and Ian to stay and get acquainted while he went to collect the luggage. Ian said he didn't want to sit down—he'd been sitting for hours in the plane—so I stood him between my knees to talk with him, and held his hands. I was wearing slacks.

Now it wasn't midnight but two thirty in the afternoon with quite a lot of people milling around generally. And it wasn't the same airport I had had my trauma in, but a much smaller one, no music and worse seats and harsh loudspeakers for the announcements, though the same sort of lighting and the same view of runways and planes. But still, now that I was looking at *him,* really seeing his eyes, everything seemed the same somehow. They both had U-V in their eyes.

I know all about light waves and reflected light and so on, and the rods and cones in the eyeballs and the aqueous humor and the retina and the rest of those things. There's nothing but physics to having one or another color in your eyes, including U-V. I haven't seen too many people with U-V eyes, and of course U-V on anything else doesn't have any special meaning for me —like that old man's tongue, for example, which just happened to have a tinge of it. But whenever I've noticed a gleam of U-V in anybody's eyes it has always had a special effect on me. They look helpless, and I *cannot* bear it.

Here was Ian answering my questions in a low voice; his hands were resting in mine with a couple of his fingers giving a little twiddle once in a while; he was wearing neat short pants and a blue jacket, and one of his knees had a scab on it; he was fair-skinned like his father and his hair was much redder; he wasn't pleading or piteous in his manner. He was being a real little man the way his father had told him to be. But when I looked into his eyes and saw the flicker of U-V there, it came over me in a rush how forlorn and helpless he was and how much he needed a good mother, and I nearly died. Because the first time I had ever seen that light in anybody's eyes, that I remember, was when *I* was standing between *his* knees, and it meant he couldn't help anything, not even leaving me. Now, with this one between my knees, it meant he was helpless too, only I was supposed to help him and what if I couldn't?

I've done everything I could for him and I think he trusts me. Lou never criticizes the way I handle him, but praises me. Even so, I see that light in his eyes a little bit once in a while, and I can't stand to have him so helpless. I know I won't let my own baby down in helping, but how can I be sure with Ian? So, I'm going to have a baby as soon as I can. Lou doesn't even make jokes about women changing their minds. He and I say I want to have a baby because I like Ian so much and he likes me so much, and that's true. But Lou knows my secret is involved in it somehow and he doesn't mind. I've thought of telling him my secret, but that wouldn't solve my problem with Ian. It's mine to handle my own personal way, and besides I like the idea of not telling him everything. It keeps him interested. He is so good to me that I simply *cannot* let his child down, but if I'm going to make it, I've got to have a burden of my own to make things easier for myself, for balance sort of—my own baby. I'm all churned up about it. But I'm so happy.

❦❦❦
❦❦❦   In a Hole
❦❦❦

I am in a hole. At first I did not want to get out of the hole. It
was a sort of relief to be in it. In my city we are prepared for
cataclysms. You cannot be sure which kind of destruction is
going to catch you, but one or another is pretty sure to. In fact,
I am lucky. I am nearly forty and this is the first one to catch me.
Properly speaking, I am not caught yet, for I am still alive and
not even injured. When I first came to in this hole and realized
what had happened and where I was, I had no impulse to get
out. I was afraid of finding the city in rubble, even though I knew
we were a tough people and would rebuild it as we had done
more than once before. My first thought was: caught at last.
Perhaps the shock had stunned me. In any case, I certainly felt
relieved of anxiety, my worry about how and when trouble was
going to find me was over.

Our city is great and strong. Yet when it was founded over
three hundred years ago, our forefathers were warned against
the location. We are at the tip of a promontory at the extreme
west of the continent, situated on a geological fault—typhoons
rake us—the land is sterile, everything worth having must be
brought to us from outside—our people are immigrants, dis-
satisfied and ambitious, we have not brought many of our an-
cestors' myths with us, we are eager to rid ourselves of customs,

284

we are unruly and rely on police to keep us in order—no matter how rich we are, no matter how hard we work, we are always overcrowded—despite the researches of our dieticians, we have many nutritional ailments, new ones springing up among us as fast as the old ones are cured. Perhaps the hardships of our location have tested us and made us tough, and our founding fathers knew this would be the case. They were stubborn in choosing this raw location. We question their wisdom, we grumble, we analyze the possibilities. But we do not seriously complain, we have no real intention of rebelling, even if we did it is dangerous to say anything but what is expected. We are too rich from trade, we are richer than we can explain, we are envied by outsiders who do not appreciate the extent and nature of our troubles. They have no idea how troubling it is not to know when and how you will be caught. One can never forget it here for long. Perhaps because of our difficulty with food, threats are always alive in our minds, ready to leap at us. No matter how much we eat, no matter what our dieticians do, no matter what chefs we import to make our food savory, we suffer from malnutrition. We are fat and undernourished. The stupid are luckiest for they do not know they lack. The wise suffer most. There are a few who make a virtue of fasting and austerity; they say they are at peace; but I have never seen one look me in the eye when he said it. They look up at the sky or out to sea, and talk of love and peace and truth. Their strict diet makes their skin rough and scaly, their nails thicken and turn blue, their eyes become vague. They do not bother people much, nobody cares enough to restrain them. We keep on trying to improve our diet, we hold conferences and symposiums on the subject, it has become the subject of our most intensive experiments.

An earthquake caught me. It was quite a severe one, but I don't think it was as bad as the one that killed a third of our people when I was a young man. I was nimble and quick, and came through with nothing worse than a few bruises. In that one, great chasms opened, whereas the hole I am in now is not more than twenty feet deep. This one caught me just as I was coming out of the telephone building.

I had gone there to argue about a mistake on my bill. They had charged me for two long distance calls to Rome the month before. Absurd! Neither my wife nor I would dream of talking with anyone at such a distance. Overseas connections are notoriously unreliable, even with our communications system, our greatest civic pride—we would be able to talk with the moon if there were anyone there to talk to. Neither my wife nor I have any friends in Rome. It is true that I have corresponded for years with a numismatist in Rome—I collect old coins—but our common interest conceals the profoundest disagreement. I would do much to avoid meeting him in person, should he ever propose such a thing, as he has never shown the slightest sign of doing. To him ancient coins are objects of trade, their value varies from time to time but at any given moment it can be agreed upon, they are commodities. I would never expose to him the slightest edge of what they mean to me, of the speculations they excite in me. (A drachma which was worth many loaves of bread two thousand years ago is now worth nothing—except to a few antiquarians like me, to whom it means a hundred times more than it did then. I looked at it unable to comprehend. If I did comprehend, it would cease to be worth even a slice of bread to me. Do all those to whom it is worthless understand something that eludes me?) The numismatist and I share no language but the code of catalogues. We would not be able to talk to one another face to face, much less over the telephone. And the length of time these supposed long distance calls went on! One lasted an hour, the other nearly as long. I went to the telephone building to complain, politely of course, but firmly. They had to prove that my wife or I had made such preposter- ous calls. They said they would find out who it was the call had gone to—both calls to Rome were to the same number. I saw they did not believe me. I knew that legally they could not force me to pay if I denied responsibility. All the same, I was not feeling cleanly victorious as I left the building.

I was thrown to the street. I remember seeing the façade of the telephone building topple out toward me in one slab, then crack and buckle. When I came to my senses, I was in this hole. There was still dust in the air. I stood up, coughed, and wiped my eyes. The rubble at the bottom of the hole was all small stuff, no boulders or big chunks of material. There was a good deal of light coming down the chimney above me; it could not be late in the day; I had not been out long. I got up, stiff, creaking a bit, but uninjured, and I inspected the hole I was in. It was shaped like a funnel, big end down. The bottom of the chimney was at least five feet above my head, and the chimney itself appeared to extend up another eight or nine feet. The walls of the cone I was in were of chunks of rock propped on one another. To remove one would risk making the whole haphazard structure fall in. I yelled. There was no answer, no answering noise, no noise of any sort. I whistled and shouted. The echo hurt my ears. I collapsed. At that moment I realized I did not want to get out. Not till light returned next morning did my forces rally.

Hunger drove me. At first, choked with dust, I suffered badly from thirst. But during the night it rained, and enough rain water dripped down for me to refresh my mouth and rinse my face. Then hunger pulled me up from my lethargy. I determined not to die alone. I would get out if I could.

But how? I yelled for help, there was no response. Once I got up into the chimney above me, I would be able to brace myself, back and knees like a mountain climber, and inch my way up. But getting myself into the chimney, that was the problem. The walls sloped back, only an experienced mountain climber with equipment would even try to climb them. There was nothing else to be done—I would have to build a pile of rocks to climb up on so that I could insert my body into the chimney. I tried to pull one of the boulders free but it was lodged too tight to budge. Another was as tight; another, another. Then one moved a little as I pulled and pushed. But when it moved, there were ominous shiftings in the wall above me, and a stone as big as my fist sprang out from just over my head, narrowly missing me. All the other boulders I could reach were wedged tight. I pulled at the loose one again. Suddenly half of it broke free and I fell on my back. It was of rotten stone, it crumbled, I had gained nothing.

I complained. If there had been anyone to hear me I would never have been so self-indulgent as to complain. But I was alone and not quite hopeless. I stood with legs spread, raised my fists, and spoke in a loud clear voice as though I were addressing myself to someone who would have understood me if he had heard me. "I have not been unwilling to be destroyed, I know how to resign myself to destruction. But why must I exhaust myself laboring to return to a world which may be in ruins and where, if it is still standing, I will be even more fearful than I was before?" As I finished speaking, a fair-sized piece of stone fell from the wall high above me onto the floor of the hole. I waited to see what else might happen. Nothing happened. I complained again, watchfully. Another rock fell. The sound of my voice was dislodging some of the upper rocks without causing the whole pile to shatter down onto me. I sang, hummed, yelled, whooped, wailed: nothing happened. I went back to complaining, in a loud clear voice and complete, rather formal sentences. Another rock fell. One of the fallen boulders was too big for me to lift, but I could roll it into place. They were of irregular shapes and would not pile easily and securely. I was going to need a great many pieces of stone of this size. I am healthy and my gardening has kept me in good condition; nevertheless, I felt myself weaker after each complaining and rock-piling episode and had to rest for longer and longer periods. My predicament did not allow me to complain mildly. I am reserved by temperament, I tried to hold back both out of inclination and out of a desire to save my strength, but I found that I could give each complaint nothing less than everything I could muster.

I did not dare complain during the night, for fear a dislodged stone would fall on me. In the daytime I watched when I talked, I could jump to one side in time. I kept trying to figure out which of my words had the power to dislodge the rocks; it must have something to do with vibrations, wave lengths.

In our city we are quite experimental. Even a private citizen like myself is infected with the spirit of experiment. I live off the income from my inheritance. My wife and I love gardening above everything. Our few friends are scattered throughout the city, we make a point of being strangers to our neighbors. Our rock garden, at the edge of a cliff overlooking a northern cove, is quite remarkable. I am sure it would win prizes and be much visited if we were interested in that sort of thing. But our friends respect our wish to keep our garden private, and our neighbors, whose gardens are severely arranged and have swept paths, do not notice the perfection of our succulents (which they think of as being no more than cliff plants anyway) nor do they see any order in the way our paths and steppingstones adapt themselves to the terrain. My wife and I have little use for most of what our city gets excited about, we are inclined to scorn prizes and fashion, I had thought I was equally indifferent to the fervor for experimentation. Now, in this hole, I have learned better.

The second night, unable to sleep well because of the discomfort of the floor, I planned experiments to try the next day. I have never heard of anyone who was in a hole like mine. Perhaps these conditions are unique. There are plenty of holes into which our citizens have been known to have fallen; sometimes they were rescued, sometimes they died before they could be got out, often no doubt they just disappeared from sight as I have done. Perhaps no one else discovered how to dislodge boulders as I did. There might be something exceptional about my voice, though no one has ever commented on it. There certainly is nothing odd about my words. They are just ordinary words used with care. Still, though I am not slovenly in my use of words, neither am I a poet. I must not let this opportunity to experiment slip from me, even though, since I need all the physical strength I have to pile the rocks up, I must work fast before I give out. During the night I planned a series of speeches to try out.

I prayed. When our city was founded, many churches were built, strong, handsome, stone structures. Our city had originally been built with walls, to withstand the assaults of pirates. To be sure, the pirates were suppressed two centuries ago, and the city grew far beyond the walls, which are now visited by tourists as museum pieces. But our churches, the best ones, which look like and once served as fortresses, have been kept in good repair, services are held in them, the choir schools still function at public expense. I knew many prayers, having been a boy soprano for a few years till my voice cracked. Neither the prayers I recollected nor the ones I made up worked to dislodge the stones.

I delivered the patriotic speeches memorized by every schoolchild—the salute to the flag, a constitution day address, the funeral oration which had been delivered by our first prime minister after the revolution had established parliamentary government, our oath of allegiance. None of them worked.

I gave an exact and full history of how I came to be where I was. I described my condition with scientific accuracy and offered every reasonable hypothesis about why I was doing what I was doing. Nothing happened.

I recited a poem, nursery rhymes, a folk tale, the prologue of our constitution. I counted to twenty in Latin, I recited as many of Euclid's axioms as I could recall. No result.

I recited a speech from a play I had acted in when I was in college. Actually I saved this till the last because the speech had become more than the character's words for me, it had come to say what I meant or at least I had come to mean what it said. The part was a small one. I was one of the lesser court gentlemen. At a crucial moment the king gives me a vital message, his throne depends on its delivery. Halfway to the nobleman to whom I am supposed to deliver it, I decide not to, and then the playwright gives me my only important speech, a soliloquy, the great speech of the play. I have no good political reason not to deliver the message, nothing but good will befall me if I do deliver it, I have never before done such a thing as I am now doing. The longer I try to account to myself and the audience for what I am doing, the stranger my action appears; I labor to find the right words, for my court language is insufficient. Twice in the history of our city this play, one of our classics, has been proscribed because of this speech, which cannot be cut out of the play, being its keystone. I recite it now in my hole. A boulder is dislodged all right, but it almost hits me. It is too large for me to lift to the top of the pile I have made. Worst, it comes from the mouth of the chimney above, enlarging it, so that now I must build up my pile even higher than before, in order to be able to brace myself in the chimney and work my way out.

I have to use our language in my own way, I have to speak for myself.

"I am in a hole, I want to get out. I don't know what I shall find when I make my way back into the city. I long to see my wife; if she is still alive and well, she will care for me while I recuperate; if she is injured, I will do what I can for her. These stones are heavy; after I put one up onto the pile, my muscles do not leave off trembling until I raise my voice to talk another rock down from the jumble about me and then hoist it into place; each time after such effort, the trembling penetrates into me deeper. I fear I will not have strength to work my way up the chimney once I have got myself into it. I want to cry, but I must save my strength for words. I do not know why I am here, I did nothing to deserve being thrown down here alone and abandoned."

So, the rocks fall.

What would happen if I did not pretend someone is listening to what I say? I know of course that no one hears my voice, but I speak as though I were being listened to. It must be that which gives my voice the right wave lengths to dislodge the stones. It obviously is neither the words themselves nor their arrangement; my experiments have removed those possibilities. In the interests of exact knowledge I should complain without audience. I know well enough that I have no audience, not a sound from outside has reached me. But I cannot imagine doing anything so unreasonable as to complain without any audience at all, even though that is what I am in fact doing. Besides, suppose when I did that, all the rocks should fall in on me at once? If I had more strength I would take the risk, I would try to imagine myself as I am. Meanwhile, I had better get on with my complaining while I still have strength and time.

ABOUT THE AUTHOR

Born in Indiana in 1918, George P. Elliott was educated at the University of California, Berkeley; he later taught English there and at St. Mary's College in California. He has also taught at Cornell University, Barnard College, and the University of Iowa, and is now on the faculty of Syracuse University. He has been the recipient of a Guggenheim and a *Hudson Review* fellowship, and, in 1964, of a grant from the Ford Foundation to work on a play. Mr. Elliott's stories, poems, and essays have appeared in many magazines, including *Harper's, Commentary, Esquire, The Hudson Review,* and the *Kenyon Review.* He is the editor of two anthologies, *Fifteen Modern American Poets* and *Types of Prose Fiction.*